"It's not a go quietly.

He circled her wrists wit their hands behind her "Oh, I think it's a very good idea."

He started to lower his mouth to hers, and, God help her, Renny stood still for the merest of seconds and waited for him to make contact. He was just so unbelievably... So extremely... So totally, totally...

His lips brushed hers lightly... once, twice, three times, four. Heat splashed in her belly, spilling through her torso and into her limbs, warming parts of her she hadn't even realized were cold. Then he stepped closer and covered her mouth completely with his, and those parts fairly burst into flames. For another scandalous, too-brief moment, she reveled in the fantasy that was Tate Hawthorne and the wild ride it promised. Then, nimbly, she tugged her hands free of his and somehow broke away to scurry to the kitchenette.

"Hey, are you as hungry as I am?" she asked when she got there.

Belatedly, she realized the glaring double entendre of the question.

* * *

The Pregnancy Affair

First

THE PREGNANCY AFFAIR

BY
ELIZABETH BEVARLY

First Published in Great Britain 2017
By Mills & Boon, an imprint of HarperCollins*Publishers*
1 London Bridge Street, London, SE1 9GF

© 2017 Elizabeth Bevarly

ISBN: 978-0-263-92808-2

51-0217

Our policy is to use papers that are natural, renewable and recyclable products and made from wood grown in sustainable forests. The logging and manufacturing processes conform to the legal environmental regulations of the country of origin.

Printed and bound in Spain
by CPI, Barcelona

Elizabeth Bevarly is an award-winning, *New York Times* bestselling author of more than seventy books. Although she has made her home in exotic places like San Juan, Puerto Rico, and Haddonfield, New Jersey, she's now happily settled back in her native Kentucky. When she's not writing, she's binge watching British TV shows on Netflix or making soup out of whatever she finds in the freezer. Visit her at www.elizabethbevarly.com.

For my grandmother,
Ruth Elizabeth Hensley Bevarly,
who told me some really great stories
when I was a kid.

I miss you, Nanno.

One

Renny Twigg threw her car into Park and gazed at the Tudor-style house beyond her windshield. Or maybe she should say Tudor-style *castle* beyond her windshield. Its walls were made of majestically arranged stones and climbed a full three stories, and they were tatted here and there with just the right amount of ivy. Its stained glass mullion windows sparkled in the late-morning sunlight as if they'd been fashioned from gemstones, and its turrets—one on each side—stretched even higher than the slate roof, looking as if they'd been carved by the hand of a Renaissance artist. The lot on which the mansion sat was nearly a city-state unto itself, green and glorious and landscaped with more flowering shrubs than a Spring Hill catalog.

There was rich, and then there was *rich*. The first

was something with which Renny had a more-than-nodding acquaintance. She'd come from a long line of powerful attorneys, financiers and carpetbaggers, the first of whom had arrived in this country hundreds of years ago to capitalize on the hugely exploitable land and its even more exploitable colonists. The Twiggs who followed had adopted the tradition and run with it, fattening the family coffers more with each ensuing generation. She'd grown up in a big white Cape Cod in Greenwich, Connecticut, had donned tidy blue uniforms for tony private schools before heading off to be a Harvard legacy, and had worn a sparkly tiara—with real diamonds—for her debut eleven years ago. Renny Twigg knew what it was to be rich.

She eyed the massive structure and its imperious gardens again. Tate Hawthorne was obviously *rich*.

She inhaled a fortifying breath and tucked an unruly dark brown tendril back into the otherwise flawless chignon at her nape. Then she checked her lipstick in the rearview mirror, breathed into her hand to ensure that there were no lingering traces of her breakfast burrito and smoothed a hand over her tan linen suit. Yep. She was perfectly acceptable for her meeting with the man her employer had assigned her to locate. *So go ahead, Renny. What are you waiting for?*

She eyed the massive mansion again. What she was waiting for was to see if a dragon would come swooping down from one of those turrets to carry her off for his own breakfast. In spite of the colorful landscaping and bright blue summer sky that framed it, the place just had that look about it. As if its owner were some brooding, overbearing Rochester who might very well lock her away in his attic.

Oh, stop it, she told herself. Tate Hawthorne was one of Chicago's savviest investors by day and one of its most notorious playboys by night. From what she'd learned of him, the only thing he dedicated more time to than making money was spending it. Mostly on fast, lustrous cars and fast, leggy redheads. Renny was five foot three in her kitten heels and had driven up in a rented Buick. She was the last kind of woman a man like him would want to stash away for nefarious purposes.

Even if his origins were pretty freakin' nefarious.

She opened the car door and stepped out onto the cobbled drive. Although it was only June, the heat was oppressive. She hurried to the front door, rehearsing in her head one last time the most tactful way to relay all the news she had for Tate Hawthorne.

Like how he wasn't really Tate Hawthorne.

Renny's employer, Tarrant, Fiver & Twigg—though the Twigg in the name was her father, not her—was a law firm that went by many descriptions. Probate researchers. Estate detectives. Heir hunters. Their services were enlisted by the state of New York when someone died without a will and no next of kin was known or when the next of kin was known but his or her whereabouts were not.

That second option had brought her to Highland Park, a suburb of Chicago for people who were *rich*. Bennett Tarrant, president and senior probate researcher, had given the job to Renny because she always found the heir she was looking for. Well, except for that one time.

And also because she was the only probate researcher available at the time who didn't have anything on her plate that couldn't be scraped off with a quick fork to the archives room. For lack of a better analogy. That breakfast burrito had, after all, been hours ago.

And although he hadn't said so specifically, she was pretty sure another reason Bennett had assigned her the job was to offer her a chance to redeem herself for that one time she hadn't been able to find the heir she was looking for. Locating someone who would be extremely hard to locate—like Tate Hawthorne—and doing so without screwing it up would make Renny a shoo-in for the promotion that had been eluding her, something that would make her father very proud. Not to mention make him stop looking at her as if she were a complete screwup.

In the meantime, Renny was proud of herself. It took skill and talent to find someone who had been buried in the federal Witness Protection Program along with the rest of his immediate family nearly three decades ago. Well, it took those things and also a friend from high school who had mad hacking skills and could find any-thing—or anyone—on the internet. But that was beside the point. The point was Renny had found the heir she was looking for, thanks to said friend. Which would, she hoped, put her back on the fast track at Tarrant, Fiver & Twigg and get her father off her back for that one tiny blip that had changed the company's 100% find rate to a 99.9999% find rate, and jeez, Dad, it wasn't like she'd lost that one on purpose, so just give her a break. *Man*.

She rang the doorbell and fanned herself with her

portfolio as she waited for a response, since, judging by the size of the house, it could be days before anyone made their way to the front door. So she was surprised to be caught midfan when the door opened almost immediately. Thankfully, it wasn't Tate Hawthorne who answered. It was a liveried butler, who looked to be about the same age as one of the founding fathers. If the founding fathers were still alive, she meant.

"Good morning," Thomas Jefferson greeted her. "Miss Twigg, I presume?"

She nodded. She had contacted Tate Hawthorne earlier this week—or, rather, she had contacted his assistant Aurora, who, Renny hadn't been able to help thinking, sounded like a fast, leggy redhead—and set up a meeting with him for the only fifteen minutes the guy seemed to have available for the entire month of June. And that was only because, Aurora had told her, he could cut short by a teensy bit his preparation for his regular Saturday polo match.

"Hello," Renny replied. "I'm sorry to be a bit early. I was hoping Mr. Hawthorne might be able to squeeze in another ten or fifteen minutes for our meeting. What I have to tell him is kind of—" *life changing* was the phrase that came to mind, but it sounded a little melodramatic "—important. What I have to tell Mr. Hawthorne is kind of important." And also life changing.

"All of Mr. Hawthorne's meetings are important," Thomas Jefferson said indulgently.

Of course they were. Hence his having only fifteen minutes in the entire month of June for Renny. "Nevertheless," she began.

"It's all right, Madison," a booming baritone interrupted her.

Renny gazed past the butler at a man who had appeared behind him and who had to be Tate Hawthorne. She knew that, because he looked really, really *rich*.

His sable hair was cropped short, his skin was sun burnished to the color of a gold doubloon and his gray eyes shone like platinum. He was dressed in a polo uniform—equestrian, not water, unfortunately, because a body like his would have seriously rocked a Speedo— in hues of more precious materials, from the coppery shirt to the chocolate-truffle jodhpurs, to the front-zipper mahogany boots that climbed up over his knees with their protective padding. All of it skintight over taut thighs, a sinewy torso, salient biceps and shoulders broader than the Brooklyn Bridge. It was all Renny could do to not drool.

Unfortunately, she wasn't as lucky in keeping herself from greeting him less than professionally. "Hiya." Immediately, she realized her loss of composure and pheromones and amended, "I mean…hello, Mr. Hawthorne."

"Hello yourself, Ms…" He halted. "I'm sorry. Aurora included your name with the appointment, but I've been working on something else this morning, and it's slipped my mind. And, well…you are a bit early."

He seemed genuinely contrite that he was at a loss for her name, something for which Renny had to give him credit. Not just because he was being so polite about her having impinged on his time after being told he didn't have much to spare, but because, in her experience, most high-powered business types didn't feel contrite about anything, least of all forgetting the name of a junior associate from a law firm they never had dealings with.

Madison the butler moved aside, and she murmured her thanks as she stepped past him into the foyer. She withdrew a business card from inside her jacket and extended it toward Tate Hawthorne.

"I'm Renata Twigg," she said. Not that she'd felt like a *Renata* a single day in her life, because Renata sounded like, well, a tall, leggy redhead. Renny had no idea what her mother had been thinking to want to name her that, or what her father had been thinking to insist it be the name she used professionally. "I represent Tarrant, Fiver & Twigg, attorneys," she concluded.

He took the card from her but didn't look at it. Instead, he looked at Renny. With way too much interest for her sanity and saliva glands. And—okay, okay— her pheromones, too.

"Renata," he said, fairly purring the word in a way that reminded her of velvet and cognac. And suddenly, for some reason, Renny didn't mind her given name at all.

"Thank you so much for making time to meet with me this morning," she said. "I know you must be very busy." Duh.

She drove her gaze around the massive black-and-white-tiled foyer to the half-dozen ways out of it—two doors to her right, two doors to her left, and one more framed by a curving staircase that led to the second floor.

"Um, is there someplace we can talk?" she asked.

For a moment, Tate Hawthorne said nothing, only continued to gaze at her in that mind-scrambling, gland-addling way. Finally, he said, "Of course."

He extended a hand to his left to indicate Renny should precede him. Which she would have done, had she had a clue where he wanted her to go. He could have been gesturing at the doors to her left, the staircase, or to the exit behind himself. He seemed to realize the ambiguity of his action, too, and threw her an apologetic smile that just made him even more charming. As if he needed that. As if *she* needed that.

"My office is this way," he told her.

He opted for the exit behind himself, and Renny followed. They passed another eight or nine—hundred—rooms before he finally turned into one that looked more like a library than an office, so stuffed to the ceiling was it with books. There was a desk tucked into a corner, facing to look out the window at a green space behind the house that was even more idyllic than the scene in front, and topped with a state-of-the-art computer and tidy piles of paperwork. Also sitting there was a polo helmet that matched his uniform, so she gathered he was in here when she arrived, trying to cram in more work before heading out to play. The guy clearly took both his business and his pleasure seriously.

"Please, have a seat," he said, gesturing toward a leather-bound chair that had probably cost more than the gross national product of some sovereign nations. Then he spun around his desk chair—also leather, but smaller—and folded himself into it.

Renny tried not to notice how his clothing seemed

to cling even more tightly when he was seated, and she tried not to think about how much she suddenly wanted to drop to her knees in front of him to unzip his boots. With her teeth. Instead, she opened her portfolio and withdrew the handful of documents she'd brought with her to support what was sure to sound like a made-for-cable movie on one of the channels that was *way* high up the dial.

"Mr. Hawthorne," she began.

"Tate," he corrected her.

She looked up from her task, her gaze fastening with his again. Those eyes. So pale and gray and cool for a man who seemed so deep and dark and hot. "Excuse me?" she said without thinking.

He smiled again. She tried not to spontaneously combust. "Call me Tate," he said. "'Mr. Hawthorne' is what they call me at work."

This wasn't work? she wanted to ask. It was work to her. At least, it had been before he smiled in a way that made clear his thoughts were closer to pleasure at the moment than they were to business. And, thanks to that smile, now Renny's were, too.

"Ah," she started again. Probably best not to call him anything at all. Especially since the only thing coming to mind at the moment was... Um, never mind. "Are you familiar with the name Joseph Bacco?" she asked.

A spark of something flickered in his eyes, then disappeared. "Maybe?" he said. "Something in the news a while back? I don't remember the context, though."

Renny wasn't sure how far Joseph Bacco's influence might have traveled beyond New York and New Jersey, but he'd been a colorful-enough character in his time to warrant the occasional story in magazines or true-crime shows on TV. And his death had indeed made national news. She tried another tack.

"How about the name 'Joey the Knife?'"

Tate's smile this time was tinted more with humor than with heat. And, gee, why was it suddenly so easy for her to think of him as *Tate*?

"No," he replied.

"'Bulletproof Bacco'?" she asked, trying another of Joseph Bacco's distinctive monikers.

"Ms. Twigg—"

"Renny," she said before she could stop herself. And immediately regretted not being able to stop herself. What was she thinking? She never invited clients to use her first name. And only Bennett Tarrant and her father called her Renny at work, because they'd both known her since the day she was born.

Tate's gaze turned hot again. "I thought you said your name is Renata."

She swallowed hard. "It is. But everyone calls me Renny."

At least everyone who wasn't tied to her by business. Which Tate most certainly was. So why had she extended the invitation to him? And why did she want to extend more invitations to him? None of which included him calling her by name and all of which had him calling her hot, earthy things as he buried himself inside her and drove her to the brink of—

"You don't seem like a Renny," he said. Just in the nick of time, too. The last thing she needed was to have an impromptu orgasm in front of a client. Talk about a black mark on her permanent record.

"I don't?" she asked, in a voice normally used only when having an impromptu orgasm. Maybe he wouldn't notice.

Judging by the way his pupils dilated, though, she was pretty sure he did. Even so, his own voice was level—if a tad warm—when he said, "No. You seem like a Renata to me."

Well, this was news to Renny. No one thought she was a Renata. Even her own parents had given up calling her that the day she stripped off her pink tutu in ballet class and decreed she would instead play football, like her brothers. Ultimately, she and her parents had compromised on archery, but still. *Renata* had gone the way of the pink tutu decades ago.

"Uh…" she said eloquently. Damn. What had they been talking about?

"Bulletproof Bacco," he repeated.

Right. Joey the Knife. Nothing like references to ammunition and cutlery to put a damper on thoughts of… Um, never mind.

"That doesn't sound like the name of someone I'd run into at the Chicago Merc," he continued.

She tried one last time. "How about the 'Iron Don'?" she asked. "Does that name ring a bell?"

The light came back into his eyes, and this time it stayed lit. "Right," he said. "The mobster."

"*Alleged* mobster," Renny corrected him. Since no one had ever been able to pin any charges on Joey the Knife that hadn't slid right off him like butter from a hot, well, knife. Though she was reasonably sure that wasn't why he'd earned that particular nickname.

"From New York, I think," Tate said. "His death was in the news a couple of months ago. Everyone kept commenting that he'd lived to be the oldest organized-crime figure ever and died of old age instead of…something else."

"*Alleged* organized-crime figure," Renny corrected him again. "And, yes, he's the man I'm talking about."

Tate glanced at his watch, then back at Renny. All heated glances and flirtation aside, the man was obviously on a schedule he intended to keep. "And he has bearing on this meeting…how?"

Renny handed him the first of the records she'd brought with her—a copy of his original birth certificate from New Jersey, much different from the one he had now from Indiana, which he'd been using since the fifth grade. The name printed on it, however, wasn't Tate Hawthorne, as he had come to be known after his stepfather adopted him. Nor was it Tate Carson, as he had been known before that. The name on this record was—

"Joseph Anthony Bacco the Third?" he asked.

"Grandson of Joseph Anthony Bacco Senior," Renny said. "Aka Joey the Knife. Aka Bulletproof Bacco. Aka the Iron Don."

"And why are you showing me a birth certificate that belongs to a mobster's grandson?"

Renny started to correct him, but he hastily amended, "*Alleged* mobster's grandson. What does Joseph the Third, or Joseph Senior, for that matter, have to do with me?"

She withdrew from her portfolio a photograph, one of several she had from the 1980s. In it, a man in his sixties was seated on a sofa beside a man in his twenties who was holding a toddler in his lap. She handed it to Tate, who accepted it warily. For a moment, he gazed at her through narrowed eyes, and somehow she sensed there was a part of him that knew what was coming. But he only dropped his gaze to the photo.

"The picture is from Joseph Bacco's estate," Renny said. "The older man is Joseph Anthony Bacco Senior, and the younger man beside him is—"

"My father," Tate finished for her. "I don't remember him very well. He died when I was four. But I have some photographs of him and recognize him from those. I assume the little boy he's holding is me."

"Yes."

"Meaning my father was an acquaintance of the Iron Don," he gathered, still looking at the photograph.

"He was more than an acquaintance," she told him. "Your father was Joseph Anthony Bacco Junior."

At this, Tate snapped his head back up to look at her. "That's impossible. My father's name was James Carson. He worked in a hardware store in Terre Haute, Indiana. It burned down when I was four. He was killed in the fire."

Renny sifted through her documents until she located two more she was looking for. "James Carson was the name your father was given by the federal marshals before they placed him and your mother and you in the Witness Protection Program when you were two years old. Your family entered WITSEC after your father was the star witness at a murder trial against one of Joseph Bacco's capos, Carmine Tomasi. Your father also gave testimony against a half-dozen others in the organization that led to a host of arrests and convictions for racketeering crimes."

She glanced down at the record on top. "Your mother became Natalie Carson, and you became Tate Carson. You all received new Social Security numbers and birth dates. The feds moved the three of you from Passaic, New Jersey, to Terre Haute, and both your parents were given new jobs. Your father at the hardware store and your mother at a local insurance company."

Renny handed him copies of documents to support those assertions, too. She'd received everything she had to support her story via snail mail at her condo a few days ago, from her high school friend with the mad hacking skills. They were records she was reasonably certain she wasn't supposed to have—she'd known better than to ask where they came from. The only reason Phoebe had helped her out in the first place was because Renny (A) promised to never divulge her source and (B) pulled in a favor she'd been owed by Phoebe since a sleepover thirteen years ago, a favor that might or might not have something to do with a certain boy in homeroom named Kyle.

These records, too, Tate accepted from her, but this time, his gaze fell to them immediately, and he voraciously read every word. When he looked up again, his pale gray eyes were stormy. "Are you trying to tell me…?"

She decided it would probably be best to just spill

the news as cleanly and quickly as possible and follow up with details in the inevitable Q&A.

"You're Joey the Knife's grandson and legal heir. In spite of your father's having ratted out some of his associates, your grandfather left his entire estate to you, as you're the oldest son of his oldest son, and that's what hundreds of years of Bacco tradition dictates. What's more, it was Joey's dying wish that you assume his position as head of the family and take over all of his businesses after his death.

"In short, Mr. Hawthorne," Renny concluded, "Joseph Anthony Bacco Senior has crowned you the new Iron Don."

Two

It took a minute for Tate to process everything Renata Twigg had dropped into his lap. And even then, he wasn't sure he was processing it correctly. It was just too far outside his scope of experience. Too hard to believe. Too weird.

Renata seemed to sense his state of confusion, because she said, "Mr. Hawthorne? Do you have any questions?"

Oh, sure. He had questions. A couple. Million. Now if he could just get one of them to settle in his brain long enough for him to put voice to it...

One that finally settled enough to come out was "How could a mobster want to leave his fortune to the son of a man who double-crossed him?"

"*Alleged* mobster," Renata corrected him. Again.

Not that Tate for a moment believed there could be any shades of gray about a guy named Joey the Knife.

"If I really am Joseph Bacco's grandson," he began.

"You are definitely Joseph Bacco's grandson."

"Then why would he want to have anything to do with me? My father—his son—turned him in to the feds. Wouldn't that kind of negate any familial obligation that existed prior to that? Or...I don't know...put a contract on my father's head?"

"Actually, your father didn't turn Joey in to the feds," Renata said. "Or any other member of the immediate Bacco family. All the information he gave to the feds had to do with other members of the organization. And he only gave up that information because the feds had enough evidence of his own criminal activity to put him away for forty years."

"*My* father?" Tate said incredulously. "Committed crimes worthy of forty years in prison?"

Renata nodded. "I'm afraid so. Nothing violent," she hastened to reassure him. "The charges against your father were for fraud, bribery, embezzlement and money laundering. Lots and lots of fraud, bribery, embezzlement and money laundering. There was never any evidence that he was involved in anything more than that. He was highly placed in your grandfather's business. Wise guys that high up... Uh...I mean...*guys* that high up don't get their hands that dirty. But your father didn't want to go to prison for forty years." She smiled half-heartedly. "He wanted to watch his little son grow up."

Tate tried to take some comfort in that. Even so, it

was hard to imagine James Carson involved in corruption. His memories of his father were hazy, but they evoked only feelings of affection and warmth. His dad, from what he recalled, was a good guy.

"Anyway," Renata continued, "because your father never fingered anyone in the Bacco family proper—in fact, his agreement with the feds stated he would absolutely not, under any condition, incriminate his family—Joey the Knife never sought a vendetta. He really loved his son," she added. "I think a part of him kind of understood why your father did what he did, so he could be with his son. But even more important, I think Joey really loved you—his first grandson. And since you had nothing to do with what your father did, he wanted you to come back and take your rightful place in the family."

As what? Tate wondered. What kind of nickname would suit the lifestyle he'd assumed instead? Bottom Line Bacco? Joey the Venture Capitalist? Somehow those just didn't have the same ring. Or did they? Renata had just said his grandfather had businesses. Maybe there was a bit of Bacco in Tate yet.

"You said my grandfather had businesses?" he asked.

She withdrew another collection of papers from her portfolio. "Several. He wants to put you in charge of Cosa Nostra, for one thing."

"Yeah, you just pretty much said that when you told me he wants me to be the new Iron Don."

She shook her head. "No, not that Cosa Nostra. That *alleged* one, I mean. Cosa Nostra is the name of a chain of Italian restaurants he owned up and down the Jersey shore."

Tate took this page from her, too, and quickly scanned the figures. Unless Cosa Nostra was a three-star Michelin restaurant that served minestrone for five hundred bucks a bowl, its profits were way too high to be on the up-and-up.

"Yeah, these places look completely legitimate," he said wryly.

"By all accounts, they are. Joey bought them with the proceeds from his waste-management business and his construction company."

Yep. Totally legit.

"Since your grandfather's death in the spring, everything's been run by his second in command, who—" she hesitated for a moment "—who's married to your father's sister."

Tate remembered then that Renata had mentioned there were other members of the "immediate" Bacco family. He'd been an only child all his life and had been under the impression that both of his parents were, too. At least, that was what his mother had always told him to explain why he didn't have any aunts or uncles or cousins, the way all his classmates did.

Of course, all these new revelations might also explain why she'd always seemed to go out of her way to ensure that he stayed an only child—not just in the birth sense but in the social sense, too. She'd never encouraged him to make friends when he was growing up and had, in fact, been wary of anyone who tried to get too close. Although he'd had a handful of friends at school, she'd never let him invite any of them home or allowed him to play at their houses. He'd never had birthday parties or sleepovers, hadn't been able to join Cub Scouts or play team sports or attend summer camp.

His childhood hadn't exactly been happy, thanks to his solitary state. He'd always thought his mother was just overprotective. Now he wondered if she'd spent the rest of her life watching their backs. He wished he could ask her about all this, but he'd lost her to cancer when he was in college. His stepfather—who might or might not have known about anything—had been quite a bit older than his mother and had died less than a year later. There was no one around who could verify any of this for Tate. No one except Renata Twigg.

"I have other family members?" he asked.

She nodded. "Your father had two sisters, both older than him. Denise is married to Joseph Bacco's second in command, Nicholas DiNapoli, aka Nicky the Pistol."

"My aunt is mobbed up, too?"

"Allegedly. His other sister, Lucia, is married to Handsome Mickey Testa, the manager of one of Joey's casinos."

Did anyone in the mob *not* have a nickname? "Do I have cousins by them?" Tate asked.

She flipped another page. "Yes. Denise and Nicky have Sal the Stiletto, Dirty Dominic and… Oh. This is different."

"What?"

"Angie the Flamethrower. Gotta give a girl credit for that. And Lucia and Mickey have Concetta."

"Who I assume is Connie the something."

"Well, right now she's Connie the economics major at Cornell. But I wouldn't rule anything out."

"So my entire family are mobsters."

"Alleged mobsters. And an economics major."

Renata gazed at him with what could have been compassion or condemnation. He had no idea. She was very good at hiding whatever she was thinking. Well, except for a couple of times when he was pretty sure she'd been thinking some of the same things he'd been thinking, most of them X-rated. Her espresso eyes were enormous and thickly lashed, her dark hair was pulled back into the most severe hairstyle he'd ever seen and her buff-colored suit was conservative in the extreme.

Even so, he couldn't shake the feeling that the image she presented to the world had nothing to do with the person she really was. Although she looked professional, capable and no-nonsense, there was something about her that suggested she wanted to be none of those things.

"So this law firm you work for," Tate said. "Does it handle a lot of, ah, *alleged* mob work?"

She shook her head. "Tarrant, Fiver & Twigg is about as white-shoe a firm as you're going to find. But, according to my father—who's the current Twigg in the name—Joey the Knife and Bennett Tarrant's father had some kind of shared history when they were young. No one's ever asked what. But it was Bennett's father who took him on as a client back in the sixties, and Bennett honored his father's wish that he always look after Joey."

"So Joey must have had some redeeming values then."

"He loved his son. And he loved his grandson. I'd say that makes up for a lot."

Tate looked down at the sheet that had his mother's original information on it. She had been Isabel Danson before she married Joseph Jr.

When Renata saw where his attention had fallen, she told him, "For what it's worth, your mother's family wasn't connected. Allegedly or otherwise."

"Do I have family on that side, too?"

"I'm sorry, no. She was an only child."

At least something his mother had told him was true.

"Her parents, both deceased now, were florists."

Finally. Something beautiful to counter all the luridness of his heritage.

"So what do my aunts, uncles and cousins think of this?" Tate asked, looking up again. "Seems to me they might all be a little put off by Joey's wanting a total stranger to come in and take over. Especially when that stranger's father ratted out other members of the organization."

"Right now, I'm the only person who knows you're Joseph Anthony Bacco the Third," Renata assured him. "Because of the delicate nature of the situation, I haven't even told the senior partners of Tarrant, Fiver & Twigg who or where you are. Only that I found you and would contact you about Joey's final wishes. I haven't told the Baccos even that much."

"And if I decide I'd just as soon not accept my grandfather's legacy?" Tate asked.

Since it went without saying he wouldn't be accepting his grandfather's legacy. He wasn't sure yet how he felt about accepting his grandfather's family, though. The blood one, not the professional one. A lot of that depended on whether or not they were accepting of him. For all he knew, they were already dialing 1-800-Vendetta.

"The surviving Baccos were all aware of Joey's wishes," Renata said. "They've known all along that he wanted his missing grandson to be found and take over after his death. He never made any secret of that. But I don't know how they felt about that or if they even expected anyone to ever be able to find you. If you don't accept your grandfather's legacy, then Joey wants everything to go to Denise and her husband so they can continue the tradition with their oldest son. That may be what they've been assuming would happen all along."

"I don't want to accept my grandfather's legacy," Tate said plainly.

"Then I'll relay your wishes to the rest of the family," Renata told him. "And unless you decide to approach them yourself, they'll never know who or where you are. No one will. I'll take the secret of your identity to my grave."

Tate nodded. Somehow, he trusted Renata Twigg to do exactly that. But he still wasn't sure what he wanted to do about his identity. As a child, he'd often fantasized about having a family. Just not one that was quite so *famiglia*. He'd be lying, though, if he said there wasn't a part of him that was wondering what it would be like to be a Bacco.

"It's my aunt's and cousins' birthright as much as it is mine," Tate said. "They were a part of my grandfather's life and lifestyle. And I—"

He halted there, still a little thrown by everything he'd learned. He searched his brain for something that might negate everything Renata had told him. But his memories of his father were hazy. The only clear ones were of the day he died. Tate remembered the police coming to their house, his mother crying and a guy in a suit trying to console her. As an adult looking back, he'd always figured the guy was from the insurance company, there to handle his father's life-insurance policy or something. But after what Renata had told him, the guy might have been a fed, there to ensure that his mother was still protected.

He conjured more memories, out of sequence and context. His father swinging him in the ocean surf when he was very little. The two of them visiting an ancient-looking monkey house of some zoo. His father dancing him around in the kitchen, singing "Eh, Cumpari!," a song Tate had never heard anywhere else except for when…

Oh, God. Except for when Talia Shire sang it in *The Godfather, Part III*.

"There are more photos," he heard Renata say from what seemed a very great distance. "Joey had several framed ones of you and him on shelves in his office until the day he died."

Tate looked at the photo in his hand again. The Iron Don honestly looked like he could be anyone's grandfather—white hair and mustache, short-sleeved shirt and trousers, grinning at the boy in the picture as if he were his most cherished companion. There were no gold chains, no jogging suits, nothing to fit the stereotype at all. Just an old man happy to be with his family. Yet Tate couldn't remember him.

On some level, though, a lot of what Renata said explained his memories. He couldn't recall taking a long road trip anywhere until his mother married William Hawthorne. So how could he have been in the ocean when he was so young? Unless he'd lived in a state that had a coastline. Like New Jersey. And there were no ancient-looking monkey houses in this part of the country. But some zoos in the Northeast had lots of old buildings like that.

He looked at Renata Twigg. "I'm the grandson of a mobster," he said softly. This time, the remark was a statement, not a question.

"Alleged mobster," she qualified again, just as quietly.

"But real grandson."

"Yes."

So Tate really did have family out there with whom he would have grown up had things been different. He would have attended birthday parties and weddings and graduations for them. Vacationed with them. Played with them. He wouldn't have spent his childhood alone. Strangely, if his father had gone into the family's very abnormal business, Tate might have had a very normal childhood.

The pounding of footsteps suddenly erupted in the hall outside his office. Tate looked up just in time to see a man in a suit, followed by a harried Madison, come hurrying through the door. When he halted, the man's jacket swung open enough to reveal a shoulder holster with a weapon tucked inside. Tate was reaching for his phone to hit 9-1-1 when his presumed assailant flipped open a leather case in his hand to reveal a badge with a silver star.

"Inspector Terrence Grady," the man said. He reminded Tate of someone. An older version of Laurence Fishburne, maybe. "United States Marshals Service. Tate Hawthorne, you'll have to come with me immediately."

"Sir, he pushed right past me," Madison said. "I tried to—"

"It's all right, Madison," Tate said as he stood.

Renata stood at the same time, though she didn't cut quite as imposing a figure as Tate was trying to achieve himself. Actually, it was kind of hard to tell if she'd stood at all, because she barely came to his shoulder. Small women. He never knew what to do with small women. They were just so…small. But Renata Twigg had already inspired a few interesting ideas in his head. Given the chance—which, for some reason, he was hoping for—he was sure he could find a few more.

Instead of responding to Inspector Grady, Tate, for some reason, looked at Renata. He expected her to look as confused as he felt over the marshal's sudden appearance. Instead, a blush was blooming on her cheeks, and she was steadfastly avoiding his gaze.

He turned back to the marshal. "I don't understand. Why should I go anywhere with you?"

Grady—maybe not Laurence Fishburne, but he looked like *someone* Tate knew—said, "I can explain on the way."

"On the way where?"

"We need to get you someplace safe, Mr. Hawthorne." And then, just in case Tate had missed that part before, he added, more emphatically this time, *"Immediately."*

Tate straightened to his full six-three and leveled his most menacing gaze on the marshal. "I'm not going anywhere. What the hell does a federal marshal have to do with—"

Hang on. Didn't federal marshals run the Witness Protection Program? Tate looked at Renata again. She was looking at something on the other side of the room and fiddling with the top button of her shirt in a way that might have been kind of interesting in a different situation. Under the circumstances...

"Renata," he said softly.

She was still looking at the wall and twisting her button, but she lifted her other hand to the twist of dark hair at her nape, giving it a few little pats, even though not a single hair was out of place. "Yes?"

"Do you have any idea why a federal marshal would show up at my front door less than an hour after you did?"

"Mr. Hawthorne," Grady interrupted.

Tate held up a hand to halt him. "Renata?" he repeated.

Finally, she turned her head to look at him. This time he knew exactly what she was thinking. Her eyes were a veritable window to her soul. And what Renata's soul was saying just then was *Oh, crap.*

In spite of that, she said, "No clue."

"Mr. *Hawthorne*," Grady said again. "We have to leave. *Now.* Explanations can wait."

"Actually, Inspector Grady," Tate said, returning his

attention to him, "you won't have much to explain. I'm guessing you're here because my grandfather was Joseph Bacco, aka the Iron Don, and now that he's gone, he wants me to be the new Iron Don."

"You know about that?"

"I do."

Grady eyed him warily for a moment. "Okay. I wasn't sure you were even aware you had a WITSEC cover, if your mother ever made you privy to that or if you remembered that part of your life. The other thing I came here to tell you is that your WITSEC cover has been compromised, thanks to a hack in our files we discovered just this morning. We need to put you somewhere safe until we can get to the bottom of it."

Tate barely heard the second part of the marshal's comment. He was too focused on the first part. "You knew my mother?"

Grady was visibly agitated about his lack of compliance with the whole *leaving immediately* thing, but he nodded. "I was assigned to your father and his family after he became a state's witness. The last time I saw your mother or you was the day your father died."

Okay, *that* was why he looked familiar. The man in the suit that day must have been a younger Terrence Grady.

"Look, Mr. Hawthorne, we can talk about this in the car," he said. "We don't know that there's a credible threat to your safety, but we can't be sure there *isn't* one, either. There are an awful lot of people interested in taking over your grandfather's position—the one they know your grandfather wanted you to assume—and it's safe to say that few of them have your best interests at heart. Last week, someone accessed your federal file without authorization, so your WITSEC identity is no longer protected. That means I have to get you someplace where you *are* protected. *Immediately.*"

"Um, Inspector Grady?" Renata said nervously. "I, uh… That is, uh… Funny story, actually…"

"Spit it out, Ms…" Grady said.

She began patting her bun again, but this time kept doing it the entire time she spoke. "Twigg. Renata Twigg. And, actually, the person who compromised Mr. Hawthorne's WITSEC identity? Yeah, that, um… that might have been, ah…me."

Grady eyed her flatly. "You're the one who told Mr. Hawthorne about his past?"

Something in his tone made Renata pat her bun harder. "Um…maybe?"

Tate was going to tell Grady that she absolutely had been the one to tell him about that, but he was kind of enjoying how her bun patting was causing strands of hair to come loose. Her hair was longer than it looked.

"You have access to federally protected files, have you?" Grady asked. "Or do you have hacking skills that allowed you to access those files? Because hacking a federal database is a Class B felony, Ms. Twigg. One that carries a sentence of up to twenty years."

She looked a little panicked by that. "Of course I don't have hacking skills," she said. "Are you kidding? I majored in English specifically so I wouldn't have to do the math."

"Well, which is it, Ms. Twigg?" Grady asked. "How

did you discover Mr. Hawthorne's identity? And why did you go looking for him in the first place?"

She bit her lip anxiously. Tate tried not to be turned-on.

Quickly, she told Grady about Joey the Knife's will and his intentions for his grandson. Grady nodded as she spoke, but offered no commentary.

When she finished, he asked again, "And just how were you able to locate Mr. Hawthorne?"

At first, she said nothing. Then, very softly, she asked, "Class B felony, you say? Twenty years?"

Grady nodded.

For a moment, Renata looked like the proverbial deer in the headlights, right down to the fawn-colored suit and doe eyes. Then her expression cleared, and she said, "Craigslist."

Grady looked confused. Tate wasn't surprised. He'd been confused since seeing Renata at his front door.

"Craigslist?" Grady echoed.

Renata nodded. "I found a computer whiz on Craigslist who said he could find anyone for anybody for the right price. He helped me locate Mr. Hawthorne."

"His name?" Grady asked. Dubiously, if Tate wasn't mistaken.

Renata briefly did the deer-in-the-headlights thing again. Then she told him, "John something, I think he said. Smith, maybe?"

Grady didn't look convinced. "And do you know if Mr., ah, Smith did anything else with this information he found for you? Like, I don't know…sold it to someone else besides you?"

"I'm sure he's totally trustworthy and kept it all completely confidential," Renata said.

Now Grady looked even less convinced. "A guy on Craigslist who says he can find anybody for anyone for money and calls himself John Smith is totally trustworthy," Grady reiterated. Blandly, if Tate wasn't mistaken.

Renata nodded with much conviction and repeated, "Totally."

Grady looked at her for a long time, as if weighing a number of scenarios. Finally he growled, "We don't have time for this right now. We need to get Mr. Hawthorne somewhere safe. And until it's all sorted out, you're coming, too, Ms. Twigg."

That finally stopped the bun patting. But it restarted the button fumbling. So much so that Renata actually undid the button, and then another below it, revealing a tantalizing glimpse of lace beneath. Which was weird, because in light of developments over the last several minutes, the only thing Tate should find tantalizing about Renata Twigg was thoughts of her having never entered his life in the first place.

"I'm sorry, but I can't go anywhere with you," she said to Grady. "I have a red-eye out of O'Hare tonight."

"You don't have a choice, Ms. Twigg," Grady said emphatically. He turned to Tate. "And neither do you. We're all leaving. Now. Once the two of you are settled in a safe house, we can get this all straightened out. But until we know there's no threat to Mr. Hawthorne, and until we get to the bottom of this security breach, both of you—" he pointed first at Tate, then at Renata "—are coming with me."

Three

Renny sat in the backseat of the black SUV with Tate, wishing she could wake up in her Tribeca condo and start the day over again. They'd been driving for more than two hours nonstop—pretty much due north, as far as she could tell—and Tate had barely said a dozen words to her during the entire trip.

He'd spoken to the marshal often enough early on—or, at least, tried to. Grady had responded to every question with a promise to explain once he was sure Tate and Renny were settled at a safe location. He'd replied the same way as he hustled the two of them out of the house earlier. He hadn't even allowed Tate time to change his clothes, hadn't allowed Renny to bring her handbag or portfolio and had made them both leave behind their electronics due to their GPS.

On the upside, the fact that Grady hadn't allowed them even basic necessities might be an indication he didn't intend to detain them for long. On the downside, the fact that they were still driving after two hours was a pretty decent indication that Grady planned on detaining her and Tate for some time.

She just wondered how far from Chicago Grady thought they had to be before they'd be considered safe. They'd crossed the Wisconsin state line less than an hour after leaving Tate's house and had kept driving past Racine, Milwaukee and Sheboygan. Like any good Northeasterner, Renny had no idea which states actually abutted each other beyond the tristate area, but she was pretty sure Wisconsin was one of the ones way up on the map beneath Canada. So they couldn't drive much longer if they wanted to stay in Grady's jurisdiction.

As if cued by her thoughts, he took the next exit off I-43, one that ended in a two-lane blacktop with a sign indicating they could head either west to a place called Pattypan or east to nowhere, because Pattypan was the only town listed. In spite of that, Grady turned right.

Okay then. Nowhere it would be.

The interstate had already taken them into a densely forested area, but the trees grew even thicker the farther they drove away from it. The sky, too, had grown darker the farther north they traveled, and the clouds were slate and ominous, fat with rain.

This day really wasn't turning out the way Renny had planned. She braved another look at Tate, who had crowded himself into the passenger-side door as if he wanted to keep as much space between them as possible. He wasn't turning out the way she'd planned, either. She was supposed to have gone to his house in her usual professional capacity, relayed the terms of his grandfather's will in her usual professional way and handled his decision, whatever it turned out to be, with professionalism.

Any personal arrangements Tate wanted to make with the Bacco family would have been up to him. Then Renny would have gone back to her life in New York having completed what would be the most interesting case she would ever handle in her professional career and try not to think about how early she'd peaked.

Instead, all her professional responses had gone out the window the moment she saw Tate, and every personal response had jumped up to scream, *Howdy do!* And those responses hadn't shut up since, not even when the guy was giving her enough cold shoulder to fill a butcher's freezer.

The SUV finally turned off the two-lane blacktop, onto a dirt road that sloped sharply upward, into even more trees. The ride grew bouncy enough that Renny had to grab the armrest, but that didn't keep her from falling toward Tate when they hit a deep rut. Fortunately, she was wearing her seat belt, so she only slammed into him a little bit. Unfortunately, when they came out of the rut, he fell in the other direction and slammed into her, too.

For one scant moment, their bodies were aligned from elbow to shoulder, and Renny couldn't help thinking it was their first time. Um, touching, she meant. Arms and shoulders, she meant. Fully clothed, she meant. But the way her heart was racing when the two of them separated, and the way the blood was zipping through her veins, and the way her breathing had gone hot and ragged, they might as well have just engaged in a whole 'nother kind of first time.

She mumbled an apology, but he didn't acknowledge it. Instead, he gripped his armrest as if his life depended on it. After another few hundred jostling, friction-inducing feet of what may or may not have once been a road, the SUV finally broke through the trees and into a clearing.

A clearing populated by a motel that was clearly a remnant of mid-twentieth-century, pre-interstate travel culture—single story, brick and shaped like a giant L. There was a parking space in front of each room, but there wasn't a single car present. In fact, the place looked as if it had been out of business since the mid-twentieth-century, pre-interstate travel culture. The paint on the doors was peeling, the brick was stained with mold and a rusty, mottled sign in front read The Big Cheese Motor-Inn. In a small clearing nearby were a half-dozen stucco cottages shaped like wedges of cheese. It was toward one of those that Inspector Grady steered the SUV.

"Seriously?" Renny said when he stopped the vehicle and threw it into Park. "You're going to hide us in a cottage cheese?"

"We've used this place as a safe house since nineteen sixty-eight," Grady said. "That's when we confiscated it from the Wisconsin mob. These days, no one even remembers it exists."

"There's a Wisconsin mob?" Renny asked. "Like who? Silo Sal Schlitz and Vinnie the Udder?"

"There *was* a Wisconsin mob," Grady corrected her. "The Peragine family. Shipping and pizzerias."

Of course.

The marshal snapped off his seat belt, opened his door and exited, so Renny and Tate did, too. The moment she was out of the vehicle, she was swamped by heat even worse than in Chicago. Impulsively, she stripped off her jacket and rolled her shirt sleeves to her elbows. Her hair, so tidy earlier, had become a tattered mess, so she plucked out the pins, tucked them into her skirt pocket and let the mass of dark hair fall to the center of her back. Then she hastily twisted it into a pin-free topknot with the deftness of someone who had been doing it for years, drove her arms above her head and pushed herself up on tiptoe, closing her eyes to enjoy the stretch.

By the time she opened her eyes, Tate had rounded the back of the SUV and was gazing at her in a way that made her glance down to be sure she hadn't stripped off more than just her jacket. Nope. Everything was still in place. Though maybe she shouldn't have fiddled so much with her shirt buttons earlier, since there was a little bit of lace and silk camisole peeking out.

But come on. It was a camisole. Who thought camisoles were sexy these days?

She looked at Tate, who was eyeing her as if she were clad in feathery wings, mile-high heels and a two-sizes-too-small cubic-zirconia-encrusted bra. Oh. Okay. Evidently, there was still at least one guy in the world who found camisoles sexy. Too bad he also hated her guts.

As unobtrusively as she could, she rebuttoned the third and second buttons. Then she followed Grady to the giant cheese wedge, telling herself she only imagined the way she could feel Tate's gaze on her ass the whole time.

"Oh, look," she said in an effort to dispel some of the tension that had become thick enough to hack with a meat cleaver. "Isn't that clever, how they made some of the Swiss-cheese holes into windows? That's what I call functional design."

Unfortunately, neither man seemed to share her interest in architectural aesthetics, because they just kept walking. Grady pulled a set of keys from his pocket as he scanned the tree line for signs of God knew what, and Tate moved past her to follow the marshal to the front door, not sparing her a glance.

Renny deliberately lagged behind, scanning the tree line herself. Though for different reasons than Grady, she was sure. In spite of the weirdness of the situation, and even with the suffocating heat and teeming sky, she couldn't help appreciating the beauty surrounding her. The trees were huge, looking almost black against the still-darkening clouds, and there was a burring noise unlike anything she'd ever heard. She recognized the sound as cicadas—she'd heard them on occasion growing up in Connecticut—but here it was as if there were thousands of them, all singing at once.

The wind whispered past her ears, tossing tendrils of hair she hadn't quite contained, and she closed her eyes to inhale deeply, filling her nose with the scent of evergreen and something else, something that reminded her of summers at the shore. That vague fishy smell that indicated the presence of water nearby. If they really had traveled due north, it was probably Lake Michigan. She wondered if they were close enough to go fishing. She'd loved fishing when she was a little girl. And she'd always outfished her father and brothers whenever they went.

She listened to the cicadas, reveled in the warm breeze and inhaled another big gulp of pine forest, releasing it slowly. Then she drew in another and let it go, too. Then another. And another. Bit by bit, the tension left her body, and something else took its place. Not quite serenity, but something that at least kept her panic at bay. She loved being outdoors. The farther from civilization, the better.

She felt a raindrop on her forehead, followed by a few more; then the sky opened up and the rain fell in earnest. Renny didn't mind. Rain was hydrotherapy. The warm droplets cooled her heated skin and *tap-tap-tapped* on the leaves of the trees and the hood of the SUV, their gentle percussion calming her even more.

With one final breath, she opened her eyes. Tate stood inside the door of the cottage looking out at her, his expression inscrutable. He was probably wondering what kind of madwoman he was going to be stuck with for the rest of the day—maybe longer. Renny supposed that was only fair, since she was wondering a lot of things about him at the moment, too.

Like, for instance, if he enjoyed fishing.

* * *

As Tate gazed at Renata, so much of what had happened today became clear. The woman didn't even have enough sense to come in out of the rain.

He must have been nuts to have thought her professional, capable and no-nonsense. Then again, he'd also been thinking she didn't seem to want to be any of those things. Now he had his proof. Even when the rain soaked her clothing, she still didn't seem inclined to come inside.

On the other hand, her saturated state wasn't entirely off-putting. Her white shirt clung to her like a second skin, delineating every hill and valley on her torso. Just because those hills weren't exactly the Rockies—or even the Grassy Knoll—didn't make her any less undesirable. No, it was the fact that she'd disrupted his life and gotten him into a mess—then made a literal federal case out of it—that did that.

Actually, that wasn't quite true. She was still desirable. He just didn't like her very much.

He heard Grady in the cabin behind him opening and closing drawers, cabinets and closets, and muttering to himself. But the activity still couldn't pull his gaze from Renata in the rain.

Renata in the rain. It sounded like something by a French watercolorist hanging in the Musée d'Orsay. But there she was, a study in pale shades, and if he were an artist, he would be setting up his easel right now.

She really was very pretty. Not in the flashy, showy, don't-you-wish-you-were-hot-like-me way that the women he dated were. Her beauty was the kind that crept up on a man, then crawled under his skin and into his brain, until he could think of little else. A quiet, singular, unrelenting kind of beauty. When he first saw her standing at his front door that morning, he'd thought she was cute. Once they started talking, and he'd heard her breathless, whiskey-rough voice, he'd even thought she was kind of hot—in a sexy-librarian way. But now she seemed remarkably pretty. In a quiet, unrelenting, French-watercolorist kind of way.

"Mr. Hawthorne?" he heard Grady call out from behind him, raising his voice to be heard over the rain pelting the roof.

Yet still Tate couldn't look away from Renata. Because she started making her way to the door where he stood. She stopped long enough to remove her wet shoes, then continued barefoot. The dark hair that had been so severe was sodden and bedraggled now, bits of it clinging to her neck and forehead, and the suit that had been so efficient looking was rumpled and puckered. Somehow, though, that just made her more attractive.

"Mr. Hawthorne?" Grady said again, louder this time.

"What?" Tate replied over his shoulder. Because now Renata was only a few steps away from him.

"Sir, I'm going to have to go into town for some supplies. This place hasn't been used for a while, and I didn't have any notice that we'd be needing it. I did turn on the hot-water heater, so there should be hot water in a few hours. But the place is kind of light on fresh food. I shouldn't be gone long."

Renata was nearly on top of Tate now—figuratively,

not literally, though the literal thought was starting to have some merit. So he stepped just far enough out of the doorway for her to get by him, but not far enough that she could do it without touching him. She seemed to realize that, because she hesitated before entering, lifting her head to meet his gaze.

As he studied her, a drop of rainwater slid from behind her ear to glide down the column of her neck, settling in the divot at the base of her throat. He was so caught up in watching it, to see if it would stay there or roll down into the collar of her shirt, that he almost forgot she wasn't the kind of woman he found fascinating. It wasn't Renata that fascinated him at the moment, he assured himself. It was that drop of rainwater. On her unbelievably creamy, flawless, beautiful skin.

When he didn't move out of her way, she arched a dark eyebrow questioningly. In response, he feigned bewilderment. She took another small step forward. He stood pat.

"Do you mind?" she finally asked.

"Mind what?"

"Moving out of the way?"

Well, if she was going to speak frankly—another trait he disliked in women—there wasn't much he could do but move out of the way.

"Of course," he said. And moved a step as small as hers to the side.

She strode forward at the same time, but she moved farther and faster than he did so her shoulder hit him in the chest, and they both lost their footing. When Tate circled her upper arm with one hand, he discovered Renata Twigg had some decent definition in her biceps and triceps.

Muscles were another thing he wasn't crazy about finding on a woman. So why did finding them on Renata send a thrill of…something…shooting through his system?

"Sorry," he said.

"No problem," she replied. In a breathless, whiskey-rough voice that made him start thinking about sexy librarians again.

She kept moving, but even after she was free of him, his palm was still damp from her clothing, and there was a wet spot on his shirt where her shoulder had made contact. Those would eventually dry up and be gone. What wouldn't leave as quickly were the thoughts circling in his brain that were anything but dry.

He watched her as she continued into the cabin, noting how the rain had soaked her skirt, too. The skirt whose length barely passed muster for proper office attire. The dampness made it seem even shorter—though it could just be Tate's overactive imagination making it do that—and it, too, clung to her body with much affection. Whatever Renata lacked in the front—and, really, no woman ever lacked anything up front—she more than made up for behind. The gods might have made her small, but they'd packed more into her little package than a lot of women twice her size.

"Mr. Hawthorne?"

Reluctantly, he returned his attention to Grady. The marshal was looking at him in a way that indicated he knew exactly where Tate's gaze had been, and if he were Renata's father, he'd be hauling Tate out to the woodshed.

"Did you hear what I said?" he asked.

"You have to go into town for some supplies," Tate replied. See? He could multitask just fine, listening to Grady with the left side of his brain while ogling Renata with the right.

"And I won't be gone long," Grady added as he made his way to the front door. "There's a phone in the bedroom, but if either of you uses it to call anyone other than me, this is going to turn into a *much* longer stay than any of us wants. Get it?"

"Got it."

"Good." Without another word, Grady exited.

Leaving Tate and Renata truly alone.

Four

Renny watched Inspector Grady leave, then scanned the cottage and decided things could be worse. The place was actually kind of cute in a retro, Eisenhower-era kind of way. The walls were paneled in honey-colored wood, and a fireplace on one side was framed by creek stone all the way around. Doors flanked it on each side, one open and leading to a bedroom and the other closed, doubtless a bathroom. The wall hangings were amorphous metal shapes, and the rugs were textile versions of the same. The furniture was all midcentury modern—doubtless authentic—with smooth wood frames and square beige cushions. On the side of the cottage opposite the fireplace was a breakfast bar and kitchenette, whose appliances looked authentic to the middle of the last century, too.

The decor reminded her of James Mason's house on

top of Mount Rushmore in *North by Northwest*. Any minute now, Martin Landau ought to come sauntering in to mix up a pitcher of martinis for all of them. Of course, then he'd try to kill Renny and Tate the way he'd tried to kill Eva Marie Saint and Cary Grant, so...

"So," she said, turning to face Tate again, "pretty crazy day, huh?"

She had hoped to lighten the mood with the question. But he only glowered harder.

She sighed. "I'm sorry, okay? For like the hundredth time, I'm sorry. Will you please stop looking at me like I ruined your life?"

"You have ruined my life," he said. Still glowering.

"I have not!" she denied. "All I did was tell you the truth about your origins. *I'm* not the one who spawned you into an alleged mob family. *I'm* not the one who tried to make you an offer you couldn't refuse. The circumstances of your birth and your grandfather's wishes are facts of your life. They have nothing to do with me."

"Yeah, but the facts of my life you dumped on me today have ruined the facts of my life that existed before. Before today, my life was fine and would have remained that way if you'd stayed in New York. No, better than fine. Before today, my life was perfect."

"No one's life is perfect," Renny said. "There's always some—"

"My life was. Until you knocked on my door."

Well, technically, she had rung his doorbell, but it probably wasn't a good idea to argue that point. Not when they had so many others to argue instead. Not that Renny wanted to argue. Tate obviously did. And maybe, on some level, she deserved the dressing-down he was about to give her.

Although she really should have thought of another phrase than *dressing-down*, since she was pretty sure he'd been doing that to her long before he discovered the reason for her visit. So maybe, on some level, she deserved the tongue-lashing he was about to give her.

Um, no, that probably wasn't a good phrase to use, either. So maybe, on some level, she deserved the, uh…harangue—yeah, that was it—that he was about to give her.

He didn't disappoint.

"A few hours ago," he began, his anger barely in check, "my weekend was going to be great. After polo, I had a late lunch with some friends to tell them about an opportunity that would have netted us each a bundle. And tonight, I had a date with a gorgeous redhead."

Ha. Just as Renny suspected.

"Tickets for a show that's been sold out for months, followed by dinner at a restaurant where it's even harder to get a table. Then back to my place for a nightcap and hours of the obvious conclusion to a night like that."

Renny wasn't sure what bothered her more. That he assumed a woman would have sex with him just because he spent a zillion dollars on an evening out—even if it did sound like a supernice evening—or the fact that he was cocky enough to think he would last for hours. With a stunning redhead.

Okay, so maybe it was actually the stunning redhead that bothered her the most. And, okay, maybe the supernice evening, too, since the high point of Renny's weekend would have been a few episodes of *Bletchley Circle* and a bag of gummi bears.

Feeling a little haranguey herself, she said tartly, "Obvious conclusion to a night like that? So the two of you go back to your place to binge-watch British mysteries on Netflix all night? 'Cause that's what I consider an 'obvious conclusion' to a night like that."

She didn't bother to clarify that that was because (A) she generally spent her weekends alone lately, and (B) she really loved binge-watching British mysteries on Netflix.

He eyed her blandly. "Find yourself going out for evenings like that a lot, do you?"

"Sure. All the time." At least once a month. Okay, maybe more like once a year. Okay, maybe more like never. He didn't have to know that, either. "I'm sure you'll have a chance to make it up to the stunning redhead."

"Not when I can't call her and tell her I won't be there. I can't even give her the tickets to the show so she can go with someone else."

He wouldn't mind his girlfriend going to the play with someone else? Did that mean she really wasn't his girlfriend? And that he might maybe possibly perhaps be open to seeing someone else? Someone who *wasn't* a stunning redhead, but was more of an ordinary brunette and—

Oh, Renny, stop. You're embarrassing yourself.

It only meant the focus of his evening wasn't the woman he was with or where they were going or what they were doing. The focus of his evening was its obvious conclusion. Meaning Tate Hawthorne was a guy with a pretty face and a gorgeous body that housed a truly superficial brain. Renny hated guys like that.

Even if they did have pretty faces and gorgeous bodies.

"I'm sure she'll understand," Renny said, "once you get back and explain what happened."

He shook his head. "How do I explain something like this? It sounds like a bad movie."

"That I didn't write," she reminded him. "Don't blame me for this."

He slumped forward a bit, as if he'd been holding his entire body too tightly for too long. Then he crossed the room and folded himself into a chair by the fireplace.

"It's just been a lot to take in, you know?" he said.

Renny moved closer, opting for the sofa. Tate stared straight ahead, but his gaze was unfocused, as if he were seeing something other than a dated but really kind of charming venue. Since his question hadn't seemed to require an answer, she said nothing. Especially since he looked ready to answer it himself.

"I've always had a plan for my life," he said. "Even when I was a kid. After my dad died, my mom struggled so much to keep a roof over our head, and I wanted to grow up and make as much money as I could so she didn't have to worry anymore. So *I* wouldn't have to worry. I hate worrying. I never worry. Worrying is for people who don't know how to make life work for them."

He turned to Renny, and she braced herself for more scowling. Instead, he looked kind of…lost? Confused?

Uncertain? All of the above? Whatever it was, it was unsettling, because until now, Tate hadn't been any of those things. On the contrary, he'd been the most cocksure person she'd ever met.

"But now I'm worried," he said. "And I don't know how to handle it. Does that ever happen to you?"

She wanted to tell him no. She'd always had a plan for life, too, even when she was a kid. Attend the same high school as her parents. Get her BA in English from Vassar like her mother and graduate from Harvard Law like her father. Then go to work at his firm, since both of her brothers had opted to work in finance, and Renny had been his last hope. Eventually marry some as-yet-nameless up-and-comer like herself. At some point, squeeze out the requisite kid or two and hire a nanny like the one she'd had. Send the offspring to the same schools with the same majors so they could go to work at Tarrant, Fiver & Twigg, too, and start the cycle all over again. It was the upper-class, suburban way. Blah, blah, blah. She couldn't remember ever planning a life that was anything else.

But she could remember *wanting* a life that was anything else. She could remember that pretty well.

In spite of that, she told Tate, "No. It doesn't happen to me. I don't worry, either."

And she didn't. Because there was no uncertainty in her life. She had a job that paid well and guaranteed her a career—provided she didn't keep screwing up. She owned her condo and car outright. She carried no debt. Even if she did lose her job, she had trust funds from both sides of the family that would allow her to live comfortably for the rest of her life. There wasn't any uncertainty in Renny's life. She really didn't have anything to worry about.

Except for those days when she felt as if she'd ended up where she was through no thought or decision of her own. Except for those days when she carried around a knot in her stomach that couldn't be anything but, well, worry.

Days kind of like today.

She pushed the thoughts away. They were silly. Her life was fine. And it would stay fine. Fine was…fine. It was. It was totally, totally…fine. There were a lot of people who would kill to have lives that were fine. No way was she in any position to worry.

"I shouldn't be worried, though, right?" Tate asked, still sounding worried. "There's no way I'm going to take over my grandfather's position. And I don't have to meet my cousins or aunts or uncles if I don't want to, do I? They'd probably just as soon I stay out of their lives, right?"

"Maybe," Renny said. "But maybe not. Especially since you don't want to inherit your grandfather's estate or take his place in the business. Once the Bacco sisters and their families know you're not a usurper, they might want to reconnect with you."

Hey, it could happen. Joey the Knife had put an awful lot of importance on family, even family who had strayed. It was possible Tate's aunts still loved their brother as much as their father had. It was possible that, in spite of everything, they'd like to see how their little nephew turned out. A lot of things were possible at this point. When Tate remained silent, she said, "You have a lot to think about. Maybe being separated from your life for a few days will be a blessing in disguise. It will allow you to mull your options without your other daily distractions."

"A few days?" he echoed, sounding even more worried. "You think we'll actually be here for a few days?"

"I think it's pretty clear we're not going home tonight. Not if Inspector Grady had to go into town for supplies."

And not if Renny continued to hide the fact that she knew perfectly well who was responsible for the security breach that compromised Tate's WITSEC identity. She was no happier to be here than Tate was. But what was she supposed to tell Inspector Grady after he said hacking a federal database the way Phoebe had could land her in prison for twenty years? And probably Renny, too, as an accessory. She'd had no idea what to say at that point. She'd been too busy panicking. Tate wasn't the only person who had a lot to think about.

"You said 'a few days,'" he told her. "Not 'overnight.'"

"Well, it *is* the weekend," she said. "Not much gets done on Saturday or Sunday in the world of bureaucracy."

"So it could be Monday before we get the all clear?" he asked.

"Or maybe Tuesday," she hedged. "Everyone in Washington could be coming back to work after a weekend at the shore or something. Takes a while to get going again after a weekend like that. I mean, conceivably, it could even be Wednesday before we—"

"Wednesday?" he bellowed. "That's four days stuck here."

Well, only if they decided by then that the hack into the WITSEC system hadn't originated with someone in the Bacco family looking to off Tate to keep him from taking over his grandfather's position. Until someone at the Justice Department realized there was no danger to him—and Renny really, really hoped they could do that without discovering the true source of the hack—he and Renny could be stuck in this dated but really kind of charming venue for a while.

"I don't know," she said in response to his question. "We can ask Inspector Grady when he gets back how long he thinks we'll have to be—"

Out of nowhere, a crack of thunder shook the cottage, a burst of lightning flashed outside the windows and the single table lamp Grady had lit upon entry flickered off, then on again. It was only then that Renny realized how uncomfortably warm it had become inside.

"Mind a little air-conditioning?" she asked.

Tate still looked a little distracted—and a lot annoyed—but he shook his head. She glanced around for a thermostat, saw one by the front door and headed for it.

"It's only for heat," she said upon further inspection.

She checked the windows for an air conditioner. Nothing. She wandered into the bedroom, which was as retro as the living room—and which also had only one bed that didn't even appear to be queen-size—but there was no window unit in there, either.

Okay, so it was an old motel that was out of use, and it was Wisconsin, where maybe summers didn't usually get that hot, but still. It was hot. They'd just have to cool off the old-fashioned way. If nothing else, rain usually brought the temperatures down.

She returned to the living room and opened one of the windows in there…only to be pelted by rain, so she closed it again. Or, at least, she tried to. But it got jammed to the point where she was banging on the window sash with both hands as water streamed down her arms, making it too slippery to get the damned thing back in its groove.

Before she realized what was happening, Tate was behind her, leveraging his extra foot of height to wrestle the window back into place for her. He surrounded her completely, his entire body flush against hers, his front to her back, his arms over her shoulders, his legs pressed into her fanny. With every move he made—and he made a lot of them—he seemed to press closer still, until Renny felt as if he were crawling inside her. And still the rain came pouring in the window, drenching them both, doing nothing to cool her off. On the contrary, the air around them fairly sizzled as their bodies made greater contact, creating a blistering friction that made her feel as if she would spontaneously combust. Finally, Tate shoved the window back into place, leaving them both wet and panting and—

And *not* moving away from each other.

Five

In fact, Tate seemed to be moving closer still. And if Renny had thought it was hot and steamy in the cottage before, it was nothing compared to the way she felt with him surrounding her, clinging to her as snugly as her clothes. Good God, the man was tall. And broad. And hard. And hot. And—

And get a grip, Renny.

He was just a guy. Just a really sexy guy. With a beautiful face. And a gorgeous body. And millions—possibly billions—of dollars. Who, she was reasonably certain, didn't like her very much.

So why wasn't he moving away from her?

She discovered the answer when she tried to retreat first, by shifting her body to the right. The moment she did, she felt it—felt him—hard and ripe and ready against her back. She wasn't the only one who'd been affected by the friction of their bodies. The evidence of Tate's reaction was just a lot more obvious than her own, thanks to his anatomy. The anatomy that, some other time, she would take a moment to appreciate but that, at the moment... Oh, all right—she appreciated it now, too. What she didn't appreciate were the circumstances that had brought both their anatomies so close, in a situation where they couldn't do anything about it.

In an effort to relieve the tension—or whatever—they both must be feeling, she tried to move a little farther to the right. But he dropped his hands from the window to cup them over her shoulders.

"Don't," he said softly. "Just...don't move."

"But I—"

"Don't," he repeated, a little more roughly.

Reluctantly, Renny stopped, but she couldn't ignore the pressure of him behind her. For one long moment, they stood still, utterly aware of each other. Then, finally, he removed his hands from her shoulders. She waited for him to take a step backward, but he stayed where he was, dropping his hands to her waist, instead.

Okay, now he would move away—or at least move her away from him. But neither of those things happened, either. Instead, he dipped his head closer to hers. She felt a warm percussion of breath stir her hair from behind, then heard the soft sigh of his exhalation near her ear.

Unable to help herself, she turned her head toward the sound, only to find her mouth hovering within inches of his. Her gaze flew to his, but he had his lowered. At first she thought he was studying her mouth, and then she realized his eyes were too hooded for that, and his focus was even farther down. What he was really looking at was... She bent her own head to follow his gaze. He was looking at her shirt. More specifically, he was looking down her shirt. At the hint of camisole lace that still peeked out of the neckline. But when she looked back up at him, he had shifted his attention again, and this time he was definitely looking at her mouth. Then he was looking at her eyes. Then her mouth again.

And then his head was lowering more, his mouth drawing nearer to hers...nearer...nearer still. Renny held her breath as she felt his hands on her hips inching forward, one up along her ribs and the other down across her belly. She realized belatedly that she was still clinging to the windowsill, something that gave him free rein over her midsection. He curved one hand under her breast and pushed the other over her skirt at the juncture of her thighs.

She spun around to face him, opening her hands over his chest to push him away. Though she didn't push very hard, and he didn't go very far, it was enough for her to regain some semblance of sanity, enough to remember she barely knew him—even if it somehow felt as if she'd known him forever—enough to remind herself he didn't like her.

"Stop," she said quietly. "Just...stop."

Although the admonition echoed his own warning of a moment ago, the fact that she still had her hands splayed open over his chest—oh, wait, her fingers were actually curled into the fabric of his shirt, as if she intended to pull him forward again—didn't exactly put a fine point on her objection.

Tate seemed to notice that, too, because he cupped his hands over her hips, pulled her close and asked, "Why? We're obviously attracted to each other. You said yourself we're going to be stuck here for a while. It would be a nice way to pass the time."

Oh, and wasn't that what every woman wanted to be to a really hot, really sexy guy with millions—possibly billions—of dollars? A way to *pass the time*? Where did Renny get in line to sign up for that?

She forced herself to let go of his shirt—it actually would be a nice way to pass the time if it weren't for that pesky *he doesn't like you* thing—and covered his hands with hers to remove them from her hips.

"It's not a good idea," she said.

He circled her wrists with deft fingers and moved both their hands behind her back, then leaned in again. "Oh, I think it's a *very* good idea."

He started to lower his mouth to hers, and, God help her, Renny stood still for the merest of seconds and waited for him to make contact. He was just so unbelievably…so extremely…so totally, *totally…*

His lips brushed hers lightly…once, twice, three times, four. Heat splashed in her belly, spilling through her torso and into her limbs, warming parts of her she hadn't even realized were cold. Then he stepped closer and covered her mouth completely with his, and those parts fairly burst into flame. For another scandalous, too-brief moment, she reveled in the fantasy that was

Tate Hawthorne and the wild ride it promised. Then, nimbly, she tugged her hands free of his and somehow broke away to scurry to the kitchenette.

"Hey, are you as hungry as I am?" she asked when she got there.

Belatedly, she realized the glaring double entendre of the question. Because there was hunger, and then there was *hunger*. And, speaking for herself, anyway, she was feeling a lot more of the latter than she was the former.

In spite of that, she asked, "You want a sandwich? I could really go for a sandwich."

Then she remembered Grady had gone into town for supplies, which meant there probably wasn't much in the cottage for a sandwich.

She spun around so she wouldn't have the temptation that was Tate Hawthorne making her want a lot more than a sandwich and opened the refrigerator. It was empty save for a couple of bottles of water and a six-pack, minus two, of Spotted Cow beer. The freezer held only a handful of indeterminate foil-wrapped things all covered with frost. She tugged on one of the cabinet doors and found plates and glasses. Another offered a near-empty roll of paper towels. Then, finally, she found some food in one. Lots of food, actually. Lots of canned food. Lots of canned food that might be as midcentury modern as everything else in the place. She pushed herself up on tiptoe to reach one in front and flipped it over to inspect the date on the bottom. Then she smiled.

"Gotta love preservatives," she said. "This will still be good when I hit the big three-oh."

There was a long stretch of silence, then an even longer sigh of resignation, then the scrape of Tate's boots across the floor.

"And when will that be?" he asked impassively.

His voice came from so close behind her Renny actually jumped. She spun about to find him doing the surrounding thing again, though this time at least he gave her a couple of inches of space that allowed for some air circulation that might dry her clothes and some thought circulation that might clear her head.

"Um, a year," she told him. "Well, a year and two months."

He looked surprised. "I thought you were fresh out of law school."

She was grateful for the change of subject and clung to it, even though the subject was her, a topic she normally avoided. Still, when the alternative was thinking—or, worse, talking—about the mind-scrambling kisses they'd just shared...

"Nope," she said. "I passed the bar six years ago. So... Beefaroni?" She held up the can for his inspection.

He grimaced. "Really? You'd eat that?"

She gaped at him. "It was only my favorite dish the whole time I was in lower school. Of course I'll eat it. It's delicious."

He looked past her into the cabinet. "What else is in there?"

She turned around and started sorting through the cans, fairly certain that none of them would compare to what he would have found on the menu of a Chicago restaurant where it was nearly impossible to get a table, which he would have been perusing this evening if he wasn't stuck in a giant wedge of cheese with Renny and Chef Boyardee.

"Let's see," she said. "There's SpaghettiOs, Mini Raviolis, beef stew, baked beans, chili mac, a variety of soups… Anything sounding good?"

When she turned back for his reply, he somehow seemed even closer than he'd been before. Judging by the expression on his face, though, no, nothing sounded good. In fact, everything sounded revolting.

In spite of that, he asked, "What kind of soup?"

She turned to check. "Clam chowder, creamy potato, beef barley, chicken and stars—"

"Is it Campbell's chicken and stars?"

"Yep."

"Fine. I'll have that."

Before she could grab it, he reached over her head to pluck the can from the shelf. Then he moved to the stove to open the drawer beneath it and retrieve a serviceable saucepan. He turned the proper burner knob to medium high without even having to check which one it was, effortlessly popped the lid on the can and plopped its contents into the pan. His moves were quick and fluid, automatic enough to make it seem as if he made canned soup in a not particularly up-to-date kitchenette every day because he had one just like it at home in his ivy-encrusted, multimillion-dollar mansion.

The only thing he did wrong as far as Renny could tell was that he added only half a can of water to the condensed soup, instead of the full can she knew the directions called for. She knew that because chicken and stars had also been a fave of hers when she was a kid. Enough that she still bought it on a fairly regular basis and hid it in her cabinets behind the jars of organic tomatoes, the boxes of steel-cut oats, the tins of gourmet green tea and the bottles of extra-virgin, first cold-pressed olive oil. Right beside the cans of Beefaroni.

Anyway, she was just surprised he knew his way around a can of soup and an antiquated kitchen. Well, knew his way around an antiquated kitchen, anyway. As for the soup…

"You should add a full can of water," she said. "The directions call for—"

"A whole can," he finished in unison with her. "I know. But a whole can waters it down. A half can gives it more flavor."

Oh. Okay. So maybe he did know his way around a can of soup, too. It was still weird, because he seemed like the last kind of guy who would have even a nodding acquaintance with either.

As if he'd read her mind, he told her, "My mom and I lived on canned stuff for years when I was a kid. After my dad died, the two of us only had her income to live on. We made regular visits to the food bank. Almost everything there came in cans."

And a growing boy's hunger must have been voracious, she thought, filling in the blanks he didn't want to fill himself. Canned food probably barely made a dent in it. Maybe that was why he turned his nose up at canned stuff now. Because he'd paid his canned-food dues a long time ago. She honestly didn't know anything about him other than the name he'd been given from WITSEC and what she'd heard and observed today.

She'd been so happy when Phoebe had sent her the info about him, something that prevented Renny from screwing up again—ha—that she immediately looked up his most recent contact info, got in touch with his assistant and booked her flight to Chicago. And when she'd seen his house, she just assumed he must have lived that way forever.

"Lower school," he said.

"What?" she asked.

"You said Beefaroni was your favorite food when you were in lower school. Not 'grade school.' You said, 'lower school.'"

It took her a moment to rewind their conversation back to where she had used the phrase. But she didn't understand the distinction he was making. "Yes. So?"

"So you must have gone to private school. Only private schools use that 'lower school' designation. Anywhere else, you would have said 'grade school.' Or 'elementary school.'"

And if Tate had grown up on canned food and his mother's solitary paycheck, then he must not have gone to private school. Renny wondered if he was one of those people who'd been so driven to succeed as an adult because he'd been so deprived as a child.

"I did go to private school, actually," she told him. Without elaborating. Since there was really no reason to rub his nose in her privileged upbringing when he'd had what must have been a pretty challenging one himself. Even if he was superrich now, no one ever left their childhood far behind. Renny knew that, because every time she had to spend more than five minutes with either of her parents, she immediately regressed into that five-year-old disappointment shedding her pink tutu.

Tate, however, seemed to want her to elaborate, because he asked, "Was it one of those really tony private schools with marble floors and mahogany paneling and farm-to-table lunches?"

"Um, kind of," she admitted. She figured it wasn't necessary to add that it had also sat on acres and acres of gorgeously manicured green space that lent itself to some really beautiful pastoral afternoons when they sometimes held classes outdoors.

Instead, she said softly, "I'm sorry about your dad."

He'd located a spoon—also in the first drawer he checked—and was slowly stirring the soup, gazing into it as if it might offer him the answers he needed to get out of this mess.

"It was a long time ago," he replied just as softly. "I really don't remember him that well. My stepfather was more of a father to me than my dad was. Not that I'm saying my biological father was a bad father," he hastened to add, glancing up long enough to see if Renny had drawn the wrong conclusion. "Just…my stepfather is the only father I really knew, you know? My mom married him when I was ten. And he was a good guy. Good to my mom. Good for my mom."

Those last sentences—and Tate's absence from them—were awfully telling. Especially considering the way he'd sounded like a ten-year-old boy when he uttered them.

"Do you remember anything about your life before your parents went into the program?" she asked.

Still stirring the soup, he said, "A few impressions of isolated moments, but nothing that puts that life into perspective."

"And your mother never gave you any reason to think there was this secret past she and your father shared?"

He shook his head. "Nothing. I mean, she was an overprotective mother—wouldn't let me do a lot of the things I wanted to do. But lots of moms are like that. I just figured she was a worrier."

Renny could relate. Her mom had worried a lot about her, too. But the reason Melisande Desjardins Twigg had worried about her daughter was because she wasn't daughter-like enough. When her mother took her to the store to order Renny her first set of big-girl bedroom furniture, they'd gone straight to the French Provincial—sorry, that was *Provençal Français*—section. Renny had uttered something along the lines of "Ew, grody" and dragged her mother to the bunk beds and desks made out of much sturdier stuff. When Renny wanted to wear a suit—with pants—to her middle school graduation instead of the white dresses the other girls had to wear, her mother had about had a heart attack. And when Renny decorated her high school mortarboard with a quote from Tupac instead of the Swarovski crystals her mother suggested, well...

Suffice it to say Renny had a long tradition of giving her mother cause to worry. At least, that was what her mother had always thought. Anyway, she could kind of relate to Tate Hawthorne at the moment.

She tried again. "Is there any chance maybe—"

"Look, Renata," he interrupted. He stopped stirring

the soup and met her gaze. "I know you're just trying to help, but right now there's so much going on in my head I don't know what to think about any of it. I'd really rather not talk about it, okay?"

Not talking about it was another thing Renny understood. Her family were the hands-down champs of not talking about stuff. So were most of her ex-boyfriends, come to think of it.

"Okay," she said. "I understand. Just…when you're done with that pot, do you mind rinsing it out? I'll use it when you're finished."

He gazed at her in silence for another moment, as if he wasn't sure how to reply to what should be a simple question. "Sure," he said finally. "No problem."

A phone suddenly rang with the shrill retro ringtone used by so many today—except this one was shriller and more retro. When it sounded again, she realized it was coming from the bedroom. She and Tate hurried in that direction, but Renny had the lead on him and made it through the door first. She followed the ringing to the other side of the bed, where a plastic rotary phone sat on the lower shelf of the nightstand. She sprang for it as it rang again, landing on her stomach on the mattress, and snatched up the receiver.

"Hello?" she said breathlessly.

"Ms. Twigg?"

For some reason, she was disappointed to hear Inspector Grady's voice at the other end of the line. Who had she expected it would be? Her mother? The Publishers Clearing House Giveaway people? Walter, the guy who'd dumped her three weeks ago after two dates—

not that she'd minded much, since he'd been so, well, Waltery?

"Hi, Mr. Grady," she said.

She looked over her shoulder at Tate, only to find that he looked a little disappointed, too. Maybe he'd been expecting a call from his stunning redhead. Then his gaze skittered away from her face and landed... Well, there was no way to deny it. He was staring at her ass. Again. She grabbed the phone and maneuvered herself into a sitting position. When his gaze wandered to her face again, she did her best to glower at him. In return, he only smiled. Knowingly.

"Ms. Twigg? Are you there?"

"I'm here, Mr. Grady."

"Look, there's been a little trouble," he began.

Oh, duh, she wanted to reply. Instead, she listened as he told her how almost immediately after he arrived in town, the roads were closed behind him from flash flooding, and how he wouldn't be able to make it back to the cottage tonight, but there was some canned food and other stuff in the kitchen, enough to get them through till tomorrow, and blah, blah, blah, blah, blah. Renny didn't register much after that except for how Grady would get back as soon as he could, and he was sure Tate and Renny would be fine until he did, since nobody was getting out of Pattypan, Wisconsin, tonight, and nobody knew where she and Tate were, anyway.

All she could do was keep repeating, "Uh-huh...uh-huh...uh-huh." When she hung up the phone, Tate was still staring at her from the doorway, now with an expression that demanded, *Well?*

Gingerly, she set the phone back in its cradle. Nervously, she moved around the bed to return it to the nightstand. Anxiously, she tried to rouse a smile.

And then, very quietly, she said, "So. Looks like you and I are going to be on our own tonight. You know how to play Snap?"

Six

A raucous crack of thunder woke Tate from a dream about Renata. Or maybe not, he reconsidered when he saw her sleeping in a slant of moonlight in the chair near the sofa where he lay himself. She looked so fey and otherworldly, a part of him wondered if he might still be asleep. Once the thunder rolled off, the cottage was oddly quiet and, save for that one sliver of silver that had found her, very dark. He could still be dreaming. Any minute, he could wake up in his bed at home, with a belly full of sushi and champagne and a tumbled redhead sleeping beside him, waiting for him to wake her and tumble her again.

But if he woke in his own bed, it would mean Renata really had been nothing but a dream. And that would mean he'd never stood behind her wrestling with a window and his libido as he inhaled great gulps of her, a combination of immaculate sweetness and earthy sexiness that had nearly driven him mad. It would mean he'd never brushed her lips with his and been startled by the explosion of heat that rocked him, a reaction he hadn't had to a woman since... Hell, he didn't think he'd ever had a reaction like that to a woman. If Renata was nothing but a dream, and he woke up back in his real life, safe and sound, then that would mean he was back in his real life, safe and sound.

But that was what he wanted, wasn't it? His real life before she'd shown up at his front door? So why was he suddenly kind of relieved to realize he wasn't dreaming at all?

Lack of sleep, he told himself. It made people think crazy things. The rain had still been coming down in torrents when he and Renata ate a dinner of canned pasta just before sundown. Which, in hindsight, he had to admit hadn't been half-bad. The dinner or the company. Renata's incessant yakking had become less annoying as the day wore on. Maybe because trying to keep track of what she was nattering about had kept Tate from having to think about all the things he still wasn't ready to think about. Like not being who he'd always thought he was. Like having a family, regardless of how sketchy their origins might be. Like how tempting Renata smelled and how weird she made him feel.

The last thing he remembered before falling asleep, he'd been flipping through a years-old copy of *Esquire*, unable to sleep thanks to the storm raging outside, and Renata had been curled up in her chair with a tattered paperback she'd pulled from a bookcase in the bedroom. Something by Agatha Christie. He'd been surprised by her choice. It was so old-fashioned.

The book lay facedown in her lap now. One of her hands was curved loosely over its spine, and the other was dangling by the side of the chair. Her head was leaning back in a way that offered a tantalizing glimpse of her neck but guaranteed she would have a wicked ache in it when she woke. In spite of that, he was hesitant to rouse her. She just looked so…

He studied her again, the elegant line of her jaw, the sweep of dark lashes on her cheeks, the lush mouth. And the errant tresses of hair that fell from her ragged topknot, curving around the gaping shirt collar that still revealed a whisper of lace beneath.

Well, there was just something about moonlight that suited her. Who was Tate to mess with that?

What time was it? Automatically, he looked around for his phone, then remembered he didn't have it with him. Which naturally reminded him he didn't have anything with him. How the hell was anyone supposed to survive without even the most basic necessities? Like a cell phone? He rose and prowled around the cottage until he located a clock in the bedroom, one of those old plastic ones with glow-in-the-dark radium numbers. It was 1:57 a.m., according to the radioactive yet once common appliance. How had anyone survived the midtwentieth century, anyway?

And just how much longer were they going to be stuck in this time warp of a place? Maybe he should be concerned about the fact that Grady had left the two of them alone, but the storm had worsened a lot after he left, so Tate hadn't been that surprised when the marshal was waylaid by flooding. He'd been heartened by Grady's assurance that he would be back tomorrow. Until the storm continued to lash for hours and the road they'd driven in on turned into a mud slide. Considering the lousy condition it was in when it was dry, he hated to think about how hard it would be to drive up the thing now, even with four-wheel drive. He and Renata could be living out of cans for a while.

Just like when Tate was a kid. Great. The last thing he wanted was to be reminded of that time in his life.

He returned to the living room and saw that Renata hadn't budged. Tate, on the other hand, was wideawake. He seldom slept more than five hours a night, but he normally fell asleep much later than he did tonight. There was little chance he would be nodding off again any time soon. Normally, when he couldn't sleep, he went downstairs to his office to work. There was always plenty of that to catch up on. Here, though…

Well, he wasn't much of a reader. Not Agatha Christie, anyway. And as nice as it was to watch Renata sleep, to do that for any length of time put him in creepster territory. What did a man do in the middle of the night when he was locked up indefinitely with a beautiful woman who also had nothing to do?

Other than that?

Shower. Yeah, that was it. After spending the day in his polo uniform, he wasn't feeling exactly springtime fresh. Then again, once he showered, he was going to have to change back into the clothes on his back, since he'd left his house with nothing but, well, the clothes on his back. But if there was food in the cottage, maybe there were other provisions, too.

He returned to the bedroom and switched on a lamp by the bed. In the closet, he found a couple of shirts— off-the-rack and 100 percent polyester, he noted distastefully—and one pair of trousers that was four sizes too big for him. The shirts were all too big, too, save for one with long sleeves, but if he couldn't find anything else, he could make do.

He had better luck with the dresser. There was a sweater unsuited to swamp weather, but also a white cotton T-shirt. In another drawer, he discovered a pair of blue jeans, even if they were as midcentury as everything else in this place. The denim was soft and faded, and they had a button fly. But they were only one size too big, which at least made them workable. And it would make them more comfortable while he had to go commando waiting for his boxers to dry after washing them.

Just to be sure, he riffled through the rest of the drawers, but the only other clothes he found were some unspeakably ugly men's pajamas and some giant Bermuda shorts. Looked like Renata was out of luck. Evidently, the overwhelming majority of people who had to go into protective custody were men. Large men, at that.

Tate thought again about his parents. What had it been like for them, leaving everything behind and moving to a place they'd never visited before, having no clue what the future held? As bad as it was being stuck here with nothing, he at least knew that at some point

he would be going back to his life and all that was familiar. His parents had had to build a new life in a new
place with strangers they'd probably taken a long time
to learn to trust—if they'd ever learned at all.

For some reason, that made him think again of Renata. In the moonlight. Looking soft and bewitching.

Shower, he reminded himself. He'd been about to
take a shower. A nice, *long* shower. A nice, long, *cold*
shower. He'd figure out the rest of it later.

Renny wasn't sure what woke her up. She only knew
she was in semidarkness and wasn't in her own bed.
When she lifted her head, her gaze fell on the book in
her lap. Right, she recalled groggily. She was in King's
Abbot with the recently deceased Roger Ackroyd. No,
that wasn't right. She was in Wisconsin with Agatha
Christie. No, that wasn't it, either. She was in Wisconsin with…

Tate Hawthorne. Right. It was all coming back to
her now.

She rubbed her aching neck and sat up straighter,
twisting to alleviate another ache in her back. Next time
she fell asleep, it was going to be in bed. Then she remembered there was only one bed in the cottage. One
bed that wasn't even queen-sized. Of course, there was
also a sofa. Which didn't look very comfortable, the
reason she'd chosen the chair for her reading.

Well, that and because Tate had been on the couch,
surrounded by his cone of silence.

She heard what sounded like a metallic squeak, followed by the cessation of a humming she hadn't noticed

until then, one she recognized as water rushing through pipes. Tate was in the shower. Or, more correctly, Tate was getting out of the shower. All naked and wet, and wet and naked, and covered in naked, wet skin. Like she really needed to have that information.

Thankfully, the only shower was in the bathroom adjacent to the bedroom, so he wouldn't come popping into the living room out of the other one all naked and wet, fumbling with a towel he couldn't quite get knotted around his waist, so it kept dipping low over his hips, under his flat waist and sculpted abs, low enough to reveal those extremely intriguing lines men had over their legs that curved and dipped down under the towel to frame what was sure to be a seriously impressive—

Anyway, that wouldn't be happening. For which Renny was exceedingly grateful. Really, she was.

She heard the bathroom door click open in the bedroom, and only then realized the reason the living room wasn't totally dark was because of the lamplight spilling in from that room. A great fist seized her insides and squeezed hard at the thought of Tate in there naked. She told herself she only imagined the scent of pine that seemed to permeate the entire cottage or the way the air suddenly turned all hot and damp. Then she heard the soft sound of bare feet on wood floor. She felt Tate moving closer behind her, then closer, then closer still.

She sat silently as he passed her chair—oh, yeah, that was definitely him causing the hot, steamy, piney thing—and seated himself on the couch. There was just enough light for her to see him, dressed now in a white V-neck T-shirt and faded blue jeans, a towel draped around his neck that he was using to scrub his close-cropped hair. She wondered where he'd found fresh clothes.

As if she'd asked the question aloud, his head snapped up, and his gaze met hers. "You're awake," he said.

"And you're clean," she replied, trying not to sound jealous. As uncomfortable as she'd been all day, it hadn't occurred to her to look for fresh clothes and get cleaned up. "You even shaved."

He lifted a hand to his beautiful jaw. "There are some disposable razors in the bathroom. If you're careful, you won't flay yourself alive with one. And there are some clothes in the bedroom that must have been left behind by previous visitors. A little big, but not too bad."

No, not too bad at all. As sexy as Tate had been in a skintight polo uniform, it was nothing compared to the jeans and T-shirt. Mostly because jeans and T-shirts were Renny's favorite attire for men. And when that T-shirt was V-necked enough to hint at the dark scattering of hair and sculpted muscle beneath, well...

"I don't suppose there was anything in my size, was there?" she asked in an effort to steer her brain in a new direction. "Something cute and comfy by Johnny Was, perhaps? Maybe some Tory Burch tomboy? Or some off-the-rack geek chic? I'd even settle for some sporty separates if they don't smell like swampland."

Because it was just Renny's luck to be trapped in the middle of nowhere with a rich, gorgeous, recently wet and naked playboy, and wearing the kind of clothes her mother would wear—which could only be made more off-putting by the added accessory of eau de quagmire.

Tate looked at her blankly. "The only part of that I understood was the word *tomboy*. If your definition of tomboy is men's shirts, trousers and pajamas that would swallow you, then, yeah. Have at it. Otherwise, the pickings are slim. But you might be able to figure out something."

Great. She could exchange clothes her mother would wear for clothes her father would wear. That was sure to make her less off-putting. Still, they would at least be clean and not stinky.

She looked at Tate again. At the curve of biceps peeking out from beneath the sleeve of his shirt. At the strong column of his throat. At the chiseled jaw now freshly shaved. And suddenly a shower seemed like a very good idea.

"Is there still some hot water?" she asked. Not that she would be using any hot water. Ahem.

"Oh, there's plenty," he said in a way that made her think he hadn't used any hot water, either. Hmm.

Without another word, she made her way to the bedroom. Tate's discarded polo uniform was folded loosely on the dresser, and his boots were on the floor below them. Quickly, she studied her apparel options in the closet and dresser, only to discover they were every bit as grim as he'd described. A gigantic man's shirt in the closet—in lavender, so apparently some criminals weren't afraid of a little color—would fall to her knees. But that was good, since she would have to wash out her underwear and let it air-dry, and she'd need something to cover her until then.

It took a minute for the significance of that to settle

into her brain, and it only did because she walked into the bathroom to see a pair of men's silk boxers slung over the towel rack, drying. If Tate's underwear was hanging in here, then what was he wearing under his blue jeans out—

There was no way Renny was going to let herself think any further about that. Or about how she would have to go panties-free herself, wearing nothing but a gigantic men's shirt that could easily be brushed aside for a quick—

Well, all righty, then. The less gigantic men's pajamas it would be. At least she could—probably—keep them hitched up by tying a knot in the waistband. A really tight knot. That would be virtually impossible for Tate *or* her to get untied.

Yeah. That's the ticket.

She snagged those from the dresser drawer—they were bilious green and patterned with little golf carts— escaped to the bathroom, closed and locked the door, turned the cold faucet handle to full blast, and stripped off her fetid clothing. So she and Tate would be without underwear for a few hours. So what? People went without underwear all the time in some parts of the world, and they did just fine.

She stepped into the cold shower and yelped.

Oh, yeah. That should do it. For now, anyway.

Seven

Tate heard a yelp from the bathroom and figured Renata was having a close encounter of the cold-shower kind much like his own. Obviously, he wasn't the only one who was thinking about the repercussions of two red-blooded adults who'd been dancing around an attraction to each other all day, being left alone for the night with no underwear.

Well, okay, maybe they hadn't been dancing around it the entire day, since he still couldn't shake the memory of that too-brief embrace. The question now was, had Renata opted for the obnoxious pajamas in the dresser, or one of the shirts in the closet? 'Cause the latter would make things infinitely easier.

Suddenly feeling restless, he rose and padded barefoot to the kitchen, forgetting until he opened the refrigerator that there wasn't much there to keep his mind off what Renata might or might not be wearing. Automatically, he grabbed one of the beers and twisted off the cap with a satisfying hiss. Then he enjoyed an even more satisfying swallow. As good as it tasted, though, it wasn't enough to keep his thoughts from wandering back to Renata. Who, at that very moment, was standing naked beneath a rush of water under the same roof he was.

He couldn't remember the last time he'd been this close to a naked woman when the two of them weren't taking advantage of that. Then again, Renata wasn't exactly his type, he reminded himself. Again. She was the last kind of woman he needed or wanted in his life. He'd survived a lot of women who showed up regularly on those "toxic types to avoid" lists—the diva, the control freak, the drama queen and his personal favorite, the material girl. But he'd never had a run-in with a member of Renata's tribe: the walking disaster.

And that one was probably the worst of the bunch for a man like him. The other types could be handled once a guy figured out which of their buttons to push or not push and where and when they liked best to be stroked. But the walking disaster? There were too many buttons with that type, and stroking the wrong part could be catastrophic. With a woman like that, there were too many things outside a man's control. Too many things that could go wrong. As had been the case with Renata from nearly the moment she'd walked into his life.

Okay, so maybe she wasn't responsible for the circumstances of his birth and had nothing to do with his biological family being a *famiglia*. She was still a disaster. There were still too many variables with her. There was still so much that could go wrong. And don't even get him started on her buttons.

He heard the click of the bathroom door and glanced at the bedroom in time to see a shadow fall across the bed. She turned off the bathroom light and, before exiting it, the bedroom light, as well, throwing the entire cottage into darkness.

He heard the whisper of bare feet, followed by a softly uttered "Ow, dammit" as she slammed something that sounded a lot like her knee into one of the tables by the sofa. Finally, she snapped on the lamp and threw the living room into warm golden light.

Okay, maybe she wasn't quite a walking disaster. Maybe she was more of a moseying disaster. She was still someone he needed to avoid.

Which was going to be even harder now than it had been before, because Renata looked... Even with her hair wrapped up in a towel like a suburban-dwelling, SUV-driving spa-goer, she looked... Even in ugly men's pajamas that would fit three of her, she looked...

Wow. Renata looked really, really... Wow.

"Sorry about that," she muttered as she steadied the lamp on the table. "I'm not so good in the dark."

Oh, Tate doubted that. She'd done pretty well in the dark so far. He'd love to see how well she did other things in the dark.

"No worries," he said.

No worries. Right. She'd rolled up the legs of the pajamas to her knees, and the sleeves to her elbows, meaning she was covered just fine, but was also intriguingly... not. And even with every button of the shirt fastened, the deep V of its placket and collar meant the garment was open to the center of her chest.

Tate was suddenly, oddly, grateful she wasn't better endowed. At least this way, he could pretend there wasn't a luscious woman underneath those little golf carts. A luscious woman who could make ugly golf-cart pajamas sexier than the skimpiest lingerie.

Renata smiled shyly at him—*shyly*, when he was thinking about things like barely there lingerie and even more barely there pajama necklines—and then, still wearing her terry-cloth turban, she moved back to her chair and picked up the book she'd left lying there. Then she thumbed through the pages until she found the one where she'd left off. And then, *then*, she did something really remarkable.

She continued with her reading. As if nothing had changed in the few minutes since she emerged from the bathroom in a cloud of prurience and pine soap and potential developments.

Fine. Two could play at that game.

"Beer?" he asked.

She threw him another sweet smile and shook her head. "No, thanks. I'm good."

Then she went back to reading. With her head still wrapped in a towel. And ugly golf-cart pajamas hiding every interesting part of her—except that tantalizing bit of skin between her breasts that had become even more tantalizing by how the shirt now gaped open

enough to reveal she was better endowed than he'd
first thought.

He moved back to the sofa and picked up the magazine he'd already flipped through. He was about to
remark on the editorial about whatever the hell it was
about when she tented her book in her lap and reached
up to unwind the towel on her head. After that, he
couldn't remember much of anything, because her dark
hair came tumbling out and spilled around her shoulders in ropes of damp silk.

He watched as she scrubbed her scalp with the towel,
something that shouldn't have been sexy but which was
unbelievably sexy. Then she draped the towel over the
arm of the chair and began to comb her fingers through
her hair. Okay, that was something that normally would
be sexy—if the woman doing it wasn't wrapped in little
cartoon golf carts—but with Renata, it was seriously
sexy. Even in little cartoon golf carts. Maybe because
of the way the top of the pajama shirt was opening and
closing in time with her movements. Or maybe because
of the way strands of her hair were clinging to her neck
and chest the way Tate wanted to be clinging himself.
Or maybe because it was nighttime, and the two of
them were stranded here alone, and neither of them was
wearing underwear.

Ah, dammit. He'd hoped he wouldn't think about
that again.

Did that even matter, though? What Renata was
doing was sexy, period. And it was sexy because she
was sexy. Hell, at this point, the cartoon golf carts were
even sexy. And if Renata gave him the smallest indica-

tion that she was thinking about the same things he was thinking about at the moment, then there was nothing that could stop them from—

"Um, Tate?" she asked suddenly. Softly. In a *very* intimate voice.

He did his best to sound noncommittal. "Yes, Renata?"

"Could you... Would you...I mean, I was wondering if you would mind if...I was wondering if you would, um..."

Whatever her very intimate question was, she couldn't seem to finish it. Which naturally made Tate think it was something really, *really* intimate. Something that obviously involved him, too. In a way she wasn't able to put into words, so she was relying on that very intimate tone of voice to convey her very intimate thoughts.

Her very intimate desires?

In an effort to help her along, he assured her, "Whatever you want to do, Renata...whatever you want *me* to do...I promise that I not only could do it, I would do it. I wouldn't mind at all, and I definitely would."

She smiled at his thorough answer to her very intimate question. At least one of them could make clear what was going on in his head. Women were just so damned circuitous.

Slowly, she stood, pushing her mass of dark hair over her shoulder. Then she took a step forward, toward Tate. He tossed aside the magazine, set his beer on the table and sat up for whatever she planned to do. He was about to lift his arms to pull her into his lap when she spun around and, without a word, headed back to the bedroom.

Well, okay, then. He hadn't pegged her as the sort of woman who would want to skip foreplay and get right to the main event, but hey, whatever. He aimed to please. Even if he did actually enjoy foreplay. Maybe next time. Or the time after that. Or the time after that. As she'd said, they could be here a few days.

He followed her to the bedroom only to discover she'd gone into the bathroom and closed the door. Maybe she was shy about undressing in front of him. Not that a woman who had just blurted out that she wanted to have sex should have been shy about anything, but...whatever.

He turned down the bed and switched on the lamp beside it, unleashing a veritable desert sun onto the bed. Well, hell. That wouldn't do. He liked to see what he was doing when he was with a woman, but he didn't want to be blinded while he was doing it. He flicked the switch again, but the lamp in the living room was as dim as the one in here was bright and barely reached the bed.

He remembered finding candles and matches in the kitchen when he was looking for a can opener. They were the stumpy white emergency kind, but they'd do. As quickly as he could, he collected them and returned to the bedroom, setting two on the dresser and two on the nightstand, then lit them all. Once they were going, he stripped off his shirt and went to work on the buttons of his fly.

He'd reached the last one when the bathroom door

opened and Renata emerged, her attention focused on something in her hand she was drying with her towel.

"I really appreciate this, Tate. My hair is just so unmanageable when it's this wet, and there's no hair dryer in this place. It's always a lot easier if someone else brushes it for me. I couldn't find a brush, but I found this comb, and it has wide enough teeth that it should work okay, but I wanted to wash it first, natch, and—"

She stopped in her tracks—and stopped chattering, too—when she saw him standing shirtless and nearly pantsless with the bed unmade behind him and candles burning beside it. "What the...?" she muttered.

"I thought you wanted to have sex," he said.

She expelled a single, humorless chuckle. "No."

She was so emphatic, the two-letter response actually came out with two syllables as *no-oh*. Then, as if he hadn't already figured out how emphatically she was saying no, she hastily clarified, "I want you to comb my hair."

"But you sounded like you wanted to have sex," he persisted, his testosterone, at least, not willing to give up the fight.

She gazed at him, mystified. "What about anything I said could have possibly sounded like I wanted to have sex?"

He replayed their conversation in his head. "Um, all of it?"

She was silent for a moment, but looked thoughtful enough that he could tell she was replaying the conversation in her head, too. For another hopeful moment, he thought she'd reply, *Oh, yeah. I guess I did sound like*

I wanted to have sex. Okay. Let's have sex! Then her expression went confused again.

"There is no way you could have mistaken any of that for me wanting to have sex."

Fine. Tomatoes, tomahtoes.

He countered, "Well, I sure as hell couldn't tell you wanted me to comb your hair."

She said nothing for another moment, then, very quietly, asked, "Could you please button up your pants?"

Tate didn't think he'd ever had a woman ask him that question before. And, truth be told, it kind of startled him to hear it now. He'd just never had a woman turn him down. Ever. Even before he'd become the success he was now, with all the showy plumage of cars and cash and castle. When he was a college student living in a dump of a loft, he'd still always had girls over, whenever he'd asked. Hell, when he was in high school, driving a beat-up Ford Falcon, his backseat had seen constant action. Women had just always flocked to him, from the time he was old enough to want them to.

Except for Renata Twigg.

His gaze still fixed on hers, he began to rebutton his jeans. And he could barely believe his eyes when she actually turned her head to keep from watching him. How could a woman who inspired such abject wantonness in a man be too shy to watch him put himself back together? Especially when he hadn't even been completely undone?

"Thank you," she said when he'd finished. Still not looking at him, she added, "Now could you put your shirt back on, too?"

He bit back a growl of irritation as he grabbed the T-shirt from the bed and thrust it back over his head.

"Thank you," she said again.

But she still wasn't looking at him. Jeez, was he that unappealing?

Then he remembered she hadn't found him unappealing that afternoon. She'd melted into that kiss with as much appetite as he had. Even when she told him it wasn't a good idea for them to continue, she'd been clinging to his shirt as if she wanted to pull him back again. And the look in her eyes... There was no way a man could mistake a look like that. Since then, more than once, he'd caught her eyeing him in a way that made him think—no, made him *know*—she liked what she saw when she looked at him.

So it wasn't that Renata didn't want him the same way he wanted her. It was that she didn't want to want him the same way he wanted her. Which actually just confused him even more.

Women were weird. Why was sex such a big deal to them?

"So I guess this means you won't help me comb out my hair, huh?" she asked quietly.

He'd forgotten that was what she'd asked him to do. Then he surprised himself by saying, "No, this doesn't mean that."

Because, in spite of her not wanting to want him, Tate still wanted her. He had no idea why. Even if no woman had ever rebuffed him before, he wasn't the kind of guy to keep after one who did, regardless of her reasons. But he still wanted to be close to Renata. He still wanted to touch her. He still wanted to inhale great intoxicating gulps of her scent. And if combing her hair would bring him close enough to do those things, he was content to do it.

He sat on the bed and patted the empty place beside himself. "Sit down," he said. Then he held out his hand. "Give me the comb."

She studied him warily, then took a small step forward and handed him the comb. He took it without hesitation, then patted the seat beside him again. She took another step, one that brought her close enough for him to tumble her to the bed if he wanted. Which he did want. But she didn't. So he only patted the mattress one last time.

Finally, she sat, the bed giving enough beneath her to send her leaning his way. Her shoulder bumped his, but she ricocheted off and turned her back. After thrusting two big handfuls of hair over her shoulders, she mumbled another breathy thank-you and waited for him to begin. Tate lifted the comb to her long, dark, sexy hair and, as gently as he could, began to tug it through the mass.

Eight

Boys were weird.

As Renny sat on the edge of the mattress with her back to Tate, she tried to focus on that thought and not the other one attempting to usurp it about how good it felt to have his fingers running through her hair. That first thought made a lot more sense than the second did, anyway. Boys were weird. Men were even weirder.

All they ever thought about was sex, and everything had some kind of sexual component to it. There was no way Tate should have thought she was talking about sex when she was talking about hair combing. She hadn't said a single word that was suggestive. On the other hand, it did feel kind of sexy the way he was combing her hair…

He was surprisingly gentle, cupping one hand tenderly over the crown of her head as he carefully pulled the comb along with small gestures. When he finished one section of hair, he pushed it forward over her shoulder and moved to another to start again. Her scalp warmed under his touch, a sweet, mellow heat that gradually seeped downward, into her neck and over her shoulders, then lower still, along her arms and down to the middle of her back.

"You're good at this," she said softly, closing her eyes.

He said nothing for a moment, then replied, just as softly, "Let me know if I hurt you."

"No worries," she quickly assured him.

Renny stopped thinking and just let herself feel. With her eyes closed, her other senses leaped to the fore. She heard the steady patter of rain on the window, smelled the clean scent of pine soap enveloping them. But most of all, she savored the warmth of Tate's palm on her head and the brush of his fingers along her neck, down her back and up again, as he untangled one strand of hair and moved it over her shoulder, followed by another. And another. And another. Again and again, his hand stroked her from her head to her waist, until all of her hair was streaming over her left shoulder, and the right side of her neck lay exposed.

By then, she felt like a rag doll, boneless and limp, her entire body evanescing into a state of serenity. Although he'd finished his task, Tate still sat behind her, and Renny said nothing to encourage him to move. On the contrary, she kind of wanted him to stay there forever, because even the slightest shift in their positions might ruin the sense of well-being that had come over her, a feeling that nothing in the world could ever go wrong again.

So lovely was the feeling that it seeped from her inside to her outside, manifesting as the brush of soft kisses along her neck and shoulders. Then she realized it wasn't she who was creating the sensation. It was Tate. He was dragging butterfly-soft openmouthed kisses over her sensitive flesh, pushing aside the fabric of her shirt as he went, stirring her already-incited senses to even greater awareness. On some level, she knew she should tell him to stop. But on another level, that was the last thing she wanted him to do.

"Tate," she murmured, still not sure what she wanted to say.

"Shh," he whispered, the soft sough a warm rush against her skin.

She opened her mouth to object again, but he nipped her shoulder lightly, igniting a blast of heat in her belly that flared into her chest and womb. She cried out softly in response, so he placed a soft kiss on the spot, tasted it with the flat of his tongue and peppered her shoulder with more caresses. Somewhere in the dark recesses of her brain, an alarm bell rang out, but the roar of blood in her ears deafened her to it. Especially when he roped an arm around her waist and pulled her back against himself, nuzzling the sensitive place behind her ear before dropping a kiss to her jaw.

It had been so long since she had enjoyed this kind of closeness with another human being. So long...

Too long.

Unable to help herself, Renny arced one arm backward, to skim her fingers through his hair. It was all the encouragement Tate needed. The hand at her waist rose higher, curling over her breast, thumbing the sensitive peak. She cried out again at the contact, the sound fracturing the stillness, and arched her body forward. Deftly, he unbuttoned her shirt and pushed the garment open, then cupped both hands over her naked breasts, kneading softly, rolling her nipples beneath his fingers. She gasped at the heat that shot through her and tried to turn to face him.

"Not yet," he whispered somewhere close to her ear.

She reached her other hand back to join the first, linking her fingers at the nape of his neck. Tate continued to stroke her breast with one hand as he dipped the other to the waistband of her pajamas. He effortlessly found the knot she'd tied in the side to keep them up, and just as effortlessly untied it. Then he dipped his hand beneath the fabric and between her legs, finding the feminine heart of her.

"Oh, God, you're already so wet," he murmured as he slid a finger inside her.

She gasped again, pushing her hips forward. He met her eagerly, driving his finger deeper, then sliding it out to furrow it between the hot folds of her flesh. Slowly, slowly…oh, so slowly…he caressed her, drawing intimate circles over her before pushing in and out of her again. He fingered her for long minutes, a hot coil inside her winding tighter and tighter as he did, until she feared she would explode from the sensations. Her breathing became more ragged, her pulse rate leaped and just when she thought she would come, he removed his hand and drew it upward again, laying it flat against her naked belly.

"Not yet," he whispered again.

In the candlelight, she felt more than saw him slip her shirt from her shoulders and toss it to the floor. But she couldn't help watching when he stood to remove his, too, reaching behind himself to grab a fistful of white cotton and drag it forward over his head. Beneath it, he was an awesome sight, muscle and sinew corded into a torso that could have been wrought by the hands of a Greek god. His biceps bunched as he undid the buttons of his fly one by one, until his blue jeans hung open on his hips, his member pushing hard against the soft denim. Then he joined her again on the bed, urging her toward the mattress until she was on her back and he was atop her, bare flesh to bare flesh. And then his mouth was on hers, consuming her, and it was all Renny could do not to come apart at the seams.

He touched her everywhere as he kissed her. He skimmed his palm along her rib cage, then into the narrow dip of her waist, then over her hip, down to her thigh and back again. Every time his hand moved over her, her pajama bottoms dipped lower, until he was tugging them out from under her and tossing them to the floor, too. And then Renny lay beneath him naked, feeling wanton, scandalous and aroused.

She explored Tate, too, running her hands over the bumps of muscle in his shoulders and arms, splaying her fingers wide over the silky skin of his back, dipping her hands beneath the loose denim on his hips to cup his taut buttocks. There wasn't an inch of him that wasn't hot and hard, especially when she guided her hand between their bodies and into his jeans to curl her fingers around his heavy shaft. He gasped at the contact, tasting her deeply and moving his hand between her legs again.

For long moments, they petted each other, matching their rhythm in languid strokes that gradually grew more demanding. As Renny drew near the precipice of an orgasm again, Tate suddenly pulled away, standing at the side of the bed.

With a devilish grin, he hooked his fingers in the waistband of his jeans and urged them down, until he was naked, too, gilded in the warm candle glow.

And if Renny had thought him an awesome sight before, now he was spectacular.

He moved back to the bed, sitting on its edge and pulling Renny into his lap to face him, straddling him. She guided her hands to his hair, stroking her palms over the silky tresses, loving the feel of having him so close. When he ducked his head to her breast, sucking her nipple deep into his mouth, she cried out again. And when he tucked his fingers gently into the elegant line bisecting her bottom to gently trace it, she gasped. But when he moved his hard shaft toward the damp, heated center of her, she drew herself backward, covering him again with her hand to halt his entry.

She couldn't quite bring herself to tell him to stop, though. She didn't want him to stop. She wanted him. A lot. It had been so long since she'd enjoyed this kind of release. It felt so good to be with him. And he was the kind of man she would never meet again. Why shouldn't she have one night with him? Where was the harm?

Oh, right. They'd had to leave without even the most basic essentials. Like, for instance, birth control.

"I want you, Renata," Tate said, his voice low and erotic, his hot gaze fixed on hers. "I really, really want you."

"I want you, too," she said. "But this is happening so fast, and I didn't exactly come prepared."

Boy, talk about a double entendre. Especially since she was less concerned about the birth control aftermath of a night like this than she was the emotional aftermath. She was at a place in her cycle where pregnancy was extremely unlikely, and her lady parts worked like clockwork. Would that she could be as confident that other parts of her body—like her heart—were as predictable.

"I didn't come prepared for a party, either," he told her. "But that doesn't mean we can't still have fun."

Before she could say any more, he dragged his fingers against her again, catching the sensitive nub of her clitoris gently between his thumb and middle finger. Renny gasped as he caressed her, heat rocketing through her body, pooling in her womb, driving all coherent thought from her brain. When he drove his finger into her again, she knew it would never be enough. She wanted more of him. She wanted all of him. She needed him inside her. Now. Her body demanded it.

That could be the only explanation for why she told him, "I won't get pregnant, Tate. The timing is completely wrong. And I want you inside me. Please. Make love to me. Now."

It was all the encouragement he needed. He pulled her close again, pressing his mouth to hers. Then he lifted her over himself and pulled her down, entering her slow and long and deep. When she opened her legs to accommodate him, he pushed hard against her, filling her, widening her even more. All she could do was wrap her arms around his neck and hang on for the ride.

And she rode him well, rising and falling on him, his shaft going deeper inside her with each new penetration. He moved his mouth to her breasts, cupping his other hand over her bottom to steady her. Faster and faster, they cantered, until he rolled them onto the bed so that Renny was on her back again beneath him. Then he rose to his knees and, gripping her ankles in both hands, spread her wide. With a few more thrusts, he drove himself as deep as he could, then spilled himself inside her until he had nothing left to give. Renny cried out at their culmination, a rocket of heat spiraling through her. She felt as if she would be fused to him forever, hoped they would never be apart again.

And then they were both on their backs, panting for breath and groping for thought, neither seeming to know what the hell had just happened. She gazed up into the candlelit darkness, afraid to look anywhere else. Part of her was already sorry she had succumbed to Tate so quickly, so easily. But part of her couldn't wait for it to happen again.

And that, she supposed, was where the root of her fear lay. That having had Tate once, she would never have him enough. Or, even worse, she would never have him again.

* * *

Renny woke to the steady rat-a-tat of rain on the window and smiled sleepily. She loved rain. Rain made the pace of a day seem slower somehow. She always let herself sleep in a few extra minutes when it rained, and she always gave herself a little more time to get ready for work, since no one at Tarrant, Fiver & Twigg ever seemed to be on time, anyway, when it rained. Today would be no exception. Why not relish a few more minutes of semiconsciousness before the day became too full? She sighed with much contentment and reached across the mattress to the nightstand to push the snooze button on her alarm clock…

Only to discover her alarm clock wasn't where it was supposed to be. Nor had it gone off in the first place. When she opened her eyes, she realized her alarm clock wasn't the only thing missing. So was her bedroom. So was her bed. So were her clothes. What the hell? Why was she naked?

She bolted upright at the memories that flooded over her, each more erotic than the one preceding it. Tate unbuttoning her pajama buttons one by one. Tate tracing the lower curve of her breast with his tongue. Tate guiding his fingers between her legs to wreak havoc on the feminine heart of her.

Oh, *that* was why she was naked.

What had she done? Renny Twigg was not the kind of woman who succumbed to a pretty face that easily, that quickly or that passionately. Even faces as pretty as Tate's that were attached to millions—perhaps billions—of dollars. Even in situations of extreme emotional upheaval like the one in which she'd found herself. Her behavior last night had been completely out of character for her.

But maybe, since the situation she and Tate were in was also uncharacteristic, she shouldn't beat herself up for that. No, what she should beat herself up for was not protecting herself by taking proper precautions. She'd told Tate the truth when she assured him the timing wasn't right for her to get pregnant, and she was confident she wouldn't. But the world was full of large families who'd tried to time that sort of thing correctly. And there were other things to worry about with regard to protection—or the lack thereof. Sure, most of them could be addressed with a simple dose of antibiotics, but still.

She had behaved irresponsibly last night. And there was no way she would let that happen again.

So…where did she put her clothes? Or, rather, where had Tate put her clothes? She had a vague memory of her pajama top cartwheeling over her head in a blur of tiny golf carts, but after that, all she could remember was—

Never mind. Best not to think about those things again. She located both the pajama top and bottoms and was knotting the latter at her waist when she registered the aroma of…bacon? Where was that coming from?

She did her best to wind her hair into something that wouldn't lead to the kind of trouble it had led to last night, then tried to look like someone who knew what she was doing as she exited the bedroom. She discovered the answer to the bacon question immediately. Tate was standing in front of the stove—barefoot and shirt-less with his jeans dipping low on his hips—stirring something in a frying pan. As she drew nearer, she saw a modest pile of bacon on a plate beside him and what appeared to be scrambled eggs in the pan. There was even something steaming in a saucepan that looked— and kind of smelled—like...the magic bean! Coffee!

For a minute, she thought maybe she was dreaming. That maybe she'd dreamed the entire frenetic night the two of them had shared, because she knew for a fact that there had been no eggs or bacon in the refrigerator the day before, never mind the magic bean. Then she thought maybe Inspector Grady had returned from town with groceries, something that would mean a potential escape from this place, but would also be mortifying for a number of reasons, few of which had anything to do with tiny cartoon golf carts on her person and everything to do with her having woken up naked in someone else's bed.

But no, her dreams had never included smells, so ev-erything, including last night, must be real. Even the part about a gorgeous guy making breakfast in his bare feet.

"Good morning," she said, hoping she injected just the right blend of aplomb and nonchalance into her voice, despite the fact that she felt neither of those things.

When Tate spun around to smile at her, though, he looked as if he felt enough for both of them, something that just made Renny feel even worse. How could he be nonchalant and aplomby about something that had been so passionate and precarious?

"Good morning," he greeted her cheerfully. "You were sleeping so soundly when I woke up, I didn't want to disturb you." He grinned devilishly. "I figured you could use the extra sleep after last night."

Wow, he was really going to go there. And so quickly, too. Renny rushed to change the subject. Last night was a place she never intended to visit again. Certainly not while the person she'd experienced it with was standing right there in front of her. So she said the only thing she could.

"Coffee. You created coffee. Out of nothing. You must be a god."

He looked a little disappointed that she didn't take his *about last night* comment and run with it. "I kind of created coffee. Out of boiling water. It's instant, so it's more like a coffee impostor. I guess that just makes me a demigod."

Renny didn't care. As long as he poured her some. Which he did. And she tasted it. And it was good.

"Where did you find eggs?" she asked after she'd ingested a few fortifying sips. "I thought Wisconsin was famous for its dairy products, not its roving bands of wild forest chickens."

For a moment, he looked as if he wasn't going to let her get away with changing the subject from what had happened the night before, because he intended to revisit it over and over again. But when he realized she was serious about steering the topic in a new direction, he turned back around to stir the eggs some more.

"They're powdered eggs," he said. "There was a package of them in the cabinet behind the canned stuff.

There's some powdered milk up there, too, if you're worried about calcium deficiency."

Oh, sure. What were powdered eggs without powdered milk to go with them? From singularly icky to doubly icky. Win-win.

"No, that's okay," she said. "But last time I checked, there was no such thing as powdered bacon. Where did you find that?"

"Freezer," he said, still not looking at her. "One of those foil bricks was what was left of a rasher. No idea how long it's been in there, but it smelled fine."

"It still smells fine," she said. "Thanks for making breakfast."

He finally looked at her again. He smiled again, too, but the look wasn't quite as cheerful this time. "You're welcome. It's the least I can do for you after last—"

He stopped before finishing, obviously remembering her reluctance to talk about what had happened, a surprisingly considerate gesture.

He looked down at the eggs again and repeated softly, "It's the least I can do for you."

So he really was cooking breakfast for her. No guy had ever cooked breakfast for Renny. Even with past boyfriends, when she'd stayed at their place, they always expected her to fix breakfast for them in the morning. It was why she'd always made sure to pick up a bag of doughnuts on her way when she knew she'd be staying over at their places.

"Have a seat," he said. "I'll bring you a plate."

She made her way to the sofa, moving aside the book

and magazine she and Tate had discarded there last night before they—

Gah. Was there no escape from thoughts of their lovemaking? Immediately, she corrected herself. They hadn't made love. They'd had sex. A purely physical re-action to a purely physical attraction. Making love was a whole 'nother animal, one she still wasn't sure she'd ever experienced. To make love, you had to be in love. And love was one of those things Renny figured a per-son didn't know until she felt it. As far as she could tell, she hadn't. Not yet, anyway.

She had just seated herself on the sofa when Tate brought over two plates with identical servings of bacon and eggs. Then he went back for two glasses of orange juice, the concentrate for which, he informed her, had also been lurking under some of the frosted foil in the freezer. A major lover of OJ, Renny enjoyed a healthy taste of it from her glass…only to realize it tasted like freezer-burned aluminum so she immediately spit it back into the vessel again. Much to her horror. The only thing worse than wearing golf-cart pajamas in front of a gor-geous guy was spitting out food in front of a gorgeous guy. Especially food he'd made. But, really, the stuff in that glass… It was way worse than golf-cart pajamas.

Tate looked dashed by her reaction, as if he'd planted, picked and pressed the fruit in his own backyard, and her rejection of it was tantamount to a rejection of him. "Is there a problem with the juice?" he asked.

"Um, no," Renny lied hastily. Even more hastily, she placed the glass back on the table. "I just remembered, uh…orange juice doesn't agree with me."

Tate didn't look convinced. He picked up his glass, filled his mouth with a hefty quaff...and immediately spit it back out again. "That tastes like the hardware store where my father worked." His gaze flew to hers. "Hey. I remembered something about my father. The store where he worked smelled like metal. Why am I just remembering that?"

Renny smiled back. "I think people's five senses are irrevocably synced with their memory banks. Most of my earliest memories are all of things I could taste or hear or smell."

He nodded, but his thoughts seemed to be a million miles away. Or maybe just a few hundred miles away. In the Indiana town where he'd grown up. Or, rather, where he'd been relocated when he was a toddler.

"Sit. Eat," Renny instructed him gently. "Maybe the bacon will taste like metal, too, and you'll remember even more."

Actually, the bacon tasted like Freon. And the eggs tasted like glue. But Renny managed to consume every bite. Because a gorgeous guy had made breakfast for her and that made everything better.

By the time they finished breakfast, the rain had diminished to a soft patter. So soft that a handful of birds were even singing. Renny went to the window and found that the clouds were less ominous than they'd been the day before. When she opened the window this time, she was greeted by a soft, if still damp, breeze, and that aroma of not-so-far-off water.

She inhaled deeply, relishing the fresh air. She liked living in New York, but some days she needed to be surrounded by green space. As bad as it was to be forcibly separated from civilization, it was kind of nice to be forcibly separated from civilization. And now that the rain was letting up some…

"We should get outside today," she said impulsively.

She turned to find Tate looking at her as if she'd just told him they should fly to Mars.

"What?" he asked.

"We should get out of the cottage for a while," she repeated. "Go exploring."

"Are you nuts? Everything out there is soaking wet."

"Then let's go fishing. If Inspector Grady doesn't make it back today—and considering last night's rain, there's a good chance he won't—then I'll make whatever we catch for dinner tonight. It's the least I can do for the guy who made me breakfast."

She might as well have told him they should drink hemlock for dinner, so repelled did he look by the suggestion.

"Really," she said. "We can't be far from water. It might even be Lake Michigan. Maybe there's a boat or something we could take out."

"You want to fish in Lake Michigan?" he said dubiously. "You want to *eat* the fish you catch in Lake Michigan? Do you know how many industries dump waste into Lake Michigan?"

"We're hundreds of miles away from Chicago. Wisconsin lake water has to be totally different from Chicago lake water."

"Funny thing about water. It does this thing where it moves around a lot. 'Flowing,' I think, is the word they use for it. That means the water—and fish—around Chicago could easily make their way to Wisconsin. Along with all the toxic waste they've consumed beforehand."

"Oh, please. You just ate bacon and eggs that might have been brought here by Donnie Brasco."

"Yeah, but that's a one-off from my usual eating habits. It's not like I eat crap every day."

"At least fish is whole food," she said. "Who knows what goes into powdered eggs? Not eggs, I bet."

He said nothing, but she could tell by his expression that he wasn't going to back down.

"Fine," she relented. "You don't have to eat what we catch. There will just be that much more for me. We're still going fishing. Because if I have to be cooped up in this cottage for another day…"

She let her voice trail off. Not because she figured an unspoken threat was a much more ominous threat, even if that was true. But because she started actually thinking about what would happen if she had to be cooped up in the cottage for another day. And it bore a striking resemblance to what had happened in the cottage last night.

Fishing, she reminded herself. She and Tate would spend the day fishing. Just as soon as she could find something to wear.

Tate had to give Renata credit for one thing. Well, actually, he had to give her credit for a lot of things. But most of those he probably shouldn't mention, since she'd made clear she didn't want to talk about last night.

The one thing he could give her credit for at the moment was that she could take a man's gigantic lavender shirt and turn it into…something else. Something without sleeves, since she'd ripped those off and tied them together to make a belt—or something—and with some kind of complicated tying maneuver at the bottom that turned that part of the shirt into shorts that fell just above her knees. Sort of. The rest of the garment was baggy and unhindered by anything resembling a pattern. To him, it just looked like, well…

"It's a romper," she told him in a voice that indicated he should know exactly what that meant.

"So it's for romping?" he asked. "Women have to have special clothes for that?" Frankly, his idea of romping worked a lot better with no clothes at all.

"No, a romper isn't for romping. It's for…" She expelled an irritated sound. "How the hell do I know what a romper is for? Some fashion designer sewed a shirt and shorts together at some point, called it a romper and it stuck. The fashion world hates women, you know. They make us buy things we don't want or need. Hence—" she swept her hands from her shoulders to her knees "—the romper." Now she settled her hands on her hips. "Hey, it beats golf-cart pajamas. Especially for fishing."

Tate battled the urge to shake his head. She really was the strangest woman he'd ever met. Not that he meant that in a disparaging way. Which was weird because, until now, he'd always considered strange people in a disparaging way. Renata brought a certain flair to strangeness. Even her romper had a certain, uh, je ne sais quoi. For lack of a proper industry term. Which probably didn't exist for an outfit like that.

They'd been cleaning up breakfast when Inspector Grady called again to tell them the roads were still out, he was still stuck in Pattypan and it could be another twenty-four hours before he could get to them. But, on the upside, the tech guys were making some headway into the computer breach that had exposed Tate's identity, and with any luck, they'd soon know exactly who John Smith on Craigslist was and just how far his crimes went.

The news that Tate and Renata were going to be stuck here for another day should have been calamitous. Instead, neither of them had been that broken up by it. In fact, it had cemented her conviction that they should spend the day fishing, and she'd gone in search of gear. A closet near the kitchen held a number of discoveries, not the least of which was a stack of board games— something she'd been so excited about she might have stumbled upon the Hope Diamond. Mixed in with them was a quartet of fishing rods and all their accessories.

Satisfied they had all the necessary accoutrements, she'd headed to the bedroom to see what she could do with the remaining clothing. Forty-five minutes later, she emerged in her current getup. He supposed it could sort of qualify for resort wear. In some parts of the world. Where people didn't have any taste.

"What about shoes?" he asked, noting her bare feet. Of course, he was still barefoot, too, but he at least had his polo boots to wear. She only had heels.

"Barefoot is fine," she said. "I love going barefoot.

I never wore shoes when I was a kid. Unless my mom caught me."

Her last statement was short, but she'd delivered it in a tone of voice that spoke volumes. Tate could relate. As much as he'd tried to please his mother and stepfather, he'd never felt he succeeded. Even before that, his mother had always given off a vibe that he was somehow disappointing her. Knowing what he did now, maybe that had had more to do with the fact that his father's family was a little unsavory. Back then, though, he had felt like it was his fault. With his stepfather, he'd always felt like maybe the guy saw him as a reminder that his mother had been involved with another man before him. Or maybe, he, too, thought Tate's origins weren't up to snuff.

Oh, hell, what did it matter? Neither of them was around anymore, and Tate had more than made a success of himself. If parts of his family tree were blighted, that wasn't his fault, was it? You couldn't blame a child for the gene pool that spawned it. Well, you could—and a lot of people did—but it wasn't fair. It wasn't right, either. Lots of people rose above humble, or even lurid, beginnings to make good.

Having obviously given up on his approval of her wardrobe, Renata collected the fishing poles and tackle she'd set aside earlier. "Come on. There's finally a break in the rain. The fish will be looking for food."

"We don't have any bait," he said, making one last-ditch effort to get out of fishing and spend the day in the great indoors instead. Now that the heat had broken—some—it might even be tolerable.

"Fish love freezer-burned bacon. Trust me."

As if he had any choice. He'd never been fishing in his life. She could tell him fish spent their days dancing the merengue in funny hats, and he'd have no way to disprove it.

"Fine," he relented. "But if we haven't caught anything after an hour, we're coming back here."

"Two hours," she bargained.

"Ninety minutes."

She stuck out her hand and smiled. "Deal."

Nine

An hour after slinging their fishing lines into the lake, they'd actually caught three fish, and Tate was itching to catch more. It wasn't Lake Michigan they'd discovered, after all, but Lake Something Else that was small enough to be ensconced by wilderness all around its perimeter. A pier extended a good thirty or forty feet from the shoreline, so they'd made their way to the end of it, sat on its edge and plunked their lines into deep water.

Renata caught the first fish within fifteen minutes of their arrival, a six-inch trout whose breed she'd recognized immediately, and which she'd thrown back in, saying it wasn't big enough. She'd handled it with a confidence he'd envied, then deftly baited the hook again, cast out the line with an easy whir and, after another ten minutes, caught a second, larger trout. Deeming it worthy of dinner, she'd stashed it in the cooler she'd also salvaged from the closet.

It had taken Tate nearly an hour to catch his fish, and it hadn't been much bigger than the first one Renata had caught. She'd been about to throw it back, too, but he rebelled, feeling pretty damned proud of his prize. So she'd smiled like an indulgent scoutmaster and stowed it in the cooler with the first. Then she'd caught the next one. She was two up on him, and hers were bigger. He was competitive enough to find that unacceptable. The next catch would be his, and it would be twice the size of her first one, or his name wasn't Tate Hawthorne. Then again, in reality, his name wasn't Tate Hawthorne, but that was beside the point.

"What's that smile for?"

He looked over to find Renata watching him with laughing eyes. "What smile?" he asked.

"You're grinning like an eight-year-old boy who just caught his first fish," she said.

"That's because I'm a thirty-two-year-old man who just caught my first fish."

She chuckled. "So there's still an eight-year-old boy in there somewhere."

Before today, Tate would have denied that. Hell, he didn't think he'd been an eight-year-old boy even when he was eight. He couldn't remember ever feeling like a child. Whenever he looked back at that time, there seemed to be such a pall over everything. His mother's fear and unhappiness, their struggle just to get through any given day, his small circle of friends that seemed to grow smaller with every passing year.

But he almost felt like a child today, sitting at the edge of a lake pier with his jeans rolled up and his legs dangling above the water. Although the sun was still stuck behind a broad slab of gray, the rain had finally stopped. Birds barnstormed the trees, warbling their happiness at being active again. The wind whispered over their heads, dragging along the scent of pine. Dragonflies darted along the water, leaving trails of what could have been pixie dust in their wakes.

And he'd caught a fish! All in all, not a bad way to spend an afternoon. He wished he'd known a few days like this when he was a kid. Or even one day like this when he was a kid.

He looked at Renata again. She sat on his left, her bare feet hovering within inches of his, her hair half in and half out of a lopsided topknot. Maybe if he'd met a girl like her when he was a boy, he would have had a few days like this one. She looked far more suited to this life—even in her ridiculous romper, which, he had to admit, was less ridiculous than it had seemed a little while ago—than she did to the one that demanded the crisp suit and hairstyle she'd worn when she'd shown up at his front door... Was that only yesterday morning? It felt like a lifetime had passed since then.

"Were you like this when you were a kid?" he asked impulsively.

He had meant for the question to be playful. He had thought it would make her smile. Instead, she sobered.

"Like what?" she asked.

He struggled to find the right words. He'd never been at a loss to describe something, but Renata defied description. "Adventurous," he finally said. Then a few more adjectives popped into his head. "Spontaneous. Unpredictable. Resourceful."

She looked more uncomfortable with every word he spoke. "I don't think I'm any of those things now."

He was about to call her on that—she was all those things and more—but he didn't want to see her withdraw further. Hoping to pull her back from wherever she was retreating, he asked, "Then what were you like as a kid?"

At first he thought she wouldn't answer that question, either. She seemed as determined to ignore it as she was what happened last night. She just reeled in her line until the hook came out of the water empty of even the bacon she had threaded onto it. She looked at the evidence of the one that got away, sighed dispiritedly, then reached into the tackle box for more bait.

And as she went about fixing it on the hook, she said, "As a child, I was...out of place."

He remembered their conversation of the day before, about how she'd attended one of those tony private schools with marble floors and mahogany paneling. He hadn't been surprised by the revelation then. Yesterday, that background had suited her. But looking at her now, he would never peg her as a product of that environment. In his line of work, he knew a lot of people who had grown up that way, clients and colleagues both, and none of them was like Renata. Then again, he wasn't sure if anyone was like Renata. He liked all those other people fine—some he even called friends. But he didn't feel he had a lot in common with them, even living in that world now himself.

He felt he had something in common with Renata, though, despite their disparate beginnings. He wasn't sure what, but they seemed to be kindred spirits. Maybe that was why they'd responded to each other so quickly. He'd been thinking last night was a result of the situation, not the woman. She really wasn't his type. Small, dark and chipper had never turned him on. But Renata did. And now that she did—

Now that she did, she didn't seem inclined to act on the attraction again. Which should have been fine with him. When it came to sex, Tate was pragmatic. Women came and went. He had fun with the ones who wanted to have fun until one or both of them grew tired of it, and then he moved on. Sometimes that happened after months, sometimes it happened after hours. It was looking like Renata was going to be one of those one-timers. So he should be in moving-on mode himself.

Strange thing was, he wasn't ready to move on. He was just starting to get to know her. And he wanted to know more. Those were both new developments. He was never the one who was finished with an encounter last. And he never wanted to know more about a woman than what was on the surface. It wasn't that he was shallow. It was just the way he was. At least, that was what he'd always thought.

It was a big day for firsts. All because of a woman who, twenty-four hours ago, he was wishing had never entered his life.

And he still didn't know what she'd been like when she was a kid. Except for thinking she was out of place.

But instead of asking her to elaborate on what she'd said, he said softly, "Me, too."

Maybe he'd been right about her being adventurous, spontaneous, unpredictable and resourceful as a kid. He could see how all those things would make her feel out of place in a world that valued tradition, orderliness and direction. Funny how he'd yearned for all those things in his childhood, without finding any of them.

They continued to fish in silence for a while, but it wasn't an uncomfortable silence. Nor was it exactly silent silence. The birds and bugs and beasts made sure of that, as did the wind and woods and water. It was almost as if time had dropped them here and stopped, freezing the moment for them because it was so damned near perfect. The only thing that would have made it better was a promise that it would go on forever.

And of all the firsts he'd experienced that day, that one was a monster. He was divorced from every single thing that gave his life meaning—his work, his home, his society, his technology—and there was a not-so-little part of him hoping to stay that way forever. How was that even possible?

He looked at Renata again. She had cast her line back into the water, but she didn't seem to be paying much attention to it. Her gaze was on the opposite shoreline— not that she seemed to be focused on that, either—and her expression was far too somber for someone who should be having fun.

Not sure where the impulse came from, Tate stretched one leg far enough to dip it into the lake, then kicked hard enough to send a small arc of water splashing over her. She squealed in indignant outrage, looking at him as if she couldn't believe he'd done what he did. He couldn't believe he'd done it, either. He was never this spontaneous or unpredictable. Then she smiled devilishly and dipped her own foot into the water. Or, at least, tried to. Unfortunately, her legs were too short to make it.

So Tate took advantage of her disadvantage and splashed her with his foot again.

"Hey! No fair!" she cried.

He was about to retort that all was fair in love and war, but since this was neither, he supposed she was right. But that didn't mean he had to play by the rules. Even though he'd lived his entire life playing by the rules.

He splashed her again.

She gaped even more incredulously. Then she put down her fishing pole and scooted closer to the edge of the pier, stretching her leg as far as it would go. She managed to get a couple of toes submerged, but when she tried to splash him back, all she achieved was a tiny blip of water that barely broke the surface. Tate laughed and splashed her again.

"Why, you little..." she muttered.

She tried to submerge her foot farther but nearly fell off the pier, righting herself at the last minute. Tate laughed some more, then watched with much amusement as she maneuvered herself onto her stomach, her arms dangling over the pier.

"Nice try," he said. "Your arms aren't any longer than your legs, small fry."

"Don't you dare call me 'small fry.' Sean Malone used to call me that, and he lived to regret it."

"Who's Sean Malone? Ex-boyfriend?"

Tate was surprised when a thread of jealousy wound through him. What did he care if Sean Malone was one of her ex-boyfriends? What did he care if he was a current boyfriend? He and Renata would never see each other again once this disaster was sorted out. Which felt less like a disaster today than it had yesterday. They'd still never see each other again after it ended. So whoever Sean Malone was, Tate didn't care. Except that he did, kind of.

"Sean Malone was the scourge of fifth grade," Renata said as she wormed her way closer to the edge of the pier again. "He had a nickname for everyone. Mine was 'small fry.' Until the day his locker started reeking with the massive stench of seafood gone bad, and he was sent to the head of school's office, where they put a mark on his permanent record. The entire east wing of Suffolk Academy had to be fumigated."

"And how exactly did the massive stench of seafood gone bad make its way to the entire east wing of Suffolk Academy?"

She grinned with much satisfaction. "It's amazing how bad a ten-piece deep-fried shrimp meal can smell if it's not refrigerated. Especially if you douse it with blue cheese dressing before you stash it in the locker of someone who's a complete slob and would never notice it until it started to reek. It took three days for it to really start stinking up the place, but once it did... Woo. And once Sean realized who was responsible, he never called me 'small fry' again. You, too, will live to regret it."

She stretched her arm as far as she could toward the water, but was still an inch or two shy of reaching it.

"Oh, yeah," Tate said. "I'm shaking in my boots."

He was about to splash her again when, with a final heroic effort, she pushed herself forward, thrust her hand into the lake and hit him with a palm-sized arc of water right in the face. Fortunately, she had small palms. Unfortunately, she also had bad leverage. He opened his eyes just in time to see her go tumbling into the lake headfirst.

She broke the surface immediately, sputtering indignantly, but quickly began to laugh. She pushed a few strands of hair out of her eyes, treaded water and said, "It was worth it to see the look on your face. I guess not too many people try to get even with you for stuff."

Tate grinned as he wiped the last of the water from his face. "I'm sure a lot of them would like to. They're just too busy."

She paddled back to the pier, and he extended a hand to help her up. She accepted it gratefully…then yanked him into the water alongside her. He had just enough time to suck in a breath before he went under, but when he broke the surface, it was to exhale in a burst of laughter. Renata was cute when she was trying to be vengeful and smug.

They paddled around each other for a moment, each trying to figure out if the other planned further retribution. Then she rolled onto her back to float and closed her eyes. She looked like someone who had all the time in the world to just drift around a Wisconsin lake without a care in the world. So Tate turned his body until he was floating, too. A curious dragonfly buzzed over him for a moment, then darted off. He watched until it disappeared into the trees, then looked up at the clouds. He couldn't remember the last time he'd gone swimming for more than laps at the gym. Hell, he couldn't remember the last time he'd looked up at the clouds. He wondered why not. Then he closed his eyes, too.

"You know," he heard Renata say from what sounded like a very great distance, "Grady could have done a lot worse by us when it came to choosing a safe house."

Her mention of the marshal brought Tate up short. He had momentarily forgotten why the two of them were here. He'd been having such a good time it felt like they'd planned this excursion months ago and finally found the time to sneak away from their jobs to enjoy it. He'd almost forgotten that, this time yesterday, they were practically strangers.

"On TV," she continued, "the cops always stash protected witnesses in some crappy no-tell motel and make them eat Taco Taberna carryout."

"Yeah, Beefaroni and powdered eggs are so much better," he said wryly.

"Don't be dissing my Beefaroni again, mister."

Tate smiled. "Sorry. My bad."

"I just meant that if we have to be held prisoner somewhere, there are worse places than a Wisconsin wilderness."

Until today, Tate would have said having to live any place whose population fell below two million would be hell. What was life without having everything you wanted at your fingertips? The Big Cheese Motor-Inn didn't even have basic cable. Talk about no-frills living. But he had to admit Renata might be right. Grady could have done worse than lakefronts and dragonflies.

"How much longer do you think we'll be here?"

He was surprised it was Renata asking the question. Then again, she didn't sound like someone who was anxious to leave. She sounded like someone who wanted to stay as long as possible.

"I don't know," he said. Funny, but he kind of sounded like someone who wanted to stay, too. "I guess until the feds locate the person who found me for you and make sure my information didn't go any farther than you."

He heard a splash in the water and opened his eyes. They'd drifted away from the pier, and Renata was swimming back to it. He watched as she gripped the edge with both hands and tried to hoist herself up, but it quickly became clear that she wouldn't be able to manage it on her own. Maybe she didn't like being called a small fry, but…she was a small fry. No shame in that. But there was no way she was getting out of the water on her own, either.

Tate swam to join her and did his best not to make it look effortless when he grabbed the edge of the pier and lifted himself up onto it. She tried valiantly to mirror his actions, but it finally became as clear to her that there was no way she was going to make it. Silently, he dropped to his knees and extended a hand to her again.

Even more effortlessly than he had pulled himself out of the water, he tugged her to the pier with him.

And instantly regretted it.

Soaked to the skin as she was, her so-called romper was clinging to every inch of her as if it was skin. And since she had forgone her still-damp underwear—as he had himself, something he really didn't need to be thinking about right now—it left absolutely nothing to the imagination. Her breasts pushed against the wet fabric, her quarter-sized areolae pink and perfect, her nipples stiff and tight. He remembered the feel of them in his mouth, so soft and hot, and it was all he could do not to duck his head to them again. Lower, the indentation of her navel beckoned, drawing his eye lower still, to the shadowy triangle at the apex of her legs. Unable to help himself, he roped an arm around her waist and covered her mouth with his, at the same time scooting his other hand down her torso to dip it between her thighs. She uttered a single small sound of protest, then melted into him and kissed him back.

Everything around him dissolved into nothing after that. All Tate registered was the feel of her mouth under his and the fabric of her shirt beneath his fingers. Hastily, he unbuttoned that part of the garment so he could tuck his hand inside. Then he furrowed his fingers into her damp flesh, catching the button of her clitoris between his knuckles before penetrating her with his middle finger. When she gasped at the invasion, he widened their mouths, tasting her more deeply. He felt her hand at his waist, unfastening his jeans, and then she was touching him just as intimately. Within seconds, he was hard as a rock and ready to rumble.

Where had this come from? This uncontrollable urge to touch her? To have her? He was never like this with other women. He was a disciplined, thorough lover. He liked to take his time. He could keep himself and his partner on a slow simmer until they were both ready to notch it higher. Hell, seduction was half the fun, even when it wasn't necessary because both parties knew they'd be in bed before the night was over.

But with Renata, there was no discipline. There was no simmer. There was just an explosion of wanting and heat and demand. One minute, he was laughing and playful, and the next, he was consumed by a need for her that was so powerful it superseded everything else. They weren't even inside the cabin. They were standing out in the middle of the world where anything could happen, where anyone could see them, even if they were, for the moment, alone. And he didn't even care. Hell, that just made it more exciting.

He withdrew his hand from her shirt long enough to unfasten the rest of the buttons. Then he peeled the wet garment from her body until she stood before him naked. He broke the kiss long enough to strip off his shirt and lower his jeans, and then…

They gazed at each other, silent save for their panting, her hands on his chest, his on her waist. No way could they make love on the pier—too many splinters. But making love in the water with the fish didn't hold much appeal, either. And there was no way he'd make it back to the motel without going off like a rocket.

He tightened his grip on her waist and lifted her into his arms. Her eyes widened when she realized his intention, but she roped her legs around his waist and her arms around his neck, then held on tight as he lowered her over his raging shaft. He slid into her so easily he might have been a missing part of her. Or maybe she was a missing part of him. He only knew they fitted together perfectly.

He bucked his hips upward as he pushed hers down, then repeated the action in reverse, relishing the hot friction. Something about the angle of their vertical bodies brought a new dimension to the sensation, and he knew he wouldn't last long. Not wanting her to be cheated, he braced one arm tightly around her waist and let the other go exploring, down over the curves of her ass, into the delicate crease that bisected it, pushing the tip of one finger into the dimple he found there.

She cried out again at this new intrusion, so he gave her a moment to adjust. She buried her head in the curve of his neck and shoulder and murmured her approval. So he jerked his hips up again, burying himself completely inside her, and gripped her bottom tighter as he deftly fingered her there.

He held off coming as long as he could, but within minutes, he was surging inside her. She tightened around him and cried out her own completion, bucking against him one final time before going limp in his arms. Carefully, he withdrew from her and lowered her back to the ground. But he didn't—couldn't—let her go. For long moments, they clung to each other, their bodies slick from their swim and the aftermath of their passion.

In the distance, thunder rumbled, silencing the chatter of the birds. The water rippled below them, and the wind whispered above them, but Tate was pretty sure its cool caress wasn't why they were both shivering.

Nothing like this had ever happened to him before. And somewhere deep inside, he knew nothing like this would ever happen again. Not the lovemaking in the great outdoors so much, but…something else. Something he wasn't sure he could identify. Something he wasn't sure he *should* identify. Because somehow he knew it had nothing to do with a Wisconsin lakefront.

And everything to do with Renata Twigg.

Ten

By the time Renny and Tate made their way back to the cottage, the sun was beginning its dip toward the trees. In the hours since leaving the motel, they'd put a half-dozen fish in the cooler, filled a T-shirt with wild blackberries, discovered a waterfall, explored a small cave and collected enough pinecones and interesting-looking rocks to fill a pinecone-and-interesting-looking-rocks room in the Smithsonian.

Oh, yeah. And they'd made love in a way Renny would have sworn wasn't possible. Not just the position, but the way it shattered her entire being, too.

She had been totally unprepared for Tate this afternoon…and yet totally ready for him, too. As quickly and feverishly as things had escalated, as wild and wanton as he'd made her feel, as far as she'd allowed things

to go after swearing she would never let them go that
far again…somehow it all seemed perfectly in keeping with the way of the world. With the way of Renny.
At least the way the world and Renny had been since
coming here. Being wild and wanton with Tate just felt
right somehow. Being with Tate period felt right. It felt
normal. With him, here in this place, she felt more like
herself than she ever had with anyone anywhere before.
And she felt as if she had been with him, here in this
place, forever. It was weird. But nice.

Maybe too nice. She was starting to kind of wish the
two of them could stay here like this forever.

Probably best not to think about it. She had dinner to make—she'd promised, since Tate made breakfast. Good thing, too, because he'd told her he'd never
cleaned a fish in his life and made clear he had no plans
to do it that didn't involve a zombie apocalypse—and
even then the whole fish-cleaning thing was iffy, since
there would be plenty of grocery stores ripe for the pil-
laging of peanut butter and jelly.

By the time dinner was on the coffee table—pan-
fried trout with a blackberry reduction—the strange heat
that had arced between them that afternoon was nearly
forgotten. For the most part. Just to be on the safe side,
Renny had changed back into her ugly pajamas after
her shower when they got back to the cottage—not that
those had been much of a deterrent the night before—
and Tate was back in his polo jodhpurs and a different
white T-shirt. Their clothes from earlier were drying in
the bathroom. Not that Renny was in any hurry to put

on the alleged romper again. Not without proper underwear next time, anyway. Ahem.

In spite of that, she couldn't quite keep herself from lighting a couple of the emergency candles and setting them on the coffee table with their dinner. Not because it was romantic, but because, um, they provided some nice ambience. Yeah, that was it. The only thing that could have made the setting more romantic…uh, she meant ambient…was if they'd had a bottle of wine to go with their meal. Then again, if previous occupants to the place and their golf-cart pajamas were any indication, it would probably have been a bottle of Wiseguy Vineyards Lambrusco, vintage last week. So maybe it was just as well.

If Tate noticed the romantic…uh, ambient…candles when he sat down, he didn't mention them. She wondered how he felt about what had happened on the pier this afternoon. About what had happened last night. About everything that had happened since the two of them arrived here. Was he as surprised and dazed as she was about their responses to each other? Did he feel the same sense of timelessness and otherworldliness about the last two days that she did? Or was all of this just an inconvenience and ordeal for him to have to get through, and he was just doing whatever he had to do to stay sane? He had told her sex would be a nice way to pass the time. Was that really all it was to him? Why couldn't that be all it was to her?

And what the hell was she supposed to do about the whole hacking thing? She could end their forced confinement here by admitting to Inspector Grady that she

knew perfectly well who had hacked the system and located Tate for her and reveal Phoebe's identity. But that
would open Phoebe up to federal charges. And probably Renny, too, for being a part of it. What was weird,
though, was that Renny was worried less about federal
charges and time in the state pen than about Tate's reaction to her admission that she could have prevented
this entire episode—or could end it at any time—by just
telling the truth. She didn't want to admit anything, and
she didn't want to end it right away. And deep down,
that had nothing to do with her fear of federal charges
and time in the state pen.

In spite of the jumble of thoughts and questions
plaguing her, Renny enjoyed her dinner with Tate.
They were so comfortable together at this point that
they could have been any normal couple eating in their
own dining room, the way they would every night—
even though they weren't a couple. Then they cleaned
up afterward in the same comfortable way. Once that
was done, however, they both seemed to be at loose
ends. Neither seemed interested in reading, the way they
had done the night before, but neither seemed willing to
broach the subject of other pursuits. Probably because
the pursuit the two of them had enjoyed together the
most since their arrival was sex. So it only made sense
for Renny to suggest—

"Scrabble," she said, once the last of the dishes were
put away. "We should play Scrabble. Everybody loves
Scrabble, right?"

Judging by Tate's expression, he didn't love Scrabble.
Even so, she hurried to the closet and pulled the game

out from the middle of a stack of other board games. When she turned back around, Tate was still standing in the kitchenette, looking like he didn't love Scrabble.

"Or there's Trivial Pursuit," she said, thinking maybe he was more of a trivia buff. "Or Monopoly." Which actually might have been the best choice, because that game went on forever and had the most potential to keep them out of trouble.

He shook his head. "Scrabble is fine."

Before he could change his mind, she scrambled to the sofa and opened the board, putting one wooden rack on her side, and the other on his. As she turned the letter tiles upside down in the box lid—the letter bag was missing, as were a number of tiles, she couldn't help noticing—Tate strode to the chair and moved it closer to the table. By the time he sat down, she had mixed up the letter tiles and chosen her seven. All but one were consonants, but the vowel was at least an *A*. Even so, it would probably be best to let Tate go first, so she could play off whatever he spelled.

"You go first," she said magnanimously.

He weighed his options for a moment, sorting his letters into different combinations. Then he used every single letter he had to spell out *P-H-A-R-Y-N-X*, with the *Y* on the double letter square. Not to mention the extra fifty points for using all his letters.

"What?" she cried. "That's one hundred and fifty-two points, right off the bat!" And of course he had positioned the word so that it was impossible for her to make it plural, even if she did manage to pick an *E* and an *S* at some point.

Tate grinned as he collected seven more tiles. "You're the one who wanted to play Scrabble. Everybody loves Scrabble, right?"

Oh, hardy-har-har-har. Fine. She'd show him. At some point. Once she picked an *E* and a *U* to go with her *C, F, K* and *R*. In the meantime, she used her *A* and *W* with his *P* to spell *P-A-W*. At least that last letter was on a triple letter square. Sixteen points. Not too horribly embarrassing. Except for it being a measly three letters.

"So obviously, you're great at Scrabble," she said. "You must play it a lot."

"Actually, no," he said as he arranged his new tiles. "I like words. I was a huge reader when I was a kid."

She remembered his description of his solitary childhood. Of course he'd been a big reader, if he was alone a lot. But Renny's youthful society had been packed with other kids and tons of activities, and she'd been a big reader, too. All the better to escape that society and those activities, inevitably the kind that had dictated specific roles for male and female alike, and the latter had too often included things like, well, pink tutus.

"What was your favorite book when you were a kid?" she asked.

"Anything with knights and castles. You?"

"Anything with pioneer girls."

He smiled. "Renata Ingalls Wilder."

She smiled back. "Pretty much. Is that why you bought your house? Because it looks like a castle?"

He'd been about to lay down another word but halted. "Noticed that similarity, did you?"

"Kind of impossible not to."

He nodded, then used the *X* he'd used in *P-H-A-R-Y-N-X* to spell out *X-R-A-Y-S*. Dammit.

"The reason I liked castles," he said as he collected four more tiles from the box lid, "was that they're impenetrable. Nobody can get to you when you're in a castle, you know? No Viking hordes in longboats. No lance-bearing Napoleonic armies. No katana-swinging ninjas. No light-saber-wielding Sith lords. Maybe I was trying to find reasons for why I was always alone myself. If I lived in a castle, of course no one would be able to enter my life."

"But you're not alone anymore," she said. A man like him must have scores of friends. "Why do you live in a castle now?"

Still looking at his letters, he replied, "Same reason."

"But—"

"It's your turn," he interrupted her.

Crap. She didn't have any vowels. Hastily, she used her *C*, *R* and *F* with the *T* she'd just drawn to spell *C-R-A-F-T* with the *A* in his *P-H-A-R-Y-N-X*. Better. But her replacement letters were all consonants again. They were definitely going to run out of vowels, unless Tate had just drawn enough to spell *onomatopoeia*. So when he used the *A* in *X-R-A-Y-S* to spell *B-A-R-N*, she knew they were in trouble.

"There," he said. "That word should appeal to your pioneer girl heart. Why were you a fan of early settlers?"

She much preferred to go back to a discussion of his self-inflicted solitary confinement in his castle—why would a man like him want to keep people at bay?—

but the look on his face made clear he was finished talking about it.

So she replied, "Because they were leaving behind society to literally forge their own path in the world. They were going someplace where the rules of culture and civilization as they knew it were changed. Not to mention they spent a lot of time outdoors doing cool pioneer stuff."

Tate chuckled. "Your pioneer girl and my knight boy probably would have gotten along pretty well."

"Only if she could have gotten past his walls. I don't have any vowels," she said before he could reply to her comment. "And we've used up all the ones that are already on the board. I'm going to have to pass."

"I don't have any vowels, either," he said. "Maybe we should just start spelling things phonetically."

Oh, sure. Now he told her. After she'd used up the letters she needed for profanity. Hmm. Even for phonetic spelling, she was at something of a disadvantage. So she used a *J* and an *F* with the *N* in *P-H-A-R-Y-N-X* to spell—

"Jiffin," she said.

He narrowed his eyes at her. "That's not phonetic for anything. There's no such word as *jiffin*."

"Sure there is. It's what you're doing when you smear a certain brand of peanut butter on your bread. You're jiffin' it."

He didn't look anywhere near convinced. But he plucked a few tiles from his rack to use her *J* to spell out *D-J-L-G*.

"What the hell is that?" she asked.

"Dijlig," he said.

"Dijlig," she echoed. "That's ridiculous. At least *jiffin* sounds like it *might* be a real word. *Dijlig* is..." She couldn't finish the sentence. Because *dijlig* didn't sound like anything. "I can barely get my tongue around that."

"It's an arcane sex act that was used by the Etruscans," he told her. With a straight face. Impressive. "Interestingly, it involves the tongue. An Etruscan man would say it when he had his mouth pressed against an Etruscan woman's—"

She held up a hand to stop him. "I get it."

He grinned. "Well, you might. If you ask nicely."

Renny felt heat creeping into her face. Among other body parts. So she quickly drew more tiles—none of them vowels—and, using the *G* he'd just placed on the board, hastily spelled out *K-M-S-G*. She was going to tell him it was a popular Korean side dish—sort of like kimchi, except with less cabbage—but he filled in the definition before she had the chance.

"Oh, *kimsig*. That's another good one from the Etruscans. Even more fun than *dijlig*, actually, because for that position, it's the woman doing it, and she uses *her* mouth and tongue to—"

"Your turn," Renny interrupted him again. Not that she wanted him to take another turn, now that he was completely fixated on the Etruscan equivalent of the *Kama Sutra*, but anything was better than hearing him finish that sentence, because the images exploding in her brain were making her want to leap across the table for a never-ending session of both *dijlig* and *kimsig*. But

when he put a *P* in front of the *S* in *X-R-A-Y-S* and she
noted he was holding a *Y* in his other hand, she quickly
rehearsed all the possible vowel combinations that might
result. Passy? Pessy? Pissy? Possy? Pus—

She snapped the board shut with all the tiles still inside. Then she shoved everything into the box, closed
it and stood.

"Scrabble is a stupid game," she proclaimed. "And,
wow, I'm exhausted. This has been such a full day. I
think I'm just going to hit the hay. I could really use a
good night's sleep."

And without awaiting a reply, Renny fled to the bedroom, closed the door and locked it behind her—since,
knowing Tate, he'd conjure an Etruscan word that meant
roll in the hay, too. And he'd be delighted to tell her—
and then show her—exactly which body parts for that
went where.

Tate grinned when he heard the sound of the bedroom door locking behind Renata. Had she done that
because she didn't trust him? Or because she didn't trust
herself? He'd noticed the candles at dinner. And he'd
seen the way she was looking at him as he described
for her the finer points of fabricated ancient sexuality.
Or, at least, tried to describe them before she cut him
off. Then again, he was pretty sure she'd gotten the gist
of it both times before ending the game. Shame, really,
since Scrabble was a lot more fun than he remembered.

She was right, though. It had been a hell of a day.
Even so, he couldn't remember enjoying one more.
Which was weird, because until his predinner shower,

he'd spent most of it wet and dirty, doing things that just made him wetter and dirtier. They'd actually found a cave and explored it. And a waterfall. Okay, so the waterfall had been only about four feet tall. It was still his first in-the-flesh waterfall discovery. Thirty-two years old, world traveled and experienced to the point of jadedness, and he'd just seen his first waterfall and explored his first cave.

Two days with Renata Twigg, confined to an area no bigger than a sleep-away camp, and he was learning and feeling things about himself he'd never been aware of before. Between this and his newly discovered family ties, it was going to be tough to go back to Chicago and pick up where he'd left off.

Then again, did he really want to pick up where he'd left off? All he'd been doing before Renata came along was working all day, seven days a week, with a break here and there on the weekends to play polo or enjoy the charms of whoever happened to be the femme du jour.

There was a reason for that, though, he reminded himself. His life was the way it was because he worked hard to make it that way. He'd worked hard for years to make it that way. And he *liked* how his life was. Of course he wanted to go back to Chicago and pick up where he left off. Neither his newly discovered East Coast Bacco relations nor his Midwestern adventures with Renata Twigg would change anything. Not unless he wanted something to change. And he didn't. His life in Chicago was near perfect. Why mess with that? Just because he'd spent a day that felt, well, really perfect?

It wasn't real, he reminded himself. The way he and

Renata had passed today wasn't the way people normally passed a day. Today was… He sighed as he remembered some of the funner things they'd done. Today was like a snow day from school. One of those happy accidents that seemed magical because it was an unexpected gift of something incredibly special—time.

He shook his head at his own weird thoughts. When had he started to think about this sojourn as an unexpected gift or a happy accident? Only yesterday, it had been the worst possible thing that could have happened. Only yesterday, he'd been blaming Renata for ruining his life. Now today he felt grateful to her for showing him how much fun a break in his routine could be.

Clearly, he needed sleep, too. Maybe Renata had done the right thing, putting a closed and locked door between them for the night. They could both recharge after what had been a tumultuous thirty-six hours and start fresh tomorrow. For all he knew, the spell would be broken by then. There was every chance the two of them would wake up fully reverted to the Manhattan attorney and the Chicago businessman. With any luck, Grady would make it back to the motel with good news and give the all clear so Tate and Renata could return to their normal lives. Maybe the dragonflies and blackberry brambles would retreat to the backs of their brains, where the two of them could visit from time to time when they had a free moment.

Yeah. That was what they both needed. As much fun as today had been, it was just a little break from reality. If every day was like today, then today wouldn't have been so special.

Tomorrow could be completely different. Everything could go back to normal tomorrow.

Even if nothing was ever the same.

Tate woke on the sofa the next morning to the sound of low thunder. He should have been angered by the sound. More rain meant the road to the motel would be at least another day away from being clear enough for Grady to return.

But hearing thunder and knowing it would rain again today didn't make Tate angry. Instead, all he could think was *There's no school today!* Or if not the actual words, then certainly the childlike feeling of delight that accompanied them. Not just because there was no school—or, rather, no work—today, but because he had another day to play, or something, with his new friend, or something, Renata.

He looked at the bedroom door she had closed and locked the night before. It was still closed. Was it locked? He rolled off the sofa and padded to it, curling his fingers over the knob. It turned easily, and he pushed the door open.

Just for a peek, he told himself. Just to make sure she was okay. Or, you know, actually there and not some fey spirit he'd conjured in a feverish dream. But no, there she was, sound asleep on her side, one hand curled loosely in front of her face, the other stuffed under her pillow. Her coffee-colored hair billowed across the rest of the pillow behind her, save for a single silky strand that streamed down her cheek.

Okay, maybe not just a peek, Tate thought. That

strand of hair was bound to become an annoyance that woke her up before she was ready. He'd just move that back to join the rest of the heavy mass so it wouldn't be a nuisance.

As quietly as he could, he tiptoed to the bed and, as deftly as he could, tucked a finger under the wayward tress. He was able to brush it back over the crown of her head without waking her, but wasn't as successful when he drew his hand away. Probably because he also couldn't resist skimming his fingertip along her cheek. He couldn't help it. He wanted to see if her skin was as soft and warm as it looked. And it was. Which was why he skimmed the backs of his knuckles across her cheek, too.

Her eyes fluttered open, looking as soft and warm as the rest of her, and she smiled. "Good morning," she said in the dreamy sort of voice women used when—

Actually, Tate wasn't sure when women used a voice like that, all quiet and husky and full of affection. He'd never been with a woman who responded to him that way—as if there weren't any face she'd rather see first thing in the morning than his. Maybe because he so seldom spent the entire night with a woman, so he rarely saw one wake up. Or maybe because the women with whom he did spend the night didn't want anything more out of it than great sex, so they didn't care whose face they saw first thing, either.

And, hell, he and Renata hadn't even spent the night together this time.

"Good morning," he greeted her back, wondering how his voice could have the same affectionate timbre as hers. He cleared his throat and tried again. "It's raining. Again. Doesn't look like Grady will be making it back today, either."

Instead of looking disappointed, she smiled. "Oh, well. Maybe today we can explore the other side of the lake."

The suggestion should have been as off-putting as fishing had been the day before. Instead, he smiled. "Then we're going to need our strength. I'll start breakfast."

Renata smiled back. "Give me a minute to wake up, and I'll help you make breakfast."

Tate leaned closer and murmured, "Give me more than a minute, and I'll help you wake up."

In response, she curled her arm around his neck and pulled him the rest of the way down to kiss him. Their lovemaking this time was slower and more thorough, as if each felt they had all the time in the world to give it. This morning, it did feel like they had all the time in the world. It was a feeling Tate had never experienced—as if he had no obligations, no responsibilities, no plans. He had only Renata. She had only him. At least for today. And tomorrow...

He'd think about tomorrow tomorrow. Today just had too much going for it, jam-packed as it was with dragonflies and waterfalls and Renata.

Eleven

It was a pattern Renny and Tate repeated for the nearly three days that followed. Wake up together, make love together, fix breakfast together. Get a call from Inspector Grady telling them the same thing—that the road to the hotel was still impassable, and the tech guys were still working on the breach. Then go exploring in the rain together, eat dinner together and play Erotic Scrabble together—or Porno Pictionary or Lascivious Pursuit—then shower together, go to bed together, make love together, sleep together and start all over again.

They were insatiable. Not just for each other, but for everything around them. Over the course of those days, the Wisconsin wilderness became less wild and more welcoming, and adversity became adventure. In a lot of ways, Renny felt more at home here with Tate than she'd ever felt back home with people she'd known her entire life. She'd always loved the great outdoors. As a girl, she'd never seen a tree she didn't climb, never met a bug she didn't befriend, never encountered a puddle she didn't jump in, never passed a rock she didn't pocket. This place was Utopia for a girl like that, and being here brought the girl right back to the surface. Except that here, that girl was allowed to run free.

And, as a woman, she'd never known a man like Tate. One who saw her and knew her the way she really was—the way she really wanted to be—and seemed to like her anyway.

No. Not seemed to. He did like her. There was no way he could respond to her the way he did if he didn't. They talked constantly, about anything and everything. They had fun. They laughed. A lot. And the night the rain clouds finally cleared, they skinny-dipped in the lake, then lay on a blanket on the pier and gazed at millions—perhaps billions—of stars, talking about nothing and everything and being the way they wanted and needed to be. Renny never wanted it to end.

But it did the morning she awoke to the crunch of gravel outside the bedroom window. Inspector Grady had finally managed to make it back up to the motel.

"Dammit, Tate, wake up," she said urgently as she rolled out of bed. "Grady is back."

Tate mumbled something incoherent as she grabbed her discarded pajamas from the floor. Then he rolled to his side and fell back asleep. She hopped on one foot, then the other, as she yanked on her pajamas and called out to him again, louder this time.

"Tate! Wake up! You have to move to the sofa! Grady is outside!"

As she thrust her arms through the shirtsleeves, she heard the bang of a car door slamming. Tate slept blissfully on.

"Tate!" she tried one last time. He didn't budge.

Fine. Let him look like a jerk, taking the bed and leaving Renny to sleep on the sofa. No way was she going to let Grady know they'd been sharing a bed—and a lake pier and a shower and a sofa and the rug in front of the fireplace—while he was gone. No way was she going to let the marshal find out what had happened during the time she and Tate were here. Not that she was sure herself what had happened. There would be time to think about that later, when she and Tate were home.

Hundreds of miles away from each other.

She let that sink in for a second—how could she and Tate live hundreds of miles away from each other when it felt as if they'd been sharing the same piece of air for a lifetime? Then she grabbed a sheet from the bed, fled the room and closed the door behind her. She had just enough time to lie down on the sofa when the front door opened and Grady announced his arrival. She used it as an excuse to pretend the noise had woken her up, rolling over to greet him in what she hoped was a convincingly slumberous fashion, even though adrenaline was pumping through her body at a rate that would have won her Olympic gold.

"Oh, hi," she said, hopefully in a slumberous manner.

She tried to rouse a yawn, couldn't find one, so opened her mouth and covered it with her hand for a few seconds. In spite of her Olympic prospects at the moment, judging by Grady's expression, she wasn't in the running for an Oscar.

"Sorry to wake you, Ms. Twigg," he said blandly—though, she had to admit, he wasn't exactly in the running for an Oscar, either, since it was clear he wasn't fooled by her sudden wakefulness. "Guess I should have called to let you know I was coming, but I still wasn't sure I'd make it up the hill and didn't want to get your hopes up. Plus, I figured you and Mr. Hawthorne could use the extra sleep."

Gee, why would he assume she and Tate needed the extra sleep?

Probably best not to think about it.

"Well, thank you for your consideration," she said. There was no reason she couldn't be just as vague as Grady.

The bedroom door flew open suddenly, and Tate appeared in the doorway wearing nothing but his borrowed blue jeans, holding his T-shirt in his hand. He looked gorgeous and virile and—there was no way to get around it—recently tumbled, and he did nothing to promote the fallacy Renny was trying so hard to cling to.

"I smell coffee," he said.

Well, good morning to you, too, she wanted to tell him. Of course, her own greeting of *Dammit, Tate* a few minutes ago hadn't exactly been romantic, either, had it? Besides, she didn't want him to be romantic. She didn't. She wanted Grady to think nothing between her and Tate had changed since the last time the marshal had been here. Even though everything had.

"Real coffee," Tate elaborated. Still not being in any way romantic. So, yay, Tate. "Good coffee. Not the powdered horror in a jar we've been having to drink every morning."

Only then did Renny notice that Grady was holding a cardboard drink carrier that housed four cups of covered coffee. When Tate noted the number of cups, his expression turned sublime. "And you brought |automatic refills." He jerked on his T-shirt, strode across the room, took the carrier from Grady and marched it to the coffee table, then uncapped one and moved it under his nose for a healthy inhalation. "Oh, baby, baby, come to Daddy."

Renny battled a twinge of jealousy that he was more in love with coffee at the moment than he was with her. Not that she expected him to be in love with her. But he could at least seem happier to see her this morning than he was caffeine.

On the upside, Grady looked a lot more convinced that her having woken up on the sofa was a credible prospect. He looked even more convinced when it became clear Tate had no intention of opening a cup of coffee for Renny. Yay again. Dammit. So she reached for one herself. There was even real cream and sugar to go with it. She couldn't remember the last time she'd had real coffee with real cream and sugar.

Oh, wait. Yes, she could. It had been less than a week ago. Saturday morning, at O'Hare. Why did it keep feeling like years had passed since her arrival in this part of the country?

Tate continued to sip his coffee in silence, so Renny

did, too. Grady set a bag on the table decorated with a logo from a place called Debbie Does Donuts, and informed them that the lemon chiffon crullers were particularly good, but not to rule out the maple bacon, because he couldn't believe how well that combination worked in a doughnut. Renny peeked into the bag and snagged a basic glazed. She wasn't feeling especially adventurous this morning.

"I've got good news and bad news," Grady said, when it became clear that neither she nor Tate would be especially talkative. "Which do you want first?"

Still looking at his coffee instead of at Renny, Tate said, "Good."

"Okay. I've been given the official all clear that there's no threat to you, Mr. Hawthorne, and you're free to go."

Tate snapped his head up to meet Grady's gaze. "Just like that?"

The marshal nodded. "You'll be home in a matter of hours. I'll drive you myself."

"Then what's the bad news?"

Grady looked at Renny. "The bad news is for Ms. Twigg."

Something cold and unpleasant settled in her midsection. All she could manage by way of a response was "Oh?"

Grady smiled, but there wasn't an ounce of happiness in the look. "Yeah, oh. Do you want to tell Mr. Hawthorne, Ms. Twigg, or should I?"

That, finally, made Tate look at her. He was clearly confused. For a moment, she could almost convince herself there was no way Grady's techs could have discovered what they had obviously discovered, since she and Tate were being given the all clear. For a moment, she could almost convince herself that the fantasy life they had been enjoying for the last five days really would go on forever.

Even though it was pretty clear Grady had discovered where the security breach originated, Renny told herself to keep her mouth shut. She was an attorney, for God's sake. Maybe she only practiced probate law, but she knew better than to say anything to a law enforcement officer that could be used against her in court. She had Phoebe to think about, too.

When Grady realized Renny wasn't going to be more forthcoming, he said, "Does the name Phoebe Resnick ring a bell, Ms. Twigg?"

Okay, it was *very* clear Grady had discovered where the security breach originated. Even so, Renny still said nothing.

"Who's Phoebe Resnick?" Tate asked, sounding even more confused.

"Also known as the Tandem Menace," Grady told him.

Yep, they knew all about Phoebe. She'd been using that nickname since sixth grade. That was when she discovered a way to get into the school's computer so it looked like the hack was coming from two places at once, only she was really coming in from a third place that didn't show up at all. No one in the administration ever figured out who was doing it or how, and Phoebe went to MIT on full scholarship.

These days, she owned a digital security company that was making her a boatload of money. She still hacked on her days off, but she used her powers only for good. She did things like move money from the accounts of despots into the accounts of human rights organizations. Or she took money from human traffickers and donated it to women's shelters and scholarship funds. Or she transferred money from the accounts of corporations that tested on animals and gave it to the ASPCA. And when a friend needed her, she did things like locate a little boy who'd been buried in a federal database.

"What the hell is a tandem menace?" Tate asked.

Grady continued to look at Renny, offering her the opportunity to clear the air with her own explanation instead of clouding it with an indictment of his own. But if the marshals had IDed Phoebe, they must know Renny was involved, too. Although she and Phoebe had only talked about Tate in person—Phoebe never left a digital trail…um, except this time, evidently—the two of them had been friends since preschool. There was no way Renny could credibly deny her involvement with the hack. And now Tate was going to—

She really didn't want to think about what Tate was going to do once he learned the whole truth. Which was another reason she didn't say a word.

Grady, however, still had plenty to say. "Phoebe Resnick is a world-class hacker who goes by the moniker the Tandem Menace on the dark web. She's the one who ransacked the WITSEC databases until she located you, Mr. Hawthorne. And, oh, yeah, she's been a friend of Ms. Twigg's since they were kids."

Renny braved a glance at Tate. He still looked confused.

"But you said it was a guy you found on Craigslist named John Smith."

Renny wanted to tell him she never would have trusted his identity to a guy on Craigslist named John Smith and at least be honest about that. But she couldn't even tell him that much. Not with Grady standing there, listening. She felt horrible now for what she had kept hidden from Tate. If she had just been honest that morning in his office when Grady first arrived...

But if she'd done that, she never would have had the last five days with Tate. And the thought of that was even more horrible. Even if she never had another day with him again—and it was more than likely that, after this, she wouldn't—there was a part of Renny that would never be able to regret her transgression.

As the truth finally sank in, Tate gazed at her incredulously. "Your *friend* was the security breach at the Justice Department?"

Renny still said nothing. She couldn't. Although this time it had nothing to do with incriminating herself or Phoebe. This time, it was because Tate was looking at her as if she were the most heinous villain in the world.

"You've known all along there was no threat to my safety?" he asked.

His anger was almost palpable. Renny remained silent.

But Tate wasn't. "This whole fiasco could have been

avoided if you'd told Grady on Saturday that you knew who was behind the breach?"

He thought this had been a whole fiasco? Had there been nothing about this week he could think of that made it only a partial fiasco? Like maybe how much fun the two of them had had before all hell broke loose? Like maybe how they'd learned about each other and themselves? Or how they'd come to feel about each other? Or how happy they'd been, if only for a little while?

Tate stood and moved to the other side of the room, though whether that was because he suddenly felt restless, or because he wanted to put as much distance between himself and Renny as possible, she couldn't have said. That became clearer, however, as he spoke further.

"Five days," he said. "Five days we've been stuck here. Five days I've been away from work. Do you know how much I missed being away from work for five days? Do you know how much it cost me to be away from work for five days?"

Renny figured she could answer that, at least, without incriminating herself. Even so, all she could do was shake her head.

"Millions, Renata. It's cost me millions. Worse than that, it's cost my clients millions. It's hurt my business. It's compromised my reputation. It's—"

He stopped pacing, hooked his hands on his hips and glared at her. Then he shook his head and began to pace again. When it became clear that the rest of his tirade would be taking place in his head—which was somehow worse than having him sling it at Renny, because she had no way to defend herself even if her actions were indefensible—she looked at Grady again.

She wanted to ask him what was going to happen to Phoebe, wanted to tell him her friend shouldn't be held responsible for any of it, since Renny was the one who put it all in motion. But she knew the law didn't work like that. The law dealt with actions, not intentions. Phoebe had broken the law. Renny was an accessory. Even if neither of them had meant any harm, they could both be looking at some hefty repercussions. And Phoebe, unfortunately, would bear the brunt of it.

Grady crossed his arms over his chest and studied Renny in silence long enough for her to mentally fit herself and Phoebe for orange jumpsuits and realize that no, orange wasn't actually the new black.

He must have realized what she was thinking, though, because he told her, "Relax, Ms. Twigg. Phoebe made a deal with us. She's going to do some favors for Uncle Sam. In exchange, Uncle Sam is going to look the other way with regard to this one…episode…and pretend it never happened. And since this…episode… never happened," Grady added, "then you couldn't be part of it, could you?"

Renny nodded. "Thanks," she said wearily.

"For what?" Grady asked.

No sense pushing it. Especially since she had a lot more to worry about where Tate was concerned. He was still glaring at her with clear disbelief and even clearer fury. She rose from the sofa to approach him, but he held up a hand to stop her.

"Don't say anything," he told her.

"I can explain," she said halfheartedly.

"I don't want to hear it."

"Tate—" she tried again.

But he turned to Grady and said, "When can we leave?"

"As soon as you're ready," the marshal said. Almost as an afterthought, he looked at Renny. "You, too, Ms. Twigg. I've arranged for a flight for you out of Green Bay, so we'll make a brief stop there on the way to Chicago. I have the belongings you left at Mr. Hawthorne's house in the SUV." He turned back to Tate. "Mr. Hawthorne, please accept my apology on behalf of the United States government for your inconvenience and discomfort this week. We only wanted to ensure that you were protected, as we promised you would be when you entered the program thirty years ago."

"Apology accepted," Tate replied automatically.

Oh, sure. He'd accept an apology from Grady, but he wouldn't even let Renny voice one. Then again, Grady hadn't actually been the person who'd caused Tate inconvenience and discomfort this week, had he? No, all of that fell to Renny. She didn't blame him for being angry at her. She was angry at herself. But she wished he would at least give her a chance to explain.

And she hoped that, someday, on some level, Tate would be able to think about the last five days as having been more than inconvenience and discomfort. She hoped that, someday, he remembered too the blackberry brambles and the pine cones and the star-studded night sky and her.

"I should shower and change," she said quietly. "I'll be as fast as I can."

Before either man could reply, she retreated to the bedroom. As she grabbed her wrinkled suit and blouse from the closet, she tried not to notice Tate's polo uniform hanging beside it and how different the two outfits were from each other. How they didn't belong together at all. How, in normal circumstances, they would never have shared the same space.

And how, now that Renny had ruined everything, they would never share the same space again.

Home, sweet castle.

After almost a week away from it, Tate opened the portcullis, strode through the barbican and surveyed his realm. It seemed a lot smaller than he remembered. And it was so empty. Even Madison wasn't around. Tate had instructed Grady to call the butler and tell him to take time off with pay until Tate returned home. Home to his castle-slash-house that he'd bought because he would be living in a fortress where no one would be able to get to him. For years, no one had.

Not until Renata Twigg.

She changed his life when she showed up with her files and photos. Not just because of what he learned about himself from those files but what he learned about himself in the days that followed, too.

He reminded himself that she hadn't just changed his life—she'd messed it up in a way that would take a long time to fix. Then again, was it really *his* life she'd messed up? Just who was Tate Hawthorne, anyway?

The grandson of a reputed New York mobster? A successful Chicago businessman? A babe in the Wisconsin woods? All of the above? None of the above? This week had left his head so full of weirdness he wasn't sure he'd ever know himself again. Not that he'd really known himself before Renata.

Just what the hell had happened to him this week?

He took the stairs two at a time, trying not to notice how the echo of his boots made the house sound—and feel—even emptier. Once in his bedroom, he stripped off the fetid polo uniform and headed for the shower. The massive marble shower with its three jets and bench for two that would have given him and Renata a lot more room to move around than the tiny stall at the motel. In a shower like this, he and Renata could—

Nothing, he told himself. He'd never see her again. She'd lied to him. She'd completely disrupted his life. She'd cost him and his clients a massive amount of money. The last five days had been a total disaster.

Okay, maybe not a total disaster, he backpedaled as he stepped under the jets. But he was happy to be home. He couldn't wait to get back to his normal life. Really. He couldn't. His normal life that would be completely lacking in discomfort and inconvenience and Renata Twigg.

Work, he told himself. He'd been too long away from the thing that gave his life meaning. No wonder he felt so weird. Working grounded him and reminded him what was really important. He needed to work.

He made his way back down the stairs—damn, the house really was way too quiet, even though this must have been the way it always sounded and felt—and made his way to his office. He had a mountain of email waiting, and at least half of them were decorated with the little red exclamation mark that deemed them Important.

But none of the Important emails he read seemed all that important.

Oh, well. He still needed to get back to work. The thing he knew best. The thing he did best. People would come and go in his life. Events would begin and end. But work... That was a constant.

Thankfully, he had enough of it to keep him from thinking about Renata and the damage she'd caused. Enough to keep him from remembering dragonflies and fireflies and picking blackberries with Renata. Enough to forget about counting stars and catching fish and playing Strip Monopoly with Renata. Oh, yeah. He was very, very thankful for all this work.

He went back to the first Important email he'd opened—even if it wasn't all that important—and hit Reply.

It was raining in New York City. Possibly the same rain that had fallen in Wisconsin earlier in the week. Renny—freshly showered and wearing silk pj's that were blissfully devoid of golf carts—gazed out her living room window at the snaking traffic of Tribeca and told herself again how happy she was to be home.

No more freezer-burned food or homemade rompers. She could binge-watch all the BBC mysteries she wanted and soak in her tub for hours. She could be with people who appreciated her for more than her ability to give them an orgasm and didn't hate her guts. She was elated to be here and not in Wisconsin. She was. Even if there was a part of her that would be in Wisconsin forever.

It was just too bad that part would be there alone.

Tate had been silent on the drive from the motel, and he'd ignored her when she climbed out of the SUV at the airport in Green Bay. Not that she blamed him. But she wished he would have at least said goodbye.

In the days that followed, Renny went about her job robotically, telling herself the reason she was so unenthusiastic about her cases was because she was just having trouble getting back in the groove.

But as the days became weeks, and her groove never materialized, she began to think a little differently. Like how maybe the reason she was the only person at Tarrant, Fiver & Twigg who hadn't always found the heir she was looking for, and the reason she'd screwed up her assignment with Tate, and the reason even the cases she didn't screw up never went as smoothly for her as they did for everyone else, the reason for all those things was because, well, Renny wasn't very good at her job. And the reason she wasn't very good at her job was because she didn't actually like her job. Not the way she should like it. Not the way everyone else at Tarrant, Fiver & Twigg liked theirs.

But after a few weeks back at work, Renny did start to think about that. Not just because of her epiphany that she might not be suited to be a suit at Tarrant, Fiver & Twigg, but because, for the first time since she was twelve years old, she was late. Not late for work. Not late for Zumba. Not late for lunch with friends. Renny

…was late as in *holy-crap-I-have-to-buy-a-home-pregnancy-test-my-God-how-did-this-happen* late.

Not that she couldn't guess how it happened. Although she'd been confident she was right when she told Tate that first time that the timing was wrong for her to get pregnant, after five days together, the timing might have been just right. So she shouldn't have been surprised one evening to find herself popping into a Duane Reade that was a few—or seventeen—blocks from her condo for some toothpaste, a bottle of biotin, a pack of AAA batteries, the latest issue of *Vanity Fair*, a six pack of Kit Kats and, oh, what the hey, a pregnancy test.

Twenty minutes after she got home, Renny was thinking she might have been better served to pick up a copy of *Parenting* instead of the *Vanity Fair*. But thank God for the Kit Kats. And once that realization set in, another quickly followed it.

HolycrapmyGodhowdidthishappen?

But she already knew how it had happened. So, really, the question she needed to be asking herself was what she was going to do. There was another human being growing inside her that was half Renny and half Tate. Knowing what she did of him, she was sure he would offer financial support. But personal support? That was a tough call. Not only was there the whole hating-her-guts thing to consider, but by now he was back to his usual routine with a work life that included weekend hours and a home office, and a social life that included leggy redheads and evenings out. Would he want any of that interrupted by the patter of little feet and a woman he didn't like? Doubtful.

More to the point, did Renny want her life interrupted? Then again, was her life what and where she wanted it to be in the first place? Not really.

She looked at the little plastic wand in her hand, with its little pink plus sign. And she wondered again what the hell she was going to do.

Twelve

A month after returning from Wisconsin, Tate's life had totally returned to normal. He was back to his normal seven-day workweek, his normal Saturday polo game, his normal Tuesday drinks with friends-slash-colleagues, who, okay, now felt a bit less like friends than they did colleagues. He was also back to his normal nights out with normal leggy redheads—though, admittedly, those nights were slightly less normal, because they always ended early for some reason and never reached their obvious conclusion. Still, except for those small factors, a month after returning from Wisconsin, his life had returned to normal. Totally, totally normal.

Except for how he had never felt less normal in his life. Almost nothing about his daily existence had changed after that brief hiccup that was five days in Wisconsin. Yet somehow everything about his daily existence felt changed.

He told himself it was because part of his life was still unsettled, since he hadn't been in contact with any of his newly discovered relatives on the East Coast. Tate's attorneys had worked with Tarrant, Fiver & Twigg to complete the paperwork necessary for him to decline his inheritance from Joseph Bacco without revealing his new identity to the rest of the family. He'd been surprised when his attorneys had informed him that his aunts and uncles and cousins wanted to meet him if he was amenable. To the Baccos, family was family, and Joey the Knife had spent thirty years wanting to bring his little grandson back into the fold. Even if Tate didn't want to join the family business, they said, they hoped he would someday see clear to join the family. When he was ready to make himself known to them, they were ready to embrace him with a big ol' Bacco hug. Tate just didn't know yet how he felt about all that.

Deep down, though, he knew it wasn't his uncertainty about his East Coast relations that was the source of his current unrest. Mostly because, deep down, he kind of knew what was the source of that. The same thing that had been the source of it a month ago. Renata Twigg.

He hadn't heard a word from her since Grady dropped her at the curb—literally—in Green Bay. Once, about a week ago, when he was up late and after a couple of bourbons, he'd Google-imaged "Renata Twigg." But when a dozen photos of her appeared on his computer screen, he spared barely a minute to look at them. Because he was suddenly sleepy enough to go back to bed, not because one of the photos was of her at some society function, looking breathtaking in a black strapless dress, with some upright, forthright, do-right kind of guy on her arm. Even if the photo had been two years old, it was just a reminder that things between them hadn't ended well. More to the point, things between them had ended. She had a life of her own half a continent away that she'd gone back to, and it doubtless had returned to normal, as well. Anyway, there was no reason for him to be Google-imaging her late at night with a couple of bourbons in him.

The next day, he'd called an event planner he knew and hired her to organize an obscenely gigantic party for him, and money was no object if she could get the damned thing put together by the following weekend, because, man, it had just been too long since he'd had an obscenely gigantic party. Which was how Tate came to be hosting a bash for a hundred of his closest friends, right this very minute, in the house-slash-castle he'd bought to keep people out, and which had been way too empty, and way too quiet for, oh, about a month now.

So why wasn't he downstairs having a blast with his hundred closest friends? Why was he, instead, standing on the balcony off his bedroom gazing down at the ones who were prowling around the grounds? Sure, he'd been a good host at first. He'd dressed the part in his best charcoal trousers and a gray linen shirt. He'd greeted everyone at the door and directed them to the three different bars and let them know the DJ would be

starting his first set at eight. And he'd made one per-
functory circuit of the goings-on to be sure the noise
level was loud enough to indicate everyone was having
a good time—it was, and they were. Then he'd fetched
a drink from the nearest bar to wait for the spirit of the
gathering to overtake him, too.

He was still waiting.

He was about to return to his bedroom when a single
guest caught his attention in the garden below. She was
standing alone at its very edge, as far removed from the
crowd as she could be without actually disappearing.
She wore a plain sleeveless dress the color of a Wisconsin wilderness, and her dark hair was shorter than
the last time he saw her, just barely brushing her shoulders. He couldn't imagine what had brought Renata to
his house—unless it was his thinking about her—but
she didn't look happy to be here. In fact, after a sweeping glance at the crowd, she turned around as if she was
going to leave.

The music was too loud for her to hear him if he
called out to her, so he ran from the bedroom, nearly
stumbled down the stairs, raced through the front door
and rounded the house on the side where he'd seen
her. Thankfully, she'd gotten only as far as the garden
boundary nearest him, so he hurried forward to stop
her before she could get away. She was looking at the
ground, though, so she didn't see him coming, and when
she suddenly began to jog away from the goings-on and
toward him, he didn't have a chance to move out of her
way, and she jogged right into him.

He was able to catch her by the upper arms before

she would have bounced backward, but the minute he touched her, all he wanted to do was pull her forward. How had he gone a month without touching her, when he'd touched her every day for—

Five days. Had they really only spent five days together? How was that possible? It felt as if Renata had been a part of him forever. And why, suddenly, was he thinking about all the moments of those days instead of the end of them when he accused her of messing up his life irrevocably? She hadn't messed up his life, he thought now. He'd only thought she messed up his life because she messed up his work, and back then— a whole month ago—work had been his life. But after those five days in Wisconsin with Renata...

Hell, she hadn't messed up his life. She'd saved it.

"Hey," he said softly as he pulled her up, "slow down. Where's the fire?" Other than in his chest, he meant. Because there was a warmth kindling there that was fast spreading.

He thought she would smile at the question, but when she looked up, her mouth was flat, and her eyebrows were knit downward.

"What, you came all this way just to glare at me?" he asked, injecting a lightness into his voice he wasn't close to feeling.

She shook her head. "No. Why I came isn't important now." She hesitated, then stepped backward, out of his grasp. "I have to go."

Before he could object—hell, before he even knew what she was talking about—she hurried past him, heading toward the front of the house. She was doing more than jogging now. She was running. Why had she come all the way to Chicago if she was just going to run away from him? Why hadn't she told him she was coming in the first place? What the hell was going on?

"Renata, wait!" he called after her. But she only ran faster.

So Tate ran after her.

He caught up with her as she was key-fobbing a sedan that was nondescript enough to indicate it was a rental. She had opened the driver's-side door and tossed her purse into the passenger seat when he caught her by the upper arm again. Only this time he did pull her toward him. Before she could stop him—and because he couldn't help himself—he lowered his head to hers and kissed her.

She kissed him back immediately, her body fairly melting into his. Just like that, a month faded away, and the world dissolved around them. All Tate knew was that he had Renata back, and for the first time in weeks, he didn't feel as if he were in the wrong place and time. For the first time in weeks, he felt as if he were exactly where he belonged.

Reluctantly, he ended the kiss. But he didn't go far. He looped his arms around her waist and bent to touch his forehead to hers. He'd forgotten how small she was. Funny how he'd always avoided small women because he thought he wouldn't know what to do with one. He and this one fitted together perfectly. Then again, that didn't have anything to do with their sizes.

"You don't hate me?" she said by way of a greeting.

"I never hated you," he assured her.

She hesitated, gazing into his eyes as if trying to see

the thoughts inside his head. Finally, she said, "That makes one of us. I hate myself for not telling you the truth right away, Tate. I'm sorry for what happened. I'm sorry I wasn't honest with you. I couldn't be. If I'd said anything in front of Grady, it could have put Phoebe in jail for a long time. But I am so sorry I—"

"I'm not sorry for any of it," he said.

For the first time, he realized that was true. Yes, Renata had lied to him. Yes, for five days, his life had been completely disrupted. If she had been honest the first day, none of that would have been the case. But those five days had ended up being the best five days Tate had ever known. In those five days, he had learned more about himself than he had in the thirty-plus years that preceded them. He'd been able to be himself in Wisconsin. He'd discovered himself there. Even more important, he'd discovered Renata. And he'd realized just how much he needed someone like her in his life to make him happy. Really, honestly, genuinely *happy*, something he had never been before.

No, he didn't need someone like Renata for that. He needed Renata.

She looked confused. "But that last day in Wisconsin—"

"That last day in Wisconsin, I didn't realize a lot of things I should have realized that first day in Wisconsin. Like how much I needed five days in Wisconsin. Especially with someone like you. Let's try this again," he said softly. "Hi."

She still looked confused. But she replied, even more softly, "Hi."

"It's good to see you."

"It's good to see you, too."

"I've missed you," he said, surprised not only to realize the feeling, but to reveal it. Not just because he'd never told a woman—or anyone—that he'd missed her before. But because he'd never actually missed a woman—or anyone—before. He'd missed Renata, though. He'd missed her a lot.

"I've missed you, too," she said.

By now her voice had softened so much he barely heard what she said. He felt it, though. He felt it in the way she'd curled the fingers of one hand into his shirt and cupped the other around his neck. And he felt it in the way she nestled her head against his chest. Mostly, though, he felt it in the air around them. As if whatever it was that made them who they were somehow mingled and joined the same way their bodies had so many times before, and now it was finding its missing pieces, too.

For a moment, they only stood entwined, refamiliarizing themselves with all the nuances of each other's bodies and spirits, remembering how it had felt to be so close, enjoying that nearness again. Tate figured he should wait for Renata to say something first, since she was the one who had traveled across half the country to get here. But she didn't say anything. She just leaned into him as if she never wanted to let him go.

So Tate started instead. "Not that I'm complaining or anything, but what are you doing here?"

She stayed silent for another moment, and he began to think she wouldn't say another word. He even tightened his hold on her a little because he feared she might try to bolt again. But she didn't do that, either. The night closed in around them, the lights of the house and grounds not quite reaching this far, the music of the party a faint burr against the darkness. There was a part of him that would have been perfectly content to stay this way forever. Finally, though, Renata lifted her head from his chest and looked up at him. She still didn't look happy. But she didn't look quite as hurt as she had at first, either.

"I need to tell you something," she said.

He couldn't imagine what. And, truth be told, he wasn't sure he cared. All he knew was that he was with Renata, and the life that had felt so abnormal for the past month suddenly felt right again.

"Okay," he said. "What?"

She freed her fingers from his shirt and dropped her hand from his neck to her side. Then she took a small step backward. But she stopped when he wove his fingers together at the small of her back to keep her from retreating farther. Her reaction wasn't exactly what he had expected. Why had she come this far only to pull away from him? Especially after he'd made clear he wanted her here.

"We need to talk," she said, not telling him what she needed to tell him.

The heat in his midsection took on a new dimension. "I thought that was what we were doing," he said, forcing a smile.

She didn't smile back. She turned to look over her shoulder at his house and the party in full swing inside and behind it. When she looked at him again, the hurt in her expression had returned.

"I should come back tomorrow," she said. "You're entertaining. It's obviously not a good time."

Was she crazy? Not a good time? Didn't she realize the minute he saw her, it was the first good time he'd had in a month?

"Renata, what's going on?" He didn't bother trying to mask his worry now.

"Seriously, it's late," she said. "I don't know what I was thinking to come here this time of night. Well, except maybe that it took me all day to gather my courage. Tomorrow would be better. I'll come back then. What time is good for you?"

She'd been here all day and was just now showing up at his door? She'd had to gather her courage to do that?

"It's barely ten thirty," he said. "That's not late. Especially on a Saturday night."

Her expression changed again, and he could tell she was weighing something very important in her head. He couldn't imagine what would be warring in there to cause her so much turmoil when, as far as he was concerned, having her here made everything fall perfectly into place. Finally, one faction must have won, because her expression changed again. But it was to something he couldn't quite identify. Resignation, maybe. Or acceptance. Of what, though, he had no idea.

"Actually," she said, "ten thirty is pretty late, even on a Saturday, for women like me. I've been turning in a lot earlier than I used to."

Okay. He'd been turning in a little earlier himself since coming home from Wisconsin. Mostly because there hadn't been that much reason to stay up. Except for insomnia. But a couple of bourbons usually fixed that. Then her wording finally struck him.

"Women like you," he repeated. "I don't know what that means. There are no other women like you."

She managed a small smile for that. The alarm bells in his head quieted some. Not a lot. But some.

"I hope you still think that when I tell you why I've been going to bed so early."

"Unless you've been doing that so you can be with someone else, I don't think it's going to make any difference in the way I feel about you."

She bit her lip in a way he remembered her doing in Wisconsin. Mostly when she was fretting over something. "Funny you should say that," she said.

His stomach dropped. No, it wasn't. It wasn't funny at all. Not if she really was going to bed with someone else.

"I have sort of been with someone else at night. Every night."

She'd been smiling when she made the comment, but something in Tate's expression must have told her just how badly he was taking the news. Because she quickly added, "Not like that! I haven't been with anyone since…I mean, there's no one who could ever… You're the only guy who ever…"

When she realized she wasn't finishing any of her thoughts—not that they needed finishing, since Tate was getting the gist of it, and the gist of it was making him feel better, if not less confused—she expelled a restless sound, took a deep breath, then released it slowly.

Finally, she said, "I've been going to bed with someone else every night because…because I'm…" She sighed heavily, and in a rush of words, she finished, "Because I'm pregnant, Tate."

Even though she uttered the comment in a hurry, it took a minute for him to hear it. And even though he heard it, he wasn't sure he heard it correctly. Maybe he'd misinterpreted. Did Renata just say she was—

"You're what?" he asked, just to be certain.

"I'm going to have a baby, Tate. Our baby. Yours and mine."

There wasn't any way to misinterpret that. Renata did indeed say she was pregnant. She was going to have a baby. Their baby. His and hers. Okay then. He waited for his reaction. Surely, it would be one of dread and panic. Any minute now, he would be overcome with both. Dread and panic descending in three, two, one…

But it wasn't dread or panic that overcame him. Instead, what he felt most was wonder.

He was going to have a baby? Well, not him, obviously, but half of it would be his. Would be him. Which was kind of unexpected. And kind of weird. And kind of… Wow. Kind of awesome. But it was also nowhere in his life plan. He'd never considered the prospect of becoming a father. He didn't even want the responsibility that came with having a pet. How was he supposed to accommodate a child in his life? Then again, no one said he had to. He could just mail a monthly check to

Renata and skip the poopy diapers and prepubescent angst and cross-country college exploratory visits. Not to mention the birthday parties and soccer games and piano lessons that ate into a successful venture capitalist's time. A lot of men just mailed checks.

Men who were complete pricks.

"A baby?" he asked.

It was a stupid question, already answered, but he honestly didn't know what else to say. The news was still winding through his brain—and, okay, his heart. But both seemed to be greeting the new development pretty welcomingly.

When Tate said nothing in response to her clarification, Renata continued, "I know that first time we… I mean…I know that first time, I told you the timing wasn't right—and it wasn't," she hastened to add. "Not that time, anyway. But after five days of…you know… And after reading that a man's, ah, swimmers can, well, swim for anywhere from three to five days after, um, jumping into the pool, something I never really thought about but clearly should have, I guess the timing kind of got right."

When he still didn't reply—because he was still processing—she roused a cheerfulness that was clearly feigned and said, "I guess I should give you some time to think about this. I'm staying at the Knickerbocker. Room 315. Call me tomorrow, and we can meet somewhere to talk some more."

She tried to pull out of the circle of his arms, but Tate pulled her close again. "Why would you want to stay at a hotel when you can stay here with me?"

She said nothing in response to that, as if she were the one having trouble processing now.

"I mean, yeah, the Knickerbocker is great," he continued, "but it's not like home."

Not that his home had felt like home, either, for the past month. Tonight, though, it was starting to feel closer to home than it ever had before.

Renata still looked conflicted. Which was fine. Tate still felt conflicted. About some things. But none of it was about her.

She opened her mouth, hesitated, then finally said, "I just thought you might want—"

"You," he finished for her. "Renata, all I want is you. In a way, I think you're all I've ever wanted. I just didn't know it until I met you."

"But the baby will—"

"Look, I won't lie. I don't know what the baby will or won't do. And you're right. I'm going to need some time to process it. One thing I don't need to process, though, is—" He pulled her closer, kissed her again, then let her go. "You being here. With me. Nothing has been clearer in my life than how much better things are when you're around."

"But—"

He let go of her, only to place an index finger gently against her lips to halt any further objections she might make. "But nothing," he said. "The days you and I spent together in Wisconsin were the best days of my life." He grinned. "At least until this one."

It occurred to him then that he didn't know how *she* felt about the pregnancy. She'd had more time for the realization to settle in than he had, but had it settled well? Or had it settled badly? And how did she feel about *him*? He hadn't exactly been kind to her that last day in Wisconsin. Sure, she'd traveled halfway across the country to see him tonight, but that was because the news she had to tell him wasn't the kind of thing you wanted to tell someone in a text. If she hadn't gotten pregnant, would she still be standing here right now?

"I mean, you can stay here at the house if you want to," he started to backpedal. "If you'd rather stay at the hotel…"

He actually held his breath as he waited to see how she would respond. For a moment, she didn't. Then she smiled. "I'd like that," she said. "If it isn't an imposition."

Yeah, right. What was an imposition was a hundred of his closest friends invading his house and yard, not to mention three full bars and a DJ who still had two sets to go.

"You know what?" he said impulsively. "I actually think a night at the Knickerbocker would be better." Before she had a chance to misconstrue, he added, "Just give me ten minutes to pack a bag."

She still looked like she was going to misconstrue. Then she smiled again. Damn, he loved her smile.

"But what about your party?"

"Madison is here. So is the event planner. They can manage without me. Hell, I've spent most of the night in my room, anyway."

"Then why are you having a huge party?"

"I'll explain at the hotel. No, on the way to the hotel,"

he said. "Once we're at the hotel, I have something else in mind."

Her smile shone brighter. "Thank goodness I packed something other than golf-cart pajamas."

It was raining in Wisconsin. Again. But as Renny gazed through the window of her and Tate's stucco cheese wedge, she smiled. The rain this time was different, a light winter drizzle the forecasters had promised would turn to snow after dark—scarcely an hour away. Which was perfect, as tomorrow was Christmas Eve. The cottage hadn't changed much since summer, save for a good cleaning and *much* better food in the kitchen cabinets and fridge, along with a fire in the fireplace that now crackled merrily against the freezing temperatures outside.

Oh, and also the ownership. She and Tate were now co-owners of the Big Cheese Motor Inn and were planning to begin renovation on it in the spring—mid-May probably, to give them both a couple of months to cope with the addition of a baby in their lives, however that addition ended up being organized. They had plans to reopen it in a couple of summers as a family-friendly vacation destination, a throwback to another, simpler time, complete with fishing, hiking, stargazing and cave exploring…and absolutely no technology to speak of.

They had been inseparable since that night at Tate's house in July. He had returned to New York with Renny long enough for her to give her two weeks' notice at Tarrant, Fiver & Twigg and to meet her parents so they could announce together the elder Twiggs' impending grandparenthood. Her mother and father had handled the news the same way Renny and Tate had, first with surprise, then with confusion, then with delight. Since then, delight had pretty much been Renny's constant companion. She'd come back to Chicago with Tate, had rented a condo in the Gold Coast and the two had begun a courtship—for lack of a more contemporary word— that was more conducive to getting to know each other in a normal environment.

Well, except for the fact that they were already expecting a baby, something that didn't normally happen in a courtship until much later.

For Tate and Renny, though, it had worked. In spite of her condition, they'd focused on each other first and foremost those first few months. And by the time she started to show, they were ready to start talking about and be excited by the baby. Neither of them had had a childhood they'd particularly enjoyed, and both were kind of giddy about the prospect of a do-over with their own offspring. They'd each furnished a room in their homes with a nursery. Tate was gradually cutting back on his hours at work—weekends in his home office had been the first thing to go. And Renny had launched a web-based business from home targeted at getting girls into the wilderness to discover the joys of fishing, hiking, stargazing and cave exploring. Among other things. She already had two full-time employees, and when the baby came, she'd hire a third and go down to part-time herself.

The motel would be the centerpiece for that business once it was up and running. For now, though, she and Tate were content to keep it all to themselves.

The front door opened, blowing in both the winter wind and Tate, bundled up in his spanking-new purchases from the North Face and L.L. Bean and carrying two armfuls of wood for the fire.

"Baby, it's cold outside," he said with a grin.

"Gonna get colder," she told him.

"Bring it. We're ready."

As he made his way to the fireplace to stack the wood beside it, Renny went to the kitchen to ladle out the hot chocolate that was warming on the stove. They'd been here for a week already, long enough to hang Christmas lights, decorate a small tree and tuck a dozen presents beneath it, and they were planning to stay through New Year's. But if the weather took a turn for the worse—which she was pretty sure they were both secretly hoping would happen—they had enough supplies to last them for a month.

They couldn't stay much longer than that, though. Tate's cousin Angie the Flamethrower was getting married on Valentine's Day, and no way would they miss that. The Baccos, once Tate had decided to approach them last fall, had been nothing but warm and welcoming to him and Renny both. Apparently, Joey the Knife had been right about family being more important than anything. The Baccos couldn't wait to include Tate—and, by extension, Renny and their baby—in their lives, and Angie's wedding had seemed like the perfect place to start. As Tate's aunt Denise told him the first time they spoke, *"Chi si volta, e chi si gira, sempre a casa va finire."* Translation: "No matter where you go, you'll always end up at home." Renny figured the saying was apt in more ways than one—and for more people than the Baccos.

She returned to the living room with hot chocolate, setting Tate's mug on the coffee table and seating herself on the sofa. By now he had shed his outerwear and was down to jeans and a brown flannel shirt. His attire mirrored Renny's—especially since the striped flannel shirt she was wearing belonged to him. In one fluid move, he picked up his hot chocolate with one hand and, as had become his habit at times like this, splayed his other open over her belly.

"So, how's it been in there today?" he asked.

"Busy," she said. "Your daughter must be learning to do the mambo before she comes out."

"She's just getting ready for all the tree climbing and log rolling you have in store for her."

"Hey, you're going to learn to do those things, too, remember. This parenting thing is going to be an equal partnership. We both decided."

He started to say something else, but Baby Girl Hawthorne-Twigg—yes, after groaning at the realization of what the hyphenated last name would be, they'd decided it was too irresistible to not use it—switched from the mambo to the tarantella, turning circles in Renny's womb in a way that had become familiar to them both. As always, they laughed. Then they entwined their fingers together. Then they kissed. For a really long time.

"Only one more trimester," Renny said when they pulled apart.

He shook his head. "It's gone so fast. Hard to believe we only have three more months left of…"

When he didn't finish, she finished for him. "Of whatever this has been between us. Whatever this *is* between us."

He set his mug on the table and turned to face her but left his fingers entwined with hers on her belly. "Yeah," he said, "we should probably start trying to pin that down."

Over the past five months, they'd talked a lot about the past and even more about the future. At least, the baby's future. What they hadn't talked about much was the present. About what, exactly, the two of them were doing right now. Probably for the very reason Tate had just described—neither really seemed to know what the present was. They'd made a million plans for the baby. But they hadn't made any for themselves.

"I'm okay with the status quo," she said. Even if she kind of wasn't.

"I'm okay with it, too," he replied. Even if he didn't sound like he was. In spite of that, he added, "The status quo is pretty great."

"It is. And no one says we have to go the traditional route, right?" she said. "Lots of people who live separate lives share responsibility for their kids and do just fine."

"Right," he agreed. "They do. But we're not exactly living separate lives, are we?"

"Well, no, but…"

"But…?" he prompted.

Actually, Renny couldn't find a reason to finish her objection. Probably because she didn't have any objection to the two of them *not* living separate lives. They'd just never talked about joining their lives, that was all. Unless that was what they were doing now...

"But..." she said again. Still not sure why. Maybe in case that wasn't what they were talking about. Wondering what she would do if it wasn't, because she suddenly liked the idea a lot and wanted to talk about it.

"So, then," Tate interjected, "maybe we should talk about that aspect of whatever this—" he gestured quickly between the two of them "—is between us."

Renny's stomach lurched at his remark, and she was pretty sure it had nothing to do with the baby. Before she could say anything else, he jumped up from the sofa, went to the Christmas tree and from beneath it withdrew a small box she was positive hadn't been there before tonight. He returned to the sofa and held it up in his open palm.

"When you were a kid," he said, "did you have that tradition where you got to open one present on Christmas Eve?"

She shook her head. "My parents never let us. Even though every other kid in the neighborhood got to do it."

"Me, neither. So I think we're both entitled to open a present the night before Christmas Eve to make up for lost time."

"Then I need to get one for you to open," she said. She started to get up—and with her growing girth, she couldn't move nearly as quickly as he did—but he placed a hand gently on her shoulder and stayed her.

"In a minute," he said. "You first. Open this one."

She would have been an idiot to not entertain the possibility that it might be a ring. The box was perfectly

shaped for it. It was Christmastime. They'd been inseparable for months. They were expecting a baby. But they
kept separate residences. They each had a room for the
baby in those residences. They hadn't once talked about
taking their relationship to another level. It could just as
easily be a Groupon for mommy-and-daddy-and-baby
music classes or something.

She looked at the gift. Then she looked at Tate. He
was smiling in a way that was at once hopeful and anxious. Probably, it wasn't a Groupon. Meaning probably,
it was a…

Carefully, she accepted the present from him. It was
wrapped in forest green foil and had a bow as silver as
a crystal lake. As she gingerly unwrapped it, the baby
began to move inside her again, probably in response to
her quickening pulse and the way the blood was rushing through her body. The crackle of the fire and patter of the rain dulled to faint whispers, and the air in
the room seemed to come alive. Tate watched her intently until she had her fingers poised to open the box
beneath the paper, but he didn't say a word. So Renny
slowly pushed the top upward.

Not a Groupon. Definitely a ring. In fact, it was the
most beautiful ring she'd ever seen.

"The stone is from one of the interesting rocks we
found that day on our hike," he told her. "The quartz
one. It was the same color as the blackberries we picked.
And I had the jeweler set it in silver because the stars
that last night were like silver. And the pattern around
the band is like the pinecones we found. I hope you
don't think it's too corny."

He sounded as excited as…well, a kid on Christmas as he told her the reasons he'd had the ring fashioned the way he had. As if she'd needed him to explain any of that. The moment Renny saw it, all those things flooded into her head—and then her heart. And now, every time she looked at the ring on her finger, she would remember and feel them again.

"It's not corny," she said softly. "It's beautiful."

He expelled a relieved sound. "Then it's yes?"

Whatever he was asking, her answer was yes. Just to be sure he was asking the same question she wanted him to be asking, though, she replied, "Is what yes?"

He looked confused for a moment, then thoughtful. "I never said it out loud, did I? I thought it like ten times while you were unwrapping the ring, but I never actually asked the question, did I?"

Not to be coy, but… "What question?" she asked.

"The one about us…you and me…getting married."

Oh, *that* question. "Depends," she said.

He looked slightly less relieved, slightly less hopeful, slightly more anxious. "On what?"

"On why you're asking. Is it because of the baby?"

He shook his head. "No. It's because of you. Because the last five months have been the best time of my life, rivaled only by five days in June that I never thought could be topped." He took the box from her hand and plucked the ring from its nest. "I love you, Renata Twigg. I think I fell in love with you the minute I saw you standing in the rain outside a giant wedge of cheese." He smiled again, and this time there was only contentment in his expression. "And I will love you until we're both food for the fishies."

Oh. Well. In that case…

"Will you marry me?" he finally asked.

"Of course I'll marry you," she was finally able to say. "I mean, I have to, don't I?"

His contentment slipped a bit. "Why? Because of the baby?"

She shook her head. "No. Because I love you, Tate Hawthorne. I think I fell in love with you the minute I saw you in those zip-up leather polo boots. That I immediately wanted to *un*zip. With my teeth."

He looked mildly shocked, then not-so-mildly turned on. "Unfortunately, I left them at home. But you know…" He arched an eyebrow suggestively. "These hiking boots aren't going to remove themselves. And neither are any of these other things."

Renny arched an eyebrow right back. "Well, in that case, what are we waiting for?"

"Nothing," he said. "We have all the time in the world."

Indeed, they did. Even better, it was a world that exceeded their wildest dreams. A world they had created together. A world where they both belonged.

* * * * *

If you loved this story,
pick up the first ACCIDENTAL HEIRS *books,*

ONLY ON HIS TERMS
A CEO IN HER STOCKING,

and these other billionaire heroes
from New York Times *bestselling author*
Elizabeth Bevarly,

CAUGHT IN THE BILLIONAIRE'S EMBRACE
THE BILLIONAIRE GETS HIS WAY
MY FAIR BILLIONAIRE

Available now from Mills & Boon Desire!

***

If you're on Twitter, tell us what you
think of Mills & Boon Desire!

As he came closer, the realization struck her like lightning.

She hadn't seen Mason Harrington in almost fifteen years. Oh, she'd wondered about him almost every day. But she'd refused to let her curiosity turn into anything more. After all, she imagined she was the last person Mason ever wanted to contact him.

It looked like the years had been good to him. Even at this distance, she could spot the telltale features she'd found so attractive: the dark blond hair cropped close at the sides but leaving just enough length on the top to showcase its inherent wave; large hands rough from working but with long fingers that could play her like the most delicate of strings; the square shape of his jaw that belied the soft curve of his full bottom lip.

He was even taller now, filled out and muscular in a way that made her uncomfortably aware of him. As did the piercing blue gaze that found her with unerring accuracy. But it was the signature black cowboy hat that he swung up onto his head that was the nail in her coffin, confirming that she faced the boy she had wronged.

And now he was every inch a man.

REINING IN THE BILLIONAIRE

BY
DANI WADE

MILLS & BOON

First Published in Great Britain 2017
By Mills & Boon, an imprint of HarperCollins*Publishers*
1 London Bridge Street, London, SE1 9GF

© 2017 Katherine Worsham

ISBN: 978-0-263-92808-2

51-0217

Our policy is to use papers that are natural, renewable and recyclable products and made from wood grown in sustainable forests. The logging and manufacturing processes conform to the legal environmental regulations of the country of origin.

Printed and bound in Spain
by CPI, Barcelona

Dani Wade astonished her local librarians as a teenager when she carried home ten books every week—and actually read them all. Now she writes her own characters, who clamor for attention in the midst of the chaos that is her life. Residing in the southern United States with a husband, two kids, two dogs and one grumpy cat, she stays busy until she can closet herself away with her characters once more.

I'm very blessed in this life to have a wonderful mother-in-law, who I watch give herself tirelessly to those around her every day. Kay, thank you for all you do for us. These books would not happen without the love, encouragement and sheer physical support you gift to me and our family day after day. I love you.

One

Finding out that the old Hyatt estate was available for purchase immediately—cash buyers only—had to be the biggest triumph Mason Harrington had ever experienced. After all, how many people got to fulfill their life's goal of owning a horse farm and get the revenge they'd ached for—all in one unexpectedly easy move?

"The foreclosure was just approved and finalized through our corporate offices," the bank manager was saying from across the polished expanse of his desk. His worried expression made him look more like a concerned grandfather than a businessman. "The family hasn't even been notified yet. There simply hasn't been time—"

"I'll be happy to handle that part for you," Mason heard himself say. *Oops! Was that too much?* From the look on the manager's face, probably. The nudge from his brother confirmed it.

Mason subtly leaned out of reach from his brother's

sharp elbow, ignoring the creak of his leather chair. Kane might resent Daulton Hyatt for his role in ruining their father's reputation in this town, but Mason had been at ground zero for the man's nuclear meltdown.

He'd never forget the humiliation Daulton had dished out with satisfaction…or the pain of having EvaMarie watch without defending him.

If the memories made him a little mouthy…

"I have to say that the foreclosure went through against my wishes. I'd hoped to help EvaMarie turn things around," the manager said with a frown that deepened the lines on his aged face.

"Why EvaMarie?" Kane asked. "Wouldn't it be Daulton Hyatt who needed the help?"

The man's eyes widened a little as he watched them from across the desk. After a moment, he said, "I'm sorry. I spoke out of turn. I didn't mean to discuss personal details about my customers." He lowered his gaze to the printed paper before him. Mason had found the foreclosure notice on a local website. The bank hadn't wasted any time trying to recoup its loss. "But I just don't feel comfortable—"

"That doesn't matter now. The bank has already listed the property," Mason cut in. "Look, we are offering more than the asking price, cash in hand. Do we need to contact someone at the corporate offices ourselves?" Surely they'd be happy to take the Harrington money.

Mason could tell by the look on the manager's face that he most certainly did not want that to happen. But Mason would if he had to…

"We can have the money transferred here by this afternoon," Kane added. "Our offer is good for only an hour at that price. Do we have a deal?"

Mason's body tightened, silently protesting the idea of

walking away, but his brother knew exactly what he was doing. Still, the thought of losing this opportunity chafed. The waffling manager was obviously trying to look out for the family, as opposed to the strangers before him, but right now Mason didn't give a damn about the Hyatts.

He cared only about making them pay for striking out at Mason and his family all those years ago.

He couldn't help but wonder how EvaMarie would look when he told her to get out of her family home...

Slowly, reluctantly, the older man nodded. "Yes. I guess this really is out of my hands now." He stood, straightening his suit jacket and tie as if steadying himself for a particularly unpleasant task. "If you'll excuse me a moment, I'll get my secretary started on the paperwork."

And he would no doubt call corporate while he went outside the office, Mason suspected, but it wasn't going to do him any good. What the Harrington brothers wanted, they often got. Usually it was from sheer bullheadedness. This time, though, they had their inheritance to back them up.

Money did open doors, indeed.

Mason still missed his dad, who had passed away about six months ago. It had been just the three of them for most of Mason's life, and they'd all been really tight. Learning of their father's cancer had been hard.

But it had only been the first surprise.

The fact that their mother had been the debutante daughter in a very wealthy family in a neighboring state had never been a secret to the boys. She'd died of brain cancer when Mason was around seven. He remembered so little about her, except how good she'd smelled as she cuddled with him and the silky softness of her hair. He would brush it for her sometimes, after she got sick, because it soothed her and often got rid of the headaches she frequently had.

Still, she'd been gone a long time. It had never occurred to either of the boys that she had left something behind for them. Hell—something? This wasn't just *something*, it was a fortune. Their father's careful money management had paid off in big ways, and he'd grown their already substantial inheritance into a monumental sum. Mason couldn't even think of the money in real dollar amounts, it was so excessive.

After all, sometimes they'd had to scrape the bottom of the barrel growing up. Like when Mason had lost his job at the Hyatt estate. They'd had to move back to his mother's hometown. Times had already been tough. Little had he and Kane known, their dad had been going without while planning for their future.

And their future was now.

After the secret came out, Mason had asked his father why he hadn't used some of the money to make life easier for him, for them. He'd said he never wanted to prove their mother's parents right—they'd always said he'd married her for money.

The brothers had been around horses all their lives. Their father had been a horse trainer with an excellent reputation for creating winners. He'd taught them everything he knew. They'd also both learned a lot from working in some of the best stables in the area, along with raising their own horses and cattle. Now, finally, they had the capital to purchase and establish their very own racing stables.

Oh, and get back at EvaMarie Hyatt for almost ruining his family at the same time.

"That look on your face has me damn worried," Kane said, studying him hard.

Mason stood, pacing the space that was relatively generous for a bank office but still left Mason feeling cramped. "I can't believe this is finally happening."

"You know Dad wouldn't want us to get back at the Hyatts for what happened almost fifteen years ago, right?"

It may have been close to fifteen years ago, but to Mason, the wounds and anger were as fresh as yesterday. Kane thought of it as a teenage crush, but Mason knew he had loved EvaMarie with everything he had at the time. Otherwise, it wouldn't still hurt so damn much.

"Yep, I know." But he could live with that. Simply seeing the shock on EvaMarie's face—and that dictator daddy of hers—would be worth a little blackening on his soul.

Right?

"Are you saying you've changed your mind?" he asked Kane.

His brother was silent, thinking before he answered. Mason admired that about Kane—it was a trait he lacked. Mason jumped first and worried about the consequences later. But as a team, their differences worked in their favor…mostly.

Kane turned to meet his gaze, his expression harder than before. "Nah. I say, go for it. But just a little warning, Mason—"

Mason groaned. "Aren't we a little old for you to jump into big brother mode again?"

"I am your big brother, but that's not it." He gave Mason a level look. "You need to keep in mind that there might be a good reason that they've lost the estate. They may not care what happens to it or who has it. I haven't heard any rumors about them financially except that they were downsizing a while back."

He shrugged at Mason's raised brows. "So I kept tabs. But we're out of the loop, except for a few old friends." He shrugged, his suit still looking out of place to Mason. They were used to flannel shirts and sturdy jeans. Dressing up wasn't the norm…but considering where this inheritance was taking them, they'd better get used to it.

Kane shook his head. "I don't know. I just have a feeling this isn't going to play out like you want it to."

Mason thought back to his awed impression of the Hyatt estate when he was a know-it-all eighteen-year-old. The opulence, the care EvaMarie's mother had put into every little touch. That house had been her life. Not that Mason had been allowed to see it. Officially, he'd seen it only once. He'd been told to take some papers to Daulton Hyatt at the big house. EvaMarie's mother had trailed after him, anxious in case he tracked manure on her antique rugs.

As though he was too much of a heathen to know how to wipe his feet. The only other time he'd been inside, there hadn't been a parent in sight.

"You may be right," Mason conceded, trying to shake the memories away. "But trust me, they care. I remember that much all too well." And he was gonna use what he knew about them to his every advantage.

It paid to know thine enemy.

EvaMarie Hyatt didn't have a clue who was driving up to the house in a luxury sedan followed by a shiny new pickup truck. But as she spied out her bedroom window on the second floor, she fervently wished that whoever it was would go back from whence they came.

After all, she was sweaty and gross after hanging insulation inside the old dressing room between her suite and the next. Plus, she had a headache pounding hard enough between her temples to rival a jackhammer. And she was the only one here willing to answer the door.

Still, she smiled with the satisfaction of knowing all of her hard work would be perfect for what she had in mind.

But this wasn't the time for lingering admiration of her handiwork. She had to get herself in gear and head their visitors off at the pass. She scurried down the back stairs, hyperaware of her parents' location. They'd be interested too, but she knew good and well they wouldn't come outside.

It was so sad to see her once social butterfly parents now housebound. Their secrecy and embarrassment made EvaMarie's responsibilities that much harder...and much more painful.

She made it to the side entrance just as the vehicles parked. Unexpected nerves tingled through her as she attempted to smooth her hair into some semblance of order. Maybe her parents were rubbing off on her...or the isolation of taking care of every last detail of their lives was turning her into a hermit.

To her surprise, the bank manager stepped out of the first vehicle, his pristine suit making her all too aware of her dust-covered T-shirt and sweatpants. But it was the driver of the truck who confounded her.

She studied him as the two men approached across the now cracking driveway. He was a stranger, yet familiar for some reason. There was something about the cocky set of his shoulders, the confidence of his stride. As he came closer, the realization struck her like lightning.

She hadn't seen Mason Harrington in nearly fifteen years. Oh, she'd wondered about him almost every day since then. But she'd refused to let her curiosity turn into anything more. After all, she imagined she was the last person Mason ever wanted to contact him.

It looked like the years had been good to him. Even at this distance, she could spot the telltale features she'd found so attractive: the dark blond hair cropped close at the sides, but leaving just enough length on the top to showcase its inherent wave; large hands rough from working but with long fingers that could play her like the most delicate of instruments; the square shape of his jaw that belied the soft curve of his full bottom lip.

He was even taller now, filled out and muscular in a way that made her uncomfortably aware of him. As did the piercing blue gaze that found her with unerring accuracy. But it was the signature black cowboy hat that he swung up onto his head that was the nail in her coffin, confirming that she faced the boy she had wronged.

And now he was every inch a man.

Mason Harrington was someone she certainly didn't want near the house…or within miles of her father. Rushing forward despite her nerves clenching her stomach, she ignored the bombshell and focused on the manager. "Clive," she said, "what can I do for you?"

"EvaMarie, I'm afraid I have some bad news."

She wanted to look at Mason, see if he knew what was going on. Which was silly. Of course he did or he wouldn't be here. "I thought we had everything straightened out last month?" Oh, goodness. Please let this not be what she feared most.

"Well, I'm afraid corporate overruled us. As I mentioned then, everything has to be approved through them."

Her breath caught for a moment, then she forced herself to speak. "But I thought you said you knew enough people up there to get them to listen."

"I know, honey. Apparently I wasn't quite persuasive

enough. I was going to call today, but got—" he glanced
at the silent man next to him "—sidetracked."

EvaMarie hugged herself as her heart pounded in
her chest. Nausea washed through her. She'd been alone
through a lot of hard times over the past five years, but
right now she wondered if there was a person alive who
wouldn't let her down. "What does that mean?"

Mason stepped forward, his boots scraping across the
driveway. "It means I'm the new owner of the Hyatt estate."

His voice had deepened. This was a man speaking. A
man taking away what he had to know meant the world
to her. She couldn't even look him in the eye. Turning
back to Clive, she struggled not to beg. "I just need a
little more time—"

"Too late."

Mason's harsh words made her cringe, but she tried to
focus only on Clive. Breathlessly she pushed the words
out. "But the mares will foal—"

Clive stepped forward, cutting off her view of Mason
with a hand on her shoulder. "You know it won't cover
more than a few payments," he said, his voice low and
firm, even though his touch was gentle. "Then you'll be
behind again. You've done the best you could, EvaMarie,
but we both know you're only delaying the inevitable. It's
time. Time to let go."

She shook her head, the words ringing in her ears.
Time to admit defeat—to Mason Harrington. Her father
would rather die.

For a moment, she almost gave in to the tears that had
plagued her for the last six months. She glanced over at
the quiet, still barn in the distance. The surrounding lush
trees had sheltered her since she'd first walked. The lake
in the distance had seen her learn to swim and fish. The

rolling hills had been her playground in her youth, her solace as she'd gotten older. Her mind conjured up memories of a time long ago when the picture before her had been bustling with employees, and horses, and visitors.

Not anymore. *No matter how hard she tried.*

Every time she'd thought she was making progress, yet another setback would stomp on her efforts. But this one was the crowning glory.

Now she zeroed in on Mason, surprised by his smug *I won* look. Obviously, he could remember a lot about this place, too. Part of her ached that he still hated her enough to find taking her home from her a worthy challenge. But a part that she didn't want to acknowledge found a tiny bit of solace in the fact that she could still touch him in some way.

She'd never be able to admit all the ways he'd changed her, even after he'd been gone. The thought was enough to have her dragging her stoic expression back into place, covering her true emotions, all of the frustration and pain she'd dealt with since he'd left, since her father became ill.

She felt so alone.

"So when do we have to be out?" she murmured, struggling to be practical. She wouldn't think right now about how it would feel, leaving the only home she'd ever known. That would lead to the breakdown she wanted to avoid.

Mason stepped fully into view, muscling his way around the bank manager. How he'd heard her, she wasn't sure. "As soon as possible would be great. You can work that out with Clive here, but first, I'd like to look over my purchase, please."

If she hadn't been struggling already, his complete lack of compassion would have taken her breath away.

EvaMarie looked at the smug man, seeing again the few traces of the boy she'd loved with all her heart, the boy she'd given her body to, even though she'd known she couldn't keep him—and wished she had the courage to punch him in the face.

Two

Mason's crude satisfaction at besting EvaMarie and her family quickly transformed to dismay as he followed her into the house.

Bare. That's the word that came to mind as he looked around the entryway and beyond. It was like a gorgeous painting stripped of all its details, all the way down to the first broad brushstrokes covering the canvas. The basic structure was still there. The silver-leafed cabinetry, the crystal doorknobs, the delicate ironwork. But a lot of the decorative china and porcelain figures and landscape paintings he remembered from that long ago day had disappeared, leaving behind bare shelves and walls that projected an air of sadness.

They had entered the house through a side door, the same one Mason had been let into fifteen years ago. The long hallway took them past the formal dining room and a parlor, then a couple of now empty rooms until they came to a sunken area facing the back of the house. Apparently the family used this as a cozier living room, if one could call the massive, hand-carved limestone fireplace and equally impressive Oriental carpeting "cozy."

Upon closer inspection, the once pristine furniture had a few worn corners. But weirdly enough, what impacted Mason the most was the flowers. Not the ones in the overrun garden outside the wall of windows, but the ones in the vase on the table behind the sofa as they entered the room.

He vividly remembered the large sprays of flowers in intricate vases from his first visit, impressed as he had been with their color and beauty. They'd been placed every few feet in the hall and several in each of the rooms he'd glanced into and entered. But this was the first flower vase he'd seen today: a simple cut-glass one. Inside was an arrangement of flowers that looked like they'd been cut from the wild gardens. Pretty, but they were obviously not the designer arrangements of hothouse blooms he remembered.

Boy, the privileged had truly come down in the world.

Glancing over to the couple seated near the fireplace, he recognized EvaMarie's parents, even though they'd aged. Mrs. Hyatt was dressed for visitors. Mason would expect nothing less, though her silk shirt and carefully quaffed hair denoted a woman who hadn't faced the reality of her situation.

The pearls were a nice touch though.

"What's going on?" Daulton asked, his booming voice still carrying enough to echo slightly on the eardrums. "Clive, why are you here?"

The bank manager shook hands with the couple, then stepped back a bit to allow EvaMarie closer. Mason had thought he'd want to see this part, to witness the lowering of the high-and-mighty Hyatts. After all, they'd orchestrated the moment that had brought his own family's downfall.

Yet somehow, he couldn't bring himself to close in, to gain an angle that allowed him to see EvaMarie's face as she gave her family the news that their lives were about to change. Afraid he was softening, he forced himself to stand tall, knees braced for the coming confrontation. He forced himself to remember how his father must have felt that day when he'd had to tell Mason and his brother that he was fired from the position he'd held for ten years at the insistence of Daulton Hyatt.

That hadn't been pretty either.

"Mom, Dad, um." EvaMarie's voice was so soft Mason almost couldn't hear it. Yet he could feel the vibration in his body. EvaMarie's voice was unique—even huskier than it had been when she was young. She'd grown into a classic Kathleen Turner voice that Mason was going to completely and totally ignore. "The bank has sold the estate."

Mrs. Hyatt's gasp was quickly drowned beneath Daulton's curse. "How is that possible?" he demanded. "Clive, explain yourself."

"Daddy, you know how this happened—"

"Nonsense. Clive…"

"Corporate took this account out of our hands, Mr. Hyatt. There's nothing I can do now."

"Of course there is. What's the point of knowing your banker if he can't help you now and again?"

"Daddy." At least EvaMarie had enough spirit to sound disapproving. "Clive has gone out of his way to help us on more than one occasion. We have to face that this is happening."

"Nonsense. I'm not going anywhere." A noise echoed

through the room, like a cane banging on the wooden floor, though Mason couldn't see for sure. "Besides, who could buy something so expensive that quick?"

Clive turned sideways, giving Daulton a view of Mason where he stood. "This is Mason Harrington from Tennessee. He and his brother started the purchase proceedings this morning."

"Tennessee?" Daulton squinted in Mason's direction. Mason could feel his pulse pick up speed. "Why would someone from Tennessee want an estate in Kentucky?"

Rolling with that rush of adrenaline, Mason took a few strides into the center of the room. "I'm looking forward to establishing my own racing stables, and the Hyatt estate is perfect for our purposes, in my opinion."

Mason could see the realization of who he was as it dawned on Daulton's face, followed quickly by a thunderous rage. He was proud to see this glorious, momentous thing that Mason himself had ignited.

"I know you," Daulton growled, leaning forward in his chair despite his wife's delicate hand on his bicep. "You're that good-for-nothing stable boy who put your hands on my daughter."

It was more than just my hands. Maybe he should keep that thought to himself. *See, Kane, I do have control.* "Actually, I am good for something...as a matter of fact, several...million...somethings..." That little bit of emphasis felt oh, so good. "And I'm no longer just a stable boy."

Daulton turned his laser look on his daughter, who stepped back as if to hide. "I told you I would never allow a filthy Harrington in one of my beds. I'll never let that happen."

"Oh, I don't need one of your beds," Mason assured

him. "I just bought a nice, expensive one of my own. I'll just take the room it belongs in."

"You aren't getting it from me," Daulton growled.

This time, Mason matched him tone for tone. "You sure about that?"

The other man's eyes widened, showing the whites as he processed that this Harrington wasn't a kid who was gonna meekly take his vitriol. "The likes of you could never handle these stables with success," he bellowed. "You'll fold in a year."

"Maybe. Maybe not. But that will be decided by *me*." Satisfaction built inside as he said it, and he let a grin slip free. "Not you."

He could tell by the red washing over Daulton's face that he got Mason's drift. The older man started to stand. Mason realized he was gripping the side of his chair with an unusually strong grip.

"Daulton," his wife whispered in warning.

But the old man was too stirred up to heed her, if he even heard her in the first place. Mason felt his exultation at besting the monster of his dreams drain to dismay as Daulton took a step forward…then collapsed to the floor.

A cry rang out, maybe from EvaMarie's mom. But everyone rushed forward except Mason, who stood frozen in confusion.

With Clive's help, the women got Daulton turned over and sitting upright, though he was still on the floor. Mason studied the droop of the man's head, even as his back remained turned to Mason.

Kneeling next to her father in dusty sweatpants and a T-shirt, hair thrown up into a messy bun, EvaMarie still had the look of a society princess when she glanced over at Mason. Her calm demeanor, cultivated through hours of cotillion classes, couldn't have been more sphinxlike.

"Could you excuse us for a moment, please?" she said quietly. She didn't plead, but her gaze expected him to do as she asked.

He'd never been able to resist that dark blue, forget-me-not gaze, always so full of suppressed emotions that he wanted to mine.

Then she tilted her head in the direction of the door to the hallway. For once, he didn't have that unbidden urge to challenge that came over him when he was faced with authority. Especially Hyatt authority. Obviously there was more going on here than he was aware of.

Turning, he let himself back out into the hall, wondering if he'd be able to forget the impression that his brother had been right. This wasn't going how he pictured it…at all.

EvaMarie could feel her hands shaking as she finally left behind the drama in the living room to face Mason in the hall. Out of the frying pan and into the fire, as the old saying went. Her body felt like she'd been put in a time machine. All the devastating feelings from that long ago confrontation in the barn—the day her teenage world imploded—had come rushing back the minute her father had raised his voice at Mason.

She'd spent a lot of time throughout her life walking on eggshells, trying not to light her father's fuse. By the time she'd grown a semblance of a backbone, the angry man he'd been had mostly disappeared. He reappeared only during times of high stress, and it was all EvaMarie could do not to give in to her childhood fears.

Now she had to face Mason—with no time for deep breaths or wrapping herself in invisible armor. Just hunkering down, enduring—just like most of her days now. The fact that he was actually here, in this house with her ight now, seemed completely surreal, but the derision on his face had been very real.

There had been no doubt in her mind how he felt about her after all these years. She should take solace in the fact that he hadn't completely forgotten her. But she had a feeling she wasn't gonna feel better about him, or this situation, any time soon.

Maybe a little diplomacy would smooth the way...

"Congratulations, Mason," she said as she approached him with measured steps, trying not to take stock of the new width of his shoulders beneath a fitted navy sports jacket that she never would have pictured him wearing, even if it was paired with a pair of dark jeans and cowboy boots. Talk about surreal...

He turned from his study of the formal dining room to face her, then raised a cool brow. How could he portray arrogance with just that simple movement? "For what?"

"Obviously, you done well to be able to afford—"

"—to no longer be pushed around by people, just because they have more money than me?"

Her entire self went very still. His words told her everything she needed to know—how Mason viewed his childhood, their breakup and her in this moment.

It told her one other thing: he was going to find a lot of satisfaction in this scenario.

Maybe it would be best to focus on business. "So, what can I do for you?" she asked, though she had a feeling he wasn't gonna make it easy...

"That tour I mentioned." He waved his hand in the direction of the stairs. "Lead the way."

EvaMarie simply could not catch a break. She could almost feel his gaze as she took deliberate steps down the rest of the hall, pointing out various rooms.

He wasn't even subtle in his gibes... "Can't say I'm

loving what you've done with the place. This version has taken the concept of 'simplify' to a whole new level, I believe."

She couldn't even argue, because she agreed with him. The state of her family home was a drain on her emotional equilibrium every day. But having someone else point it out…well, it certainly hurt.

Should she admit she'd sold off all but her mother's family heirlooms to keep them afloat? Yeah, his reaction to that would be fun. Just one more thing to mock her with.

So she kept silent on that topic, instead launching into a knowledgeable diatribe on the parquet floor pattern, imported tile and other amenities her father had spared no expense on. All the little details she'd spent a lifetime learning that would be useless once she was driven away—but for now she could use them to keep herself from admitting the truth.

She'd done what she could, but the estate was going under, and there wasn't a whole heck of a lot she could do to stop it.

"You're getting a good deal," she said, trying to keep any emotion from her voice.

"A great deal," he conceded.

Color her shocked.

They stood at the top of the back landing, facing a large arch window that gave a clear view to the stables and beyond. It was a mirror of the front of the house, which looked out over the drive and the wooded property between the house and the highway.

Mason studied the view. "Gardener?"

"Um, no," she murmured. "Not anymore."

"That explains a lot," he replied.

Stiffening, she felt herself close off even more. Though

she shouldn't be surprised that he just couldn't leave it with the question. From the first words out of his mouth, she had expected his judgment.

"My brother and I would like to offer anyone on staff a job," he said, surprising her. "No need for them to be worried about their incomes because the place has changed hands." He stepped back to the landing, studying the first floor from his higher vantage point. "And we're obviously going to need some help getting things in order."

Yeah, no need for the staff to worry...only her family worried about living on the street... She ignored the implication that the property would need a lot of work to whip it into shape. She'd done the best she could. "That's very generous of you," she said, struggling not to choke on the words and the sentiment. "Currently we only have one employee. Jim handles the stables."

Mason stared at her, wide-eyed. "And the rest?"

"Handled by me."

"Cooking? Cleaning?"

EvaMarie simply stared, not liking where this was headed. Sure enough...

"Well, someone has definitely grown up, haven't they? I can remember days of you being waited on and pampered..."

Unbidden, she flushed. "If that's a backhanded compliment, thank you." She turned away, breathing through her anger as she stepped over into an open area that branched off into hallways to the various rooms. "The rest of this floor is bedrooms and baths, except for this sitting area."

"Your parents occupy the master suite?" he asked, his voice calm and collected.

Of course it was. After all, he wasn't the one being typecast.

"No. The stairs are too much for my father anymore. There's a set of rooms behind the kitchen. They sleep there." They were originally staff quarters, but she left that unspoken.

"I'll see the master suite, then."

She gave a slow nod, then turned to the short hallway on the left.

"Your father's illness?" he asked, for the first time using a gentle tone she didn't trust at all.

"Multiple sclerosis, though he prefers not to speak of it," she said, keeping her explanation as matter-of-fact as possible. No point in exhibiting the grief and frustration that came with becoming a caretaker for an ill parent. "We've managed as well as we could, but the last two years he's steadily lost his mobility and physical stability."

Her mother had declined also, though hers was from losing the stimulation, social gaiety and status that she had fed off for most of her life.

The grandeur of the master suite swept over EvaMarie, just as it always did when she entered. It was actually two large rooms, joined into one. Both were lined and lightened by hand-carved, floor-to-ceiling white wooden panels strategically accented in silver-leafing, the same accent that was used throughout the house.

With thick crown molding and a crystal chandelier in each area, the space left an indelible impression. Even empty as it was now.

She stepped fully inside as Mason strolled the cavernous space, his boots announcing his progress on the wood flooring. "There are his-and-hers dressing areas and bathrooms on each end of the suite," she explained. "Though the baths haven't been updated in some time."

"I'm sure we will take care of that," he said, pausing

to turn full circle in the middle of the sleeping area. One wall was dominated by an elaborate fireplace that Eva-Marie could remember enjoying from her parents' bed as she and her mother savored hot chocolate on snowy days.

She thought of the ivory marble bathtub in her mother's bathroom, deep enough that EvaMarie had been able to swim in it when she was little. It didn't have jets in it like the latest and greatest, but it was a gorgeous piece that would probably be scrapped, if the latest and greatest was what Mason was looking to put in.

Unable to handle any more of memory lane, she turned back toward the door to the hallway.

"And your room?" Mason asked from far too close behind her.

"Still on… On the other side of the floor." She held her breath, waiting on him to insist on seeing her room. Between them was Chris's room—*please, no more*. She wasn't sure how much longer she could hold herself together.

In an attempt to distract them both, she went on. "The third floor has been empty for years. There're two baths up there. A couple of the bigger rooms have fireplaces. Oh, and the library, of course."

His pause was significant enough to catch her eye.

Did he remember the one time that she'd snuck him in to show him her favorite place in the house? Long ago, she could have spent entire days in the library, only emerging when her mother made her come to the table. Maybe Mason did remember, because he turned away, back to the stairs.

"Another day, perhaps," she murmured.

As they hurried down the stairs, he didn't look back until he reached the side entrance, his hand wrapped around the Swarovski crystal handle.

"If there are any problems, I'll have my lawyer contact you."

She let her head incline just a touch, feeling a deep crack in her tightly held veneer. "I'm sure."

"It was good to see you again." His sly grin told her why it had been—because it had served his purpose.

She wished she could say the same.

Three

"The signing date is set. The property is almost ours." Mason grinned at his brother, then turned back to the lawyer. "You've been great. We really appreciate it."

James Covey grinned back, looking almost as young as them, though Mason knew he was a contemporary of their father. "It's been my pleasure. I'm thrilled to be able to help y'all like this."

His smile dimmed a little, and Mason knew what he was thinking...what they were all thinking. That they wished their father hadn't had to die for this to happen. Kane's hand landed with heavy pressure on Mason's shoulder, and they shared a look.

It wasn't all a bed of roses, but they would honor their father's memory by establishing the best stables money could buy and talent could attain, using everything he'd ever taught them.

It was what he would have wanted.

"So are we going to be running into the Hyatts every time we turn around in this town?" Kane asked as they exited the lawyer's stylish brownstone in the upscale part of downtown that had been renovated several years back. Slowly they made their way down the steps.

Kane had been gone for a week and a half, starting the process of training their new ranch manager to take over their Tennessee stables. They weren't leaving behind their original property, though it wouldn't be their main residence any longer.

"I don't think so," Mason said.

"Good, because that would be awkward."

Mason rather thought he would enjoy rubbing their newfound success in Daulton Hyatt's face, but he preferred not to confirm his own suspicions that he was a bad person. "I'm not even sure what's going on out there," he said. "When I went to tour the stables, no one was there except the guy we're taking on, um, Jim. I haven't seen the Hyatts…or EvaMarie…around town."

"Well, don't look now."

Mason looked in the same direction as his brother, spotting EvaMarie immediately as she strolled up the wide sidewalk headed their way. The smart, sophisticated dress and heeled boots she wore were a definite step up from the sweatpants he'd seen her in, yet he almost got the feeling that she'd put on armor against him.

He wasn't that bad, was he? Okay, maybe he was…

She paused at the bottom of the steep concrete stairs, her dark hair falling away from her shoulders as she looked up at them. "The landlady told me where to find you."

"Um, why were you looking?" Mason asked, ignoring Kane's chuckle under the cover of his palm. He also tried to ignore the way his body perked up with just the sound of her husky voice.

EvaMarie ignored his question and nodded toward the office behind them. "He's good."

"I know." *So there's no getting out of the deal.*

EvaMarie was obviously not daunted by Mason's refusal to relent. She extended her hand in his brother's direction. "You must be Kane?"

His traitor brother went to the bottom of the stairs to shake her hand and properly introduce himself, then he glanced at Mason over his shoulder. "Gotta go. I'll see you back at the town house tonight."

What a wimp! Though Mason knew Kane wasn't running; he was simply leaving Mason to deal with the awkward situation of his own creation. The odds of EvaMarie simply happening by here were quite small, even though the town was only moderately sized with a large population of stable owners in the area.

Sure enough, she waited only long enough for Kane to disappear around the corner before turning back to him. "Could I speak with you, please? There's a café nearby."

A tingling sense told him he was about to be asked for a favor. Not that the Hyatts deserved one. After all, Daulton had shown no mercy when he'd had Mason's father fired from his job and blacklisted at the other stables in the area. He hadn't cared at all that his father was the sole support of two children. He'd only wanted revenge on Mason for daring to touch his daughter.

Mason would do well to remember that, regardless of how sexy EvaMarie might look all grown up.

The café just down the street was locally owned, with a cool literary ambience that was obviously popular from the crowd gathered inside. Bookshelves lined a couple of walls, containing old books interspersed with teapots and mugs. Tables and ladder-back chairs shared the space with oversize, high-backed chairs covered in leather. He glanced at EvaMarie, only to see her gaze sweeping over the crowd in a kind of anxious scan.

Though he refused to admit it, seeing her do that gave him a little pang. It seemed as though things hadn't changed too much after all. She still couldn't stand to be seen with him in public.

Struggling to stuff down his fifteen-year-old resentments, Mason was a touch short when he snapped, "Grab a table. I'll order the coffee."

"Oh." She glanced his way, her smile tentative. "Could I just get an apple cider please?"

Apparently she hadn't chosen the place for the coffee. As he took his place in line, he couldn't help but think how strange this was. EvaMarie wasn't someone he'd had a typical relationship with—though she'd been the only woman he'd had more than just sex with. That was a first—and definitely a last.

But they'd never been on a real date, just his graduation party with his high-school friends. Never really out in public. Mostly they had gone on trail rides together, holed up in the old barn loft and talked, sneaking stolen moments here and there when no one was looking.

Once he returned with their drinks, she fiddled with the protective sleeve on the cup, moving it up and down as if she couldn't decide if she wanted to try the drink or not. But she'd requested this meeting, not him, so he waited her out in silence.

Which only made the fidgeting worse. Why did he have to feel such satisfaction over that?

"I found a place for my parents," she finally said. "They'll be moving tomorrow."

"That's nice—is something wrong?"

Just as he'd known it would, his question only made her more nervous. She started to slowly strip the outer layer off the corrugated paper sleeve.

"No," she said, then took a big swallow that was probably still very hot, considering the way she winced. "I'm fine. I just…well, I didn't realize there would be so many people here at this time of day."

"Still embarrassed to be seen with me?" he asked. Then wondered why in the hell those words came out of his mouth.

She must have wondered too, because her eyes widened, her gaze darting between her drink and his. "No, I mean, that isn't the issue at all."

"Could've fooled me." He wasn't buying it. Especially not with too many bad memories to back up his beliefs.

"And my father's reaction didn't teach you any differently?"

That gave him pause, almost coloring those memories with a new hue. But he refused to accept any excuses, so he shrugged.

"Anyway—" she drew in a deep breath "—they chose to move into a senior living facility so my mother would have help with my dad. The cost of getting them settled is more than I anticipated. I wondered about an extension on the house?"

"Nope."

He caught just a glimpse of frustration before her calm mask slid back into place. "Mason, I can't afford first and last month's rent on a place to live and to pay someone to move all of our stuff."

"Don't you have friends? You know, the old standby— have a nice pizza party and pickup trucks? That's how normal people do it. Oh, right, you aren't familiar with normal people—just the high life."

She looked away. He could swear he saw a flush creep over her cheeks, but he certainly saw her lips tighten. That guilty satisfaction of getting under her skin flowed through him.

She turned back with a tight smile. Boy, she was certainly pushing to keep that classy demeanor, wasn't she? "Honestly, I've spent the last two years taking full-time care of my father. I don't have any—many close friends. And while I'd like to think of myself as capable, even I can't move the bed or couch on my own. I just need—"

He opened his mouth, ready to interrupt with a smart-ass answer, when a woman appeared at EvaMarie's side.

"Oh, EvaMarie, you simply must introduce me to your handsome friend."

"Must I?"

EvaMarie's disgruntled attitude made him smile and hold out his hand to the smiling blonde. "Mason Harrington."

"Liza Young," she said with a well-manicured hand laid strategically over her chest. "I don't believe I've heard of you—I would most certainly remember."

The woman's overt interest wasn't something Mason was comfortable with—he preferred women more natural than Liza—but rubbing EvaMarie the wrong way was worth encouraging it. Besides, he and his brother were gonna need contacts. Liza's expensive jewelry spoke to money, her confident demeanor to upper class breeding. "I'm new to the area." He glanced across the table so he could see EvaMarie's face. "Or rather, returning after a long absence."

"Oh? And what brings you here?" So far she had completely ignored EvaMarie beside her, but now she cast a quick glance down. "Surely not little EvaMarie Homebody."

Okay, this wasn't as fun. Mason narrowed his gaze but kept his smile in place. For some reason, it was perfectly acceptable for him to pick on EvaMarie—after all, Mason justified that he had a reason for his little barbs—but this woman's comment seemed uncalled for.

"The area's rich in racing history," he explained. "My brother and I are setting up our own stables."

"Oh, there's two of you?"

No substance, all flirt. Mason was getting bored. "Lovely to meet you, but if you'll excuse us, we were discussing business."

"Business?" She threw a sideways glance at EvaMarie, who looked a little surprised herself. "Well, that makes more sense."

Liza giggled, leaning forward in such a way to give Mason a good look into her not-so-modest cleavage. He couldn't help but compare the in-your-face sexuality and lack of subtlety in a woman he had just met with the image of soft womanhood sitting beside her. EvaMarie was smartly dressed, and yes, he detected a hint of cleavage, but she hadn't flashed it in his face in order to get what she wanted. Of course, that thought reminded him of just how much of her cleavage he'd seen…and how much he'd like to see it again. Sort of a compare-and-contrast thing. He remembered her as eager to learn anything he'd been willing to teach her—did she still need a teacher?

Mason quickly reined himself in. There was no point in going there, since he had no plans to revisit that old territory. No matter how tempting it might be. Besides, EvaMarie was looking stoic again. Maybe he should relent—a little.

He stood, then pulled a business card out of his inner jacket pocket. "Well, it was a pleasure to meet you, Liza," he said, handing the card over. "I hope I'll get to see you again soon."

Liza grinned, then reached into the clutch at her side for a pen, wrote on the card and handed it back. "So do I," she said, then flounced back to a table across the floor where several other women were waiting.

EvaMarie had turned to watch her go, then groaned as she caught sight of the other women seated at Liza's table, all of whom were craning their necks to get a good look. "Well, I hope you're ready to announce your presence, because it's gonna be all over town in about two hours."

"That's the plan," Mason murmured. A glance at the card revealed Liza's cell phone number. With a grin because he knew how much it would annoy EvaMarie, he slipped the card back into his pocket. "Now, where were we?"

The pained look that slipped over her face as she opened her mouth, probably to start from the beginning, made him feel like a jerk. So he broke in before she could speak.

"Let me see what I can do," he said. Not a concrete answer, but he needed time to think. And a few more days of worry wouldn't hurt her.

Dang it!

How come Mason Harrington had to show up every time she looked like a dusty mess? Here she was desperately trying to pack like a madwoman with only five days to move, and he was interrupting with his loud, insistent knocking.

She seriously considered leaving him there on the doorstep, especially since it was raining. Her nerves were strained from the physical labor, emotional stress and learning everything she needed to navigate while losing their home, but a lifetime of training had her opening the door.

But she only forced herself to produce a strained smile. After all, she was exhausted.

"Mason, what can I do for you?"

His lazy smile was way too tempting. "That's not very welcoming."

It wasn't meant to be. And she refused to be lured in by his teasing—a long time ago it had been a surefire way to shake her out of a bad mood. Instead of saying what she thought, she simply focused on keeping her smile in place. But she didn't move.

He didn't own the place yet.

"Come on, EvaMarie. Let me in," he added, a playful pleading look to his grin. "I have an offer that will make it worth your while."

She hesitated, then stepped back, because continuing to keep him out was bad manners. That was the only reason. Not that she should care, but a lifetime of parental admonishments kept her in check.

Mason took a good look around the high-ceilinged foyer with its slim crystal chandelier, then walked farther down to peek into a few other rooms on either side.

"Wow. You've made progress." His voice echoed in the now empty spaces.

That's because I'm working my tail off. But again, that was impolite to say, so she held her tongue. She didn't bite it, because she had enough pain right now. Though she'd taken on a large amount of the physical work around the estate, it had not prepared her for all the lifting, dragging and pulling of packing up her childhood home. Her muscles cried out every night for a soak in her mother's deep tub, but even that didn't relieve the now constant ache in her arms, thighs and back. Definitely hard on her back but great for weight loss.

He glanced down the hallway toward the back of the house. "Is your father here?"

She shook her head. "Why? Worried?"

"Nope." Again with the cute grin, which was making her suspicious. Why was he being so nice? "Just didn't figure it was good for him to get all riled up."

For some reason, she felt the need to defend her parent, even though Mason was right. "He hardly ever does anymore. Not like he used to. He had a heart episode about six years back that forcibly taught him the consequences of not controlling his temper." She gave him a saccharine smile. "I guess you're just special." Or inspired a special kind of hatred maybe.

"Always have been," he said. If he'd caught the insult, he let it roll off him.

His nonchalant handling of everything she said made her even angrier. Luckily, she was used to holding her emotions deep inside.

"Actually, I finished moving them to an assisted living facility yesterday."

Mason's raised eyebrow prompted her to explain. "I chose to put them there because at least I'll know there's someone to look out for them. Even though I feel that someone should be me." The place had cost a small fortune, but she was hoping being out from under the crippling mortgage payments would help. Now, what did she do about herself? Well, she hadn't figured that out yet.

Hopefully she'd find something soon, or she might just break down in a panic attack. She hadn't been kidding when she said the first and last month's rental deposits put most places out of her range. The fact that she didn't even have friends she could call on to let her sleep on their couch made her feel lost and alone.

"Do you work?" Mason asked.

The change in conversation came from out of the blue. "What?"

"A job. Do you have one?"

His tone implied she didn't even know what one was. She certainly wasn't going to tell him about the new career she was building. He would probably think she was crazy or arrogant to believe she could make a living off her unique voice.

"Taking care of my parents and this place was my job," she answered, even though most people didn't view it that way. Mason probably wouldn't either, even though it had been damn harder than a lot of things she could have done. And asking one of the families they knew in the area for a job would have meant exposing her parents' failure to their world. She'd chosen not to go against their wishes.

True to form, Mason asked, "How'd that work out for you?"

"I did the best I could," she said through gritted teeth.

"Think you could do better with a better boss and actual resources?"

Now she was really confused. "What?"

He turned away, once again inspecting the rooms. "My brother and I have plans—big plans. To establish our stables is a simple matter of quality stock, training and talent." He turned back, giving her a glimpse of his passion for this project. Guess buying this estate wasn't only about revenge.

"Establishing a reputation—that's a whole different story," he said, his gaze narrowing, "and we don't have the breeding to back it up."

She knew all too well how hard it was to keep and make contacts within society here—after all, her father had kept his illness a secret in order to protect his own social reputation. It took two things to break into the inner circle around here: breeding and money. Preferably both. But they'd accept just the money if someone was filthy rich.

"We can fast-track it—after all, money makes a big first impression."

A surreal feeling swept through EvaMarie. Honestly, she couldn't imagine she was talking to the same boy who'd held her so long ago. Sure, he'd talked horses and racing. She'd known he'd wanted to own his own stables one day—but money had never come up. Then.

They'd both been naïve to think it hadn't mattered.

"Which means we will be turning this into a show-place," Mason said, sweeping his hand to indicate the room.

"What does that have to do with me?"

He cocked his head to the side, a lock of his thick hair falling over his forehead. "You've lived here all your life?"

She nodded, afraid to speak. His sudden attention made her feel like a wild animal being lowered into a trap.

"I bet you know this place better than anyone."

"The house and the land," she said, feeling a pang of sadness she forced herself to ignore.

"So you could come to work for me. Help with the renovations. Prepare for the launch. I'll even give you more time to move everything."

Her heart started to pound as she studied him. "Why?" Revenge? Everything in her was saying to run. Why else could he possibly want this?

"I need a housekeeper. I'm assuming you need a job," Mason said with a nonchalant shrug. "You need time to figure this all out. That's what you were asking for, right?"

Regardless, working with him every day? Watching him take over her only home and never being able to show her true emotions for fear he would use them as a weapon against her? The last few encounters had been experience enough. *No, thank you.*

She shook her head. "I don't think that's a good idea."

"You don't?" He stepped closer. "Seems to me you're about to be out of a home, income… What's the matter? Afraid your friends will find out you have to get your hands dirty for money?"

That was the least of her worries. Her parents had feared that—yes—but not her.

He moved even closer, giving her a quick whiff of a spicy aftershave. Why was he doing that? Suddenly she couldn't breathe.

"I'll give you a job and a place to live. Sounds a whole lot better than the alternative, don't you think? And in return I get someone who can make this renovation move even faster."

Looking into his bright blue eyes, she wasn't so sure she agreed. There had to be a catch in there somewhere… but she truly wasn't in a position to turn him down.

Four

EvaMarie smoothed down her hair, wishing she could calm her insides just as easily when she heard Mason come through the side door. From the sound of other voices, he wasn't alone.

This time she was prepared.

Or so she thought. First she caught sight of Mason's brother, Kane, who had filled out just as much as his brother. The two men were like solid bookends; carbon copies with broad shoulders and muscles everywhere. If only Mason's shoulders were available for resting on. How incredible would it feel to have someone to rely on for a change? To lean against his back, feel his bare skin against hers, run her fingers down along those pecs—

Whoops. Not the direction she should let her mind wander down right now. Especially as the three men before her all turned their attention her way. The middle one—slighter than the brothers—looked vaguely familiar.

Kane stepped forward, intimidating in his size and intensity, until a smile split his serious look. "Hello, Eva-Marie. I'm Kane."

"I remember," she murmured, and shook his hand. What a surprise. No smart remarks. No ultimatums. Looked like at least one brother could be reasonable. "Mason didn't say when you'd be joining us." She could sure use a buffer from his brother.

"Oh, I won't be moving in right away. I'm still tying up some loose ends at our base camp, and we invested in a town house when we were scoping out the landscape." He shared a glance with his brother. "But I'll be here soon enough."

The thought of being here alone with Mason set off a firestorm of nerves inside her.

"After I get the chance to work my magic on this place. I've been waiting years," the slender man said as he moved forward. He didn't have the bulk of the other two, but she could tell he made up for it with loads of personality. The good kind.

"Hello, EvaMarie," he said, holding out his hand. "It's been years since we've seen each other, so I don't expect you to remember me. I'm Jeremy Blankenship."

"Oh, yes. I thought you looked familiar. It's good to see you again..."

Now that she had a name to go with the face, her memories clicked. Jeremy was a son of one of the active horse racing families who had decided to go completely against the grain and attend school for an interior design degree.

"Can we move past the pleasantries and get to work, please?" Mason groused.

"You'd better get used to pleasantries and small talk if you plan on socializing much in this town," Kane warned.

Jeremy nodded his agreement before turning his gaze

back to EvaMarie with questions in his soft brown eyes that had her tensing. "When I heard the Harringtons had bought the estate, I didn't expect to find you still here."

Before she could answer, Mason cut in. "EvaMarie will be overseeing a lot of the daily work and details for me."

Jeremy looked between them for a moment. "Oh, so are y'all together?"

"No." Mason's voice was short, but EvaMarie wondered if that was a hint of satisfaction she heard. "When I say she'll be working, I mean it literally. As in, for me."

There it was... EvaMarie felt her face flame, blood rushing to the surface as she wondered how many other people he would find satisfaction in telling her new status to. Part of her wanted to crawl away in defeat, but she forced her shoulders back, projecting a confidence she was far from feeling. With any luck, this job would be a gateway to a new life for her. One that wasn't going to be at the same level as she'd had growing up, but despite what a lot of people were probably gonna think, she was fine with that.

At least she'd be one step closer to this life being *hers*.

There was no point pouting over what she couldn't change...yet. That was one thing life had taught her. The key was to simply put her head down and power through. "Jeremy, would you like a look around?" she asked, assuming that's why he was here.

"Would love it. After all, I can't interior design if I haven't seen the interior, right?" He smiled big, as if to show her his approval, then linked his arm through hers and led her down the hallway.

She might just like having him here.

Most of the rooms were just going to need new wall treatments, updated lighting and furniture. Uncomfortable at first, EvaMarie soon put forth a few tentative ideas and received an accepting reaction from all but Mason, who remained aloof though not outwardly antagonistic. She directed the little party around the downstairs, then into the kitchen and family room.

"This would be a great place for a leather sofa and big screen television," Kane said. "Right next to the kitchen. Perfect hang out space."

The discussion devolved into name brands and types of electronic equipment that had EvaMarie yawning. Then Kane climbed the three steps to the main kitchen area. The rest of them followed. EvaMarie tried not to cringe. This room had been in desperate need of a make-over for years. Its mustard yellow appliances and farm motif dated it from the early eighties at the latest.

"I want more extensive work in here," Kane said. "Stainless-steel appliances, new granite countertops, the whole shebang."

"My brother," Mason interrupted, "in this area, I give you free rein."

"That's because you don't want to starve," Kane teased.

Mason winked, pointing at his brother. "You are correct, sir."

Without thought, EvaMarie said, "Well, looks like one of you learned to cook."

The men glanced her way. Once more she felt that tell-tale heat in her cheeks. Maybe she'd gotten a little too comfortable—the last thing she should have alluded to was her one and only trip to the Harrington household when she was a teenager. That's when she'd realized that the extent of Mason's cooking skills included opening a box and the microwave door. Of course, hers weren't comprehensive, but her mother had the housekeeper teach her the basics. She'd enjoyed it so much she'd taken home ec and some specialty classes once adulthood allowed her to pursue a small number of her own interests.

"Well, we will definitely coordinate these two spaces so they flow together," Jeremy said, smoothly glossing over her sudden embarrassed silence. He gestured back toward the living area beyond the bar that served as a divider between the two spaces. "Do you gentlemen want a true man cave here or something more subtle?"

"Man, too bad there isn't a place for a big game room," Mason said. "We can at least watch the Super Bowl on a big screen here, but something more intense would be a great addition."

Kane nodded. "Pinball machines, a poker table, a wine cellar. Wouldn't that be awesome?"

"What are the odds of us getting something that's awesome?" Mason asked Jeremy with a grin.

"Well, all of these first-floor rooms are open to the hallway. How true to the style of the house do you want to hold to?"

The guys bantered back and forth, Mason's smile breaking through full throttle. For the first time, EvaMarie caught a true glimpse of the Mason she remembered. Oh, he was older, more ruggedly handsome. But that smile showcased the fun-loving, friendly resonance of his youth.

She'd missed it, as much as the thought scared her.

As they talked more and more about what would make a really cool splash in the house, EvaMarie could feel her stomachache growing. Ideas sparked in her brain...as did the voice of her father calling her a traitor. The push and pull of what should be clear family loyalties confused her. After all, her family had had a difficult time with what life had thrown at them. While losing their home was just part of that life, losing it to the Harringtons was unforgivable to her father.

She shouldn't be helping them. But she needed to do a good job, right?

"What about the basement?" she asked, the words bursting forth before she'd actually made up her mind.

The three men shared a glance, then Jeremy asked, "What basement?"

EvaMarie offered the interior designer a tentative smile despite her guilt and led the way back out to the breezeway. On the far side of the stairwell was a regular door that opened to a fairly wide set of stairs. She could feel Kane as he leaned around the doorway. "Looks promising," he said.

"What it's gonna look is dusty," she said as she started down, flicking the light switch on as she went. "I can't even remember the last time anyone was down here."

She'd actually forgotten about the space, which was currently used for storage. Probably a good thing. Thinking about packing and moving all the stuff down here too might have thrown her over the edge of what sanity she had left.

Funny the things you could block out to protect your mind in a precarious state, she thought.

"Wow. This is incredible," Jeremy was saying as his dress shoes clicked on the concrete floor.

"The open space runs under this half of the house," EvaMarie explained, relaxing a little in the face of his enthusiasm. "Since the house was built into the hill, they finished this portion for the square footage. But with only the three of us, there wasn't any need for it."

As Mason's expression darkened, she decided it was time to keep her mouth shut again. The men explored, brainstorming all the cool things they would do down here, sparing no expense on Mexican tile and glass block room dividers and yes, a place for pinball machines. Her input was no longer needed. Not wanting to get in the way, EvaMarie wandered back the other way to the one room on the other side of the stairway. A large open entryway framed the room beyond like a picture.

The long-mirrored wall reflected the ballet bar attached at a child's level. She could also see her elaborate doll house closed up in the corner. The few stuffed animals she'd kept were resting safely in the wooden toy chest. This had been her own space when she was a little girl—a safe haven from her father's unreasonably high expectations and her mother's silent pressure to conform.

A safe haven, until her mother had created the library on the third floor the year she turned twelve. It had been her birthday present.

"Havin' fun?"

Mason's voice right behind her head caused her to jump. Her heart thudded, even though there wasn't any danger. Was there?

She glanced over her shoulder to meet his gaze. "Sure."

"Just don't have too much fun. You're here to work, remember?"

I don't think you'll let me forget, will you? Probably not the most appropriate response to an employer...

Kane paused on his way to the stairs to pat Mason's shoulder. EvaMarie could hear Jeremy's shoes on the steps as he ascended.

"This is gonna be great," Kane said with a grin before he headed up.

EvaMarie had marveled at the camaraderie between the brothers. After all, she hadn't had a sibling in a long time. Certainly not as an adult. Would Chris have stood by her through thick and thin? He'd been extremely protective of her, so she had a feeling he would have.

Only he'd never gotten the chance.

"You're lucky. It's wonderful that you have a brother like that," she said, her gaze trained on the stairs though her eyes remained unfocused, wishing for something she couldn't have.

"Actually, it's wonderful to have someone at your back when the world turns on you."

The sharp tone penetrated her thoughts, the pain catching her attention. She glanced Mason's way to find his glare trained on her, close and uncomfortable.

"Yes," she whispered. "Yes, it is."

As if he knew he'd made his point, Mason walked away, leaving EvaMarie with the uncomfortable knowledge that she'd reminded him exactly why he was here... and why she was here too.

For a few minutes she'd forgotten, and that could be detrimental in a lot of ways.

Then he glanced over his shoulder to deliver another dictum. "The furniture for my bedroom will be here tomorrow. You'll set it up good for me, right?"

Sure. She had no problem performing what should be a perfectly normal task. So why did it feel so intimate to her?

A few very rough days later, EvaMarie bent from the waist and let her upper body hang toward the ground in an attempt to stretch her aching back. Since the work in the basement was scheduled to start simultaneously with the upstairs renovations, she had a week to get it completely emptied.

Which wasn't nearly long enough to handle the relics

from two generations—all by herself. Regardless, she still had to be ready for the moving team in two days.

Faintly she heard something through the sound of her own exertions and the radio she'd turned on to help keep her mind off how lonely this job was. Standing up straight, she cocked her head to the side, trying to get her bearings as the blood rushed down from her brain. *Was that footsteps?*

Crossing the room, she cut off the radio just in time to hear her name coming from the direction of the stairs.

Great. Just what she needed—Mr. High-and-Mighty, probably showing up to give her just one more task to demean her pride and heritage. He'd been unbearable these last few days.

Even though it irked her no end, sometimes she could almost understand. Being at someone else's mercy wasn't fun. And knowing that person could control the fate of your entire family? Definitely scary. Mason must have been so angry and petrified when he'd left here as a teenage boy.

But the constant interruptions and subtle—or not so subtle—digs as he demanded she clean out the garbage disposal, bag up and carry out trash, and clean his toilet, all while he watched with a smug expression had worn out her patience long ago. Hell, her father wasn't even this obnoxious.

She hadn't realized when she agreed to take this job that she'd be serving as his whipping boy.

"I'm in here," she called as she heard him walk past her childhood playroom.

He stopped in the doorway with a hard step, back tight, frown firmly in place. "Why didn't you answer me?" he demanded.

"I didn't hear you."

"What do you expect when you shut yourself away down here with a radio on? Anyone could have waltzed right on in and made themselves at home."

She studied him for a minute, trying to figure out where this irritating attitude had come from. "You told me to come down here and clean it out so Jeremy could get work started," she said, keeping her voice calm but unable to control lifting an eyebrow. "That's what I'm doing."

"Part of working for me is being available."

Okay, she'd had about enough. "To do what? Kiss your feet?"

"What?" he asked, his head cocking to the side.

"Look, this high-and-mighty attitude is getting old—"

"You don't like the new me?"

Not really...if he just weren't so darn sexy.

"Ah, can't say anything nice, huh?"

If you can't say anything nice, don't say anything at all. How many times had her mother admonished her with those words? "It's just unnecessary. I know you hate my guts, but wouldn't it be more pleasant to be civil?"

"No," he said with a grin that was just as smug as it was sexy. "I'm enjoying this just fine."

"I'm sure you are."

He took a few steps closer, managing to appear menacing even though the grin never left his face. "If you have a problem with me, you're welcome to leave. I'll even give you a day to get all of your stuff, and your family's stuff, out."

Right. She just stared, feeling her mask of self-preservation fall into place. She'd let him see way too much of herself by arguing with him. It accomplished nothing other than giving him more ammunition for pushing her buttons.

"What can I do for you then, *boss*?"

Mason smirked. He knew he had her right where he wanted her. "Come with me. You're gonna love this."

Probably not, but what choice did she have just yet? Soon though. Soon she'd have enough savings and steady work in her new career lined up to make it on her own. Until then, she simply needed to keep her head down and endure.

Of course, it didn't stop her exhausted mind from questioning what task he had in store for her now—and whether her already taxed body was up to snuff for it.

The worry didn't set in good until they'd already traversed the length of the upstairs hallway. Then she followed him out the side door and across the parking area in front of the four-car garage. They passed the gleaming pickup truck he drove and her own much older sensible sedan. Then he turned onto the path to the stables.

This couldn't be good.

EvaMarie had taken on a lot of physical labor since her daddy had gotten sick, but one thing she'd never done was the heavy lifting in the stables. Feed the horses or brush and ride them—sure. But that was the extent of it.

Plus, she'd already worked all morning packing in the basement. And the day before that, and the day before that…

Mason finally paused beside the stall where EvaMarie's mare Lucy resided. The satisfaction marking his face told her his anticipation was high. Too bad it was all at her expense.

No matter what, she wouldn't cry in front of him.

"We're bringing in our best mare later today from the home farm. Kane should be here this evening. I'll be back in three hours to make sure this stall is cleaned and ready for her."

EvaMarie studied him for a minute. Surely he was joking, pulling a mean prank. "But Jim's not here."

"You are." His expression said he wasn't budging.

Stand up for yourself. Automatically, her stomach clenched, nerves going alert just as they had her entire life. Taking a stand did not come naturally to EvaMarie. Her daddy had squashed that tendency when she was knee high to a grasshopper. "I don't do stables."

"Says who? Is that written down somewhere that I missed?"

Her jaw clenched, but she forced the words out anyway. "You know it's not."

"Welcome to the world of manual labor." He skirted back around her, heading for the barn door. Even the sight of that high, tight butt in fitted jeans didn't lift her mood. "Have it done in three hours," he called over his shoulder.

"I can't!"

Mason turned back with a frown. "Princess, employees shouldn't try to get out of work. It doesn't look good on their evaluations."

"But I'm already working. In the house."

"Good. Then you won't mind getting dirty."

Five

This was gonna be so much fun...

Mason eyed the man in the dark suit who stood near the side door to the house, staring at it as if he could divine who was inside through the exalted abilities of his birthright alone. The tight clench of Mason's gut and surge of anticipation told him that his body remembered this man well...and the role he'd played in the destruction of Mason's family all those years ago.

He hadn't actually seen Laurence Weston since he and Kane had returned to town, but Mason had hoped he would have the chance to rub the snitch's nose in his success at some point.

He just hadn't planned on doing it here at the Hyatt estate.

"May I help you?" Mason's words were polite. His tone...not so much.

Laurence turned to face him with an expectant expression that reminded Mason of his own youthful expectation of having everything go his own way. Laurence had felt the same, only exponentially, and he'd made it a point to let those "beneath" him know their purpose was to serve—and not much else.

"I'm looking for EvaMarie."

"Right." Mason turned for the stables, leaving Laurence to follow if he wanted.

At least, Mason assumed she'd still be out here. Was she capable of cleaning out a stall in three hours? A month ago, Mason would have answered with an emphatic "no," but he grudgingly admitted that EvaMarie had changed a lot since he'd last seen her. Other than knowing how to saddle a horse, the teenage girl he'd fallen hard for wouldn't have known how to work the business end of a shovel, or pitchfork, or rake… Though he hadn't been there to see the actual work, the adult EvaMarie had made some impressive headway inside the house this week, without any help that he could tell.

Which just irritated him even more. Why was she working so hard, staying so loyal to a family who had obviously taken her hard work and obedience for granted? Which led him to do stupid things like put her to work in the barn…

A glance into the stall showed that she was indeed capable of cleaning one in a few hours. The straw bedding and buckets were fresh and clean. There wasn't even a hint of manure in the aisle for Laurence to step in, darn it—Mason would have loved to see those Italian loafers ruined.

Petty, he knew. Just like giving the princess the job of cleaning the stables. But this man—when he'd been a boy—had deliberately told EvaMarie's father where to find them together, simply because he'd wanted EvaMarie for himself. Considering they weren't married now, it must not have worked out the way Laurence had planned.

As they moved farther into the cool, dim depths of the stables, Mason heard the low hum of a husky voice. His entire body stood up to take notice. Man, that siren voice had played along every nerve he had when they were dating, lighting him up better than any drug. Sometimes just talking to EvaMarie on the phone was as good as seeing her in person. Now he felt the same physical charge— no other woman's voice had ever affected him like that.

More's the pity.

She'd grown into its depth though. As she came into view talking to one of the mares in a stall farther down, he compared the wealth of hair piled on her head and strong, curvy body to the delicacy she'd possessed as a young woman. His daddy had said she wouldn't stand up to one good birthing.

Then.

Now she was a strong woman capable of handling what life dished up to her—*so why was he piling on the manure?*

Before he could do something stupid like voice his thoughts, EvaMarie glanced up, spying him over the horse's back. Her features expressed the weight of her exhaustion, emphasized by the dirt smudging her cheeks and the pieces of hay sticking out at odd angles from her hair. But her words were as polite as always. "The stall is ready."

Which was what he'd wanted, right? He'd set out to demonstrate the hard work he'd done for her father once upon a time. Teaching her a lesson was his aim in keeping her here, wasn't it?

So why didn't seeing her like this, exhausted and dirty, make him happy?

"Why the hell are you cleaning stalls?"

As Laurence's voice exploded in his ear, EvaMarie looked to Mason's left with wide eyes. "Laurence?" she asked.

The other man stepped around Mason and got a good look at EvaMarie's disheveled state. "What is going on, EvaMarie? You don't answer the phone. You don't show up for this week's committee meeting. And now this?"

Mason could feel the hairs on the back of his neck lift, hackles rising as another male attempted to assert himself in Mason's territory. And he wasn't at Laurence's mercy like he'd been as a kid.

"Shouldn't you be asking me that?" Mason said, stepping around to take a stand between Laurence and the stall door. "After all, I'm the boss around here."

Laurence's incredulous glance between the two of them almost made Mason laugh. Obviously this was something he couldn't comprehend. Finally Laurence asked, "And who are you, exactly?"

Mason wanted to smirk so badly. In fact, it may have slipped out before he caught it. "I'm Mason Harrington."

It took a minute for the name to register. After all, what need would Laurence have had for that nugget of information all these years? Then his eyes widened, his gaze cataloging the adult Mason. "And you're the boss, how?"

Behind him, Mason heard the stall door open, but he wasn't about to let EvaMarie deprive him of the joy of putting Laurence in his place. "I'm the new owner of the Hyatt Estate."

Laurence trained his hard gaze on EvaMarie. "How is that even possible?"

The rich never wanted to believe that one of their

own could fall...unless the fall worked to their advantage somehow.

"The estate went into foreclosure, Laurence," Eva-Marie said in a hushed tone. "We were forced to sell."

Mason braced his legs, arms crossing firmly over his chest. "And I simply couldn't wait to buy."

"Wasn't your dad just a jockey? A trainer of some kind?"

If anything, Mason's spine stiffened even more. "He was a one-of-a-kind trainer whose career you ruined with your little disclosure to EvaMarie's father all those years ago."

Laurence's gaze narrowed, but Mason wasn't about to let him get away without hearing the facts. "But it didn't matter in the end. Upon his death, my father left Kane and I enough money to buy this estate and start our own stables. Probably five times over." He took a step closer, edging the other man back. "We may have been easy targets back then, but threatening us now would be an unwise move...for anyone."

Laurence stood his ground for a minute more, though Mason was close enough to see the staggering effect his current situation had on Laurence. "How is that even possible?" he asked.

"I know it's hard to imagine someone bettering their circumstances through hard work—" and a lot of deprivation "—but the truth is, I earned it."

I earned it.

Those words rang in EvaMarie's ears as she ushered Laurence back toward his Lincoln. Mason was right—he'd always worked hard. Since she'd been working for them, it had become very obvious he and Kane had no plans to rest on their laurels and simply enjoy their money.

She couldn't help comparing Mason to Laurence, who had gone to a good school thanks to his daddy's money, coasted by and gotten a job in his daddy's real-estate business where he sold off of his personality when he actually tried, and let someone else handle the paperwork for minimum wage.

She wasn't immune to his faults, but he was the one friend who had stuck with her all this time, despite knowing some of the realities of the Hyatts' situation. He was also the only one her parents had let see what was really happening to them. Even though they were holding out hope she'd eventually give in and marry him, this was the one area of her life where she'd built a wall of resistance.

"How could you let this happen, EvaMarie?" Laurence asked, digging his expensive heels into the driveway to bring them to a halt. "All you had to do was call me. I could make all of this go away. Easily."

Only if she accepted his conditions. In that, he and Mason were very similar—every offer came with strings. Why Laurence was so insistent that he wanted her, she couldn't fathom. With his uninspired track record when it came to work, he should have given up long ago.

"I told you I can handle myself."

"By losing the family estate? Great job."

That stung.

"Why didn't you call me?" he went on. "Tell me you were in this much trouble?"

"It was my dad's decision whether or not to share. You know how careful he is. He didn't want word to get around."

Laurence shook his head, hands on his hips. "He's

not gonna be able to hide it for long with those yahoos horning in."

That sounded like sour grapes to EvaMarie. "Regardless," she said, "I'm simply staying until everything is up to standards. By then, my plans will allow me to support myself."

"Plans to do what? Work yourself to death?" He grabbed her forearm. "Spend your days dirty?" He used his hold to give her a good shake. Her irritation shot through the roof. Laurence's voice rose to match. "Where do I stand in those plans?"

EvaMarie felt her backbone snap straight despite her fatigue. "Don't. Start."

His grip tightened, as if he was afraid she'd escape. He crowded in close, giving her an uncomfortable view of his frustration. Memories of several such confrontations with her father caused her stomach to knot.

"You know I can give you the life you deserve," Laurence insisted, his breath hot on her face. "Pampered and taken care of instead of cleaning up after your parents and that guy." His expression tightened with disgust as he assessed her with a sharp glance. "I mean, look at you."

Yes, look at me.

For a moment, just a brief moment, she was tempted to stop fighting and let someone handle life for her for a change. Tears of exhaustion pushed their way to the fore.

"It's what our parents always wanted," Laurence said, his voice deepening. It was low and husky in a way that left her cold. It shouldn't…but it did. But he was insisting… "We'd be perfect together."

Until the thrill of getting what he wanted wore off. Through years of dealing with Laurence, EvaMarie had learned he was like a big child who wanted a toy to entertain him and an adult to handle all the hard stuff.

After the goal was accomplished, EvaMarie would simply be left taking care of Laurence, just as she did everyone else, and be expected to make his life as easy as possible.

Hers would be just as hard. Just as lonely. But he didn't see it that way.

"Everything okay?"

EvaMarie glanced to the side and saw Mason eyeing Laurence's hand on her arm.

Laurence glared, refusing to budge. "Yes," he insisted.

Ever the diplomat, EvaMarie reached up to pat his hand with hers, wincing at the unexpected pain in her palms. "Everything's fine," she agreed. Then she gave Laurence a hard look. "Goodbye, Laurence. I'll see you at the library committee meeting next week."

He looked ready to protest, but then adopted a petulant expression and let go of her arm. Because it was easier. Because in the end, he was still an overgrown child.

Which was evidenced by his defiant gunning of his engine on the way out. EvaMarie rubbed her arm, once again feeling that sharp pain in her palm. She glanced down, but one quick peek at the red, raw patches on her skin had her hiding her hands by her sides.

"Seriously?" Mason asked. "That guy is still around?"

EvaMarie tried to hide the exhaustion that was now starting to weigh her down like a heavy blanket. She just wanted a shower and her bed. If she didn't get inside soon, the shower wasn't happening. "Laurence is a friend of the family."

"But not part of the family? Bet that's a disappointment to your father."

He had no idea. The only thing her father continued to badger her about these days was Laurence. Though he wouldn't say it explicitly, Daulton saw Laurence as the answer to all of his problems. No matter where that left EvaMarie.

Too tired for more politeness, she headed for the door. Mason could follow or not. "There's a great many things I do that are a deep disappointment to my father," she mumbled.

Her choices had always been wrong—ever since her brother had died. The smiling, applauding father had long ago turned into the disapproving dictator. Illness and age had quieted him, but not mellowed him. "Anyway, Laurence is just looking out for me."

"Don't you mean looking out for his investment?"

She skidded to a stop on the tile in the foyer. "What?"

"Well, he's put a lot of years into pursuing you. Wouldn't want all of that effort to go to waste."

"Effort isn't even a word in his vocabulary." If Mason thought any different, he didn't know Laurence at all.

But she might have underestimated Mason. He quirked a brow as he said, "Ah, I see you've gotten to know him quite well. Took you a while."

No, she'd always known how Laurence was. Only no one had trusted her to make the right choices, only the easy ones. They'd expected her to give in to her parents' demands and marry the man they wanted for her. She might have given up a lot in her lifetime, but that choice was not one she was willing to let go of. She did have boundaries, even if no one else bothered to see them.

Or respect them.

Wearily she made her way up the stairs, her feet feeling like lead weights. If only she could pull on the banister for support, but she had a feeling her hands wouldn't appreciate the pressure. "Good night, Mason."

"Wait. Why are you stopping for the night?"

Because I can. She didn't answer at first, just kept on going with all the energy left inside her.

When she reached the landing, she finally repeated, "Good night, Mason," and dragged herself to her room.

That man was like arguing with a brick wall.

Six

Mason winced as he bumped into the banister in the dark, then wondered why on earth he didn't turn on the lights before he fell down the back staircase.

Nightlights were placed at intervals along the hallway, but didn't help him with the unfamiliar spaces and shadows. Lightning from the thunderstorm beating the house from outside lit up the nearby arched window, giving him a chance to locate the light switch. The hanging chandelier lent its glow upstairs and down, allowing him to make better progress on the stairs and in the hallway.

As he approached the family room, he heard a noise. Looked like it was time for a little midnight tête-à-tête with his roomie.

As he made his way through the darkened family room into the kitchen, with only a faint light burning above the stove, the muffled sounds he'd heard morphed into husky curse words that were creative enough to raise his brows.

Apparently the princess had gotten herself an education while he'd been gone.

This should be interesting.

Flicking on the overhead lights, the first thing he noticed was legs. Bare legs.

EvaMarie stood next to the bar in a nightgown that barely reached midthigh. Beside her were open packages and what looked like trash strewed across the counter. She blinked at him in surprise...or maybe it was just the bright lights.

Mason stepped closer. "Problem?" he asked, unable to keep the amusement from his voice.

If she'd been a kid caught with her hand in the candy jar, she couldn't have turned redder. Her body straightened; her hands slid behind her back.

"Nope. Everything's fine."

Right. Her shifting gaze said she had a problem, just one she didn't want him to know about.

He stalked to her, even though he knew being close to all that bare skin wasn't the best idea he'd ever had. But seeing the first-aid kit in the midst of all the wrappers, he realized this wasn't the time to play.

"All right. Let's see it," he said, his tone no nonsense. "After all, we don't have time for you to be off duty."

Those dark blue eyes, so thickly lashed, couldn't hide the wash of tears that filled them. Alarm slammed through his chest. He could handle a lot of things, power through just about every situation. But put him in the vicinity of a woman's tears, and he was hopeless.

Luckily she blinked them back, but then murmured, "It'll be fine." Her lashes fell and skimmed the flushed apples of her cheeks. "I'll be fine by morning. Just go back to bed."

Even Mason wasn't that self-centered. Gentling his voice, he said, "Just let me have a look, Evie. Okay?"

Her eyes connected with his. He saw his own surprise reflected there. He hadn't called her that name in too many years. But it worked, because her hands slipped from behind her back, as though she instinctively trusted that connection.

For once, he refused to use it against her. She didn't need that right now.

Or ever, his conscience chastised him.

Pushing his conscience aside to deal with later, he cupped her hands in his and turned them over so he could see the palms. "Holy smokes, EvaMarie. Why didn't you wear gloves?"

He could feel her stiffen and try to pull back. Her fingers curled as if to protect the wounds from his judgment. "I did," she insisted. "The only pairs I could find were all too big. They kept slipping against my skin."

Alarm mixed with a darker emotion, deepening his voice. "I can see that. Looks almost like you have carpet burn on your palms. Let me have a better look." As he led her over to the stove so he could get some direct light, she said, "I cleaned them as best I could in the shower, but the soap burned—"

"I bet."

"My wounds weren't that dirty. The gloves kept the dirt out for the most part. But I think they need to be wrapped." She glanced over her shoulder at the mess on the bar. "Only it's kind of hard to do one-handed."

And it hadn't occurred to her that there was now someone else in the house she could ask to help her. Why should it? His conscience flared up again. He'd proved pretty well so far that his job was to make her life harder, not better.

He cradled one of her hands in both of his, bending closer for a good look. Memories of holding her hand abounded, but he couldn't remember if he'd ever examined her there in this much detail. He was pretty sure those calluses on her palms and fingertips hadn't been there before. The skin along the back still felt silky smooth and smelled faintly of lilacs. Was that still her favorite scent?

And when he noticed the faint outline of curvy, muscled legs down below the bar, his body went a little haywire. The mix of past and present was throwing him off balance.

For a moment, he could almost understand her father's protective nature, the desire to shelter her from harsh reality—though Mason could never forgive the lengths her father had gone to achieve that aim. No one deserved to have their life ruined like that, not Mason, not his father.

As he surveyed the abraded skin, the damage done by his own selfishness, a strange compassion kicked in. One he almost resisted, almost ignored. Man, it sucked to realize his brother had been right. They'd been joking with each other, but Mason *had* done a bad thing.

"Let's get these wrapped up so they don't get dirty. I think they'll heal in a few days, but we don't want infection getting in where the skin is broken." He turned back to the bar, breaking their physical connection. The cool air he drew into his lungs cleared his head. The sound of the rain outside ignited thoughts of starting over.

As long as he didn't let himself get too close, get drawn into the attraction that flirted behind the edges of his resentment. Therein lay the real danger he needed to protect himself from.

"Then how about I make some hot chocolate?" he

asked, remembering it as her favorite drink. "That'll warm us up before trying to sleep."

"So you have learned to cook?" she asked, cautious surprise lightening her voice.

"No, but I make a mean microwave version."

EvaMarie held herself perfectly still.

Her insides jumped and shivered with every touch of Mason's fingers against hers, but she refused to let it show. Part of her wanted to relax into his newfound compassion. After all, she remembered an all-too-nice version of Mason that she wished would come back.

But the bigger part of her couldn't forget his behavior since his return. Better not to trust that this version would last longer than it took to feed her hot chocolate and send her to bed like a child.

Maybe that was the key—treating her like a child. After all, he didn't seem to care for the grown-up version of her too much.

His touch was amazingly gentle as he applied a thin coating of antibacterial ointment to each palm, then set about wrapping her hands in gauze and tape. Memories of other times he was gentle, like the night she offered him her virginity, pushed against the barriers she had erected to block them out of her brain. What good would it do to relive those times? After all, he hated her now. Thinking about it would get her nothing but grief.

But she'd pulled out the memories of their loving often over the years. Mason had been her first, and best, lover. Her one experiment in college to replace those memories had proved a disappointment. So her time with Mason was all she had to live on during the long, lonely nights of her adulthood. But she had learned one lesson from that lackluster experience in college: settling for something less than what she'd experienced with Mason wasn't worth the trouble.

Which had kept her from making several stupid choices that would have easily gotten her out of this house years ago. Like marrying the man who had pestered her to do so since she'd turned eighteen.

EvaMarie's suspicions grew as Mason deposited her at the nearby table, cleaned up all the wrappers and discarded bandages, then went to search in the pantry. Some food had been delivered on the same day as his furnishings and personal items, but she didn't remember any hot chocolate mix. But sure enough, he pulled out a round brown canister with gold lettering: a specialty chocolate mix, her one indulgence.

The awkward silence in the room, broken only by the sounds of Mason and the rain outside, urged her to do the polite thing and speak. But what subject wouldn't be fraught with unexploded land mines? As she studied the expert wrapping on her hands, she knew she had to try.

"So I suspect that your purchase of the estate is the talk of the town, or will be soon," she said, her voice hushed in deference to the night and the storm outside. For some reason it just seemed appropriate, even if a touch too intimate. "It's really incredible, Mason. I'm proud of you and Kane for being so successful."

And she was. Her one visit to the Harrington farm when they were dating had shown her just how different their lifestyles were. Mason's family hadn't lived in poverty, but their situation had probably been what EvaMarie now knew as living paycheck to paycheck. Mason's dad had cooked her a simple meal of homemade fried chicken, and macaroni and cheese from a box. It had been good, and the atmosphere around the table had been friendly and welcoming.

Mason hadn't been able to understand when she said it was the most comforting night of her life. He hadn't understood what life was really like for her…and she hadn't wanted him to know the truth.

"I know your dad must be too," she added.

Mason turned away from her as the microwave dinged. "Actually, my father's dead."

"Oh, Mason. I'm so sorry."

He was silent for a moment before he asked, his voice tight, "Are you?"

"Yes. He seemed like a nice man."

"He was. He didn't deserve the lot he had in life. Constantly undermined and unjustly ridiculed by people who didn't even know him, but who had all the power."

The spoon Mason used to stir the hot chocolate clanked against the side of the cup with a touch more force than necessary. EvaMarie winced, knowing that he was talking about her father, and his father's former employers. She held her breath, awaiting a return of the snarky, condescending man he'd shown her since his return. Instead, he crossed the kitchen and set the mug before her without comment.

She wasn't sure how to respond, so she remained quiet. The steam from the cup drew her. She wrapped her aching hands around the outside, letting the heat slip over her palms into the joints, then up her arms. So soothing… "So he left you an inheritance?" she asked, hoping to steer him away from the touchy subject.

"Actually, it was my mother."

EvaMarie nodded, though she'd never heard much about the woman before. Lifting the cup close, she breathed in the rich chocolate scent. The comforting familiarity cloaked her in the very place where familiarity seemed to have gone out the window. This was her kitchen, the one she'd drunk hot chocolate in all her life, but it wasn't hers anymore. And the man next to her wasn't hers either.

"We moved back to Tennessee where she was from, though my grandparents on her side wouldn't have anything to do with us for the longest time. My grandfather never did come around."

"Why?" She couldn't get out more than a whisper and found herself grasping the mug just a little tighter.

"They were high society, lots of money." His glance her way said *sound familiar?* "They never approved of the marriage, or the fact that their daughter died after he took her away."

The level of Mason's resentment after all these years was starting to make a little more sense. "They wouldn't come see her?"

Mason shook his head, his hands clenching where they lay on the table. "My father even sent a letter after receiving her diagnosis. He knew it was bad. My grandmother later told him her husband refused to allow her to open it. They didn't see her before she died."

A stone-like weight formed in EvaMarie's chest. "How awful."

"My mother had a sizable trust fund created for us. Over time, my father managed to grow it out of proportion to what she left us. But he never touched it."

Considering how much they had struggled after his father lost his job, EvaMarie couldn't imagine that kind of sacrifice. But she daren't mention it for fear it would make Mason angry again. This small moment of civil conversation was a gift she didn't want to squander.

"He told us about it after his first heart attack. Helped us decide what to do and taught us how to manage it. It was—" he paused, shaking his head "—*is* still amazing to me."

"That's an incredible gift," she said.

"Yes. And he was an incredible man."

Indeed. To have taken such care with his wife's gift for her sons, even when it made his own life harder than it had to be—that was a true father. EvaMarie struggled not to make a comparison to her own father, to the lack of foresight he'd exercised, but her heart remained heavy.

As she sipped, the downpour outside quieted to a light, steady rain, soothing instead of boisterous. The ache in her palms had subsided some beneath the warmth and care of her bandages. And Mason had surprised her. They hadn't talked, truly talked, in many years. She shouldn't be enjoying it this much.

Her eyelids drooped. The day had been a long, hard one. And she'd start an even busier one tomorrow on even less sleep. As much as she wanted to savor this truce while it lasted, it was time she headed back to bed.

Standing, she glanced across at Mason, only to catch him surveying her bare legs. Almost as quickly he looked up, but she pretended not to notice. "Um, I think it's time I headed back upstairs," she said. Then trying to smooth over the awkwardness, she asked, "Is your room set up all right?"

"Yes, thank you, EvaMarie."

She tried to squash the glow that blossomed at his words, but couldn't. Tomorrow, he'd kill the glow soon enough.

"Well, good night. Thank you for the hot chocolate and, well…" She nodded toward her hands.

Mason stood, as well. "It's the least I can do, EvaMarie."

She took a few steps back, then paused. "Until tomorrow." She turned and made quick progress toward the hall. She'd almost made it when she heard him behind her.

"EvaMarie."

Heart pounding, though she knew it shouldn't, she glanced back. "Yes?"

"You have a storage building already, correct?"

And just like that, they were back to boss and employee. Why did tears feel close all of a sudden? "Yes. I promise all arrangements have been made and the moving guys will be here on Wednesday to have everything out in time for the renovations to start."

He stepped closer, looking mysterious as the darkness hid his expression. "Actually, a moving crew will be here tomorrow to help you. All you have to do is direct."

The bottom dropped out of her stomach like she'd taken a fast-moving elevator. "What?"

He didn't move, didn't speak for a moment. Then he let out a deep sigh…one she'd almost mistake for regret. "Just consider it hazard pay."

Seven

"I'll be on the second floor if you guys need me for anything, okay?" EvaMarie said.

"No problem. Thanks, Miss Hyatt."

With a deep breath, EvaMarie headed up the stairs from the basement, skirting the carpenters already measuring for their plans to widen the entryway. Sad to say, but she'd rather be down there helping with the packing, even with her sore palms. But she had another job waiting for her.

With the extra help, her family's belongings were going into storage a lot quicker than she'd anticipated. Which meant she had to get her brother Chris's room cleaned out ASAP. She was surprised Mason hadn't asked about the other empty room on this floor, but she was grateful. She didn't want movers in there.

Yet cleaning it out herself wasn't a task she was looking forward to.

Her hand trembled as she reached for the doorknob. As if this wasn't gonna be hard enough.

"Is this where you'd like the boxes, Miss Hyatt?"

EvaMarie almost jumped, but caught herself before turning back to the young man. "Yes, please." After he set them and some tape down in a neat pile, she added, "Thank you so much for bringing those upstairs."

"No problem."

His gaze flicked to the still-closed door before he turned back toward the stairs. He might be curious, but he wasn't going inside. No one had been inside that room except her and her mother for over twenty years. Not even her father.

Turning back, she took a deep breath and forced herself through the door. A quick glance told her everything was the same. A small part of her had wondered if her mother would take something from the room with her when she left, but it didn't look like she had.

In fact, the room remained exactly as it had been when Chris had died in a tragic car accident here on Hyatt land. He'd been fifteen. The emotions of that day stood out so vividly in EvaMarie's mind, though the actual images were mere shadows now. She'd been angry with her brother because it was one of those rare times he'd refused to let her tag along on his adventure. It was one of the few times he'd disobeyed their father. He wasn't supposed to be in the vehicle unsupervised.

While he was out, he'd lost control of the truck, and it plunged headfirst into a ravine. His chest had been crushed against the steering wheel. By the time anyone found him, he was gone from her forever.

But his room remained full of old-school video games and a huge television, the best model from that time. Horses were everywhere, whether it was pictures or his collection of carved wooden figures. While Chris had been a typical teenage boy, he'd loved the family's animals and looked forward to taking over from their father someday.

A Tennessee football bedspread and pillowcases. A BB gun and his very first rifle on the gun rack above the bookcase. Even a pair of discarded cowboy boots peeking out of the barely open closet door. How did she even begin to pack away the life of someone she loved and missed so much—even to this day?

She picked up the photo box she'd brought in the other day, along with some trunks to pack away the more valuable keepsakes, and walked over to the wall beside the bed. Pictures of Chris at various sporting events and horse shows, some of him alone, some with her or their parents, were barely hanging onto the wall. The tape had deteriorated over time. One by one she took them down, removed what adhesive was left and packed them away in the box. Her mom might not want them now, but eventually she might. EvaMarie had long ago made secret copies of the originals for the scrapbook she kept in her room.

"Whatchya doing?"

Whirling, EvaMarie tilted off balance before righting herself for a good look at Mason. "Oh, I thought you were gone for the day."

He shrugged, but his gaze steadily cataloged the room around them. Her hands tightened on the box until the edges cut into her bandaged palms. She didn't hide her wince soon enough.

"I took care of some stuff in town," he finally said. "Then I came back to see how things were going. Looks like they are making steady progress in the basement."

Her voice was breathless as she tried to justify herself. "Yes, I planned to get back down there—"

Again that nonchalant shrug. "You did fine. They were

very clear on what you wanted done. You've gotten everything pretty organized."

"I try," she murmured. It felt weird to acknowledge the compliment, as if she needed to search for some hidden insult. After last night, she wasn't sure what to expect.

Or quite how to react.

"How're the hands?"

"Better." She gestured with the box. "Awkward."

"I'm sure. Let me know when you need some new bandages."

Which just reminded her of the two of them in a dimly lit kitchen and how she had been half-dressed. That had been an ill-timed choice, but when your hands were on fire and you needed to get to the first-aid kit, putting on pants moved low on the priority list. At least he hadn't seemed to mind...

A flush swept up her body and bloomed in her cheeks. She nodded and turned away, anxious to hide her reaction.

Behind her, she heard him moving, prowling the space. She bit her lip. Though she knew the reaction was unfounded, part of her ached to stop him. Her mother wasn't here to care that there was a stranger in Chris's room, but it still felt wrong.

"Can I ask whose room this is?"

Despite his gentle tone, despite last night, she was still afraid to say. Afraid of the condemnation or judgment that might come from the revelation. But it wasn't as though she could hide it with him standing right behind her.

Gathering the last of the pictures into the box, she carefully put the lid on top and laid it on the desk near the door. "This room belonged to my brother, Chris."

Mason's slow nod didn't give her a clue as to his thoughts. "You've never mentioned him before."

No, she hadn't. Not even when she and Mason had been close. So his accusing tone was justified—this time.

How did she begin to explain that it was a barrier her parents had put up that she was almost afraid to cross? Especially since her own grief, never properly expressed, might have broken through the dam if a crack had ever appeared. Even now, she wasn't sure what openly experiencing her grief would have been like.

"My parents—" she cleared her throat, trying to loosen the constriction "—they never talked about him."

He shook his head. "How is that even possible? Not to talk about your own child?"

Now it was her turn to shrug, because she didn't understand it as well as she wished she did. Even now, she couldn't explain her tight throat or pounding heart. It made no logical sense, but the sensations were there, nonetheless.

Still, she forced herself to speak. "Once we came home from the funeral, he wasn't ever talked about again. Everything about him disappeared, except this room," she said, glancing around with a covetous look. "As if he didn't exist—at least, it felt that way."

She stroked a finger down a picture of Chris on his favorite horse that sat framed atop the desk. "Only I know that wasn't true. At least, not for my mom."

"How?"

She pursed her lips before she spoke. "Because mine is the next room over. I could hear her crying in here some nights." She took a shuddering breath, remembering the eerie, sad sounds. "But no one mentioned it in the morning."

Behind her, she could hear him moving but was too caught up in her emotions to turn around.

He asked, "So you were old enough to know him, to remember it?"

EvaMarie turned around and nodded. "He was quite a bit older than me, but the age gap didn't keep us apart. Chris took me everywhere with him. Taught me to ride horses, swim. We were rarely apart. He was my champion." Her voice trailed to a whisper. "My protector."

He'd protected her from their father and his demands for perfection, even at her young age. After Chris's death, her father had become her jailer. For a long time, she'd understood the need to keep his only living child safe. Until Mason. Until she'd become desperate to finally live.

"I don't remember hearing about his death, but then I'm only a couple of years older than you."

"It was sudden, a car accident here on the estate. When something isn't talked about by the family, and no one dares ask, it becomes a matter of out of sight, out of mind."

A few steps brought him closer, almost to within arm's length. EvaMarie was amazed at how desperately she wanted him to close that distance, to hold her against him until the sad memories dissolved.

"But why would *you* never tell me?"

Her gaze snapped up to meet his. Unnerved by the intensity of his stare, she swallowed. For a moment, she considered giving some kind of flippant, casual answer. But something about that intensity demanded a true reason.

So she gave it. "You'd be amazed, I'm sure, at how deeply a family's darkest moments can be buried. When something makes you happy, the last thing you want to do is remember the bad times."

Which was why she'd never been completely honest with him about her father, even. Yes, she'd warned him they needed to be careful. That she wasn't allowed to date. That her father would probably run Mason over with his truck if he caught them together—if he didn't get his gun first. But she'd never told him that her father scared her. That he controlled every last second of her life, demanding that she be the perfect, compliant child.

Because she didn't want to taint their time together with the darkness she lived with every day.

Her chest tightened, threatening to cut off her air supply. Time to change the subject. "Thank you, Mason."

"For what?" he asked with a slight tilt of his head.

"For listening, letting me talk about him." The words were rushed, but if she didn't get them out quick, they wouldn't come at all. "Though I wish I'd had more years with him, I try to remember how he lived while he was with me."

His slight smile told her he could relate. "My father always said, the least we could do to honor my mother was to keep her alive through our memories, to keep her a part of our family. He talked about her until the day he died."

"I wish we had." EvaMarie's heart ached as she looked over her brother's possessions. "I'm so out of the habit now…it feels weird." She lifted her head. "And it shouldn't."

And somehow, she'd find a way to change this…just like she was changing a whole lot of other things in her life. So with a deep breath, she got started packing.

Mason followed his brother into Brenner's, breathing in the smell of grilled meats and a real wood-burning fire. This wasn't a touristy place but had a huge local following—off the beaten path.

Though they had a varied menu, their steaks and Kentucky microbrewed beers were a superb version of man food.

Kane stretched in the booth, taking in the roaring fire nearby and the authentic aged brick walls. "Can you believe we're here and eating at a place like this?"

"As opposed to the cheap burgers that were a treat growing up?" Mason shook his head. "Kinda hard to believe, even now. But dad would have loved this."

Mason thought of the man who had worked so hard, taught them so much, and had still laughed and had a beer with them… He shifted, uncomfortable comparisons with what he now knew of EvaMarie's childhood rising up in this mind. But before he could mention anything to Kane, the waitress appeared.

By the time their orders went in and their foam-topped beers had come out, Mason thought better of sharing. After all, it really wasn't his story to share. Since EvaMarie would be working with Kane some too, he didn't want her to be uncomfortable if Kane let his knowledge slip.

While he and his brother both sat in thoughtful silence, Mason couldn't help but think about the changes in their circumstances that were so unexpected, so welcome, and yet made him long for the man who had made it all possible. Their lives could have been very different if their father had been a different kind of man.

As if on the same wavelength, Kane raised his mug. "To the man who sacrificed so we could have all this."

They tapped beers and drank. The smooth amber liquid had just enough bite for Mason's satisfaction. "Dad loved us," he said. "That much is clear."

"Was always clear," Kane agreed.

Again Mason came back to EvaMarie, her childhood,

her family. He'd had something she'd never had for all her privilege: the unconditional love of a parent.

Kane went on, "I'd like to think he'll be happy with us naming the stables after him. He was so excited when we told him what we wanted to do."

But not about them moving back here. The one and only time Mason had mentioned that idea, his father had become visibly upset. Maybe through the years he'd realized just how hard the persecution had been on Mason, and had probably known that if he got within a hundred miles of the Hyatt family, revenge would be the only thing on his mind.

"You okay, Mason?" his brother asked.

Suddenly he realized he'd been staring into his drink. But the last thing they needed right now was his confused thoughts on the Hyatts complicating their vision for their racing stables. "Yeah," he said. "Harringtons. Quite an upscale ring to it, I'd say."

They shared a grin before Mason raised his glass once more. "We'll make it everything he would have wanted." If he could have had what he wanted in life...or rather taken their money to build what he'd wanted. "He was a selfless man, you know," Mason said, preaching to the choir. "Makes me wonder if I can even attempt to live up to the man he was."

Kane raised a brow in query at the sudden turn of the conversation. "Living in the same house with EvaMarie got you thinking a little differently?"

"How'd you guess?" Mason hated a know-it-all.

"Brother, there's a reason I opted to oversee the transition at the home farm when we decided to buy the Hyatt estate. You need time to work through things, good or bad."

"I didn't expect it to be good. Didn't expect…" *Her*. He shook his head. "This isn't going how I planned."

"Told ya so."

Mason had a suspicion his brother was making fun of him. Now the smirk made it obvious. "I'm glad you're enjoying this."

"Then we're both happy."

"Smart-ass."

"And practical." Kane winked. "EvaMarie seems like a nice, capable, intelligent woman. How can she possibly complicate your life that much?"

"You'd be surprised," Mason mumbled.

"Then I guess you shouldn't have hired her then, huh?"

Mason hated it when his brother had a point. Luckily the waitress brought their food just then, filling the table with enough plates of steaks and sides and bread to keep them busy for quite a while. Then she headed back for another round of beer.

Mason was savoring his first bite of succulent meat when Kane's grunt drew his attention. Kane's gaze followed the activity over Mason's shoulder.

A quick glance and Mason wanted to grunt himself. Daulton and Bev Hyatt were making slow progress across the main part of the restaurant floor, patiently accompanied by the friendly hostess who was chatting with the one and only Laurence Weston. Mason's very own kryptonite, all at one table.

He turned back to his food. "Well, that's great."

And it only got worse. The hostess was making for a table not too far away. In fact, it was directly across the fireplace from the booth Mason and Kane occupied. Right on the edge of Mason's peripheral vision.

So much for enjoying dinner.

He pushed back, wiping his mouth with a few rough strokes of his cloth napkin. "I'm done."

"Admitting defeat already?" Kane asked with an arched brow.

Why did his brother have to be such a voice of wisdom? "Are you thirty-two or eighty-two?"

Kane shrugged, that trademark Harrington grin making another appearance. "Not my fault someone has to be the adult."

He wasn't joking, no matter what that smile said. Only two years Mason's senior, somehow Kane always played the adult role. He wasn't prone to the same emotional outbursts as Mason. Very few people had seen his serious side—and they definitely regretted it when they did. When crossed, snarky, joking Kane turned cold and calculating.

A scary thing to see, even for Mason.

So he acknowledged his brother's point with a short nod and returned to his food. No reason why the other family had to impact his and Kane's dinner, which had started on such a bright note.

The brothers' conversation turned desultory before they regained their normal rhythm. Their refreshed beers helped.

But it wasn't long before the weight of unwanted attention settled on Mason. He considered ignoring it, but he just wasn't that kind of person. A casual glance to his right showed him that, sure enough, the Hyatts were staring. Laurence had his gaze trained almost defiantly on the couple, as if he refused to lower himself to looking Mason's way.

Mason dipped his chin in a single nod of acknowledgment, then returned his attention to Kane. "Was that adult enough?" he asked, hoping to lighten the mood.

Kane grinned. "Sure."

But apparently it wasn't enough for Daulton. Within minutes, snippets of the conversation across the fireplace struck them like pellets from a BB gun.

"—just a shame, in this day and age, people like that can come in and steal everything you've worked for."

The low rumble of other voices answered. Mason met Kane's look across their table. His brother sighed. "This is going to be interesting."

Mason tried to ignore it. He really did. But Daulton Hyatt had no compunction about slandering the Harringtons in a public restaurant. At all.

"In my opinion, there's a reason God lets people be born with no money. Everyone has a station in life. That's an indicator. And a predictor of future behavior."

The bright flush radiating from Bev Hyatt's cheeks was almost painful to see, but Mason noticed she never made an attempt to quiet her husband. She simply worried the edges of the cloth napkin beside her plate. Laurence's remarks must have been more moderate in tone, since Mason couldn't make out the words, but whatever he said seemed to spur Daulton along.

"Those Harringtons don't even know what to do with a horse, much less a stable of them," he said loudly enough to turn a few heads from the tables around him. "You mark my words," he said, adding emphasis by shaking his steak knife, "they'll be a complete failure within a year."

Kane was on his feet two seconds quicker than Mason expected. He followed, eager to provide backup.

"I'm not sure I heard you correctly," Kane said. "Did you mean we'd be as much of a failure as you were?"

The older man straightened, obviously unused to being challenged. "I am not a failure."

"Really?" Kane wasn't backing down...and he chose

not to lower his voice either. "Because your stables were in bankruptcy when we bought it. Was that from mismanagement? Lack of knowledge? Or sheer laziness?"

Oh boy. Kane was dangerously calm as he went on. "You mark *my* words, old man. We aren't afraid to fight dirty, so I'd pull my punches if I were you."

Daulton Hyatt turned to his companions. "Listen to how they talk to me. Guess their father was as inept a parent as he was a businessman."

Mason quickly sidestepped to force his body between Kane and the table. Otherwise, Mr. Hyatt would have been counting his broken teeth. Unconsciously, he reached for his own form of ammunition.

"That's a strange attitude for you to have, considering your daughter is working for me now," Mason said with a deadly quiet reserve that he knew wouldn't last for long. Unlike Kane, he enjoyed yelling.

He could see the surprise knock Daulton back a little, but he never looked away. Bev glanced across at Laurence with wide eyes. Whatever she saw there made her swallow hard.

"My daughter would never betray me by working for you," Daulton blustered. "She got a job at the library."

"Sure about that?"

Daulton must not have liked what he saw in Mason's eyes. "EvaMarie is a good girl. Too good for the likes of you. Or did you somehow trick her into doing this like you tricked us out of our house?"

Now it was Kane's turn to restrain his brother. His hand on Mason's arm was the only thing that kept Mason from slamming his palms on the Hyatts' dinner table. "You know, EvaMarie is a good person, a good *woman*."

His emphasis on the last word did not sit well with EvaMarie's parents. Their eyes widened, full of questions. Questions that Mason would never stoop to answering.

"It's amazing that she's turned out as well as she has," he went on, "considering the overbearing, manipulative father she's put up with all her life."

"Overbearing? Dear boy, that's the last thing I am." Daulton's chest puffed out. "I made sure my child learned right from wrong, how to be a true lady and how to conduct herself with respect. Which is more than your father ever taught you."

Kane's deliberate removal of his hand from his brother's arm signaled exactly how hard that blow hit. But this time, Mason used words instead of fists. He leaned onto the table, getting close to Daulton's face even though he didn't lower his voice. "My father was more of a man than you'll ever be. He cared for his family instead of browbeating them." He shook his head, driven to break through the man's steely facade. "He would never have completely erased a son from his life simply because he had the gall to die on him."

"Mason!"

Jerking around, Mason found himself facing EvaMarie. The flush of her cheeks and slight sob to her breath told him if she hadn't heard everything, she'd heard more than enough. But it was the accusation in her eyes, the betrayal in that look that cut past his defenses.

For once, it was more than deserved.

Eight

"How could you disgrace us by working for that man?"

The Harringtons were barely out the exit before the interrogation started. A quick glance around at their fellow diners only reinforced EvaMarie's wish that her father would lower his voice. After all, she was only across the table from him.

With few other options, she modeled a lower tone. "That man and the job he offered me—a great paying job along with room and board—are helping us get through our…situation," she insisted.

"I don't see how," Daulton said, leaning back in his chair and crossing his arms over his chest. It was a stubborn pose if ever she saw one. A pose she'd seen him adopt often in her lifetime.

She knew, just looking at her father, that Mason's outburst wasn't his fault alone. Her father could provoke the calmest of people. And right now, her own anger was rising hot. Anger at Mason. Anger at her father. It was threatening to crackle the paint off her inner walls, walls that had locked away years' worth of emotions and kept her calm and collected for far too long.

She leaned forward, crowding over the table. "*You* can't afford to live in that facility, Dad. I know you'd rather not face it, but that's the reality." Her heavy sigh might seem mild to most people, but was a risky move with her father. "When are you gonna face how life really is, Dad—for you and for me?"

As her father's expression closed off even more, her mother joined the conversation for once. "But to tell Mason those things—personal things about us…"

Sadness and guilt mingled within EvaMarie as she watched her mother clutch her cardigan together at the vulnerable hollow of her throat. Compassion softened her response. "I'm sorry, Mother. Mason found me clearing out—" she choked slightly, still unable to speak her brother's name in front of them "—the room. I gave an explanation. It never occurred to me—"

"That he'd use it as ammunition?" her father interjected. "How naïve are you, EvaMarie? That's the kind of man he is."

Laurence nodded. As much as EvaMarie wanted to argue that Mason wasn't like that, that she'd seen him laugh with and support his family, show compassion even to her when he probably didn't feel like she deserved it, she'd heard his accusation herself.

"How could you lie to us, darling?" her mother asked. "We thought you were working at the library?"

"Shocked me too," Laurence added.

With a quick sideways glance, EvaMarie mumbled, "You aren't helping."

But Laurence wasn't backing down. He loved stirring the pot. "Honey, you weren't born to clean barn stalls."

The surround sound gasps told her he'd gotten his point across. That was the problem with Laurence…always had been. He was only willing to further his own agenda.

"No daughter of mine—" her father started.

The smack of her palm on the table sounded impossibly loud to EvaMarie. No one else in the restaurant even looked in their direction, but she felt like she suddenly had a 1000 kilowatt light shining right on her.

It was always that way when she dared defy her father.

"Yes, I will." She enunciated clearly, hoping she could get her point across in one try. The quiver in her stomach told her the chances were iffy, but at least a numbness was starting to creep over her raw emotions, giving her a touch of distance as she delivered what was most likely her long-needed declaration of independence.

"I will do whatever I'm told by Mason. I'm not a princess, not anymore—face it, Dad. I'm a worker bee."

The breath she drew in was shaky, fragile. "This is my life. One I am struggling to resurrect out of the gutter after years of trying to keep us afloat. What did you think would happen when you left me to clean up the mess you left behind? I'm doing the best I can with what I have to work with here."

Shocked silence was a new response from her parents. A novel one, in fact. Thank goodness, because she wasn't sure she'd have been able to withstand any dictums to sit down and shut up. Instead EvaMarie stood, palms firm on the table to keep her steady. "I thought you'd be proud of me, Daddy. After all, you're the one who taught me not to argue with authority."

The reality of what she'd said didn't honestly hit Eva-Marie until she was on her way home. Then she had to pull the car over until she could get her shaking limbs under control. How could she have talked to her parents like that? But then again, every word had been honest.

Though her father regularly wielded his honesty like a sword, EvaMarie had never been allowed to own hers.

Her emotions were in turmoil, overflowing until she didn't know how to contain them. Especially when she ran into Mason on the upstairs landing. Suddenly she had a target for her deepest emotion: anger.

"How dare you," she demanded, stomping across the landing to crowd into his space.

He straightened, withdrawing only an inch before staring down at her intently. EvaMarie felt her emotions go from hot to supernova.

"Your dad was deliberately pushing my buttons," Mason said, for once the calm one in the situation. "You should have heard what he said before you got there."

She shook her head, her mind a jumble of thoughts and questions, but one stood out from the rest. "Why would you talk to him in the first place?"

His incredulous look didn't help matters. "How could I not? He made sure he spoke loud enough for the whole restaurant to hear."

Well, that did sound like her father. "That's no excuse."

"Actually, it's enough of an excuse. I'm not gonna sit by and let him malign my family and keep my mouth shut."

"But it's okay to retaliate by throwing his dead son in his face?" She stomped closer, close enough to feel Mason's body heat. "I trusted you with that information—something I've never done with another living soul. Why would you turn around and tell it to anyone? Much less use it as a weapon against my father?"

"I got angry," he said with a shrug. "Kinda like you are right now, only you're much cuter."

EvaMarie wasn't sure what happened. One minute they were facing off. The next the knuckles on her right hand burned and Mason gripped his left arm. She'd...oh man, she'd hit him. Her whole body flushed.

When Mason pushed forward, she instantly retreated. Standing her ground wasn't something she'd ever been good at, especially when she was afraid. If he decided to retaliate, she certainly deserved it.

Then her back met the wall. His body boxed her in. She looked up into his face, fear gripping her stomach, only to have his lips cover hers.

This wasn't a teenage kiss. It was rough, powerful, and had EvaMarie's body lighting up all on its own. Leaving anger far behind, she wanted nothing more than to drown in the hot rush of need that overtook her in that moment.

Suddenly his teeth nipped the sensitive fullness of her mouth. Her gasp gave him free access. He pressed in, those vaguely familiar lips giving her a good taste of what he was capable of as an adult. This was no innocent exploring. Instead he conquered. With every brush of those lips, every stroke of his tongue, her body bowed into his without compunction.

Without thought, she pressed her palms against his sides, her fingers digging into his rib cage to urge him closer. Images of his body covering hers forced tiny mewling sounds from her throat. How had she lived this long without having him again?

Suddenly he pulled back. Bracing his hands over her head on the wall, he rested his forehead against hers. The sound of their rapid breathing was loud in her ears. *No, please don't leave.*

She should be embarrassed by her need, ashamed to want a man who had set out to make her life miserable. But she couldn't find the self-preservation to care. It was hidden somewhere beneath the desire that had lain dormant in her body for fifteen years—and was now clamoring for fulfillment.

Then his hand pressed up on her chin, forcing her to face him. By sheer will, forcing her to open her eyes and see the man behind the touch.

"I know I'm a safe outlet for your anger, EvaMarie. Much safer than your family," he said, still struggling to get his own breath under control. That gave her more than a hint of satisfaction. As did the deep timbre of promise that resonated in his words.

"But remember, that doesn't mean I won't retaliate."

Mason awoke the next morning with the taste of EvaMarie on his lips and the scent of her in his head.

Still.

That fresh taste of guilelessness with a dark undertone of desire was like rich chocolate, igniting Mason's hunger for more. But there was too much history. Too many complications.

Yeah, he just needed to keep telling himself that—no matter how many times his body reminded him just how soft she'd felt, how much fuller she was as a woman, with intriguing curves that he ached to spend a night exploring.

Nope. Not gonna happen.

Grabbing a pair of jeans, Mason dressed quickly and headed downstairs. He could hear the faint sound of workmen from the basement. But there was no EvaMarie in the dining room, family room or kitchen, and no fresh coffee either. He made quick work of getting it set to brew, and stared broodingly out the window.

He shouldn't want to see her, but here he was searching around every corner. What was his problem?

Jeremy called to him from the hall. "Morning, Mason. Hope we didn't wake you."

"Nope. That basement has great soundproofing."

His friend grinned. "Good thing, considering the sound system you guys want installed."

"Oh yeah." That was gonna be fun.

Jeremy nodded toward the hallway. "Wanna take a look at the wall treatment going in the formal dining room? It's about halfway done."

"Sure." Mason paused long enough to fill a coffee mug, then followed. "When are the new floors going down?"

"Two weeks."

He grinned. "I'll make sure I'm absent that week."

"I don't blame you," Jeremy said, then presented the room under construction with a hand flourish worthy of Vanna White.

After admiring all the improvements Jeremy had gotten done in a very short amount of time, Mason finally got down to what he really wanted to know. "Have you seen EvaMarie this morning?"

Jeremy nodded. "Sure. She was in the barn when we got here this morning. She came over to let us in, then she went back." A frown marred his young face. "Looked like she'd had a rough night. You haven't been making her clean out more stalls, have you?"

Mason paused, eyeing his friend over the rim of his coffee mug. "Told you about that, did she?"

Jeremy eyed him back. "That was not nice."

And Mason wouldn't be allowed to forget it. "I know. Of course it won't happen again."

Jeremy looked skeptical but let his line of questioning dry up.

As soon as he could escape, Mason dragged on his

boots and headed for the barn. Jim's truck was in the drive, which made EvaMarie's presence in the stables that much more of a mystery.

As he stepped into the cool darkness of the large building, he heard the faint murmur of EvaMarie's voice. Just like the other day, all his senses stood up and took notice. The farther he walked, the clearer the words became until he realized she was singing a lullaby. As he walked past Ruby's stall, the mare had her head out of the box, ears pricked forward as she stared down the aisle toward the source of the soothing tones. Apparently Mason wasn't the only one entranced.

The sound originated from the double stall down on the far left. As he reached the half-door, Mason couldn't see EvaMarie's upper body because the mare had crowded over the half-door to her stall to rest against EvaMarie's shoulder as she sang. He could see a delicate hand resting on the horse's neck, the flash of blunt-cut nails as she lightly scratched in time with her song.

An ache shot through him, so strong his knees went weak.

Swallowing hard, Mason watched that hand—so graceful yet so capable—until the horse pulled back to glance into the stall behind her.

Jeremy had been right—EvaMarie was a mess. He'd go so far as to say she looked worse than when she'd cleaned the stall. Almost as if she'd slept all night on the barn floor.

"Yes," she crooned at the animal, unaware of his observance. "You have a pretty, pretty baby."

"That she does," Jim said, appearing from the other side of the stall door. "Very pretty indeed."

A baby. The mare had foaled during the night...which explained a lot about EvaMarie's appearance. Jim grinned when he saw Mason standing there.

"She delivered about two hours ago," he said, bringing EvaMarie's attention his way. Mason wanted to grin as she suddenly smoothed a hand over her hair, then plucked out a piece of straw, but figured she might not appreciate that he found her disheveled state cute.

"Why didn't you come get me?" he asked instead. "I could have helped."

"She's not your horse," EvaMarie replied, quiet but firm. "Besides, Lucy did the work. We were just here in case of trouble."

The reserve he heard in her voice was clear. Mason just wasn't sure if she was still angry with him, or embarrassed by their confrontation the night before. He couldn't resist teasing her to find out.

"Sure looks like you worked hard to me...all night long." He let that grin slip out. "Jeremy accused me of making you clean out stalls again."

Her cheeks flushed pink. He would swear he heard her mumble as she turned away, "You'd think they'd never seen a woman get dirty before..."

Oh, Mason hadn't...at least not in the way he wanted.

Funny how EvaMarie could do the simplest of things and it would crack his resistance like a sledgehammer—like laugh with Jeremy, blow across a cup of hot chocolate, bristle at Mason's comments. Every move was way sexier than it should be—or maybe he just had a really dirty mind.

As she disappeared from his range of sight, Jim inched closer. "She told me about the argument with her father."

"Yes?"

Jim didn't look angry, so maybe Mason wasn't in too much trouble.

"Well, there's lots of time to talk while you're waiting and watching for a birth to happen. Anyway, Mr.

Hyatt has always been a difficult man. I almost quit more than once."

"Been here long?" Mason didn't remember the older man from his brief stint here as a teenager.

Jim nodded. "I was here for a while, then moved to Florida for several years to care for my wife's parents. We moved back after they both passed away."

Mason knew he shouldn't ask, didn't have the right to, but he heard himself asking anyway. "Were you here when Chris died?"

"Yes," Jim said, his tone low as he glanced toward the stable entrance as if seeing something that wasn't there. "I watched Mr. Hyatt carry that boy's body out of the woods himself. It was a tough time for everyone, but especially for EvaMarie."

"Losing a brother must have been hard, especially at that age." Mason couldn't imagine a tiny EvaMarie with no one to hold her, comfort her in her grief.

"It was." Jim met his gaze. "Losing her parents right along with him was even harder."

Mason zeroed his attention in on the other man. "What do you mean?"

"He wasn't always like this, you know. Mr. Hyatt was tough, and had a quick temper, but he loved his kids. Spent loads of time with them...until the day they lost Chris."

Mason instinctively glanced toward EvaMarie but couldn't see her anymore. How confusing must the change in her father have been? On top of never being able to mention the brother she'd idolized...

"It rocked her entire world," Jim murmured, seeming lost in his own memories of that time.

No doubt it had lasting repercussions for her... Mason's own loss at a young age had hit him hard, left lasting scars, and he'd had his brother and father to lean on.

EvaMarie had been all alone.

Suddenly Mason was hit with the realization of how long they'd been standing there talking…and how quiet EvaMarie was. He glanced over Jim's shoulder again but didn't see her.

Taking his lead, Jim moved away to look behind the open part of the door, then he gestured Mason in with a smile.

Some internal instinct had Mason entering with quiet steps. As EvaMarie came into view, Mason's heart melted. She sat curled against the barn wall in a thick pile of hay, fast asleep. He remembered how she could sleep anywhere, but this had to be a first.

As much as he didn't want to, as much as he wanted to hang on to the distance and anger, Mason couldn't look at her without seeing a gorgeous woman, grime and all. Not only that, he saw a woman who had endured a lot, who had stood on her own two feet without a hell of a lot of support, possibly none.

A woman he wanted the chance to know, even if it was complicated. But he doubted he'd ever be able to see her as the enemy anymore.

Mason glanced toward the stall, listening to the soft sounds of the horses as mama and baby got to know each other. "Everything good here?" he asked.

Jim nodded. "The mare's a pro, and she handled the birth like one." He eyed Mason a moment, then looked over at the sleeping beauty. "I think EvaMarie already has a buyer. The stables will be cleared soon enough. She's gonna miss them though, and vice versa."

Thinking back to what he'd seen when he entered the barn, Mason completely understood. "Once you get the mare settled, text me, then go home."

Jim's eyes widened. "But boss—"

"No." Mason's voice was firm, carrying through the aisle. "You've been here all night. I'm more than capable of watching her." *Both of them.* "Go get some rest. There's nothing here that can't wait until tomorrow. I'll get EvaMarie inside."

"Poor thing is exhausted. When she's devoted, she's all in—and she wasn't leaving until they were both okay."

From what Mason had learned, that sounded about right.

Nine

Carrying a sleeping woman was a unique experience for Mason. He hadn't expected it to be quite so emotional—and it wasn't, not in a soft, mushy way. The feelings rushing through him were fierce, protective and full of demanding need. Add in yesterday's ups and downs and a fitful night's sleep dreaming of this woman's lips, and he had a feeling he was about to be in a very tough spot.

He skirted by the dining room without being noticed by anyone inside. As he climbed the stairs, EvaMarie began to stir, but didn't open her eyes until they reached the landing.

Even then, a sleepy haze covered her baby blues. They barely opened as he watched her fight her body's normally heavy sleep mode to handle whatever trouble she'd landed herself in now.

If her habit had stayed the same all these years, EvaMarie slept like the dead once she got going.

He carried her to her room, smiling at the feminine touches and soothing green color on the way through to her bath. Once inside, he eased her down onto a little padded bench and kneeled before her, slightly uncomfortable when the comparison to a prince before a princess came to mind.

"EvaMarie, honey, you need to wake up."

Her brow furrowed, but those sleepy blues cracked open once more. "I'm sorry," she murmured, "I'm just so tired."

"Not sleeping will do that to you. But you're also dirty."

Her eyes widened, and she looked down at her dusty clothes. Then he heard a soft sigh. "I almost don't care," she said.

Mason wasn't falling for that. "But you'll blame me when you wake up in dirty sheets, so let's go."

"Go where?" Her lids slid closed, and she slumped toward the wall.

"Oh, no, you don't." Mason pulled her forward with a tiny shake. "EvaMarie, you have to shower."

"With you?"

Mason's world stopped. "What, Evie?"

He saw her eyelids flicker, but it took a minute for her to brave opening them.

"Will you stay with me?" she finally whispered.

His hands tightened, his need to tear through their boundaries seriously compromising his resolve. "That's not a good idea," he managed to say. "For a lot of reasons."

The barest sheen of tears made her eyes look like damp blue flowers, catching him off guard before she closed them once more. "You're right. I'll be fine."

But *he* wouldn't be.

He hadn't been fine since Evie had come back into his life—and for just a little while, he wanted a taste of what they could be together once more.

Slow but sure, he reached out and started working on the buttons down the front of her flannel shirt.

"What are you doing?"

The simplest answer was the best, because he wasn't entirely sure what he was doing. Going out of his mind, maybe? "Undressing you."

Her breath caught, then she said, "You don't have to do this."

Just as he had yesterday, he reached out and lifted her chin with his knuckles until there was nowhere else for her to look but at him. "No, I don't have to. I want to."

I want you.

Layer by layer he peeled away her clothes; she'd bundled up to keep herself warm. Pulling that last T-shirt over her head to reveal skin and lingerie had him sucking in his breath. Blood and heat pooled low. EvaMarie had filled out into some serious feminine curves. The combination of creamy skin, pink lace and the scent that was uniquely hers sent his heartbeat into overdrive.

This was really happening.

And it looked like he'd found the perfect thing to wake EvaMarie. Though her lashes were lowered, she still watched him. The throb of her pulse at the base of her neck served as a barometer for her response. As did the quiver of her bottom lip.

He eased her to her feet, eager for more. One thing about Mason, once he committed to a cause, he was all in. This time, his entire body agreed.

Before he could get carried away, he turned on the shower to let the hot water work its way up to the second floor. Then he stripped off his own sweatshirt and thermal undershirt. Her eyes drank in every inch of flesh, giving Mason an unaccustomed feeling of pride. He worked hard. His body showed it.

And he was more than happy for EvaMarie to enjoy the results.

Stepping closer, he reached for one of her hands, lifted it for a light kiss, then rested it right over his heart. Suddenly she curled her fingers, scraping her blunt nails against his skin. Just as he'd ached for in the stables.

His body flooded with desire, hardening with need. Soon. Soon.

Without preamble, he unzipped EvaMarie's jeans and shoved every layer beneath down to her upper thighs. He didn't give her time to object, but guided her back down onto the bench and made short work baring her legs and feet. She had shapely muscles—obviously he wasn't the only one who worked out. And painted toenails—just like always. He grinned at the burgundy polish with gold flecks. A sexy mature choice compared to the neon pinks she'd been into when she was young.

As he lifted her to her feet again, he kissed each of her flushed cheeks. "There's no need to be embarrassed, Evie," he murmured against the smooth slope of her jaw. "This is just you and me."

She curved her fingers over the front of his waistband as if holding on for dear life. "It's been a long time, Mason…you might not like—"

He cut her off with a kiss, tasting her with lips, tongue and purpose. Just as he had last night. Only this time he let the rest of his body join in the game. He tilted slightly, rubbing his chest against lace and skin. The friction drove him crazy. So did the clutch of her hands around his biceps, urging him closer.

He made quick work of his own jeans, but he couldn't

bring naked skin to naked skin soon enough. Evie's gasps and groans filled the air. Reaching around her, he placed a hot and heavy palm on each of her butt cheeks to pull her flush against him. The breath seemed to stop in her chest. She held herself perfectly still. His body throbbed hard, demanding more.

"I'm scared, Mason," she murmured.

He knew she spoke the truth, and was probably asking for reassurance at the same time. But this was something she needed to choose willingly.

Stepping back, he retreated out of her reach. Her expression shattered, but he refused to be swayed. Sliding back the glass door, he stepped into the shower, fighting a shiver when the hot water hit his back, adding to the overload of sensations.

"Join me, Evie," he said, and held out his hand.

Her choice. His chance. His only thought as she took his hand was *hell, yes*.

The last vestige of sleepiness fled as EvaMarie stepped beneath the onslaught of hot water. She'd thought taking off her bra had been hard. But in the steamy space her skin went tight, her nipples even tighter.

How could she want him this much and be so afraid at the same time?

Her desire was dampened by her fear, her self-conscious awareness of the changes in her body and her life. She wasn't a teenager anymore, but she barely had more experience than all those years ago. Would she disappoint him? Would he find her boring?

Still she couldn't walk away from this chance to have Mason one more time. Tears flooded her eyes, forcing her to blink. She needed this. Needed him. He waited patiently, quietly. Though tentative, she reached out her hand to his chest, her eyes closing as she savored the textures of skin and water together.

This was new, exciting. Her heart pounded in her chest; her blood pounded lower. No matter what happened later, she simply couldn't stop.

A step closer, and she couldn't resist glancing up. Mason watched her with a hooded gaze. His body told her he was more than interested. And that look—it conveyed the primal need of an adult male. She was more than happy for him to take what he wanted...so why didn't he?

She caught her bottom lip between her teeth. "Mason?"

"Come to me, sweetheart. Show me what you want."

But that wasn't what she wanted. She needed him to direct, to take...to overpower her so she could stop thinking for once and just feel.

Again he tilted her chin up with his knuckles. She should hate that, resent being manhandled. Instead the gesture made her feel cherished, seen.

"We're gonna do this together, okay, Evie?"

Mesmerized by the intensity in his blue eyes, she nodded.

"Then touch me however you want. Learn whatever you like."

Somehow, his permission loosened her inhibitions. She pressed close, gasping as every inch of her met every inch of him. Slick, steamy, sexy. She explored his body with her own until the friction had her parting her thighs.

Mason took full advantage to thrust his leg between hers. She rose against him, entranced by the feel of hard masculine muscle against her most sensitive skin. Again and again she lifted against him, dragging out the sensations, aided by the guidance of Mason's hands pulling and pushing her hips. His touch added just enough force, and a ton of excitement.

Her whimpers echoed around them. Her body flushed hot as she rode him. With each glide, the friction of his body against her core made her insides tighten with delicious anticipation. Little mini-explosions prepared her for the fireworks to come. Somehow her nails were digging into Mason's shoulders. She should stop, but she couldn't. He wouldn't let her.

Then his hot, open mouth covered the side of her neck, sucking, drawing her orgasm to the surface until she exploded with a cry she couldn't hold inside. His hands pinned her hard against his thigh. His masculine growl vibrated against her sensitive skin, prolonging the ecstasy.

And Mason wasn't about to let that be the end.

He switched places so that her back slammed flush against the tile wall. He rubbed against her, his movements rough, urgent. "Oh, Evie, yes."

Every nerve ending seemed to answer his call. She arched against him, needing, demanding. Lost in sensation, she somehow managed to open her eyes to find his damp drenched blue eyes cataloging her every expression.

"Mason, please," she begged.

His trademark grin made an appearance. "With pleasure." He ripped open the condom packet he'd pulled from his jeans earlier and made quick work of covering himself. His groan as he pulled away for mere seconds made her body soften that much more. He didn't ask, didn't wait for her to comply.

He simply did what he wanted with her. All of her.

Lifting one of her legs at the knee, he hooked his arm beneath it. Opened her wide. Left her vulnerable to whatever he needed of her. The wall and her hands on his shoulders gave her leverage, but Mason wasn't about to let her fall.

Bending his knees, he made a place for himself right where she wanted him. He eased himself barely inside her. She gasped, tilting her hips in an attempt to accommodate his size. It had been too long. She was embarrassed at how long.

"Easy, baby," he murmured. "Let me make it good."

Just like that, she relaxed. Mason worked his hips, opening her little by little, filling her. The sounds he made lit sparks inside her. His groans, grunts and masculine cries carried the wordless emotions straight to her heart. She pushed her hips toward him, her body now more than eager for his full possession.

As he slid in to the hilt, he moaned through gritted teeth. With a shudder, his whole body strained, his head falling back in a kind of ecstasy that mesmerized her. The pressure between her thighs anchored her to him, to this experience. She thought he would make quick work of it now, driving himself to oblivion.

Instead he paused. Those big hands left her hips to cup her face, and she felt her soul crack a little as his mouth covered hers in a soft, sensual taste that belied the strain of his lower body. His eyes remained open, creating a connection that EvaMarie vaguely thought she might regret later but couldn't turn away from in this moment.

Then he trailed his hands back down, tweaking every sensitive spot along the journey. When he regained his hold, she braced herself for the ride. Sure enough, his body took over, demanding its due.

Every thrust forced her up on her toes, but she didn't notice as sparks flew through her body. She strained with him. Eager. Tense. They both moved on instinct alone until Mason pinned her hip to hip. As their cries mingled in the steam, EvaMarie knew she'd never be the same.

Ten

Horse—check. Workers—check. Food—check.

Mason balanced the tray with care as he made his way back upstairs. The house was not only quiet, it was empty. He'd sent everyone home a couple of hours early tonight, eager to have the place to himself.

What awaited him in EvaMarie's bedroom would be a challenge. He had no doubt.

She'd been asleep before he could get her head on the pillow. So Mason left her to rest while he took care of the work crew and checked a couple of times to make sure Lucy and her foal were getting along well. He knew EvaMarie would want an update when she woke. And hopefully she'd want other things, as well.

But he had a feeling his little filly would be having second thoughts the minute her eyes opened.

He let himself into the darkened room and stood for a moment, soaking in the stillness and the sound of

Evie's breathing as she slept. He should be having second thoughts, too. Way more than EvaMarie. So why wasn't he shaking in his boots? Instead he was bringing replenishment to the woman so he could—hopefully—have his way with her again.

God, being with EvaMarie had been nothing like when they were teenagers. Before she'd been tentative, untried. Her hesitation this morning had made him think she'd be the same, but soon she'd been as hot as the water and as responsive as hell. He could still hear her cries echoing off the tiles in the bathroom.

He wanted to hear them again.

Setting the tray on the chaise in her room, he shucked his jeans before easing back the comforter. Suddenly EvaMarie sat straight up. "What are you doing?" she gasped.

Distracted by more bare skin than he'd hoped to see this soon, Mason spent a moment trying to pry his tongue from the roof of his mouth. Noticing the direction of his gaze, Evie gasped again, this time jerking the comforter up over her nakedness. Which was a shame.

He tried to tease her with a grin. "I'm coming back to bed," he said, his voice gravelly with the desire evoked by just the thought of being with her again. "But we can go to my bed if you'd prefer. It's a little bigger. More space for rolling around."

Her eyes widened, and he could just see the images she was tossing around in her mind before she blinked. With innocence overlaying a deep river of sensuality, she was so damn intriguing.

But then panic engulfed her expression. She scrambled back to sit against the padded headboard. "Mason, look, I'm so sorry."

Hmm… Was she sorry she'd slept with him? Because he'd never push her for more than she was willing to give. Or was it something else? This time, her expression wasn't telling the whole story. He let a raised brow speak on his end.

EvaMarie swallowed hard. "I realize you're my employer, and I did not mean to throw myself at you."

Ah, this he could answer. "You didn't."

"I remember asking—" The blush that bloomed over her cheeks was bright enough for him to see in the dim light coming from behind the pulled curtains. Luckily she looked away and didn't notice his smile. He didn't want her to think he was making fun of her. He was simply, well, to his surprise, he was simply enjoying the ins and outs of being with her again.

"And I remember accepting," he finished for her. "I consented way before any clothes came off." He crawled onto the bed to get closer, though he left her with the protection of the comforter. "And I'm really glad I did."

A quick cut of her gaze his way showed him her surprise. "Um. Thank you?"

He chuckled, easing the tension enough for her to meet him face-to-face again.

"Is this gonna be awkward?" she asked.

"Depends."

When she tilted her head to the side, a waterfall of tangled hair spread over her bare shoulder. As the image of burying his face in that silky mass came over Mason, he almost groaned.

But she wasn't done asking questions. "Depends on what?"

"On where this goes now." He flicked his tongue over his suddenly dry lips. "I know what I want, but I'm not gonna push you into anything you don't want to do. Anything that makes you uncomfortable."

"What do you want?" she whispered.

Which only made him think of what other words he wanted her to whisper to him.

"I want the chance to take you to bed."

It wasn't romantic, he knew that. But it was honest. Besides, "romance" and "relationships" came with a lot of complications—especially with EvaMarie.

To his surprise, she said, "On one condition."

This was new. "What's that?"

"That there're no obligations in the end. And no rules as we go."

To Mason's surprise, a trickle of disappointment wiggled through his gut. Why in the world would he be disappointed? EvaMarie was offering him every man's dream—unattached sex with a sensual, beautiful, responsive woman living right in the same house with him. "That's not anything like dating, you know."

She shrugged. "That's not what I'm looking for."

Me, neither. He crawled toward her on all fours, enjoying the widening of her eyes as he stalked her. "But that's two rules, not one."

Her giggle was spontaneous and went straight to his nether regions. He buried his face against her neck. "Then I guess we can have dessert before dinner, right?"

EvaMarie plopped down on the staircase a couple steps up from the bottom. Long minutes of pacing had worn her out, yet parts of her still felt all jittery. The nerves were getting to her.

Mason had left this afternoon to meet with Kane and their lawyer, who had then taken them to dinner. Which was perfectly fine. A weekend in bed together couldn't last forever—nor should she want it to.

She was simply eager for him to see the storage system that had been added to the wine cellar today. That's all.

Oh, who was she kidding? Sure, Mason had been happy to take her up on what she'd offered, and the memory of her request had her face flaming hot. He'd even been complimentary, patient and enthusiastic, which had led to the most incredible two days of her life and done wonders for her ego.

But the minute he'd walked out the door this afternoon, doubt had set in. Her impulsive actions had been the result of a whopper of a few days—the argument with her father, then Mason, then lack of sleep and seeing the foal being born. She certainly hadn't been thinking straight, but couldn't bring herself to regret it.

She simply wasn't ready for it to end.

Since there were no rules, she wasn't sure what to expect. Then tonight, he hadn't come home…no phone call or even a text to let her know where he was after ample time for dinner. Her fingers were crossed Mason wasn't simply avoiding her because he'd had his fill and now he was done.

She shifted on the hard stair. Wouldn't that be a humiliating conversation?

Yes, asking him for some no-strings-attached time had been unprecedented, as well as unpremeditated. But she'd realized that she wanted Mason, without the complications that had come before—and now she could have him.

But for how long?

Mason had agreed…but did he regret his decision the minute he'd left her? Had he told Kane? Were they even now trying to figure out a way to fire her…to get her to leave without angering her enough to file a sexual harassment suit?

Just as her panic reached fever pitch, she heard a key in the front lock. Her stomach clenched hard enough to force her to swallow, but she couldn't tell if it was fear or anticipation. Then she heard—wait, was that a woman?

The wave of nausea rushing over her kept her immobile, so when the door opened she stood and continued to stand there like a scared rabbit, shaking in her sweatpants. *Busted.*

The wave of relief to find herself facing a group of people, and not just Mason with some woman he'd brought home, was short-lived. Because she knew these people. Mason. Kane. John Roberts. And Liza Young.

Liza's gaze swept up the stairs and right to EvaMarie with her bare feet, baggy sweats and T-shirt. A wave of heat followed that look, lighting EvaMarie with embarrassment everywhere it touched.

"Wow, EvaMarie," the other woman said in an exaggerated drawl. "Whatever are you doing here?"

The heat and nausea combined caused EvaMarie to break out in a sweat. She glanced at Mason, hoping for a little help, but he remained silent, his expression a touch perplexed. Her smile felt sickly, but she offered it to the rest of the group anyway. "Could you all excuse us a moment?"

Surely Mason got her point, but he only went as far as the stairs, even when she moved as if to go farther down the hallway. His frown didn't bode well. Kane and John spoke in a low murmur, but Liza never looked away. With the uncomfortable feeling that her oversized T didn't cover nearly enough, EvaMarie pulled at the hem.

She returned her attention to Mason, and her nerves flared. "Couldn't you have let me know you were bringing people home?" she snapped.

His right brow shot up. He'd gotten pretty good at the haughty look for someone who hadn't grown up using it. "I didn't realize I needed permission to bring people to *my* house."

Nerves gave way to pain as the remark hit her like a slap to the face. Then a giggle came from right behind Mason's shoulder. They both turned to find Liza listening, her overly mascaraed eyes wide, taking it all in. Her grin turned EvaMarie's stomach, because she'd seen it before—whenever Liza knew she'd just landed a juicy bit of gossip that she could use to her advantage.

"Well, Mason, I thought this was your place now," she said, blinking as if her remark was innocence itself. "But that does make me curious as to what she's doing here…"

Mason glanced back at EvaMarie with a look that said since this situation was all her fault, she could get her own self out of it. Quelling the unexpected urge to smack him, she quietly filled the silence. "I work here."

Liza's exaggerated gasp made EvaMarie want to cringe, but she maintained her stoic expression with the last ounce of her strength.

"Whoa," Liza said, throwing a look around the room as if to include everyone there. "Did y'all hear that? From princess to pauper. Bet that's a big change."

Mason's frown deepened. Luckily this time it wasn't directed at EvaMarie. He turned to face Liza. "Nonsense. EvaMarie knows this place better than anyone," he said. "And she's quite talented with organization and interior decorating."

Kane chimed in too. "She's doing a great job overseeing the renovations. Let's go look. After all, that's why you're here."

Mason led the way. John Roberts was quick to cross the foyer and offer his arm to Liza, but she was just as quick to get in her parting shot. "Well, she's dressing the part, isn't she?" The words were whispered to her partner, but echoed off the walls of the cylindrical room.

The hitch in Kane's stride said he'd heard, but still he paused right below EvaMarie. "Join us?" he asked.

Words wouldn't come right now. As much as EvaMarie knew she'd be the object of ridicule every time she met someone of Liza's caliber in the future, that didn't mean it didn't hurt. She was too soft-hearted, her daddy had always said. But truly, it was Mason's response that had hurt her more. If she went with them, she'd probably do something stupid like cry. So she simply shook her head.

The pity in Kane's look quickened her getaway. Her hope to witness the excitement on Mason's face when he saw the new wine cellar pieces didn't matter anymore. Climbing the stairs proved tortuous, as did the whirl of her thoughts. She could go to bed, but Mason would just find her there later—probably crying. Or maybe not.

After all, he didn't seem very interested in her at the moment.

There was only one thing she could think of to soothe herself. A deep breath helped her pull on her big girl panties...along with jeans and a pair of boots. She'd known she was naïve, but not how much until this very moment.

Now she knew. When Mason said this wouldn't be like dating, he hadn't been lying. This definitely wasn't dating...it wasn't even friendship.

Eleven

Mason gritted his teeth against Liza's inane chatter as he walked their little party back down the promenade to the foyer.

"What, no EvaMarie to see us out like a good girl?" she asked, her giggle scraping Mason's nerves. The glasses of wine she'd had at dinner had combined with the sampling they'd had downstairs to celebrate their renovations, pushing her into the just-inebriated-enough-to-lose-any-claim-to-class stage of drunkenness.

She'd been an unfortunate discovery as John Roberts's dinner companion when their lawyer had introduced them to the stable owner who was also a fellow lawyer. About ten minutes ago, Mason had reached his utmost capacity for stupid and catty remarks for the evening—even if they had learned quite a lot about a few key players in the local upper echelons tonight.

From his increasingly stoic expression, it looked as though Kane felt the same.

"I can't wait to tell the girls that juicy story," the woman rattled on.

"Liza." John Roberts's soft rebuke didn't have any backbone to it.

Mason didn't have the patience to be that soft. His voice came out a low growl. "Excuse me?"

"You know, the whole privileged-daughter-is-now-the-hired-help story," Liza gushed.

Mason had to wonder how long she'd been holding this in. Maybe she'd taken his silence earlier this evening as permission.

"She's always been such a Goody Two-shoes." Liza threw a sly glance at Mason. "At first, I thought maybe she had a totally different reason for being here, but she certainly wasn't dressing to entice anyone, was she?"

Like you would have? Clenching his jaw to keep the words inside, Mason had a sudden epiphany. EvaMarie hadn't been dressed to entice, but she'd definitely been waiting for someone. Crap. That's why she'd been upset that he'd brought people home. She didn't want advanced warning because she felt any kind of ownership over the house or him. She'd wanted the common courtesy of being able to prepare herself before someone came in—something Mason wasn't used to dealing with, so it hadn't occurred to him.

Man, he'd better get these two out of here before he said something he shouldn't...and gave away more than EvaMarie would appreciate.

Aiming for a distraction, Mason ushered them out the door, then watched as John Roberts gallantly helped Liza down the stairs and out to his car. Halfway across the driveway she ditched her heels, leaving her date to pick up the pieces.

"That woman's laugh could be used as a torture device," Kane said from beside him.

Mason allowed himself a chuckle before turning away from the departing couple. He faced Kane, the man he'd always been honest with. "I screwed up, didn't I?"

"I believe so."

He'd just seen EvaMarie's haughty expression, heard her irritated tone and snapped back in kind. And reacted like the moody teenager he used to be.

Mason stared out into the night as he thought about the implications of tonight's encounter. "Do you think she's told anyone that she's here, working for us?"

"I doubt it." Kane rocked back on the heels of his cowboy boots. "Her parents have taught her the exaggerated importance of preserving her privacy."

"Yeah."

"Did you see her face when Liza made that snide remark about her clothes?"

"No." He hadn't even heard the remark. He'd been too intent on showing off, which meant getting the others downstairs and away from a situation he wasn't sure how to handle.

"Don't think I've ever seen a face go that blank."

EvaMarie's parents had drilled their version of acceptable behavior into her so thoroughly that making a scene or standing up for herself never would have occurred to her. She'd taken what Liza dished out without a complaint, though he noticed she hadn't joined them downstairs.

"I'd better go check on her," Mason said.

The brothers parted with a quick hand slap, and Kane headed for his truck. Mason went to EvaMarie's room, but she wasn't there. Stumped, he stood on the threshold for a moment.

Maybe she was in Chris's room? After all, he'd bet she was more than upset. But no. She wasn't there either.

You're a smart boy, Mason. Figure it out.

A sudden memory rose of watching a young EvaMarie saddle her horse with tears flowing down her rounded cheeks after yet another dressing down from her father. Did she still love to ride to clear her head? Did she still sit by her favorite tree on the side of the stream that flowed through the middle of the estate into the lake?

He bet she did.

After a quick change into jeans and boots, Mason confirmed his suspicions when he found one of the mares' stalls empty. He quickly saddled up Ruby, groaning as he swung into the saddle. It had been too many days since he'd been on a horse. His growing business activities here cut into his riding time.

He needed to change that.

The ride felt good, free. He moved with the horse, limbering up and clearing his head as he gained speed, though he didn't push the mare too hard in the dark. Since he hadn't been back in the wooded area along the creek as an adult, Mason dismounted and led the horse down the still-clear path he remembered from all those years ago.

The soft whinny of EvaMarie's horse corrected his course just a little. She didn't glance his way as he broke from the tree line. He tied Ruby near Lucy and cautiously approached the blanket EvaMarie was reclining on. "Hey," he said softly, not wanting to startle her if she'd slept through his arrival.

"Hey," she replied.

Which gave him nothing to go on. After all, EvaMarie had evolved into a master at hiding her emotions. Unsure what else to say, Mason lay down next to her in the darkness. The blanket provided a thick barrier over the mixture of bare dirt and clumps of grass beneath them. The trickle of water from the stream reminded him of the soothing sound when they'd lain here and held each other so long ago. The sky showcased an array of bright stars framed by tree limbs that he didn't remember from his last visit here.

Of course, they hadn't come here for the stargazing back thcn.

"I wasn't demanding anything from you, Mason," she finally said, her voice sounding huskier, deeper than before. "I don't think I should have to demand the common courtesy afforded to anyone living in the same house—like normal roommates."

Whoa. Though she'd spoken quietly, Mason recognized an unfamiliar tone in EvaMarie's voice. It wasn't even the same tone she'd used when she'd spoken to him in anger the other day. Instead, it was the simple assurance that the facts were in her favor—the facts that called him an overreacting idiot.

Before he could formulate his thoughts, she went on. "I realize that might not be a courtesy given to paid employees—"

"Shush, will ya?"

Leaning up on his elbow, Mason stared at the oval shape of her face, but had trouble making out the details in the dark. "There's no need to play the martyr, EvaMarie."

He rushed on when she opened her mouth to parry with him. "It was thoughtless of me to bring people home without letting you know. Hell, it was thoughtless not to tell you we'd gone to dinner after our meeting, then had drinks. I'm sorry."

She must have been as surprised as he was, because she didn't speak.

"I'm not used to having to think about those things, about other people. Kane and I never had company much except our weekly poker game with the guys. And half of them were stable hands. They just walked in off the job for dinner."

"Thus the poker room, huh?"

Smart girl. "You got it."

He heard her take a deep breath. "I'm sorry, Mason. I was just embarrassed, I guess."

Should he warn her she'd be even more so if Liza had her way? He'd face that tomorrow. For better or worse, Mason didn't want to shatter the now lighter mood.

But it seemed as though she was going to do it for him. "I don't think this is gonna work, Mason," she said, what sounded like regret weighing down her voice.

Was that the same emotion sinking like a rock into his stomach?

He didn't want it to be. Still he asked, "Why?"

She stood, presenting her back. "I know I asked for this, but honestly I don't know how—"

The strangled sound that choked off her words resonated with him—because he didn't know either. His history of plenty of one-night stands and a couple of longer stretches with the same woman didn't match anything in his situation with EvaMarie. Here, he was with a woman he knew, but didn't know just the same. He suspected she didn't know this side of herself very well either.

But he wanted to know her, every part of her, with a desire that was more than likely dangerous.

"Haven't you ever wanted to make your own rules?"

What prompted his question, he wasn't sure. But he sensed that something inside Evie was changing, breaking free, and he wanted to encourage it.

She responded with a huff of a laugh. "Only forever."

With a firm hand, he reached for her arm and turned her to face him. "Then we'll do that here. Together."

"Why are you doing this?"

He hadn't expected the question or the aching sadness in her voice. But he couldn't ignore it. "We were friends once, long before—" He cleared his throat. "We were friends first. Let's remember that." Especially in this place that had seen so much of that young love— not just the sex, but talking, laughing and the sharing of dreams. He owed that time something.

"Like friends with benefits?" she asked with a giggle.

"Oh, I definitely hope so."

She seemed to sober, though he couldn't see her features really well. "How?"

Good question. "One day at a time."

"That simple?"

"That simple. And the first rule should be that common courtesy rules the show. Agreed?"

She didn't speak but simply nodded.

"And rule number two…" He pushed forward, meeting her chest with his, combining their body heat with explosive results. Her gasp said she felt it too.

Breathlessly she asked, "Rule number two?"

"Let me show you."

And boy did he.

Drawing her up to her knees, Mason moved in close before she could catch her breath, leaving just enough room for his hands. Very busy hands. All too soon he'd taken her shirt off, and the cool night air kissed her bare skin. The brush of his shirt against the tips of her breasts had her gasping for air.

Then he efficiently removed that final barrier, and heated skin pressed to heated skin. If EvaMarie remembered nothing else from their time together, she knew that first moment of full body touch would stand out above all else.

But she wasn't content to wait on him this time. Her own urgency pushed her to grasp his muscled shoulders, to pull him as close as possible. One of his knees slid between hers, the length of his thigh pressing her jeans roughly against her feminine core. Her moans mingled with the sound of the water nearby and the rush of the wind, all intertwining to heighten EvaMarie's acute senses.

Reaching around, Mason cupped her jeans-clad bottom with his large hands, pulling her up along his leg, then pushing her down until her knees once more touched the ground. The force of his touch and the strain of his body told her this was happening quickly.

His breath deepened, the sound accelerating with the beat of her heart in her ears. His urgency fed her own. Her grip tightened. Her core ached. And her brain short-circuited in her pursuit of making any sense of what was happening.

Better to just feel. Thinking was overrated.

His mouth devoured hers. Nibbling, sucking, exploring. EvaMarie was ready to do a little exploring of her own. Her hands traveled down his back, laying claim to the smooth territory below his waistband. More than enough to overflow her palms, his butt cheeks were squeezable and oh, so sexy. The muscles flexed as he did what he wanted with her body, previewing the dance they would indulge in all too soon.

Suddenly he sucked at her neck, causing everything inside her to tighten—including her fingers. Her nails dug against his skin. In return, he set his teeth against the tendons running along her throat. Their groans filled the air.

"Again," he gasped.

The combined tension and need left EvaMarie light-headed on a runaway train. And she wouldn't have had it any other way.

The same need had Mason fumbling with the button of her jeans. His combined chuckle and growl of frustration floated over her nerve endings like an electrical current. The sheer sensations of being with him like this pulsed beneath her skin.

Within minutes of getting naked, Mason lay back on the blanket. "Take what you want, Evie," he gasped.

To her surprise, the idea inspired her, though her natural hesitation still reared its ugly head.

"Now, Evie."

The force of his words unlocked her barriers. Instead of the slow and careful advance she would have expected, her body leaped into movement. Crawling over him, relief spread through her as she straddled his thighs. Relief, and a rush of desire so strong it was almost a cramp.

Mason was ready for her, but he didn't reach out to help. He positioned himself like a platter on display, eager for her to avail herself of his bounty. So she did. With a single swift move, she made them one. Her entire body gasped at the intrusion, her mind overtaken with the sensation of fullness. Her muscles clasped down in ecstasy.

Mason's moan played over her ears, heightening her experience.

In fact, every response to her movements held her breathless. Never had she felt such a sense of power or responsibility—she could do whatever she wanted with his permission, yet what she wanted was to make it good for him too.

Her body adopted a natural rhythm, one learned through a lifetime of riding. Mason grasped her hands in his, leveraging her up yet keeping them connected. She could watch his face as she moved, learning what entranced him, what ramped up his need and what sent him over the moon.

Before long they were both gasping, playing along the edges of ecstasy without falling over. All too soon, Eva-Marie couldn't hold back. She thrust hard. Once. Twice. The explosion catapulted her into a feeling of flight.

Mason reared up, wrapping his arms tightly around her. His guttural cries against her skin sparked shock waves in the aftermath. A sound EvaMarie knew she'd never forget.

An experience she'd carry with her for a lifetime.

Twelve

"Jeremy, do you know where EvaMarie went?" Mason asked as he stepped into his bedroom.

The crew had repainted the room the day before and was now addressing the crown molding, among other upgrades to the dressing area and adjoining bath.

Jeremy glanced up from his clipboard and blinked, but didn't answer.

"I saw her car leave as I headed back from the barn," Mason prompted.

"Ah, EvaMarie, yes," Jeremy said. "She headed over to the library, I believe."

The library? She'd always been a reader, but—suddenly her father's voice came back to him, *"She got a job at the library."*

Mason tried to continue the conversation casually, but in the back of his mind, unease grew. More than that, his worry unsettled him.

Within twenty minutes he hit the road. The main

branch of the town's library wasn't too far from the house. When he entered the building, two librarians eyed him as he walked past, but he continued on his hunt. Finally, a husky, resonating voice led him to...the children's room?

The door to the glassed-in room remained open, but Mason didn't need to stand right on the threshold. Eva-Marie's voice carried, so he stood to the right so he could watch her from outside her line of sight. Mason let go of the words and simply focused on the cadence of her voice. As much as he adored that sound, what struck him the most was her expression. Calm. Happy.

She's enjoying herself.

Since his return, the closest he'd seen EvaMarie to happy had been during their discussions about the house, and with the horses. Their most intimate moments together were about a different kind of enjoyment. And he'd seen all too many instances of the blank mask she used to hide her emotions. But this, he could only describe as carefree.

Her guarded look returned as soon as story time ended. Their gazes met through the glass, and Mason could almost see the barriers go up, which told him more than she probably wanted. It meant this place, this time, meant something special to her. Remembering how much she'd loved books when he'd known her before, seeing all the books around her rooms since his return, and her joy in being among these children, he'd have to be completely clueless not to have figured it out.

And he was glad she'd taken steps to create something meaningful in her life.

But her cautious approach said she might not have been ready to share it with him. "Hey. What are you doing here?"

The tone wasn't exactly accusatory. He couldn't put

his finger on it, but definitely the caution was there. And for once he wasn't quite sure how to answer...because saying he'd rushed down here because he was afraid she was interviewing for another position would make him more vulnerable than he was ready for.

"Miss Marie?"

Mason looked down to find a little blonde sprite between them. Her arm wrapped around EvaMarie's thigh, as if to claim her in the face of the big bad man across from them. He glanced up at EvaMarie with a questioning look.

"My full name is too much for some of the younger ones to pronounce," she said with a rueful grin.

"Is he your daddy?" the little girl persisted.

"What?" Mason's tone conveyed a wealth of *hell no*.

He immediately recognized his response as a bit too much when a slight wash of tears filled the wide eyes watching him. Unlike him, EvaMarie knew exactly how to handle the situation. With natural ease, she bent down. "He's my friend," she said in a soothing tone. "Like Joshua is your friend."

"Do you play together?"

This one Mason had an answer for... "All the time."

EvaMarie shot him a glare, even as her face flamed.

But the little miss wasn't done yet. "Sometimes Josh will pull my hair."

Mason choked back his laugh as best he could. EvaMarie's skin almost glowed in her embarrassment. But this time Mason bent to the little girl's level. "Well, you tell him that's not how girls like to be treated. He needs to be a gentleman and treat you like a lady."

The little girl preened, her smile saying she liked that idea. Then her mother called from across the room, so she hugged EvaMarie quickly and left them with a cute little smile.

"Whew," Mason said, "that was getting tricky."

EvaMarie raised her brow in a nice impression of a Southern belle. "You brought it on yourself."

He had to concede with a grin. After all, he was fully aware of his shortcomings. Instead, he waved a hand toward the rapidly emptying room. "Why this?" he asked.

"My degree is in early education, and this is a helpful way to put it to use," she said as she started straightening up the room.

"Degree?"

Her grin was self-deprecating, but there was also disbelief mixed in over his surprise. "Yes—believe it or not, I did go to college."

"Oh, I believe it. You always liked to learn." Which reminded him of his one unauthorized visit inside the Hyatt house as a teen. "Is the library still in the turret tower?"

He caught a glimpse of sadness crossing her face right before she turned away to fit the book she'd read back on the shelf. "The room is there, but the movers helped me pack away the books and store them."

She didn't have to tell him she missed it. The turret library had been her favorite room when he'd known her. Her escape, other than the horses.

She turned back to face him, more questions in her eyes, but then her expression changed. "Hello, Laurence," she said, looking over Mason's left shoulder.

"EvaMarie," the other man said, offering Mason a short nod but keeping his gaze on EvaMarie. "I was just down here discussing the Derby festivities for the children's festival." His eyes narrowed. "Could I speak with you, please?"

Mason wasn't sure what came over him exactly. Masculine pride? The burn of competition? But he couldn't stop himself from saying, "Actually we're on our way to lunch. You can call her later." He didn't even look at EvaMarie to see what she thought.

Of course, Laurence wouldn't be a worthy opponent if he didn't protest. "I prefer—"

"Is it urgent?" Mason asked.

"Well, no."

"Then call later." *Or not at all.* Mason hooked his arm through EvaMarie's. "See ya."

Then he ushered her outside.

They were almost to her car when she asked, "Was that really necessary?" Instead of the angry tone he expected after his interference, she sounded almost giggly. He glanced over to see her suppressing a smile.

"Got a problem?" he asked playfully. "Because I can take you back in."

"Right, like I'm looking forward to the lecture I was in for for associating with the… No way." She shot him a look that arrowed straight to his groin—sassy, sexy and something he'd never expected to see from EvaMarie in public. "But I guess this means you owe me lunch."

If this was punishment for opening his big mouth, he'd do it every time. "I'd never dream of going back on my word."

Mason parked on one side of the historic square downtown, and EvaMarie was able to pull into the spot right next to his. They didn't touch as they walked along the sidewalk, but their connection felt almost tangible to EvaMarie. She didn't need his touch to know that he was aware of her, which was an empowering, heady experience.

After last night, she'd felt almost revived, set on a new

course, a better course. But she didn't have the overall plan yet.

As they strolled past Mr. Petty's antique shop, something she glimpsed through the window made EvaMarie pause. Her instincts urged her to look closer, check it out, but maybe it wasn't her place to do so. Only she hesitated a moment too long.

Mason joined her. "What is it?" he asked.

So far Mason and Jeremy had been the driving forces behind the renovations. EvaMarie had been present at most of the discussions and had offered her opinion, but never had she taken the initiative. She worried her lip with her teeth for a moment, trying to decide. Finally she offered a small smile. "Let's go inside."

He nodded and held the door for her. Stepping across the threshold to the jingle of the doorbell, EvaMarie made her way straight to the piece she'd seen through the window: an old-fashioned sign for a gentleman's sports lodge, weathered with age, but in good repair. She pointed to the sign. "Mason, wouldn't that be great in the poker room?"

"Hell, yeah." He grinned up at the sign. "This is perfect. Good eye."

She tried to ignore the glow of pleasure blooming in her belly. "We could carry the dark wood theme from the wine cellar into the game room, kind of give it a hunting lodge-type feel."

"I've got more where that came from, if you're interested."

EvaMarie turned to see the proprietor had found them. "We're decorating a game room. What did you have in mind?"

Half an hour later, they had purchased the sign, wall rack, poker table and wine rack in varying degrees of restoration. It was a job well done. It felt good, and Mason's deference to her opinion left EvaMarie glowing.

They continued down the sidewalk to a popular corner café at a casual stroll. "So where did you go to college?" Mason asked.

"An exclusive women's liberal arts college in Tennessee. Father wanted me to study so I would be articulate and ladylike, but he didn't really care what else I actually learned there, so I decided on something I thought I would enjoy doing one day." How different she'd dreamed her life would be, even then. "By the time things went downhill and I needed to get a job, my degree was years old. I'd need some updating and to pass my teaching certification exam. There was always so much to do, I just never seemed to find the time to enroll."

Many people, Mason included, saw her from the outside and expected days filled with directing staff and having her nails done. When the actuality of running a household, caring for a sick parent, and bolstering up another weak parent were like two full time jobs in only one twenty-four-hour period. "What about you?" she asked, curious about Mason's life after he'd moved away.

"I majored in business management. Dad insisted, even though I didn't see the point in a full four-year degree. We always knew we wanted to run our own stables, and had plenty of hands-on knowledge, so I thought shorter, more specific studies would be more appropriate."

He smiled at the hostess as she seated them. To EvaMarie's surprise, he took the chair right next to her instead of the one across from her, bringing them closer, creating a more intimate atmosphere that matched their conversation. She forced herself not to acknowledge the tingles low in her core at his nearness, his attention.

Seemingly unaware, Mason went on. "Now I know why he did so many things I didn't understand. Kane and I both needed the knowledge, ways of thinking and maturity that came from college to not only maintain our own businesses, but build the reputation that will help sustain us in such a public arena."

"And then you cut your teeth on the stables back home."

Mason nodded, then smiled at the waitress as she delivered their drinks and an appetizer of fried green tomatoes with corn-bread muffins. He waited until she'd taken their lunch orders to answer. "We started those stables with our dad. There's also some cattle ranching, but it's not a huge herd because the property isn't big enough to sustain it. Our big focus there is horse breeding. As we developed those lines, we were on the lookout for stock that would be our start into racing. I'm proud to say our dad helped us pick out our first mare and stud."

The smile they shared felt like more—more personal, even intimate in the midst of a crowd. What they were discussing might have seemed mundane, but EvaMarie knew how much it meant to Mason. She remembered him talking about running his own stables when he was a teenager, and had watched him soak in everything the other stable hands and manager had been willing to teach him.

As much as it saddened her to leave her home, she could actually see that it would be in good hands with the Harrington boys. "You're gonna do great," she murmured.

Surprise lit up his eyes. "Your dad would call that kind of talk sacrilege."

"Of course he would. That doesn't make it any less true."

His gaze held hers. "Thank you. That means a lot to me."

The very air between them seemed to grow heavy, leaving EvaMarie breathless and a little confused. Mason blinked, then focused on the plate in front of them. He snagged one of the tomatoes and lifted it toward her lips. "Taste this. I had some the other day, and they're great."

She wasn't about to tell him the treat was nothing new to her. Instead, she clamped down on her surge of need as he fed her the crispy tart bite, then took one of his own. Definitely not the kind of response she should be having in public.

"Well, this doesn't look much like business. Now does it?"

Liza's cutting, accusatory tone belied the saccharine smile plastered on her face as she stood beside their table. How long she'd been there, EvaMarie couldn't have said. She'd been too caught up in the magic of Mason's attention.

Silence reigned for a moment. After last night, Mason was probably afraid to touch the remark with a ten-foot pole, so EvaMarie adopted a closed expression and answered just loud enough for the group of women watching from a few feet away to hear her. "We just finished buying the decor for the new game room at the shop next door. Antiques will give the room real depth, I believe. Don't you agree?"

Liza's eyes widened, as if she didn't know how to take this polite response to her tasteless interruption.

"I agree," Mason finally chimed in. "Mr. Petty has some unique pieces in his store. I'll probably go back for other things for the house, but what we ordered today is perfect for that room." The grin he offered Liza sparked some nasty jealousy, but EvaMarie ignored it. Because Mason wasn't hers to be jealous over.

"Still a man cave," he went on, "but with class."

The attention helped Liza recover. She offered him a smile seemingly loaded with double meaning. "As if you could be anything but classy." Stepping a little closer, she rested her hand on Mason's shoulder. Her red nails seemed to dig just a touch. EvaMarie might have been imagining that from this angle. But she wasn't imagining the husky quality that colored Liza's voice. "I had such a good time last night."

I'm amazed she remembered it...

Meeting Mason's gaze with her own, EvaMarie could have sworn she saw the same thought reflected there. He gave a slight nod and her heart pounded. Being on the same wavelength with him was certainly a heady experience. Then he turned back to look up at Liza.

"How's John Roberts?" he asked.

Liza frowned. "How should I know? He dropped me off after a lecture on—" Stopping abruptly, she flicked her gaze between Mason and EvaMarie, then shook her head. "Anyway, I haven't seen him today. The girls and I are just out for some shoppin' and strollin'."

"Well, I see the waitress headed this way with our lunch," Mason said, "so if you don't mind…"

Sigh. What woman couldn't see that Mason wasn't interested? Of course, just the thought made EvaMarie worried that she was also the type of woman who read more into what was happening between her and Mason than what was really there. Things she really shouldn't want but couldn't quite turn away from.

"Of course," Liza said, never taking her eyes from him. "But I do hope you'll remember that preseason party we're having. It's gonna be the biggest thing around here. Anyone who is anyone will be there. Please tell me you'll come."

"You said you hadn't even sent out the invites yet."

The other woman's sweet smile made EvaMarie slightly sick.

"Mason, dear, you don't need an official invite. You're welcome anytime."

After her parting salvo, Liza turned without a good-bye and headed for the table her shopping companions had claimed…right within line of sight. Mason ignored the final part of the conversation and dug into his food with the gusto of a hardworking man.

But EvaMarie was left with the knowledge of the role reversal between them. For the first time, he was invited to the party she wouldn't be considered good enough to attend.

Thirteen

"Girl, aren't you about done with all this work for the day?"

EvaMarie gasped, her heart automatically jumping at the sound of a man's voice despite knowing Mason was out of town. "Don't scare me like that!" she scolded Jeremy.

He leaned against the threshold to what used to be the walk-in closet off her dressing room—now her sound studio. "You know you're too protective of this," he said. "If you'd just tell Mason, he'd fix it so you could continue to work here."

She looked around the surprisingly roomy space. At least, it was roomy for what she needed. When she'd started creating the studio, she'd given away and stored tons of clothes that she'd held on to since she was a little girl. Her current wardrobe resided on a portable rack in her dressing room.

In here, she'd stripped the walls down to the Sheetrock and installed a layer of insulation. She'd planned to refinish the walls, but then Mason had bought the estate. The space left provided enough room for a small desk that held her recording equipment, scripts, a small lamp and office supplies.

Just what she needed to build her career narrating audiobooks.

She'd never brought Mason in here, and he'd never asked.

What she was trying to do here, and the hope it represented for a new life, a new independence, felt fragile to her. Mason had always gone after whatever he wanted and damn the consequences. He'd probably see her efforts as weak, shadows of his own mighty conquests. Hopefully she could finish out her time in her childhood home without having to expose this part of herself.

It was the very first thing that was all her own. Her parents didn't know. Neither Laurence nor any of her friends knew. Jeremy had only divined the truth after wiggling his way in. To her surprise, he'd become her fiercest cheerleader. She simply hadn't been able to share it with Mason yet. It was too personal, too risky. If she failed, she wasn't gonna do it in front of an audience. "I know things aren't going to end well with him," she argued. "They can't. This, I mean, I haven't even told my parents about this. How could I—"

"You gotta have positive thoughts, girlie."

"No." She turned his way, giving him a hard glare. "No positive thoughts. Not in this. My father almost ruined Mason's family. No matter how much of a good time we're having…" She stumbled over the words.

Jeremy gave her a knowing grin. "And a very good time it is, indeed."

"Shush. It won't last." She glanced around the small

room. "This—I need in my life. I need to accomplish this, to support myself, okay?"

"So if this thing with Mason isn't gonna last, why do you have this out?"

From the rack beside the door, Jeremy lifted up a formal dress in a garment bag. EvaMarie's heart thudded. Jeremy knew what the dress was—they'd discussed it when the movers were cleaning out a storage room downstairs. She should have sent it to the storage unit, but she hadn't been able to. She shouldn't have tried it on, but she hadn't been able to resist. She shouldn't have had it cleaned this week, but she hadn't been able to quiet the hopeful voice inside that said Mason would ask her to go to Liza's family's ball the day after he returned.

She knew he had a new suit. She'd taken delivery on it when it had arrived.

"I don't even know why I have it out. He hasn't mentioned taking me." She slumped into her chair, disgust rolling through her to wash all the starch from her posture. "Why am I torturing myself like this?"

Because this had been the best few weeks of her life. No parents to judge or criticize her. Purpose and meaning in her work. And a man who made her feel sexy and wanted.

Even if he didn't really want her for the long term.

"So just go yourself and show him what he's missing," Jeremy said.

Her grin was rueful. "Can't. I didn't get an invitation. Except—"

"Except what?"

"Laurence has asked me to go with him, as a friend."

Jeremy was already shaking his head. "Don't do it."

"I'm not." But she wasn't sure that she wouldn't. The thought of Mason being there without her, not even realizing he could have invited her, stung. She might just be selfish enough to give in to Laurence.

Jeremy lifted the bag once more. "This would fit you perfectly. And there's nothing wrong with hoping, Eva-Marie."

"Except feeling shattered when your dreams don't come true," she replied, but her tone held little heat. Deep inside, a small part of her was already resigned to never finding someone who would accept all of her, including her family obligations and who she truly was and wanted to be as a person. Those guys seemed few and far between.

But it was the dream dress—her mother's from her "debut" on the local scene. It fit EvaMarie perfectly... Who was she kidding? She wasn't going to any stupid dance, so she should stop mooning around about it like a teenage girl from an after-school special.

"Did you need me?" she finally asked, doing her best to forget the complications and focus on reality.

"Do you have time to show me where the furniture needs to be placed in the study?"

"Yeah. I've got about an hour's worth of recording left, but I need to give my voice a break first."

Her current project was a blessing in many ways. It had come in the same day Mason had left to go out of town—it was also her longest project to date, by an author she'd never worked with before, so she hadn't been entirely certain how many hours would be involved. But the author was a bestseller with lots of connections. If she liked EvaMarie's work, this could lead to some good things for her budding career.

But she'd delayed jumping into the project because she'd been nervous about doing a good job. A few false starts, though, and she'd been ready to go.

Jeremy glanced over the equipment she'd painstak-ingly paid for, piece by piece, and treated like the most delicate of babies. "I think this is so cool," he said. "With your voice and attention to detail, you're gonna be a star."

"I'll settle for financially stable, but thank you."

She was gonna miss the little studio when she was forced to move. Despite the half-finished walls and need for secrecy, the alternative would likely be a tiny closet or bathroom in an apartment complex, with all the noise complications that came with it, so—

"You should still tell him," Jeremy said, nagging her. "I thought you were moving into a whole I'm-going-after-what-I-want stage of life?"

The reminder had her standing up straighter, but she knew the minute she looked into Mason's eyes, her words would die unspoken. She enjoyed having sex with him— hell, that was an understatement. And not just the physi-cal part, but the exploration and intimacy of being with Mason. She even enjoyed living with him—his smart, funny approach to life kept her guessing and on her toes.

But she refused to use the L word. Because if she couldn't trust Mason with the most important things in her life, like the career she was struggling to build book by book, then he wasn't truly the man she wanted for forever.

Was he?

EvaMarie took a deep breath and braced herself before she even stepped out of her car. The doors of the assisted living center where her parents now resided weren't quite far enough away for her liking. She hadn't seen her par-ents since the blowup at the restaurant. Heck, she'd barely even talked to her mom, and not at all with her dad.

Maybe she should put this off for another day?

But her mother had needed a few things from storage and given her a few niggling reminders that EvaMarie hadn't been to see the place since they'd gotten settled and—boom! Here she was...

I'm such a sucker.

Trying for a positive attitude, she pushed through the door with purpose and smiled at the girl behind the reception desk who directed her to the Florida room. According to her mother, their new afternoon routine included cool drinks with friends before dressing for dinner. Her parents were happy. Settling in. Her job was done.

Except walking through the spacious rooms with their lush, real plants and unique pieces of artwork only heightened the sense of pressure to perform. Her parents couldn't truly afford to live here without digging deep into the savings that needed to stay untouched in case of a rapid decline in her father's health. So EvaMarie was supplementing his disability checks.

Something she'd need to continue doing, which meant achieving her goal of becoming a successful voice artist was of the utmost importance. And after her time with Mason was done, she'd probably have to take another part-time job, as well. Some days she thought she would never know what it was like to live without the performance pressure.

"EvaMarie, there you are," her mother said as soon as she reached the door. Her mother met her halfway with a kiss. "Darling," she murmured, "you couldn't have dressed up a bit more?"

Since when was she required to "dress" to visit her parents? She'd thought her jeans and nice shirt were perfectly presentable.

They approached a table where several other residents were seated. As soon as her mother started to introduce everyone, EvaMarie changed her mind. Maybe dressing up would have bolstered her confidence in the face of so many people. Her father rose to stand beside her, an arm around her shoulders. It was a pose they'd adopted many times through the years. The picture of the perfect family.

To EvaMarie, it only reminded her just how far from perfect they were.

"If you all will excuse us a moment," her mother said, "I wanted to introduce EvaMarie to Mrs. Robinson."

EvaMarie moved along with a smile, then said, "Mother, I really need to bring in your clothes and stuff—"

"Nonsense. There's plenty of time for that."

They came to a table closer to the floor-to-ceiling windows occupied by an elderly woman. She appeared awfully frail, but her expression was alight with intelligence when she turned to them. At her direction, they were seated and her father flagged down a waiter for a round of iced sweet tea.

"You were absolutely right, Bev," Mrs. Robinson said. "Your daughter is beautiful."

EvaMarie murmured her thanks, while her mother beamed. Though it made EvaMarie feel like she was three, the compliment pleased her mother. After chatting for a few minutes, her father stood. "Bev, let's go arrange to move your things to our apartment."

But when EvaMarie started to rise, he waved her back. "We can take care of it. You stay and chat."

"Um…" Her parents seemed all too happy to make a hasty retreat. But the silence wasn't awkward for long.

Mrs. Robinson chuckled. "They aren't subtle, those two, that's for sure."

"I'm so sorry."

"Don't be, child. I did actually want to meet you, and

now that I have, I'm very glad." Her smile softened the angular edges age had added to her face. "In this instance, I think your mother was dead right."

"About what?" EvaMarie asked, caution leaking into her voice.

"Why, I'm looking for someone to hire to take care of my place."

Surprised, EvaMarie stared for a moment. "Your place?"

"Yes, child. I had to move here about six months or so ago when I started having some bad back issues. My nephew has been staying at my home since then. Keeping everything in good repair and making sure no one starts thinking it's empty."

"That's nice of him."

Mrs. Robinson laughed again. "Well, I paid him to do it. I don't expect anyone to uproot themselves out of the goodness of their hearts. Plus, the house is a good enough size and filled to the brim with antiques, so there's always something that needs looking after. But now he's been offered a really good job in Nashville, and I need someone to take his place."

EvaMarie stilled. "You want to pay me to watch over your house?"

"Well, you'd need to live there. Your parents mentioned you would need to move out of your own situation posthaste. That's perfect for me. Not that I expect you to give up your normal activities. Just stay on top of things and come out here once a week for us to go over what's happening and any expenditures."

Mrs. Robinson glanced over EvaMarie's shoulder. "Ah, I see your parents heading this way, so I'll hurry. Despite what they may say, dear child, there's no pressure. But if you think you'll be interested, please let me know soon. You can call the front desk and ask them to transfer your call to my suite."

She reached across the table with one frail hand, prompting EvaMarie to take it. "You let me know. All right?"

EvaMarie had to clear her throat to get her words out. "Thank you, ma'am."

"My pleasure," the elderly woman said just as Eva-Marie's glowing parents returned.

Another fifteen minutes of casual conversation was punctuated by her parents casting pointed glances her way. Somehow EvaMarie managed to ignore them, and Mrs. Robinson gave her a pleased nod as they left. They didn't even make it around the corner before her mother started in.

"Isn't it a wonderful opportunity?" she gushed. "The old Robinson place is one of those gorgeous antebellum homes in the historic district. Very prestigious looking. You couldn't ask for a better situation."

"I thought you didn't want me taking care of other people's homes," EvaMarie asked, the dry question going right over her mother's head.

"Don't be silly, dear. We'd just prefer for you to work for someone whose reputation would enhance your own. Why, this would hardly be work at all."

"But I do have obligations right now—"

"Nonsense," her father barked. "You don't owe anything to a cheater. He manipulated you into taking that job."

Maybe, but still… "But it was a job that I needed. And I'm grateful for it."

Her mother, always eager to soothe over what might turn into an argument, said, "But this would be much less awkward. And you'd start right away. Mrs. Robinson is a lovely lady. This is perfect for you, dear."

"What idiot would turn it down?" her father added, probably to combat the resistance he could sense was growing inside her. Or maybe he was just mad that she hadn't automatically poured gratitude all over Mrs. Robinson and them for the opportunity they'd handed her.

Take what you want, EvaMarie.

"I'll discuss it with her a little more before I decide," she hedged, a little ashamed that she wasn't truer to the memory of Mason's words echoing in her head.

"What's to discuss?"

She tuned out the rest of whatever her father said, a skill she'd long ago perfected.

Twenty minutes later, when she managed to escape to her car, her ears rang with her parents' strident insistence that she contact Mrs. Robinson tonight and accept her offer. And even though it smacked of giving in, Eva-Marie had to admit that they had a point.

It would be an easy job that she'd be paid for—a lot easier than overseeing the renovations. She'd have the space and privacy to build her career without interference or worry. And she could put an early end to the probably unhealthy reliance she was developing on Mason's touch, Mason's presence.

So why did the very thought of accepting make her so sad?

Fourteen

Mason frowned as he waited one more time for Eva-Marie to answer her phone. He'd called twice already—once at dinnertime, then again a couple of hours later. Both calls had gone straight to voice mail.

If everything hadn't been just fine when he'd left, he'd think she was avoiding him.

"Hello?"

Boy, one breathless word and Mason was wishing away the hundreds of miles between them. How had he become addicted this hard this fast? "Hey," he replied, his own voice deepening with his desire.

She didn't speak, and her very hesitation magnified his uneasiness from earlier. He focused on the sound of her breathing. "How has your day been?" he finally asked.

Oh, that deep sigh could mean so many things.

"Well, Jeremy's crew completed the first-floor tiles."

Mason had known the job was next on the list, but

he hadn't expected them to get to it this quickly. "That's great."

"Yes. But I finally had to leave," she said with a soft chuckle. "I couldn't handle the sound of them cutting. No matter where I hid, that high-pitched whine chased me down."

The noise could be piercing. Not to mention the commotion caused by the extra crew Jeremy had brought in to get the entire floor done quickly. Good thing Mason had been out of town. "So did you ride out to the stream so you could fantasize about me?"

His little joke didn't garner him the laugh he was looking for. "Actually, I went to visit my parents."

"Bummer."

"Mason."

How could even her preschool teacher voice sound sexy? "Hey, you know you need someone to brighten your day. I'm just trying to help that along."

Her huffy sigh expressed a depth of exasperation that told him his playful mood was not winning him any points. He probably shouldn't ask if they'd spent the entire time lecturing her on quitting her job. Maybe he'd try a different tactic.

"I actually did want to talk to you about something."

"Really?"

He grinned as excitement entered her voice, softening the irritation.

"Yep. Kane and I have a new job for you."

"Oh."

Mason rushed on, his enthusiasm for their idea pushing to the surface. "We've decided to host a big bash at the house. After all, there will be a lot to show off, right? Introduce ourselves to the racing community, entertain in the new spaces downstairs, have a buffet in the formal dining room…" It took a while for him to realize that EvaMarie wasn't responding. "What do you think?" he demanded.

"If being seen is what you want, that will make a big splash."

"We need to be seen and make contacts…it's good for business."

"This will definitely be good for business."

So why didn't she sound excited? "We want you to put it together for us. I told Kane that no one would know better what to have and who to invite. You'll do great."

"Sure."

Maybe she was simply overwhelmed. "I know you've got a lot going on with the renovations, but this will be fun. And great for us."

"It will be my pleasure to organize a party for you."

But it didn't sound like a pleasure. Her voice was stiff, not husky and molten like when he usually spoke with her. Maybe he should change tactics. "I think I'll be back by Thursday."

She was silent so long he wondered if they'd been disconnected. "EvaMarie, are you okay?"

"Sure." She still didn't sound convincing, but at least she was talking. "I'm just tired, I guess. A lot on my mind."

"Anything I can help with?"

"I doubt it."

He wasn't sure, but he had a good guess what the problem was. After all, in twenty minutes her parents had totally screwed up his head. He could only imagine what they could do to hers in an afternoon. "Did you spend all day fighting off new suitors or better job offers?"

"No," she snapped back. "Nothing like that."

"Come on…work with me here," he crooned. He'd

never seen her in this kind of mood, but he was more than up for the challenge. "I'm very good at distraction."

"And that's helping, how?"

"Do I look like Dr. Freud? Don't kill the messenger. I'm not the obsessive worrier here, am I?"

Now he garnered a laugh, small one though it was. "Well, I can't deny it, as much as I'd like to."

"See?" It felt good to make her feel good, even over the phone. Almost as good as making her feel awesome in person.

And she wasn't letting him off the hook. "Well, if you want to help, you may need to work a little harder."

"Oh, I'm perfectly capable of working it hard if you need me to." He let his voice deepen into a playful growl.

"Mason!"

There we go. Time to have some fun. "Well, maybe not from this far away...but I can make it work for you."

"What did you have in mind?" That breathlessness from earlier had returned. Even though they were only connected by phone, her husky voice worked its way along his nerve endings to set them all abuzz.

"Just talking. You like talking to me, right?"

"Of course."

Her response was too matter-of-fact. He needed to shake her up. "Then tell me your favorite part of what we do together."

"Um, what?"

She sounded so innocently shocked he wanted to laugh...or kiss her thoroughly. "Come on, baby. Tell me what you like." His body throbbed as he waited for her answer.

"I don't know," she whispered, leaving silence to hang between them.

"I'm waiting."

"When you…" He heard her clear her throat. "When you kiss and suck at my neck," she finally murmured.

Mason's mind conjured up explicit details of him doing just that. "And I love how you respond. Moaning. Nails digging in. Your hips lifting to mine."

Every word brought a new picture. His body tightened, and he desperately wished she were there for him to hold close right now.

She felt it too. He could tell by the acceleration in her breath. Was she eager to play? "Now tell me how you like to be touched."

"With hands…" she said, quicker now to respond, "hands that are rough, calluses on them."

Just like his.

"Firm. Guiding me. Supporting me."

Just like he wanted to.

"Digging in." Her voice was almost deep enough to be a moan. "Not to hurt, but in the excitement of the moment."

Just like his did when he felt her climax around him.

Mason broke out in a sweat, hands clenching into tight fists. Not from the images she was conjuring. But from the fear that after playing with fire, he'd never again be free of his need for EvaMarie.

"I thought we agreed you wouldn't go to the ball with Laurence?"

EvaMarie paused in her attempt to work one of her amethyst earrings into the hole in her ear. She hadn't worn them in forever. There wasn't any need for fancy jewelry at the few places she went. But they went perfectly with her mother's debutante dress, so EvaMarie hadn't been able to resist.

"I'm not, actually," she replied to Jeremy. The frown

that appeared on her face in the mirror didn't go with the filmy cream layers of her dress or the elegant upsweep of her hair. Why did he have to ruin her anticipation? She was having a hard enough time hanging on to her composure as it was.

She caught the pointed look he directed her way via the hall mirror. "I'm going on my parents' invite, okay? They insisted. I might be meeting Laurence there, just as friends."

After all, how pathetic would she look without a date? And the fact that she had to worry about that, when she had a man who had no problem climbing into her bed every night, ticked her off.

"But you're really going to be spying."

"I don't know," EvaMarie said. Her frustration from the past week boiled over. "He didn't say if he was going, okay? Didn't say if he was coming home tonight. Didn't give me any indication whether me going with him was even an option at all." She huffed, blinking back tears. After all, she didn't want to ruin her mascara.

At least, that's what she told herself.

"Why didn't you ask?" Jeremy said.

Ask? "Why didn't I ask? Because wouldn't that leave me looking pathetic when he said no?"

"So it was easier not to ask than it was not to know?"

"I…" Maybe so. Maybe not. "I'm just confused."

Jeremy moved in close, looking suave and elegant in the mirror in spite of the casual clothes he wore for working on the estate. He settled warm hands on her bare shoulders. "Sweetheart, you are worthy of an answer. If you don't get one, you have to demand one."

"But—I can't…" In her world, demands were always punished. "That's just not me."

"Isn't it? Isn't that what this is all about?" He waved

a hand over her dress. "A way to demand Mason answer your unspoken questions without having to come right out and ask them?"

Her hands clenched into the gown at her sides, as if fearful someone would try to tear it from her. "Are you saying this is wrong?" she asked.

"Absolutely not," Jeremy said, meeting her gaze in the mirror. "I just don't want you to sell yourself short. Have some self-respect, EvaMarie. You've earned it the hard way. But you'll never build up your stockpile if you keep letting people steal it from you..."

The image that statement created in her mind held her in awe for a moment. She could literally picture a pile of gold bars that her father and mother and Mason and Liza all kept stealing from...and she did nothing to stop them.

"All right," she said, a glimmer of understanding rapidly expanding in her mind. "I just want to see if something happens...if he responds. Wouldn't you?"

Her restlessness this week had coalesced into a fierce curiosity to see just how Mason would react to her in a public setting. After all, they weren't dating. But somehow, some way, she'd still thought he would invite her to go to Liza's ball with him.

She'd been sorely disappointed.

But she didn't know the why of it—at least, a why that she could accept. That's what was eating at her. Along with the job offer she'd had. She hadn't been able to bring it up with Mason...but she needed to make a decision before the opportunity slipped through her fingers.

Jeremy kissed her on her temple. "Girl, yes, I would." He squeezed her arms to encourage her. "You look beautiful, sweetheart. I just don't understand why you think things couldn't work out with Mason. Any man would be lucky to have you."

EvaMarie shook her head, blinking back tears. "It can't work. There's too much history, too much—"

"Seems to me like it's working now. I don't see what the past has to do with anything."

She met his gaze straight up. "Can you honestly see my father walking me down the aisle to meet Mason? I'm not ready to spend a lifetime separated from the parents I still love."

Like Mason's mother. Had it been wrong of her to walk away from her family for love? Had she regretted it? EvaMarie knew her parents would be the same, forever condemning her for that choice. But then again, they might not cut her off completely. They'd become quite dependent on her these past few years.

If her parents weren't an issue, would she make a different choice?

"I'll see you at the party," Jeremy said, turning to go as if he knew he'd said enough.

She nibbled on her lip as Jeremy's footsteps echoed down the hallway and then down the flight of steps to the basement.

She could tell herself she was going because she wanted to, but deep down, she knew what she really wanted was to see Mason there—and be seen by him. But she did have some pride. If he ignored her, she would not push the matter.

To make her nerves worse, Mason hadn't made it home the day before as planned. She knew he was heading out sometime today, but he hadn't said when, hadn't called her when he left, nothing. So this was probably just a tournament of nervous tension for nothing.

Stop mooning and go if you're going.

So she did. Only stepping out of her car was a bit more difficult than she'd anticipated. After all, she'd always come to these events *with* her parents or *with* Laurence. Never on her own. And people could talk about lifting your chin and storming a room with pride…but it was actually a damn hard thing to do.

But she pictured that pile of gold bars and knew she didn't ever want to be with someone who wouldn't add to that pile. Which meant, if she were to continue living with herself, she better get to work.

Because she was worthy of way more than a pile of gold. She was worthy of respect—and tonight she would demand it.

Fifteen

Mason stumbled, exhausted, into the side entrance when he got home around seven on Friday. Over twenty-four hours after he should have been here. He hadn't even been sure he'd make it in tonight. The long drive over, after some last-minute meetings this morning, had about done him in. But as much as he wanted to hole up underneath EvaMarie's cozy down comforter, he needed to put in an appearance at Liza's party.

Kane hadn't been able to leave at all, making it all the more imperative that Mason serve as the lone rep for their debut tonight in Kentucky racing circles. Liza's family was both prominent and well-connected in the local racing scene. Mason needed to get his name—and even better, his face—circulating.

But first, he wanted to see EvaMarie. She hadn't sounded right when he talked to her on the phone yesterday, and something told him she was upset. Hopefully not with him, but she hadn't wanted to talk about it. He could tell by the hesitation in her responses and how distracted she'd sounded.

EvaMarie wasn't the type to spill her guts, even after all they'd shared. If Mason wanted to know, he'd have to coax it out—something he hadn't wanted to do over the phone. He was much better at it in person.

He looked around the downstairs, noting the sleek elegance of the new tiled floors and the finished dining room. No sounds came from the basement, so Mason assumed they were done for the day, though Jeremy's car was still in the drive.

Mason took the stairs two at a time, hoping to find EvaMarie in her room, but all was quiet. As he searched, the ticktock of time passing niggled in his brain.

No EvaMarie. Maybe she was in the barn. Would she be able to shower quickly and throw on a dress? Did she even own a formal dress? Surely she did, but he wasn't sure how long it had been since she'd worn one.

He'd spent years dreaming of her living the high life on her parents' money. But in actuality, her life had been very different.

In clear detail, Mason now saw the drawbacks to his decision not to mention the party to EvaMarie. He might have been worried he wouldn't make it home, but if she was here somewhere, he hadn't left her a lot of time to get ready.

Of course, he'd also felt some confusion over whether he should ask her at all. Despite the incredible intimacy they shared, they weren't technically dating. They'd agreed on that. Mason didn't want her to feel like she had to go with him if she wasn't comfortable making a public appearance on his arm.

But by God, he wanted her with him tonight.

He reached into his pocket for his phone to call her,

all while stomping across her rug to the dressing room he knew was on the other side of her bathroom. As he entered the room, he saw a rack of clothes to one side, which seemed odd. No formal dresses there, though. He reached for the door to the closet. Maybe she kept things she didn't wear much in here.

But what he found inside had nothing to do with clothes. What the hell?

"Girl, why are you back already? Did you forget something?" Jeremy called from the bedroom. "Or did the thought of facing an evening with dull Laurence make you change your mind?"

Ducking back out of the closet, Mason came face-to-face with the other man.

"Oh, snap," Jeremy said. He swallowed hard. "I don't think you're supposed to be in there."

"It's my house," Mason said, stalking closer. His exhaustion faded in the face of his growing anger. "I can be wherever I want."

Jeremy inclined his head, holding his hands up in surrender. "Also true."

"What's this?" Mason asked, jerking his head back toward the closet.

The walls had been covered in insulation, and the shelves were empty of clothes. A table and a filing cabinet had replaced the closet's usual function. If he had to guess, what looked like sound equipment was the key to the mystery.

Jeremy worried his lip as his averted gaze told Mason he didn't want to answer.

"You obviously know," Mason said. "Spill it. Does princess have a ham radio obsession I'm not aware of?"

Jeremy laughed, then slapped a hand over his mouth.

When he finally removed it, he was sober under Mason's glare. "Well, she has an incredible voice, right?"

Mason couldn't argue that. "What does that have to do with—"

"She needs a way to support herself," Jeremy rushed to say. "A mutual friend of ours is an author, and she put EvaMarie in touch with some people in the audiobook industry. She's been working very hard to build a foundation…"

Jeremy's voice trailed off as he noticed Mason staring. Mason couldn't help it. His brain had short-circuited the minute he'd realized EvaMarie was building a career. Not a job, not a hobby. A career. One she hadn't bothered to mention to him—at all.

"Where is she?" he demanded, not caring that his voice had roughened.

He could tell from Jeremy's face he wasn't going to like this answer either.

"She left about forty-five minutes ago for Liza's party."

Liza's party. Without him. Yet another thing she hadn't mentioned. "With dull Laurence?"

Jeremy shook his head but paused under Mason's look. "Well, she drove herself, but she was meeting him there. As friends."

Mason gave a sound of frustration and anger all mingled together.

For once, Jeremy didn't pause. "Well, what did you expect, man? *You* certainly didn't invite her."

No. No, he hadn't. He'd thought to keep everything separated into neat little compartments. But that didn't mean he wanted to hear about it from someone else. "I don't think I need you to tell me how to handle this—" He'd almost said relationship, but that wasn't what he had with EvaMarie, was it? Not really.

"Well, you certainly need someone to tell you," Jeremy said, gaining bravado and not backing down beneath Mason's glare. "She's not just your housekeeper, now, is she? She's your woman…or is she just convenient?"

Shock jolted through Mason. "Is that what she thinks?"

"Should she?"

"Should I?" Mason demanded, gesturing back toward the modified closet.

Jeremy frowned. "I'm sure she has her reasons for keeping certain things private, but I think EvaMarie isn't the only one who needs to be honest around here."

Mason wanted to rail some more, work out his aggression here and now. As if he knew that, Jeremy didn't even give him the chance. He simply left.

Mason glanced back into the darkened room with its pile of sophisticated equipment. He'd kept business and pleasure and emotions completely apart from one another. Like a picky child who thought the piles of food on his plate would contaminate each other if they touched. Obviously Mason had been too good at keeping things separate. And while he could forgive EvaMarie for going to the party without him, he refused to take responsibility for her keeping this a secret. That was all on her.

And Mason wanted an explanation.

EvaMarie slowly relaxed into the rhythm of the evening. Laurence had been just attentive enough when she had arrived to soothe her secret ego, but seemed to lose interest quickly. Which wasn't unusual for him. Her parents had been welcoming, without finding any little faults to disapprove of… All in all, she was having a much better time than she'd expected.

Except for the urge to look toward the entryway every ten minutes to see if Mason was going to show up.

She'd already checked her phone once to see if he'd texted or tried to call, but had put it away again when her mother frowned in her direction. Her parents weren't fans of the current trend to have cellular phones constantly in hand. To them, parties were for socializing with the people actually at the party.

Normally, EvaMarie didn't have a problem with that. Tonight was a whole other matter, in more ways than one.

Suddenly her father announced, "I need to sit down."

Her mother assisted him with a concerned look that encouraged EvaMarie to stay close. If her father started having difficulty or limb pain while in the midst of all these watching eyes, her mother wouldn't cope well.

"I'm fine, Bev," he barked as her mother hovered over his left shoulder. "Just tired, all of a sudden. EvaMarie, get me some champagne."

Laurence half rose from his chair. "Would you like me to—"

"Nonsense," her father said in a gruff voice. "She's perfectly capable of fetching me a drink."

Concerned, EvaMarie hesitated, but her mother gave a quick nod in the direction of the bar. It wasn't until she was in line that the first inklings of unease appeared. Several feet away, Liza stood, holding the attention of a court of young ladies. EvaMarie knew them all. They'd grown up together.

What bothered her were the frequent glances in her direction, accompanied by giggles and whispering.

Despite the ache in the bottom of her stomach, EvaMarie took a deep breath and turned slightly away to ignore them. Whatever was happening, she refused to feed the fire by granting it her attention. That was often the thing Liza was looking for—a way to be the center of attention in any given situation. She didn't need Eva-Marie to accomplish that.

But the longer she stood there, the louder the giggling grew. EvaMarie didn't think the women were getting louder...they were simply getting closer. She ordered her father's drink and turned to go back to the table with relief.

But Liza had no intention of letting her escape. She'd barely taken half a dozen steps before the woman moved into her path. "EvaMarie, it's so nice to see you here," she cooed, the sugar-sweet tone grating on EvaMarie's nerves. Liza leaned forward as if to impart a secret, only she didn't really lower her voice. "Although I don't remember seeing your name on the guest list, if I recall correctly."

The women behind her giggled, reminding EvaMarie of a gaggle of geese playing follow the leader.

She wasn't going to give Liza the satisfaction of justifying her presence. It was a pointless exercise when Liza knew that EvaMarie could have arrived with any number of people here.

"I was just telling the girls about your new job," she said, her overly mascaraed eyelashes wide enough to show the whites of her eyes. Not the most flattering look, in EvaMarie's opinion.

"Yes?" she said. She was a working woman now. No point in hiding it, which she didn't want to do.

Earning her own living, learning exactly what she was capable of, left EvaMarie feeling pride—not shame. And looking at the women before her, the very epitome of unoccupied children without purpose in their lives, made her glad. This was what her parents had wanted for her when she was young. But it wasn't what she wanted. Her work at the library had given her a taste of creating meaning in her life by helping others. And as hard as the work with Mason had been, EvaMarie ended her days satisfied instead of empty.

"So you're living up there all alone?" one of the women asked over Liza's shoulder.

EvaMarie squinted. "I'm not sure what you mean."

"You know," the woman elaborated, "just the two of you in that big ol' house."

EvaMarie almost expected a *wink, wink* to be added. Was this really what they'd spent their time discussing? "There are a lot of workmen up there. I'm simply directing the renovations for the Harringtons."

"The Harringtons, huh?" Liza giggled. "But you and *Mason* are up there alone at night, right? At least, from what I saw." She glanced over her shoulder at the lemmings behind her. "Gives a whole new meaning to live-in help, if you know what I mean."

"No, I—"

Laurence appeared at her elbow. "Your father wants to know what's taking so long." He lifted the champagne flute from her hand.

"What do you think, Laurence?" Liza interjected. "I'd bet the odds that EvaMarie is securing her job with *the Harringtons* in more ways than one."

EvaMarie felt her cheeks flush as Laurence didn't jump in to immediately defend her. Instead, he cast an inquiring look in her direction.

And even though EvaMarie knew her time with Mason wasn't like that, she couldn't stop the red hot glow from spreading down her throat and chest. "That's not what's happening at all," she choked out, even though her brain told her this wasn't junior high and she didn't need to justify herself to anyone.

"If it was me," Liza said, though her tone made it clear

she'd never have to stoop that low, "well, let's just say I wouldn't blame you for milking that relationship for all it's worth. You get to hold on to your home and garner the attentions of one sexy man…although I notice he wasn't the one who brought you tonight. Now was he?"

Just like that, EvaMarie felt her innermost fears laid bare for this uncaring group to dissect and make fun of at her expense. Even Laurence, who'd always stood by her despite her decidedly outcast role in recent years, continued to eye her as if he could see all her secrets behind her fancy retro gown. Finally he asked, "Well, he certainly does have himself a sweet deal, doesn't he?"

"Laurence." Anger started to replace the nerves she felt in the pit of her stomach. "That's completely uncalled for." Regardless of whether or not it might be true. "I keep my job the same way any employee does. I work hard, and go above and beyond for the Harringtons."

"Do you now?"

Mason's voice from right behind her should have been a relief. But the hard tone didn't reassure her at all. Before she could turn, he stepped in close to her back and spoke to the others. "If you all would excuse us, please?"

Then his hand encircled her wrist, a perfect pivot for him to turn her to face him. She had a brief glimpse of Laurence's angry expression before Mason whisked her out onto the dance floor.

His sure touch guided her into a loosely modified version of a modern waltz that allowed them to slowly traverse the lightly populated space. Most people were still enjoying the hors d'oeuvres and drinks and hadn't taken advantage of the live music yet.

The glitter in Mason's blue eyes as he stared down at her didn't calm her unsettled nerves. She'd wondered how he would react to seeing her here. She was about to find out.

"So, was Laurence right? Seems to me you've gotten quite a few perks out of this deal. Though it hadn't occurred to me that you might be milking every opportunity to get exactly what you wanted…until tonight."

"I don't understand…"

"I went into your closet tonight."

Her stumble could have been disastrous, but Mason's smooth save kept them upright and floating across the floor. The whirl of the crowd on the periphery of her vision made EvaMarie a little nauseous.

As if he could read her understanding in her expression, Mason gave a nod, then went on. "So you do understand? How many other secrets have you been keeping from me?"

"What? None." This new assault from a completely unexpected direction left EvaMarie grasping for a response. "Look, I wasn't ready to talk about what I was trying to do…"

"Right." His expression turned into a glare. "It would be a shame for me to encourage you."

"Would you have?"

Mason didn't answer, just continued with his unrelenting glare. EvaMarie wasn't sure exactly what was happening here. She'd made a mistake not telling Mason about her narration job, but they really hadn't had a lot of time to build that kind of trust. Especially in a situation that had an end date in sight…

When he still didn't speak, EvaMarie gave in to her own internal pressure to explain. "I'm just trying to build some sort of career."

"A career based in my house."

His resentment was becoming clearer. "Actually, I can

do it anywhere. You know as well as I do that I needed a place to stay—"

"—and work."

"And it helped to be able to continue to work, but that's not why—"

"Why you slept with me?"

The emotions that stopped EvaMarie in her tracks were too complicated to untangle. She found herself searching Mason's face, desperate for any sign of the lover and, yes, friend she'd spent the last few weeks with. The man who had let go of the need for revenge that he'd shown up with on her doorstep. "Is that really how you see me? As a woman who would sleep with you for the chance to stay in my childhood home and—" nausea tightened her throat "—get paid for it?"

In the back of her mind, she realized people were starting to watch them, listen to their conversation. And all of Liza's suspicions were being confirmed. But what mattered right now was Mason and the realization that he hadn't changed as much from that vengeful man as she'd thought.

"Well, you haven't really let me get to know you, the real you, have you? So I can't really say."

"Are you kidding me?" she asked, incredulous. "I keep one thing a secret and now I'm hiding from you? Is that how you really view me? Or is this just an excuse to push me away now that other people are starting to talk?"

"I'm not the one who's always cared what other people think. Am I?"

No, he wasn't. But that didn't really answer her question.

EvaMarie was immediately struck by the sudden awareness of how quiet the other conversations in the large room had gotten. And as much as she'd like to say she didn't care, that didn't mean she longed to air her dirty laundry in front of all of these people.

Without answering, she turned on her heel, stalking back to her parents' table. "EvaMarie," her mother said fretfully as she approached.

She ignored her, ignored her father's hard stare, ignored Laurence's arrival right after her. Instead, she reached for her clutch and shawl. She'd had enough partying for one night.

But Mason wasn't done. "So let's just get one thing straight," he said, the sound of his angry voice scraping across her nerves. "Did you or did you not work with me, sleep with me, so you could stay close to your very nice, very free studio in order to build your new career?"

"No," she snapped.

"Then why the secrecy?"

Before she could tell him to go to hell, her father bellowed, "What's he talking about?"

"Nothing."

Still he struggled to his feet, always willing to use his large stature to intimidate an answer out of her. "Why would you need a career?" he demanded. "We agreed you're taking the job with Mrs. Robinson."

"A job?" Mason's voice had gone deadly deep, shaking EvaMarie far more than her father's at his worst. Mason moved in closer, right over her shoulder. He left no space for her to turn and face him. "What? No two weeks' notice? Or do you only grant others that kind of courtesy when it suits you to do so?"

Sixteen

Mason should have been satisfied as he replayed the memory of EvaMarie running from the Young house, the fragile vintage gown pulled up away from her heels. Instead, he clenched his fists around the steering wheel and hit the gas with considerably more force.

He'd walked away from a blustering Daulton as he demanded EvaMarie tell him what was going on. Their little family drama didn't interest him. She'd run past him across the large main foyer as he'd made his apologies to Liza's parents for disrupting their party. But he had the uncomfortable feeling that the argument hadn't bothered them the way it had Mason.

After all, he'd just made them the talk of the town without any effort. Though Lord only knew what this would do to the Harrington reputation. Probably enhance it, considering how backward things like this worked in the world.

Now he let himself into the house and paused a moment to listen to the stillness. EvaMarie's car was in the drive, not in the garage where she normally parked it.

Was she in her room? The kitchen? Was she planning to continue their discussion? Maybe offer him something special to tease him out of his bad mood?

Mason shook his head. As angry as he was, he recognized that wasn't the EvaMarie he knew. Yes, he'd lashed out and accused her of sleeping with him to get what she wanted. But deep down he didn't want to believe that could be true.

But he wasn't sure the woman he'd come to know as an adult was real. Had she been hiding behind what he wanted to see in order to hold on to the life she hadn't been ready to give up? Even worse, he wasn't sure what to do about that.

Right now, he just needed some freakin' sleep.

Only it didn't look like he was going to get it. As he approached the darkened back staircase, Mason looked up to see EvaMarie seated on one of the upper steps, a pool of frothy material puddled around her. She stared out the arched window opposite, giving him a decent view of streaked mascara and the luxurious wash of hair she'd let down to cover her bare back.

Did she have to be so lovely?

He clenched his fists, wishing he could eradicate all sympathy, all regret from his emotions right now. If only she didn't look like a Cinderella after the ball, after her world had gone to hell in a handbasket. If only she didn't make his heart ache to hold her just once more—even when he knew he shouldn't.

The silence lasted for long minutes more as he stared at her from the bottom of the stairs. Maybe he'd been wrong. Maybe she was justified in keeping her secrets.

But what about the job? Or rather, the new job. That familiar anger and hurt flooded his chest once more.

Just when he'd thought she wouldn't, EvaMarie spoke. "I'll be out by Monday."

He drew in a deep breath, but she didn't give him an inch of ground.

"I'd be out sooner, but everything was going so well, I sort of forgot I was supposed to be packing."

"So did I."

And he had, because deep inside, he hadn't wanted to think about EvaMarie leaving. Because her leaving would have made him wonder why being without her left him lonely, why laughing with her made him happy and why knowing she'd kept even a small part of herself from him made him angry.

Because he'd fallen in love, all over again.

She stood, the fall of the gown reflecting the scant moonlight from the window opposite. A few steps was all she gained before she turned back. "I'm sorry, Mason. I know you probably won't believe that. Probably don't even care. But I need to say it for myself. I'm sorry that I kept things from you."

Her huff of a laugh resonated with a sort of despair that startled him. "I thought everything I'd done for you, with you, would have told you what you needed to truly know about me. But I forget that's not the way life works. It never has been. At least, not for me. I've spent a lifetime protecting myself, and old habits die hard, regardless of whether they are serving you well or not. And that's my fault."

"No, EvaMarie." Without thought he moved to the bottom of the stairs, gripping the newel post in his hand. "No, I just didn't expect—"

"That the young, innocent girl you knew would grow

up into such a complicated woman. So needy. So scared."
Her hand was a pale blur as she waved it to indicate the
house at her feet. "After all, I had the perfect life. The
least I could do was meet your expectations."

She moved down a step, then stopped to hold herself
in frozen stillness as if realizing she'd made a mistake.
"That's what everyone else wants. So you should too.
Only I thought you wanted me to grow, wanted me to
break out from my past—" her voice rose to echo around
the black space "—wanted me to take what I wanted." A
small sob escaped her throat. "But no one really means
that. They just say it to be nice and take it back when it
doesn't go the way they expected."

She turned away once more, not speaking again until
she reached the top step. Mason's gaze traced the fragile line of her spine where the dress dipped to midback
below the fall of her hair, remembering the feel of it
against his fingertips.

Her words floated down without her turning her head
toward him. "Jeremy was right. No one will ever respect
me, because I don't respect myself. So from here on out,
I'll accept nothing less…only I figure that means I'll
spend a lifetime alone. Funny how that works, huh?"

In that moment, Mason realized he'd let EvaMarie
down far worse than anything she'd ever done to him
when they were kids. Then, she hadn't stood up for him
because she didn't know how. Now, he'd taken advantage
of the fact that she wouldn't stand up for herself to exor-
cise his own anger and conflicting emotions.

Guilt gripped his throat, refusing to let him call out to
her as she walked away. He heard the door to her room
close, then the distinct click of the lock.

She was done talking, leaving Mason to spend the night
contemplating just how big of a jackass he truly was.

* * *

She's really done it.

Mason came around the corner of the house to find a long horse trailer parked before the stables. Jim came out the arched entryway leading Lucy, her foal not far behind. Somehow, seeing the horses loaded up with their new owners—without EvaMarie anywhere in sight— told Mason's brain more than anything else that she was gone.

When she'd left him a note telling him she wouldn't be back, she'd meant it.

He hadn't seen her after that night. Her room had been empty the next day, save for a stack of moving boxes in one corner and the furniture. If she had been at the house since that night, it hadn't been while Mason was present. He suspected Jeremy was helping her co- ordinate her movements, though the other man hadn't said a word.

All of her belongings, including her sound equipment, had been loaded into moving trucks the third day by a group of burly men in uniforms. But it still hadn't seemed real. Until the horses...

EvaMarie had loved those horses. He'd just assumed she would be here to say goodbye to them.

Kane appeared beside him. "What's going on?"

Mason bumped his chin in the direction of the stables. "New owner is here for the Hyatts' horses. Got the sta- bles all to ourselves now."

Kane grunted. "We're gonna need to hire on some help for Jim." He was quiet again for a moment, then said the very thing Mason didn't want to hear. "You okay with this?"

"Hell, yes." But he wasn't. And that was eating away his insides.

"No," he finally conceded. "Hell, no."

Kane slapped Mason's shoulder. "About time you admitted that."

"Why? So you can gloat?"

"Would I do that?"

"Yes." And that was an understatement.

"Nah! But I might have to indulge in at least one *I told you so.*"

As much as he'd like to, Mason couldn't begrudge him that. "You were right."

Kane clutched his heart in a mock death grip. "And you admitted it? Is the world ending?"

"It will for you if you don't drop the theatrics."

Kane chuckled, a sound so rare it startled Mason. "I can't resist."

"Try."

Mason frowned as Jim and the new owner checked over the inside and outside of the trailer to make sure the horses were safe and secure. "This didn't go how I thought it would."

"Life is full of surprises, Dad used to say."

"And not all of them good, if I remember correctly."

"He did mention that a time or two. And as much as you showing up here was a nasty surprise for the Hyatts, I think it was a good thing for EvaMarie."

"I doubt she'd agree with you now."

"You sure about that?"

Mason studied him.

"Do you remember the year I was in sixth grade?"

"Yeah. That was a pretty miserable year for you." It was before Kane had gotten any height on him. He'd spent the year being picked on by a particularly burly boy at school. "Why?"

"I learned something that year. Oh, I didn't learn it

right then. But many years later, looking back, I was taught a massive life lesson."

"That bullies need their asses kicked?"

Kane smirked. "Besides that. I learned that the job of a bully is to make you cower. Not just outside, but inside. To make everything you are shrink until it disappears, including the very essence of who you are."

Mason could see where this was going, and it wasn't helping him feel any better.

"EvaMarie lived with a bully her entire life," Kane went on. "The thing that amazes me to this day is the amount of strength it took for her not to give up, not to lose who she really was. She buried it, and protected it, until the time when it was safe for her to bring it back out."

"So I could stomp all over it." Mason watched the truck and trailer disappear down the drive. Jim raised a hand in acknowledgment before heading back into the stables. They really had to get that man some help. "I completely screwed up. How do I change that?"

"It's easy…"

"For you to say."

Kane squinted as he gazed across the rolling hills behind the stable yard. "Nope. You've just got to help her be who she should have been all along."

Seventeen

"Jeremy, come on," EvaMarie hollered. She couldn't help it. Wondering if Mason was gonna walk in at any minute had her stomach cramping.

Jeremy finally came around the corner from the basement with a grin that made her want to smack him. "Seriously, you could at least be curious as to how the game room turned out."

Oh, she was. More than anything she wanted to take a leisurely stroll downstairs to see all the cool goodness Jeremy had been able to put in place. She wanted to see how the plans they had all discussed and dreamed about had come to life... She wanted to see how the furniture she and Mason had picked out looked in the game room. She wanted to talk party plans and food and music...but that wasn't her place anymore.

"I just want to get my stuff from the safe and go," she insisted, ignoring what she wanted but could no longer have.

"Well, why didn't you go on up and get it?"

Because it was weird.

She knew Mason had now moved the focus of the renovations to the second floor. Honestly, she'd be surprised if he hadn't gutted her room. He probably wanted absolutely nothing to remind him of her. Probably the entire floor was unrecognizable now. What had they done with Chris's bedroom? The thought left her cold. She wasn't sure she wanted to see.

Jeremy watched her closely, seeming almost amused. "I told you Mason left the safe on purpose once I explained you'd forgotten some things in it."

"I'm amazed he didn't blow it out of the wall," she mumbled.

"Oh, stop fussing and get a move on."

She totally wasn't in the mood for his attitude. "Now who's in a hurry?" she challenged.

But she did want to get done before Mason arrived. In the three weeks since she'd left her childhood home, she hadn't seen Mason once. Not driving around town, not out shopping and certainly not here at the estate.

The few times she'd returned for her things, Jeremy had arranged for her to show up when Mason wasn't home. Whether her former lover approved of this strategy or not, she wasn't sure. When she realized that she'd forgotten to get the few real pieces of jewelry she still owned from the wall safe in her closet, it had taken a whole week for Jeremy to find a window for her to come by.

But standing around here in the hall that had seen all the ups and downs in her life made her sink even further into the morass of sadness that darkened her life at the moment. She needed out. As a matter of fact, she almost gave Jeremy the code and asked him to get her stuff from the safe, but she'd done enough wimping out for the day. This she needed to do for herself.

Hard as it might be.

So she forced herself to climb each step, focusing on Jeremy's leather shoes at her eye level in front of her. They shouldn't be so fancy for all the work he did in construction zones, but somehow he managed to pull it off without a single scuff. Amazing.

With a grimace, she acknowledged that she was in deep avoidance mode, but she still refused to look right or left as she crossed the landing to her old room. Her brother's room pulled at her senses, but what good would looking do? He was gone. So was her childhood. Wandering these halls to reminisce about either would probably throw her into a depression she could never crawl out of.

"How are the parents?" Jeremy asked, as he paused outside the door to her old bedroom.

"Currently refusing to speak to me," she confirmed. "Once I told them they could agree to my terms or not see me, they immediately set about breaking every rule I put in place. We're in what I call the tantrum stage."

"Ah, the terrible twos."

"And threes and fours and fives…I feel like it's never going to end."

"It will."

"I hate to say it, but I agree. The minute my dad has his first big health scare and they need me, they'll come calling. I'll just have to remind them that I mean business on a regular basis." Just the thought exhausted her sometimes, but this was life with her parents, since she wasn't willing to cut them out altogether.

Jeremy echoed her thoughts. "I know it's hard, but stick to your guns."

She hated to admit it, but being away from her parents right now was easier than going along with all their demands had ever been. But remembering that would help her keep her backbone strong. It would have been nice to have someone by her side, giving her encouragement and support while she dealt with all of this, but she'd lost that chance the night of the ball.

Without voicing her complicated thoughts, she nodded. "All right. Let's see it."

Jeremy opened the door and stood aside, telling her something had definitely changed beyond the threshold. As much as she dreaded it, this was another good thing. A hard thing, but she needed to remember that this was no longer her home. The past was gone. She couldn't go back.

Especially now that her room had been turned into an office. Her first thought was that it had been turned into Mason's office, but the pale purple of the walls didn't really scream "masculine." With a quick glance, she scanned what appeared to be an antique rolltop desk, a modern ergonomic desk chair covered in a leather that matched the desk's finish and some bookshelves. She didn't look closer. She didn't want to.

Definitely not.

The pale purple had been carried over into the dressing room, but unlike the other space, this one remained unfurnished. Then she opened the door to the walk-in closet and gasped.

Instead of the stripped walls she'd expected, all the surfaces had been reinforced with cushioning covered in some kind of leather. Decorative tufting had been created with upholstery buttons. At the far end, a custom-built shelving unit and desk took up the entire wall. An L-shaped addition on one side was filled with equipment that made the woman who had poured over sound equipment sites to find the best of the cheapest drool.

"Oh my God, Jeremy," she breathed.

"Do you like it?"

That deep voice wasn't Jeremy's. Barely able to breathe, EvaMarie turned in a slow circle until she faced Mason in the doorway. A remote part of her brain recognized that she'd started to shake, but the rest of her was simply working to keep herself upright.

"Um..." *Oh, real intelligent, EvaMarie.* "It's wonderful."

He stepped farther inside, sending a jolt through EvaMarie's core that she struggled to hide. When his gaze narrowed, she wasn't sure she'd succeeded.

"I'm glad you like it," he said, that deep, soothing tone gliding over her like a calming wave. "I did it with you in mind."

Um, thanks? She could have happily gone years without knowing that she'd inspired a room in his house. Was he crazy? "I don't know what to say," she murmured.

"Say you'll use it to record that sexy voice for me and the world to listen to."

She must not have heard him right. "What?" she gasped.

"I built it for you, EvaMarie."

She could swear she'd heard him wrong, but the acoustics in here were excellent. Perfect for her business. "I lined up two new authors this week," she said, the inane trivia the only thing her brain could cough up. Then she winced. Her "career" was probably the last thing he wanted to hear about.

"That's because you're excellent at everything you put your mind to," Mason said, surprising her.

A deep breath helped her gather the unraveling threads of her cognitive abilities. "That's what you said the last time I saw you. That I'm as good at secrets and lies as I am at cleaning up after the construction crew."

"And this is my way of saying I'm sorry."

She glanced around the impressive space, awed for a moment. "Pretty expensive apology."

"It's worth every penny if it means you'll at least talk to me again."

"Again…it seems like a lot for talking." She just couldn't let it go.

"You're gonna have to grovel, my man!"

"Go away, Jeremy!" Mason yelled back toward the bedroom. "I don't need an audience."

EvaMarie struggled not to smile. What had happened between them wasn't funny, but her emotions were never straightforward with this man. But confusion quickly overtook all her other thoughts.

She shook her head. "I don't understand."

"Understand what?" Mason took a step closer, which didn't clear her thoughts at all.

"I mean, I really don't understand. You hate my family. You hate what I let them do to me. You think I was using you for a place to live and work." She stepped back, struggling to breathe. "After all that, why would you do this?"

Tears threatened to surface. What she'd wanted all along seemed right within her reach, but she couldn't take it, because she couldn't live with him thinking of her that way.

"Remember, we said no other rules. Right?"

Not trusting herself to speak, she nodded.

"Well, I was wrong. There is a third rule."

"What's that?"

"We have to respect each other."

And just like that, her heart shattered. Mason would never respect the woman he thought she was.

"Do you respect me, EvaMarie?"

That was easy. She'd seen the man he'd become—a fierce opponent when fighting what he believed was wrong, utterly loyal and still as hardworking as he had been when he was young. "Of course."

"Even with my faults?"

She'd had enough time to get some perspective on that. "We all make mistakes." Hadn't she?

"And I more than most." This time he moved in close, not giving her a chance to back down. "I built this room to show you that I respect and support the woman you are now." His hands gripped her upper arms, anchoring her to the reality of what he was saying. "The woman who takes the time to read to children, who isn't afraid of hard work or to challenge me when I'm being a total ass."

She tried to smother her grin, but he caught it anyway, shared it with her despite the seriousness of what he said.

"The woman who pays attention to details, and sings to calm the horses. The woman who, even now, is struggling to teach her parents better manners while refusing to abandon them in their time of need."

"Jeremy told you?"

Mason nodded. "He told me. And I'm proud of you."

With that, she could no longer hold back the tears.

Ever so gently, Mason tilted her chin up so her watery gaze could meet his. "Let me be the first to say, EvaMarie, that I'm very proud of you. I know it's not easy. You could have continued to keep the status quo, but you saw that it wasn't the best thing for any of you, and you did something about it."

EvaMarie couldn't explain how his words made her feel. It wasn't just love. It wasn't just about soaking in the rare bit of praise. It was her heart blossoming as she realized someone could get her for the first time—warts and all.

"So you want to, what? Go back to how we were before?" She wasn't sure that's what she wanted anymore.

He buried his hand in her hair, bringing that sculpted mouth so close to hers. "Oh, I want what we had before… but I want much, much more."

His kiss left her reeling, so it was hard to coordinate her feet when he pulled her back toward the door. When they reached the office, she saw a dress hanging from one of the bookshelves. "That wasn't there before."

"Nope."

It was a vintage style with a close-fitting bodice and a full, frilly skirt. The crisp teal cotton was complemented by the lace-edged crinoline beneath the skirt. On the shelf above was a stylish hat with a matching teal ribbon woven through the brim.

EvaMarie pressed her palm hard against her stomach to quiet the butterflies that had taken up residence there. "What's that for?"

"Well, I was hoping you'd still help us with our open house when we put it on."

Her heart sank, and it was a literal, physical feeling. She eyed the dress with longing, wishing it represented so much more than it appeared to.

"As my fiancée."

Turning to look at Mason, EvaMarie found him on one knee right there in her old bedroom. His hand was lifted up to reveal a gorgeous white gold and amethyst ring with a circlet of tiny diamonds supporting it. "Mason?"

"I don't want there to be any more misunderstanding between us, EvaMarie. We're both products of our upbringing, but we're our own people too. And personally, I think you've turned into something incredible. Can you forgive me for letting the past get in the way of the present?"

Heart aching, she stepped in close, pulling his head

to her chest. "Only if you can help me be the person I should be."

Mason looked up to meet her gaze. "No, but I can help you be the person *you want* to be."

Standing, he kissed her again with a soft reverence that made her heart ache. Then he pulled her close against his body. As she looked over his shoulder, the pictures on the bookshelves became clear for the first time. Framed pictures of her and her brother. "Mason, how?"

"Jeremy got them out of storage for me. I never want you to feel like you can't talk about your life. All the parts of it."

"I promise this time I will."

Mason scanned the busy rooms on each side of the hall, looking for his fiancée in the midst of the open house chaos. People stopped him frequently. He had to consciously tamp down his impatience with the interruptions. They'd staged this party to make themselves known and extend memorable hospitality.

Mason would just enjoy it more with EvaMarie by his side.

His hunting skills proved apt when he tracked her to the kitchen. There she was in her gorgeous dress, busily helping the caterer fill trays. He watched her for several long moments.

She wasn't anything like he'd expected when he'd shown up at the estate that first day. Instead, she was more.

"Woman, what are you doing?" he finally asked.

She glanced up, giving him a glimpse of her round blue eyes beneath the rim of her hat before dusting off her fingers. "I'm sorry, Mason. I just worry about everything getting done."

Secretly he was amused, but he couldn't resist the

blush staining her cheeks. He stepped closer, running his knuckles lightly down the flushed skin. "I understand. But you're the lady of the house. And this dress is not meant for the kitchen."

They left the room to the chorus of giggles from the catering crew. "When you said you weren't big on parties, I thought you were just saying that because of the last time you went to one," Mason said as he led her through the people meandering between the front rooms and the hopping activities in the basement.

"Honestly, I've never been big on them. Not nearly as much as my parents," she murmured, sticking close to his side. Mason was amazed at how good that felt. "I'd much rather be upstairs with a book."

The turret library had been bumped to the front of the restoration checklist. They'd returned a large number of EvaMarie's books there, along with Mason's own smaller collection. They spent a lot of quiet evenings in that room, before Mason coaxed her down to the master suite.

He snuggled her closer to his side, bending to her ear to say, "As much as I was looking forward to this event, I'd rather be upstairs too…for a completely different reason."

She gasped as he whisked her partway up the stairs. "Mason, we can't."

A quick maneuver and she was in his arms as they looked out across their guests. Sunlight from the arched window opposite highlighted her cheekbones, reminding Mason of the angel he'd allowed into his life. "I'm teasing you, Evie," he said, grinning at her knowing look.

She knew him all too well.

A particularly loud guffaw had Mason glancing toward the ballroom, which they could see a sliver of from their elevated position. EvaMarie's parents held court in one corner of the room. "Your father is in his element."

"Amazingly." EvaMarie shook her head. "I can't believe they're actually here."

Mason had done his best to support her as she struggled to establish her relationship with her parents on a new footing. There'd been many a time he'd wanted to step in, but he rarely had to do that. EvaMarie, perfectionist that she was, knew exactly what she wanted and stuck to her guns in order to get it.

"You did it, love," he said, kissing her temple. "The house is gorgeous, the party is a hit and your career is gaining momentum. I'm damn proud."

"Thank you."

The tight squeeze of her arms conveyed her heightened emotions. Mason continued to be amazed when she admitted she needed help from him. The admissions were few and far between, but each one made him feel like a superhero as he attempted to give back even a fraction of the support she granted him every day.

"Where's your brother?" she asked.

Mason swept his gaze over the floor once more. "He must still be at the stables. There was a problem getting the stud settled in."

She nodded. "Soon the stables will be set—"

"And we will be the newest stables to win a Kentucky Derby. Just you see."

Her smile gave him the biggest boost. "I'm sure I will."

"It's gonna be beautiful. Just like you."

"No," she said, leaning her head against his chest. "Like us together."

* * * * *

MILLS & BOON®

Desire™

PASSIONATE AND DRAMATIC LOVE STORIES

sneak peek at next month's titles...

In stores from 9th February 2017:

Billionaire's Baby Promise – Sarah M. Anderson *and*
Seduce Me, Cowboy – Maisey Yates

Reunited with the Rancher – Sara Orwig *and*
Paper Wedding, Best-Friend Bride – Sheri WhiteFeather

Just can't wait?
Buy our books online before they hit the shops!
www.millsandboon.co.uk

Also available as eBooks.

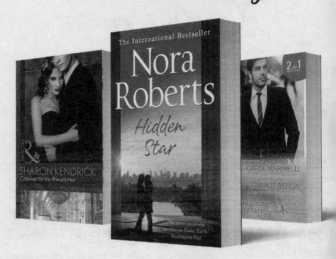

Join Britain's BIGGEST Romance Book Club

- **EXCLUSIVE offers every month**
- **FREE delivery direct to your door**
- **NEVER MISS a title**
- **EARN Bonus Book points**

Call Customer Services
0844 844 1358*

or visit
illsandboon.co.uk/subscriptions